THE
FRAGILE
KEEPERS

Natalie Pinter

Hellbender Books

Mechanicsburg, Pennsylvania

HELLBENDER BOOKS

an imprint of Sunbury Press, Inc.
Mechanicsburg, PA USA

FIRST HELLBENDER BOOKS EDITION: October 2020

Set in Garamond. Interior design by Chris Fenwick | Cover by Cory Pinter | Edited by Chris Fenwick.

Publisher's Cataloging-in-Publication Data
Names: Pinter, Natalie, author.
Title: The Fragile Keepers / Natalie Pinter.
Description: First edition. | Mechanicsburg, Pennsylvania : Hellbender Books, 2020.
Summary: When a pair of siblings discover a mythical creature, she grants them both sublime gifts and horrific curses.
Identifiers: ISBN 978-1-62006-356-9 (softcover).
Subjects: BISAC: FICTION / Fantasy / Contemporary. | FICTION / Fairytales, Folk Tales, Legends & Mythology. | FICTION / Fantasy / Thrillers / Supernatural.

Continue the Enlightenment!

Also by Natalie Pinter:

More Time,
a Brief Anthology of Indie Authors

For my mom, who plants seeds.

That holy dream—that holy dream,
While all the world were chiding,
Hath cheered me as a lovely beam
A lonely spirit guiding.

— *The Dream* Edgar Allen Poe

PART ONE

CHAPTER ONE

June

The bell chimed as the giantess walked into the Chestnut. Andromeda Waters looked up from the invoice, immediately alert. The giantess was a phantom customer. Her appearances in the store were rare—like a glimpse of Sasquatch—and not always with the same employee at the helm. She was the only person Andre had ever seen in real life who was somewhere north of seven feet tall. The woman's hair was in a scarf that covered her ears. She wore a black dress and moved like a statue gifted with life. Andre had no idea how old she was. Large sunglasses—which she kept on despite being inside—shielded her eyes.

"Let me know if I can help you find anything," Andre said.

"Thank you." The woman's voice held overlapping timbres. She moved down the aisle, scanning the dried goods.

Most people in Arroyo went to the Safeway a mile down the road for their grocery shopping, but the yuppies and hippies kept the Chestnut busy. The tiny store was nestled in a shopping center between an Indian restaurant and a massage parlor. Local produce was crammed into small refrigerators against one wall. Supplements were on cluttered shelves next to flower essences, herbal tinctures, incense, and a plethora of liver, kidney, and colon cleansers. There was a spinning fixture with dreamcatchers, wind chimes, and crystals—"the sparkle stand"—as Andre and Merri referred to it. In one corner was a small bookshelf and a rack of New Age magazines.

Perched on the stool behind the counter, Andre opened a bag of expired gluten-free pretzels she'd pulled off the shelf that morning and marked off in the waste log. She finished with the invoice and flicked through a catalog while stealing glances at the giantess, who had moved over to the corner with the bulk bins. A few minutes later, the woman walked up to the counter with a large bottle of honey and a jar of aloe. The giantess paid with a card and held out a tote bag for Andre to put her items in and left with a nod.

☙❧

That evening, Andre pulled a brush through her hair as she stared out her bedroom window. She'd long since smoothed out all her tangles, and the brush fell through the jet silk without resistance. Her posture slackened as she prepared to fall onto her pale blue bedspread. The ritual of brushing her hair until it was silky and then lying in bed on her side was set since childhood. As a young girl, she'd imagined she was going to sleep half-submerged in a shallow pool, and her hair was water.

Only a salt lamp on her dresser cut through the darkness. A bookcase took up half the wall between the closet and the window. On her dresser sat little treasures: a small porcelain jewelry box with a faerie painted on the lid; a picture of Andre and Ryan in the redwoods, her legs around his waist, piggy-backed. There was a framed photo of Amy and Andre from when they were four years old, wearing a wreath of flowers in their hair.

She scooped her hair over her shoulder and looked at the waning moon over her yard and the forested Arroyo hills, which were a dark smudge of shadow. Ryan would be back on Saturday. Maybe they would go to the lake, pack a picnic, finally move some more of her stuff to his apartment. Her thoughts were scattered by the appearance of a bright sphere—a shimmering, zapping ball of electricity, the size of a classroom globe, bobbing just outside of her window. Andre yelped and crouched down, squeezing the handle of her brush. Her heart hammered and her first lizard brain thought was that there was about to be an earthquake or an explosion. She stood up and gaped at the light zig-zagging around. It moved from her window and down the side of her house, drifting out over the backyard toward the shed.

Ben had stopped playing his keyboard twenty minutes before, but it was too early for him to be asleep. He was lying on his bed, looking at his phone when Andre burst into his room without knocking. "Oh, my god. You gotta see this. C'mere."

He didn't move. "What?"

"There's this weird light outside. It's crazy. Hurry. There's like this orb moving around. C'mon, hurry. I've never seen anything like it."

They turned on the back porch light and walked around the yard. At first, it seemed to have disappeared, but then it shot out from behind the shed before popping over the backyard fence and out into the park beyond.

"What the hell *is* that?" Ben opened the fence, and they walked a little way down the path, but the ball had moved quickly. There was no sign of it anymore, and they'd need flashlights to go any farther.

"I don't get it," he said as they went back inside. "It was like CGI, you know? Crap, I didn't get a picture. Did you get a picture of it?"

"No. It happened too fast. I didn't grab my phone. So freaking weird, right?"

They spent the next hour looking online. When they came upon a phenomenon known as "ball lightning," they decided they'd found the closest thing to an answer.

Andre tossed her purse onto the passenger seat the next morning, plopped into the car, and observed the sunny, innocuous morning suspiciously. Her gaze drifted up to Ben's window. He would be asleep for a couple more hours. Her phone buzzed, and she pulled it out of her purse. Ryan. "*Morning,*" he'd texted and sent an emoji of a bee. She sent him a smiley face.

Ten minutes later, she pulled out her keys to unlock the glass doors of the Chestnut, losing herself in the vines and flowers and art nouveau–style lettering of the store's name painted on the glass. Andre liked to pretend she was opening some special chamber, some magical apothecary with her special keys. It was a habit of her perception to make the mundane more interesting. When she pumped gas into her car, she pretended she was feeding her large, sentient beetle with wheels. But she didn't need her keys. The door was already unlocked, and she could see some of the lights on down the length of the store.

Merri had beaten her there, and the morning's produce shipment had already arrived. "Hey." Merri nodded at her and set a wooden crate of radishes down in front of one of the refrigerator doors. Fortunately, it looked like she was almost done. Andre disliked this part of her job because handling the cold food and being in and out of the refrigerator and freezer made her hands ache. She was one of those small girls who was always cold. She helped Merri put away the last bags of chard and kale on the bottom rack.

Merri glanced at her and spoke hesitantly, "So, um, I was wondering . . ." She took a deep breath and clasped her hands beneath her chin in a supplicating gesture. "Can you do me a huge favor and work for me tomorrow? Pleeeease?"

"I haven't had a Saturday off in ages." Andre's voice was too loud as if one of her ears was plugged. "I specifically asked your mom for it off. Ryan and I were going to do something. Maybe go to the lake." Merri's mom, Vivian, owned the Chestnut, but Andre and Merri usually ran the shop.

"I know, but there's the overnight festival at the Shrine tonight, and The Maze is going to play, and Amy has an extra ticket for me." She was wringing her hands. "She assumed you wouldn't want to go because of the crowd. You could just open the store. I'll come by in the afternoon?"

Andre sighed. "Okay."

"Thanks. I love you." Merri hugged her. "I really appreciate this. I will make it up to you. Do you, um, do you know if Ben's going?"

They wandered behind the counter to open the registers. "To the show? He didn't mention it to me. Probably, if he has a ticket." Andre grimaced and pressed her hands to her abdomen. "Ugh. My stomach is upset." She'd gone to bed soon after seeing the ball lightning and wondered if she'd started to feel queasy then. She couldn't remember. "Hey, have you ever heard of ball lightning?" She pulled out her phone to look it up. "I think I saw this last night. It was kind of like this one." She pointed to an image of a glowing sphere. "It was the strangest thing I've ever seen. I thought I was hallucinating."

"Weird," Merri said. "That's kinda cool, though."

"Yeah." Andre grimaced again, leaned over the counter, and put her head in her hands.

"Are you okay?"

She took a few deep breaths before answering. "Actually, no. Could you do me a favor right now?"

"Sure."

Andre straightened. "Could you hold down the fort today? My stomach is upset, and I feel like I'm getting a fever."

"We don't have anything here to help you?"

"I'll drink some ginger tea, but I think I just need to go home."

"Okay, yeah . . . sure."

"Thanks." Andre broke into a chilly sweat as she walked out to her car. Her stomach churned. She sat down in the driver's seat and took deep breaths until the feeling passed. She pulled out her phone. There was another message from Ryan:

Could not find my phone.

It was in my coat pocket.

So now it's okay.

She smiled. They had started a couple of months ago when they were all drinking one night, and Amy was saying how nobody wrote love poems anymore. Ryan said he'd start sending Andre a poem every day, and so they'd devolved into one dumb haiku a day. She wanted to tell him about what she'd seen, but not in a text. Setting her phone down to check herself in the mirror, she noticed how pale she looked. As she was leaving out of the parking lot, a silver Mercedes pulled up and parked in front of the store. Andre watched in her rearview mirror as a moment later, the door opened, and the giantess unfurled from the driver's side.

Ben's car was still there when she got home. After parking, Andre sat for a moment and closed her eyes, picturing the ball lightning. She half expected to hear music when she went inside, but the house was quiet. Ben might still be sleeping. He was a night owl and usually wasn't in bed before 2 a.m. or awake before eleven. She poured a glass of water, went up to her bedroom, and faced her window. The sky was blue and cloudless. Mount Domingo looked like an azure sandcastle in the distance. Their house was on a small hill, and she could see beyond the woods to the golden hills spotted with clumps of trees. The fact that they had a house at all in this part of the county was something of a miracle. Three millennials—two who worked menial jobs and one who was usually unemployed (Amy)—would never have been able to afford a house in Arroyo. But they'd inherited their home from their dads who'd inherited it from Ben's paternal grandfather.

Feverish and achy, Andre laid down on her bed and fell asleep.

She woke a couple of hours later with visions of ball lightning. She'd dreamed of the crackling, silvery-gold energy hovering outside her window. She gulped water from the glass on the bedside table and went downstairs. Hammer, Ben's mutt, came nosing after her. His eyes were watery, and his padded feet made a scratchy sound on the floor. "What about you?" She rubbed the fur along his neck. "Did you see anything strange last night?" She tried not to consider that her sickness might be connected to the light.

Andre went around the side of the house. Overgrown bougainvillea bunched around half the perimeter of the fence. She crossed the yard, opened the fence, and stood for a moment, looking down the hill to the park. The small valley of trees containing streams from the Shellara eventually rose up another, higher hill. She liked to imagine it was wild land, untamed, unexplored. Beyond those hills might be anything. There were not many vistas these days that allowed such a suggestion. Even this one was flawed. If she turned her gaze just a ways to the left, the blemish of the interstate would slice into the picture. She felt a prick of anxiety.

She walked a bit more, uncertain of what she was looking for. Ben took Hammer here all the time, but it had been at least a few weeks since she'd entered the park. The sequoia trees grew denser overhead as she moved down, and the land plateaued. There was a stream just a little farther in. When Andre got to it, she knelt on a rock and stuck her hand in the cold water. Her phone got a message. She stood, wiping her hand on her jeans, and pulled it out of her pocket. Amy: *"Her car is here, but where is Andre?"*

Back at the house, the fence was open, and Amy was waiting for her at the end of the yard. Andre was disconcerted to find she was panting from the short trek back up. "I need to exercise more," she muttered, wiping her forehead with the heel of her palm. She looked at the shed to the right of her and watched a daddy longlegs traipse down the side, lose its footing, and fall to the grass.

"What's up? Why aren't you at work?"

"I don't know. I was looking for . . . something." Andre breathed deeply. "I left early. I don't feel well." They walked back into the house together, and Andre told her twin about the light.

"That's bizarre. Maybe it was an alien trying to make contact or something."

Andre smirked. "Yeah, maybe . . . what are you up to right now?" Amy only lived with Andre and Ben about a quarter of the time. She was a bit of a local nomad, and the last few weeks she'd been with Ricardo, but his apartment was already pretty crowded.

"I was bored. We didn't have any food, and I don't feel like grocery shopping." They sat in the living room now. Amy frowned at her phone. "Do you know where Ben is? He's not answering his phone or my texts, and I need to know if he's coming with us to the Shrine tonight. If he's not, I'm giving his ticket to Ricardo's friend."

"He's not here?" Andre sat on the couch. She took one of the cushions and set it on her lap, pressed it against her stomach, and leaned over. She took a deep breath and willed her nausea away again. *God, don't let me be pregnant.*

"He's not in his room."

Andre shivered. "That's weird. His car is outside."

"What's wrong with you?"

"I don't know. I feel nauseous. I think I have a little fever." And it suddenly bothered her, acutely, that they didn't know where Ben was. "Ben was here last night. I heard him playing right before I went to sleep."

"Maybe he went on a walk . . . " Amy frowned, looking at Hammer a few feet away from her lying on the threadbare blue rug in front of the kitchen window—his favorite spot. "Without Hammer?" Amy yawned. "It's a mystery." She reached her arms up high and cocked her head to either side, tiny popping sounds emitting from somewhere in her neck. "I've got to stop by Ricardo's to drop off his ticket. You want to come with me?"

Andre wanted to lie down again, but she felt strongly disinclined to stay at the house alone.

"I hope Ben can make it," Amy said in the car. "Merri will be disappointed if he doesn't come." She gave Andre what was probably a sly look, but it was hard to tell with her sunglasses on.

"Why?"

"You've never noticed how moony she gets when he's around?"

Andre watched the trees and telephone poles drifting past the window. "No, but that's . . . sweet." Dreamy, orphan Ben with his shaggy sable hair and piercing, wary black eyes—dark features from his Mexican mother. She'd died of breast cancer when he was four. At twenty-four, he was very thin despite a sedentary lifestyle and a steady diet of beer. They'd lived together since the twins had moved out west thirteen years ago. Their fathers had been unmarried partners, but Ben was more of a sibling to Andre than her real half-brother.

Ricardo, Genevieve, and Raf lived on the top floor of a tiny apartment on the border of Arroyo and Darryville. Amy parked, shoved her sunglasses back up onto her head, and shuffled through her backpack. Andre followed her twin up the stairs. Amaryllis was beautiful. Not normal beautiful, but a freak–unnerving, startling. Andre was weirdly proud of it. It amused her to introduce Amy to people and watch them blink and gape. The physical differences between them bordered on comical. Andre was nine inches shorter with straight black hair down to her waist. She was small and compact, built like a gymnast and flat-chested. Amy was five-ten with turquoise hair and large, tapered limbs half covered in tattoos. She had huge fawn eyes, and her face was ridiculous– otherworldly. Her sculpted bone structure alone was a gift from the gods to humankind. Andre was average looking, maybe pretty, but next to Amy, everyone was plain.

Immediately following Amy's loud knock was the sound of high-pitched barking. "Down, Pippin! Pippin! Down!" Genevieve, buxom, also heavily inked, opened the door, blocking the fiercely yapping Pomeranian with her leg before bending down and scooping him up. "Hi! Come in." She stroked the dog aggressively and pressed her face into its fur. "Why do you *always* have to freak out, huh?"

They stepped into a cluttered living room that smelled of sandalwood incense and pot. A Chagall print sat over the sofa: two people—pancake-flat—suspended in the air. Genevieve set Pippin down. He barked a couple more times and scuttled around, sniffing Andre's and Amy's ankles.

"Are you coming tonight?" Amy asked.

"No, I have to study. Raf can't go either. He's working. Are you?" she asked Andre.

Andre shook her head. "I work tomorrow morning. I picked up Merri's shift for her. It's not really my thing. I don't like crowds."

"Hey, twinsies." Ricardo appeared, shirtless and wearing sweatpants. "Who's doing what?"

"They aren't going tonight, but I am," Amy said.

"Is Ben coming?" Ricardo moved some magazines off the couch and sat down, then stood back up. Andre didn't understand band politics, but Ben and Ricardo used to practice together, and now they didn't. She never sensed tension between them but hadn't asked Ben outright about it. Amy shrugged and then followed Ricardo back to his room. "Good question. I'm trying to get a hold of him, but he's unfindable at the moment."

Andre hugged herself and sat down with a whimper.

"Are you okay, sweetie?" Genevieve asked, putting a hand on Andre's back.

"Yeah, sorry, no, my stomach is upset." Andre looked up, and her gaze floated along the tiger lily tattoo on Genevieve's arm.

"Want some tea? The water is still hot," Genevieve said, moving towards the tiny kitchen. "I just made some."

"Sure, thanks." Andre's phone rang—Ben. "Hey, where are you?"

"*Andre.*" She'd never heard so much desperation poured into the two syllables of her name. She went still.

"What's wrong?"

"Where are you?"

"I'm at Genevieve's with Amy. Everybody's looking for you."

"Don't tell anyone I'm on the phone. Can you come home?"

"Yeah, as soon as Amy's done here. Ugh. I need to get home. I'm sick."

"You too?" He muttered something she didn't catch, then said, "Fuck."

"What's wrong with you?" she asked, anxiety niggling at her more the worse she felt.

"Just get home, please. It's important."

Genevieve appeared in front of her holding a mug with a monkey arm handle. Andre smiled apologetically but stood up and shook her head. "Okay. I'll be there as soon as I can."

"Listen, don't tell anyone that you've talked to me. I can't talk to anyone else right now."

"Got it." Genevieve shrugged and disappeared back into the kitchen. Andre spoke quietly, "What's going on? You're freaking me out."

"That light we saw last night brought something with it."

"What—"

"Just get here." He hung up.

CHAPTER TWO

Ben stood on the deck in the backyard, smoking a cigarette and guzzling a beer. He hoped, with a sort of imploring fervency that was almost prayer, that Amy would drop Andre off and not come inside too. It wasn't that he didn't want Amy to know, but if he was crazy and wrong about what he'd thought he'd seen, Andre would be less likely to give him a hard time and make a thing of it.

They were taking forever.

His fingers shook as he brought the cigarette to his mouth. Staring at the shed fifteen feet away, he finished his beer. It was probably not the best thing for him at the moment, after vomiting off and on the last couple of hours, but Ben was having trouble dealing with reality sober. He stubbed the cigarette out and flicked it over the fence. Unforgivable. He'd not been so thoughtless in years, but now everything was different. The world might be coming to an end.

Andre opened the back door so quietly it startled him. "Hey." Hammer had followed and stood panting by her legs. She stroked his ears absently, looking around. "Sorry it took so long. Amy . . ." She made a flicking motion with her hand and rolled her eyes, and this somehow indicated Amy's flightiness or fault. "She had to pull over. I threatened to throw up in the car. I almost did. She went back to Ricardo's." Andre grimaced, crossed her arms over her chest. "I don't get it." She licked her lips. "I feel like shit. Like, poisoned."

Looking over his shoulder at the shed, Ben turned to go back inside the house. "C'mon." He crossed the living room into the kitchen, threw his beer can into the recycling, and went to the fridge to pull out another. He opened it and took a long drink, avoiding her eyes. "I'm glad you saw that crazy ball lightning shit last night. It will make this easier to take."

Andre frowned. "Weird. I can see the vein in your neck like, pulsing. You know, I was starting to think I'd imagined it or exaggerated how it was. But I'm pretty sure it's a real phenomenon, just super rare." She poured a glass of water. "But . . . you're kind of scaring me. What's going on?"

When he opened the fridge again, pulled out another beer, and held it out to her, she said, "No way. How can you drink right now?"

"You should have one. Here, seriously, it'll make things easier."

"Ugh. No. I've barely eaten today, and it's stupid to drink when you have the stomach flu."

"We don't have the stomach flu."

She sighed. "What is going on? Stop acting all traumatized and mysterious and just tell me, please, so I can go lie down."

"Sorry. I don't know what's wrong with us, but I think it had something to do with the light." He rubbed the bridge of his nose. "I was freaked out this morning. I thought maybe the light was radiation. Because this morning I'm sick as hell and the power was out, and the internet was down. And then I couldn't stop thinking about the light." At her horrified expression, he shook his head. "It's better now. I haven't thrown up in an hour, and I don't feel sick anymore. Just—just wired."

"I . . . don't think the power was out for me this morning. I don't remember if I turned on any lights or anything then. No one else saw anything that I can tell, and there's nothing on the news, right? I mean, not that I've found . . ."

"It's not that," Ben said. "Or, there is more to it." His forehead glistened with sweat in the late afternoon light. He rummaged through a drawer by the sink and pulled out a small blue flashlight. "C'mon."

Andre followed him out to their backyard again. "What are we doing?"

He didn't answer but stopped at the shed. "Shh!" He turned to her, so serious with a finger to his lips. She laughed.

There was a thudding sound from inside the shed. They both jumped. "I came out here this morning, and the door was open . . . I found something," he said finally.

"Something?"

"Someone. I don't know."

"Wait! What?" Andre tugged at his shirt as he went to open the door. "Whoa, maybe we should call the police, or animal control, depending on whatever you're talking about."

He opened the door.

It was a huge shed, made years ago by Ben's grandfather. It smelled of must and childhood. Ben's old tricycle leaned against the wall towards them. There were crates with tools stacked haphazardly on makeshift plywood shelves; an old lawn mower; folded deck chairs; rusted patio furniture; a small, round trampoline; boxes of mason jars. In the far corner was an old deck swing, tiny and rusted. A shaft of weak, brownish light drifted down from the small window in the corner.

Seconds passed while Ben waved the light around. "There!" He shined the light in the far left corner, below the window.

"Did you move stuff?" Several boxes had been stacked together and shifted to the right to make a free space where a sort of nest had been formed from an old tablecloth and an opened umbrella.

"No. It made itself at home, I guess."

"It?"

Andre took a step closer. Something small huddled beneath an old picnic tablecloth. Ben clenched his hands into fists, experiencing the same intoxicating rush he'd had the first time he'd seen it, but now he was emboldened by the presence of Andre and the alcohol in his system. And there was some validation, too. He'd not imagined it.

"What the . . ." Andre stepped forward, squinting.

A figure could barely be made out behind the tablecloth covering it. After a moment, it moved, and there emerged the suggestion of a shoulder, and pale, gossamer hair. The figure was small—too small. The rest of it was slumped down on its knees beneath the tablecloth leaning against the wall. The face was turned away. The top of the tablecloth shifted slightly. Andre blinked and stepped farther into the room, frowning.

What they were seeing did not make sense. Ben's heart started hammering again, and the whole world turned sideways. He was seasick.

"Maybe . . ." Andre said softly. Then she balked. "Let's go." She stumbled back and knocked over a ceramic desk lamp. It didn't break, but the noise caused the figure in the corner to peek out from beneath the blanket. And then they couldn't move once they saw a glimpse of its eyes.

"I don't think it's dangerous," Ben said breathlessly, taking a step closer. "Just God. Just look!"

Andre whimpered, her knees wobbled, and she dropped onto them. Ben placed one hand on her shoulder. With his other, he adjusted the flashlight so as not to put a direct spotlight on what was beneath the tablecloth. Andre turned to look at him, and their eyes met for a moment, soaking up the sacred strangeness of it all. The moment had a personality. It was self-aware, poised, and graceful, a drifting soap bubble saying, *"Look at me, remember this. Remember when everything changed."* Then Andre's phone vibrated loudly in her pocket. She pulled it out and silenced it. Ben took a step closer to the figure. He'd only glimpsed the face beneath once, and now the figure was shielded under the tablecloth again.

"Hello?" Andre spoke in an exceedingly gentle voice and shuffled on her knees forward until she was only a few feet from it.

Ben experimented, turning off the flashlight and trying to see with just daylight behind them through the open door and the one tiny window. "It might not understand us," he whispered. It was too dark without the flashlight. He turned it back on.

"Why do you keep saying 'it'?" Andre whispered. On her hands and knees, she slowly resumed moving closer and passed Ben. "Hey there," she said softly. "We're not going to hurt you."

And then Andre was only a foot away. Ben cracked his knuckles. Andre reached over to remove the tablecloth, but Ben put his hand on her arm to stop her. Dark possibilities tumbled around in his mind's eye—talons reaching out, acid being spewed at them. Glacial seconds ticked by. Finally, the creature moved a little, and the cloth dropped from the left side to reveal the flash of a huge golden eye peeking out. It covered itself immediately again.

Andre licked her lips and looked back and forth from Ben to the figure. "I'm going to move this tablecloth, okay?"

He swallowed and gave her a little nod. Andre gently tugged the tablecloth down.

Ben looked away. He heard Andre's sharp intake of breath and then, softly, "Oh my god." He finally looked again. At first, the puffy hair concealed most of its face. It wasn't until he leaned in and saw, really saw, that he could confirm he'd not imagined that first impression. Several hours earlier, he'd stumbled out of the shed in blind terror, a singular panic lancing through his nervous system.

It was not right.

Before them was something like a person, but the eyes were too big in proportion to the rest of the face. The overall shape of the head and face was impossible, like an ostentatiously perfect and beautiful figurine come to life. Large pointed ears rose like beech leaves from either side of the head. The most irrefutably inhuman quality was the diminutive size of its body. It was like a living puppet—larger than a doll, smaller than a child, and lean as an adult.

"Oh my god," Andre murmured over and over until it turned into a chant. "Oh my god, oh my god, oh my god." She finally put one hand over her mouth and held up the other in a gentle, conciliatory gesture. "It's okay. It's okay." It wasn't clear if she was talking to the being in front of them or to herself. The creature looked back and forth between them. There was never a question of intelligence. Gears of sophisticated thought obviously worked behind those huge shimmering eyes. "What?" Andre shook her head, unable to fully form a question. "Oh, you're not possible."

Ben was relieved to see that awe had trumped terror in Andre's case. The creature lifted a small hand with long slim fingers up to mirror Andre's. They didn't touch. "So." Ben cleared his throat and, modulating his voice very carefully, said, "I think they must be connected to the light, right? So, it's like, an . . . alien?"

"An alien? From outer space?" Not moving her hand or taking her eyes off the creature, Andre began to giggle. For a minute, she covered her mouth to contain the bubbles of hysteria that were threatening to surface and foam out of her. Eventually, she took a deep breath and sat back on her knees, sniffling. "Look, I'm sorry. I just don't understand." She looked from the creature to Ben and then back to the creature. "I don't understand what I'm seeing. I'm waiting for this to be a joke, but I don't understand how that"—she pointed—"could be a joke. It's just . . . it would be too expensive."

"It's not. At least I don't think it is. I wouldn't know. I hope it is."

She looked up at him. Her eyes were wet, but from what emotion, it wasn't clear. "You do?" She sighed and gazed at the intruder with rapture. "Not me. I've been waiting for this my whole life."

The tablecloth had come down to reveal a neck and shoulders.

Andre glanced anxiously at Ben and then smiled. "What is your name?" she asked it. "I'm Andromeda. Andre for short," Andre said, pressing her hand against her chest. "*Aaann*dree," she repeated.

It gave a tiny nod. Andre turned to Ben and looked at him expectantly.

Ben lost it then too. "Me, Ben." He hunched over and teared up with laughter, finally feeling some of the beer he'd consumed. "Aw, c'mon," he said at Andre's scowl. "It's so cliché." He gestured at the creature, and his laughter trailed off.

"Ben."

They both started at the sound. It was one syllable, but the voice was like seeing a new color. The pitch was suffused with preternatural beauty. If a pink star diamond or the buds of a cherry blossom could speak, it might sound something like what they'd just heard. A delicate finger pointed to Andre. "Aandree."

Andre beamed and nodded. "Yes." She licked her lips and scooted a little closer to the creature. "What is your name?"

It looked from one of them to the other and then down. Andre wondered if it understood, or maybe didn't know the answer, but then it touched its forehead and slowly dragged a finger down the middle of its face, along the bridge of its nose, continuing over mouth and chin. It closed its eyes, opened them slowly, and said, "Shae."

The sound of the voice made a pleasant shiver run down Ben's spine. Notes of music chimed in his head, like bright colored leaves being swept by the wind and flowing down a dull-colored, vacant street.

Andre took a deep breath. "Why don't we get some of this shed cleared out? It's a mess." She wrinkled her nose. "And . . . I'll find something for it to wear?"

"Yeah, that's a good idea," he said quickly. Compelled by a notion that it was basic, cursory etiquette to offer a guest somewhere comfortable to sit, he said, "Why don't you sit here, Shae?" He motioned to a child's beach chair that was open and just a few feet to the right of where Shae was crouched.

Apparently understanding, Shae stood, and the tablecloth fell away. Shae was naked, female, and not a child. Ben dropped his eyes.

"The fuck?" He rubbed his forehead, keeping his eyes averted. He looked around as if taking in his surroundings for the first time. "Yup, I'm going to start moving all this crap out of here. She needs somewhere to stay." He propped open the door with a fifteen-pound metal weight he found lying nearby. Some years ago, lifting them was supposed to have become a daily habit. He began grabbing items at random and moving stuff out to the yard.

"Are you sure you want all that stuff out here?" Andre asked. "Where are we going to put it?"

"It was your idea."

"Oh, yeah." She laughed giddily.

Jesus Christ, we're in shock right now. Ben heaved a heavy-looking box with newspaper sticking out of the top that touched the bottom of his chin. "It's mostly junk. I'll dump it off at the thrift store or the dumpster." He stepped outside, set the box down, and looked at Andre, plaintive. "Could you find something for her to wear?"

Andre nodded and then looked pained and slammed her hand over her mouth. She ran out of the shed and back into the house.

Over the next hour, Ben pulled almost everything out of the shed, avoiding looking at or getting too close to Shae while Andre was sick in the bathroom. When she finally reappeared in the backyard, she looked much better, elated almost. She clutched a flowered, sleeveless shirt. "It might fit her as a dress."

Ben followed as she stepped back into the shed and stood in front of Shae, who sat in the beach chair with her knees up, arms clasped around them–a relaxed pose, and yet she seemed ready to spring at any moment.

"Want to try this on?" Andre asked.

Shae looked at Andre, at the shirt/dress, then back to Andre. Andre bit her lip. "We usually wear clothes." She indicated her garments, running her hands over her jeans and tugging lightly on the fabric beneath her armpit. The shirt was snatched from her.

"I'll be back." Ben wiped at his forehead with the heel of his hand and went inside the house for another beer. He was agitated and feeling the effects of alcohol on an empty stomach. Drinking more wasn't wise, but a part of him genuinely feared he was losing his mind. He felt taut as a bow and was courting hysteria. He didn't know what that would look like full-blown and didn't want to find out.

It was as if a curtain which had surrounded him his whole life, to the point he was unaware of its existence, had been lifted away to reveal he didn't know *anything*. It made him inexplicably angry. Like he'd been lied to. He was an animal who'd spent its life believing the large, comfortable cage it dwelled in was the world entire, only to be released into a vast and unending country. He didn't trust the ground under his feet to remain solid.

He doubted Andre was angry. She seemed okay, all things considered. He wondered what Amy would say. No doubt, she would find out eventually, yet the thought of telling anyone else frightened him for reasons he didn't look at closely.

The door opened, startling him. Andre poked her head into the kitchen. "You coming back out?"

CHAPTER THREE

The girl-alien-thing looked kind of cute. The shirt was too big for her—like a burlap sack—and she wore it as a dress. Andre had contrived a belt out of a ribbon.

She frowned. "I'm gonna have to buy some little kid clothes and alter them? I'm not much of a seamstress."

They stepped back out of the shed once it was satisfactorily clear and moved a few paces into the yard and out of sight of Shae. "Do you think this is safe?" Ben pulled out his phone and checked the time. It was almost four. Where had the day gone? He scratched his head. "I mean, should we just leave her alone, or do you think we should, you know, keep an eye on her?"

Andre gave him a funny look. "You think what, she's dangerous?"

"No. Well, I don't know. I meant more like I'm concerned about her getting out and . . . hit by a car or something."

Andre looped her hair around her fingers. "Yeah . . . well, there is no protocol in this situation, but I think she's capable enough not to get hurt." She frowned. "We have no idea, actually."

"Yeah."

"But, you left her alone all morning after you first saw her."

"I almost pissed myself when I first saw her. I didn't think about whether or not leaving her alone was the right thing to do."

"Wherever she's come from, I imagine she's traveled far. I bet she's tired. I'm going to ask her if she wants to sleep," Andre said decisively. He followed her back into the shed, where she squatted down in front of the space Shae had made for herself. "Would you like to sleep?" Andre pressed her hands together and turned her head to the side, a childlike miming. Shae blinked slowly and gave no response, but Andre took this as an affirmative and turned to Ben. "Yeah. I'm going to get her some blankets and a pillow." She passed by him. When she got to the door, she said. "I don't think it would be wise for you to drink any more alcohol."

He stared at Shae while Andre was upstairs. She kept her gaze down in her lap. He felt like he should say something, offer some words of comfort or hospitality, but nothing came.

Andre returned, a comforter and two pillows wedged beneath her arms. She shrugged the comforter out over the length of the now nearly-empty storage shed, in front of the chair. Without any prompting, Shae lay down, wrapped the bedding over herself completely, and disappeared into a tight little ball. They stepped out quietly, shutting the door but for a crack.

They sat at the kitchen table. The house looked different. The prosaic blended odor of a dog, semi-clean furniture, and residual garlic that permeated their little home was comforting but more noticeable now than it usually was. Ben rubbed his face and contemplated getting another beer. Andre took the teapot, filled it with water from the tap, and soon they sat over steaming mugs of chamomile.

For a few minutes, they shared the silence. It was monumental, not even worth attempting to put into words right away. Andre blew lightly over her drink and took a sip. "I don't think we should tell anyone," she said.

"Me neither."

"At least not yet." The rectangular clock of brass and wood that Ben's grandfather had made struck the half-hour. "I'll peek in on her a few more times before I go to bed tonight, but I think that's all we can do right now." Andre removed her hands from the mug and held them out before her. They trembled like she had palsy. "We should—I should have offered her water or food or something but . . . I think she's asleep now, and I just can't. I just can't." She started hyperventilating.

"Shhh."

"*What the hell.*"

"Yup," he agreed.

She took a few, shaky breaths. "Where were you anyway, today when I first came by?"

"In the woods. I went there after I saw her. I don't know why. I thought I'd maybe find some sort of explanation out there."

"Huh. I went out there too. Guess we missed each other. I just got as far as the stream before Amy texted me."

"I forgot to bring my phone. I went like a mile. I think I was in shock and just needed to keep moving. I didn't find anything either, though."

She tilted her head back and took a deep breath. "Crap. I told Merri I'd cover her for work tomorrow. Look, I don't fault you for getting wasted all day, but you've got to shape up. I have to go in at least and open. You've got to be around for her." Ben sensed Andre had the same overwhelming conviction that they needed to watch out for the creature, keep her safe.

"What about Amy?"

Andre bit her lips. "I've got to think . . ."

"Okay. And Ryan?"

She shook her head. "Oh god, I can't imagine keeping this from him for long, but he's in Arizona right now for work. He's back tomorrow morning. I'm not going to just text him a picture." She smiled suddenly. "I feel so weird right now."

"I feel weird, too," Ben said.

"We must still be in shock, right? This doesn't happen every day. Maybe it's never happened to anyone ever before." She smiled again, dazed. "It's so freaking cool! What do you think it means? What *is* she?"

He shook his head. "An alien? We found her the morning after that light. She must have come with it. She's like . . . a bona fide alien, right? Like a gray alien, except . . . a little different?"

Andre leaned forward and blew on the fragrant steam, frowning. "I don't know. I think she looks like a faerie." Nodding, she pocketed her phone and stood up, grabbing her tea. "I mean, you see it too, right?" She didn't wait for him to answer. "I'm going to see what I can find online."

Andre went into her room and turned her laptop on. Most of the websites proved useless: flashy images of half-naked winged women or faerie children, poems with inspirational quotes, links to Wiccan sites, dribbles of mythology, and Celtic history. She reviewed some things she was already familiar with: the Tuatha De Danaan, Morgan Le Fay, the disappearance of Robert Kirk, the poetry of Yeats.

She perused until the screen made her squint, and her mouth was dry. She scribbled notes in her book and wrote down a few questions to ask Shae. Andre was pretty sure the name Shae was Irish. And Ireland was associated with faeries. The West Coast of North America had some Native American faerie tales, but Andre couldn't believe there were any ley lines in Shellara Regional Park. She'd half grown up here. She would have felt it before now, wouldn't she? After making notes of some books that might be helpful, Andre closed her laptop.

She needed a little mission—the feeling she was taking steps to get answers and not just sitting around while a world-shattering secret sat in that backyard. She took a shower and brushed her hair, and lay in bed for a long time, trying to sleep. For as long as Andre could remember, she'd been waiting for something extraordinary to appear around a corner. All her life, she'd hoped for and dreamed of something like Shae. Of course, there was more to life than this conveyer belt of work, play, sleep, rinse, repeat. Of course, there would be something impossible and wondrous one day. That day had finally come. Her eyes filled with tears. And now that Shae was here, Andre *needed* to know where she'd come from. She wanted to penetrate the barrier and see that world. That night, Andre dreamed she had wings.

CHAPTER FOUR

I lay staring at the shaft of light—different from the rich-orange rays I know—slanting down through the small, high window of the box. Everything is different. The air is acrid and saturated with filth. I look down and run my fingers over the ungainly garment. I have only a fuzzy memory now of what I am supposed to do. I no longer have my name. But I've spoken and made a sound for them—"Shae"— and so now there is something.

I scarcely remember what my task is. I am to bestow gifts: give them their greatest desires and then . . . kill them to collect the tithe? I'd been out of myself when I arrived; in a fugue from the passage between worlds. I wonder what plan the court has for me to carry out. What will it look like in the end?

I curl my fingers in frustration. They'd played songs for me right before I'd left, the cricket drums and pipes making the most fetching sounds, and with the music came a compulsion: *"Do your work! Do your work! Find the one upon which to bestow songs! Find the one to become! Do your work! Change their world! Give them these gifts and snatch those sweet young lives for our payment!"*

As the chosen one, I was led down the path flanked by trees I'd known since time immemorial. Then over the bridge that spanned the glittering waters, I loved to play in. And on, through the pleached alley and into the mountain beyond where there lay the cave of lightning. I was surrounded by all kinds: big and small, the bony and thorny and diaphanous. They gave me my last shot of sweet nectar, and then they'd done that most awful thing, stripping my name. I cried out for it, a part of my essence gone forever. *"The only way you can travel so far,"* they'd hissed. And the last thing one of them had muttered, *"You, little one, will change."* And I'd felt fear as they shoved me into that silvery, stinging vortex. And right before the ball of lightning sealed, when there was scarcely space for it, a woodwalker slipped into the vessel with me, hitching a ride. I don't know why it would do such a foolish and dangerous thing. But it's a foolish and dangerous creature. And then the vortex had brought us to this place.

They'd not said anything of what I was to find here. I didn't know how confused I would be when I arrived. How much it stank here. How different the air and how ugly the creatures. While they share a basic blueprint with me, they are clumsy next to my winged, utilitarian frame. And base though they are, I am abashed at the thought of killing them. They seem welcoming enough and have not tried to harm me. But it is my task to collect the tithe. Not the woodwalker's. If I were a creature given to shedding tears, I might, but instead, I feel the surge of music and channel it off to the boy.

Ben rolled over, so his face was in the corner of the couch. A song was inside him, running through his sleeping brain and into his veins. He was buoyant, surfing on the melody. It dipped and curved—pleasure pulsed through him. The music looped over in the most exquisite combination of notes, and he followed the shimmering path of sound. He was beginning to awaken but resisted opening his eyes. He wanted to stay in this auditory wet dream forever.

Ben had passed out around midnight—earlier than usual. He'd barely eaten and was frightened and sick and vomiting *before* drinking a bunch. He cleaved to sleep, dimly knowing full consciousness would be painful, and he would spend the day a squinting, miserable sponge of alcohol. The quiet of the house and the less familiar bed of the couch led to his awareness that this was an earlier hour than he was used to waking. He groaned as the vestiges of sleep funneled away. The song was softer now, but it still pulsed. He felt a relieved thrill to have caught it, like a slippery, jeweled fish. He opened his eyes. Despite the hangover, he was itching to get his hands on his keyboard and guitar and bring it to life.

He bolted up and looked around the living room. The music flushed out of his head, and his heart took up the familiar hammering of the day before. *Fuck!* The faerie-girl thing. What time was it? Where was Andre? How come she hadn't woken him? He found his phone in his pocket: 8:45. Andre must have just left. She was just opening the store, she'd told him. She would be back as soon as she could.

Parched, Ben went to the kitchen and poured a glass of water from the tap. He gulped it down and started the coffeemaker.

Hammer eyed him sleepily from his spot in the sun on the blue rug. Ben wanted to go out and open the shed to make sure she was still actually there, but he also wanted a shower before he did anything else. He'd not taken one after getting sweaty moving all the stuff from the shed. He quickly showered and dressed, went back downstairs, and poured a large cup of coffee. There was a text from Andre: *"You up, okay? Let me know when you see her."* Drumming his side and gritting his teeth, he headed out back through the junk-cluttered yard to the shed.

Before yesterday, the wonder and depth of possibility Ben had known as a child was long gone. He fondly recalled a time when he could play outside and make his reality: be a ninja or a pirate and then come home for lunch. But the supernatural was supposed to stay in films, books, and video games. It wasn't supposed to punch through to the present—to reality—and he was struggling to face it again.

Steeling himself, he knocked on the shed, waited a few seconds, and then slowly opened the door. The night before, they had gone in to look at Shae and talked quietly over her, watching her shallow breathing. They'd spoken her name while Andre shook her shoulder. They had considered that maybe she was doing something when she appeared to be sleeping. Perhaps she was in a restorative hibernation or mining a deep database she had to be unconscious to have access to. They discussed this possibility, and also that she might be like some exotic animal, and that when taken away from her native flora and fauna, would not survive.

Ben stood hesitating, afraid that he'd open the door to the musty odor of decaying insect, or the putrid tang of just turning flesh. It would be awful, not just because she'd been a sentient creature, but the holy fucking grail. She was the most important thing ever to happen, and they'd not asked her any questions. *And I would never get to hear that voice again.* He grimaced and opened the door.

The air was humid. Shae lay on her side exactly as she had the night before. He lingered in the doorway, letting his eyes adjust to the weak light leaking through the window. Then he squatted down and studied her profile. She looked no different. Her chest still rose and fell shallowly. "C'mon, wake up," he whispered.

Her eyes opened. She stared at nothing, at the space in front of her.

"Um, so hi." Ben smiled tightly. It was difficult to look and harder to look away. The impossibility of her made his eyes bounce around a bit.

She sat up. "I'm still here."

She could talk! In English! *How the hell did that work?* And that voice . . . it was like she pulled out some lustrous ribbon and waved it through the air. And God, she sounded so *sad* about it.

"Wow. That makes things easier." He realized he was continually nodding his head and forced himself to stop. There was so much to ask—too much. He didn't know where to start. "Where did you come from, and what the hell are you?" felt a little uncouth. "Are you hungry?"

He slowly held out a hand. "You want to come inside?"

Shae put her fingertips to her temples, closed her eyes, and whispered something. Then she looked up at him. "I'm trapped here."

"Uh, what do you mean, trapped?"

She didn't answer but began rocking back and forth—apparently the universal sign of having a fit. She dropped her head between her knees and made a sad little squeak. Then she slumped back down into the blankets.

Ben waited a moment, unsure of what to do. "I—I'm sorry?" Then he touched her, very gently, on the shoulder. "Do you want to come inside?" he asked again.

Shae stood with lazy, feline grace and looked up at him. She was impossibly small and exquisite. Her eyes were a greenish-gold like sunlight through pond water. He could see her better since she was close to the door and under the sunlight. He observed that her hair wasn't quite white–where the light hit it, hues of green, orange, and violet shimmered like the surface of an opal. The volume on the song in his mind turned up suddenly, and for a few seconds, his head bobbed. "Yeah, let's go inside."

Ben tried to gauge her reaction to the house when they entered the living room, but if she was surprised or disturbed or interested, he could not tell. "Here." He walked through the den from the back door towards the kitchen. He held out a chair at the kitchen table for her, which she quickly climbed up and stood upon. Hammer rose at the sight of her and waddled over. Shae lifted a hand and massaged behind the dog's ears. A little sound came from her throat—something between a purr and a sustained chirp. "That's Hammer. He's a good boy. Aren't you, Hammer-man?" Ben squatted down and roughly rubbed Hammer on the side and patted him, silently thanking him for not barking.

"Um so . . . are you hungry or thirsty or something?" He made motions of eating, feeling ridiculous, and resentful towards Andre for not being there. Before Shae replied, he poured her a glass of water and placed it on the table. "Here." He nodded, forced a smile.

Shae grasped the glass with her tiny hands and drained it in two impossibly huge swallows. She set it down, her eyes half-lidded in obvious relief. He refilled the glass and set it down again, but Shae shook her head. "It is bitter, but thank you. I was thirsty."

He realized he was trembling and forced himself to stop. "Are you hungry?" He went to the fridge. "I'm not sure what kind of food you eat, so I guess I'll show you a few things and let you pick." Andre did most of the shopping at the Chestnut, so they were usually stocked with healthy food. He was going to start taking things out of the refrigerator but saw Shae's eyes widen at the jar of honey sitting in the center of the table. She grabbed it, opened the lid easily, and began drinking it. Ben texted Andre: *Get more honey.*

"You want anything else?" Ben asked when she set it down. When several seconds passed without her replying, he said, "Okay, well, just let me know if you get hungry."

He almost texted Andre that Shae could speak, but decided she'd find out soon enough. He made toast for himself and sat down at the table with his toast on a paper towel and held the phone out. "It's a cell phone." He was feeling pleased with himself as if he could take credit for the existence of this object. Still sitting at the table, Shae leaned over and stared. The screen was dark. "Here, see." He tapped the button on the bottom and dragged his finger across, waking it up. "It's got everything—games, the Internet, pictures, music . . ." He tapped a few icons to show her. "But it's a phone. You use it to communicate with people far away." He cleared his throat. "Here, go ahead. You can play with it."

She hesitantly tapped on it. He noticed something peculiar about her hands and suppressed a shudder. Her delicate fingers had three joints instead of two. She went to his pictures and swiped through a few. "Strange," she said simply.

God, her voice. He ate quietly, wondering what it would be like to encounter a cell phone for the first time: a glowing screen, tiny pictures, and video . . . it would be insane. Or maybe it was primitive to her. But he didn't get that impression. Maybe because Andre thought she was a faerie. She did look like one, and the images of them were usually in a natural context: forests and meadows, dainty beings communing with plants and animals, flitting through the trees. They were from another time as well as another place, somewhere devoid of technology and pollution, a quasi-medieval fantasyland.

After a minute, she lost interest in the phone, climbed down from the table, and went up to the window, putting her hand against the glass. He put the phone back in his pocket and glanced at the flat-screen TV in the living room. Would it frighten her if he turned it on? The coffee buzzed in his head, and Ben experienced a sharp moment of clarity. *That creature is right there in front of me. Oh, fucking Christ.* His mind scrabbled for an explanation.

Perhaps it was some quirky disease—some genetic, exceedingly rare, but still documented condition. There were so many strange diseases out there. He'd seen a special about primordial dwarves on TV once. There were conjoined twins, giant people, those super-hairy people, the poor beasts that filled the Mutter Museum, folks who could pop out their eyeballs, hold their breath for twenty minutes . . . all manner of talented and tragic freaks. Perhaps once they contacted whatever authorities handled missing person situations, an explanation would surface, and he and Andre would look foolish. They might even be in trouble for keeping her any length of time before alerting anyone. Why were they keeping her? Why had they both just assumed she would stay?

When Shae turned back and looked at him, those thoughts evaporated. She was not deformed. She was not ill. There was nothing wrong with her. He could not alert the authorities. In the best-case scenario, she would become a celebrity of sorts, maybe a political pawn. In the worst, she would disappear, and he and Andre might, too. Who knew what the powers that be—those people in white coats or black suits and sunglasses he imagined—were capable of? Perhaps they were all that stood between Shae and vivisection. A headache loomed in his temples, but then the song rose within him and pushed out pain and worrisome thoughts. It rejuvenated him and provided a dramatic soundtrack to the conviction he now had to protect her. *She came to our home for a reason*, he thought. *We're supposed to keep her safe. Now . . . what to do with her?*

He tossed away his paper towel and brushed crumbs off the table. "You want to go back outside?" Ben looked out the window and winced a little at the bright day. He grabbed his sunglasses and baseball cap from the small table next to the front door, went to the back door, and turned to her. She went ahead of him, and he saw she had a strange way of walking. There was too much time between her steps.

Ben felt a flicker of annoyance at the state of the yard. He hadn't considered that he'd have to make multiple trips to the dumpster and thrift store to get rid of all the stuff in the shed. It was a decent yard when it wasn't cluttered with crap. The bougainvillea that grew in along the edge of the house provided a colorful, pink border, and their little lemon tree was full of the sun-yellow fruit. There were a few potted succulents on the porch.

Hammer snuffled out from behind them, trotted over to his doghouse, and went inside. He reappeared a second later with an ancient gray baseball in his slobbery mouth. He padded up to Ben, panting. For the next few minutes, Ben played catch with Hammer while Shae walked around the perimeter of the yard, keeping close to the fence. He tried to get a glimpse of her bare, narrow little feet.

When he sloppily threw the ball a few feet from her and Hammer got a hold of it, the dog went to her, tail wagging, and dropped it at her feet. "Hey, boy!" Ben clapped his hands. "Leave her alone. C'mere!"

Shae picked the ball up and turned it over in her hands. Then, with more force than Ben would have thought she had in her arms, she chucked the ball over the fence. Hammer toddled over, turned back to Ben, and barked. Shae looked at Ben expectantly.

He hesitated. They were safe behind the fence. But once they were out in the woods . . . It was unlikely that they would run into anyone before they reached the main park, and he liked to think if they heard or saw anyone approach, they would have time to hide her or turn back, but it was still an uncomfortable thing to do. He took off his baseball hat and wiped his forehead.

"Okay." He opened the latch.

Beyond the fence were miles of parkland. It had been an idyllic place to wander as a kid. Ben had spent a good deal of his life in these woods, playing alone much of the time except when Mateo came over to hang out. He'd been a quiet only child, back when Andre and Amy lived with their mom on the East Coast, and he only saw them once or twice a year.

Ben closed the gate and turned around to face trees he knew well. Shae did not wait for him but plunged down the path, Hammer trotting along beside her. Ben looked up at a tiny pin of an airplane trailing through the cobalt sky. For a moment, the world was not filtered through his jaded twenty-four-year-old perspective, but something more expansive. Then he half skidded down as the path dropped and came back to himself. She was getting far ahead. He longed for a cigarette though he'd been trying to quit. There'd been few in a pack at the back of his dresser, but he'd consumed them all the day before in the few anxious hours before Andre came home. He wondered if there were more floating around somewhere in the house. He patted himself down out of habit and picked up the pace.

The trail soon grew narrower; clusters of sequoia rose higher and became denser. Shae blazed through, and Ben saw there really was too long a pause between her steps and too much space covered.

She stopped abruptly, and Ben caught up with her. "I used to hang out here all the time as a kid. There is a stream a bit further." It was hard to tell if she was listening or not. She dropped her head back, closed her eyes, and stuck out a pink tongue that was too long and wagged it in the air. Hammer, who was a few feet ahead, trotted back to them, the baseball still in his mouth. Shae opened her eyes, turned to Ben, and said, "A dangerous one is here."

He shuddered. He couldn't look directly in her eyes, so he looked around her. Her hair was seafoam, and her skin was seamless. She was a paradox; she fit in the world, and she didn't. Hammer nudged up against him. "What? What's dangerous?"

When she spoke, he nodded at the words, but it was seconds before he comprehended them. The drug of her voice distracted him. "I had hoped it would die in the vortex, but a gray Unseelie followed me here. A bad one—a woodwalker."

A breeze rolled through, stirring the tops of the trees. *Great. Now she's saying creepy shit.* Ben knew he should be asking questions, but right then, he just wasn't ready to know. He was trying to power through his hangover and not lose his mind. "Oh," he managed.

"I'm going to look." Shae tugged off her sleeves and dipped out of the shirt-dress.

Wings sprouted from her back. They were not feathered as a bird's or powdery-velvet like a butterfly's, but sinewy. And like a dragonfly's wings, there were shimmers of glassy color: orange-pink, blue, and green. She pumped them back and forth a couple of times, hopped into the air, and was gone as smoothly and quickly as an errant balloon.

Ben sagged against a tree and whimpered. Hammer trotted around him in a circle and barked once before nuzzling up beside his legs. "Oh god, oh god," he mumbled. He defended himself to Andre in his mind, *What the hell was I supposed to do?* Eventually, he straightened up slowly. "Okay." He nodded and chanted: "Okay. She flew away, but it's okay. She flew away, but it's okay." He rubbed Hammer's head. "You saw it too, buddy? I'm not totally fucked in the head, right?" *She said she was going to look.* He reasoned she would likely return once she finished looking. She didn't say she was going away. She was looking for a "dangerous one," which she'd determined was nearby, after *tasting* it in the air.

Ben pulled out his phone and checked into the comfort of the real world. A European politician whose name sounded familiar had been killed in a car accident. There was a wildfire being contained several hours north. The hammering in his heart slowed at seeing the mundane. He needed to make the last payment on his keyboard; there were a few more "likes" on a picture of Hammer he'd posted. It occurred to him they'd not gotten a picture of Shae, and while it would have been a questionable thing to do, he regretted it now. If he and Andre never heard from her again, he would start to question his sanity.

Then he realized they hadn't yet explained to her to stay out of other people's way. What if she didn't know her appearance was alarming? He started sweating. He picked up her dress and paced around in figure eights a few times before finally setting off in the general direction she'd gone.

Up in the trees, I wonder, *what is my name?* How could they take it from me? Surely it is still somewhere? And what am I supposed to do now? The Woodwalker could be a problem. And how am I supposed to collect the tithe? I won't just bash their heads in with a rock, getting myself messy. I don't feel like killing anyone. And I need more time too because they have to get their gifts first, right? It is all becoming confusing. I want to go home. I want nectar and music and mischief. This place doesn't suit me at all. Though . . . at least there are trees. I sense the serious one is agitated, and I funnel the song to him.

The melody filled Ben's mind again, and his panic eased. He reached the stream in a few short minutes as his head swayed, and his hands drummed his sides. He threw the ball a couple of times for Hammer and clambered awkwardly on a chunky boulder of a rock that he'd pretended was the fist of a giant when he was a kid. His dog waddled over to him. There were white hairs now all around Hammer's muzzle and where his eyebrows would be if he'd had eyebrows. Ben scratched him behind the ears. He'd gotten Hammer as a month-old puppy, the summer of his eleventh birthday. Hammer was an old man now, but he usually still wanted to play catch even if he couldn't last more than a few minutes. He padded over and found a comfortable-looking spot to sit.

Mateo texted. *"You went to the show? Awesome! How was it? I'm jealous you saw NS."* Ben didn't reply. He didn't think he could partake in an ordinary conversation.

He was just about to call Andre and inform her that he'd lost their guest when Shae landed on a rock a few feet away. Hammer lifted his head, glanced at Ben, and then rested his head back on his paws. She was facing him so he couldn't see exactly what happened when her wings retracted, but he got the impression of them closing like a jagged, Japanese fan, folding into neat ridges halfway down her back.

When their eyes met, he thought he saw a flicker of understanding. *Maybe she gets it*, he thought. *She knows how weird this all is.* He picked up a pebble and plunked it into the water. "Did you find what you were looking for?"

"I caught its trail for a while, but . . . it hides." She looked into the water as she spoke. "I didn't know if you were coming back." He tried to ignore the fact that she was naked again. Part of him wanted to grab her. He had the hopeful, slightly shameful feeling of a child trying to catch a butterfly or a little frog who kept hopping away. "Did you see anyone? Any people?"

"A man. Sitting by the water."

Every time she spoke, he felt a trickle of euphoria. "What was he doing? Did he see you?"

She shook her head. "I was up." She pointed.

"Oh, good." He averted his gaze to the water. "Um, you know you shouldn't let anyone see you?" He cleared his throat, stood, and held the dress out to her. "It's probably not a good idea. It could be dangerous."

She threw the dress on over herself, inside out, a hint of defiance in her movement. "Yes, I know. And do not tell anyone about me."

"Okay." He nodded. "Sure." After a moment, he asked. "No one? We . . . have some friends, and my other stepsister, Andre's twin, she lives with us." *Sort of.*

She squatted down on the rock, leaned over, and stared into the water. "No."

A few quiet minutes passed, and Ben could not tell if they were peaceful or uncomfortable. He wondered what she was doing, studying the minnows and pebbles and bits of creek-side flotsam so intently. He checked his phone again and saw Amy and Ricardo had sent pictures from the festival. "Umm. Hey, do you want to head back now? I've got something to show you."

Ben couldn't tell if the television was as impressive as he'd thought it would be. He had Shae sit on the couch while he stood and explained that he was going to turn it on, and she was going to see and hear lots of things, but not to be alarmed because it wasn't real. He rapped on the surface. He didn't want her smacking into the screen, trying to jump into any inviting pictures. He held out the remote. "These buttons"—he indicated the up and down arrows—"that's how I change the channel. We can keep pushing these until we find something we like." Shae ran a finger along the edge of the remote.

"Here we go." He turned the volume down and then slowly back up while an attractive woman in a cardigan wiped up a blue puddle on a counter in a pristine, sunlit kitchen. Shae's eyes widened. Her hands were clenched at her sides. "This is a commercial—an advertisement. I'm going to change the channel now." A weatherman stood in front of a map with swirling imagery, clouds, and precipitation. "This is the news. He's giving the weather forecast." He licked his lips and turned up the volume, let it linger to learn that the next week was going to be perfect: sunny, mid-seventies, highs in the low eighties. Then there was a political news show where cranky-looking men barked at each other. Each time he changed the channel, he looked to see a reaction. Shae didn't move or comment, but there was an erectness in the way she sat that made her seem tense.

Ben rubbed his temples. A stretching, hot and sparkling pain filled his brain as long-held views of normal and right and possible were shredded a little more.

He changed the channel again to a nature show and then turned at the sound of Andre opening the front door. "Dude, she speaks English, and she can fly."

Keeping her head turned, so her eyes remained on a documentary about bats, Shae stood up off the couch and turned her back to them, briefly demonstrating; her wings opened, and she lifted a few feet off the floor. Andre felt the fine hairs all over her body stand on end. Then Shae turned to her, and they stared at each other. Andre gasped as she felt a sharp sting, deep behind her eyes. For a flicker of an instant, Andre saw herself through Shae's eyes; she felt a muted panic at being in a new strange place. She felt a tugging concern about the gray one who was out there looking to kill things and trying to find a tithe. Andre shook herself, trying to make the feeling dissipate. *What the hell just happened to me?*

Shae pumped her wings and turned back to the bats as Andre swallowed down tears of awe and envy. She pulled a notebook from her purse. "I thought it would be a good idea if I started keeping notes." That morning she'd written down a physical description of Shae and then made two columns: the first highlighted the qualities she considered to be human, in the other were "supernatural" qualities. She pulled out a pen and added "wings" to that column. A part of her knew it was busywork, but it was an anchor and gave her a slim sense of control.

Ben disappeared upstairs and returned a minute later with his acoustic and set to plucking a stirring, melancholic refrain.

Andre's phone vibrated, and she pulled it out of her pocket. Ryan: *"Still, sick?"* He sent a green-faced emoticon.

"It's Ryan."

Ben kept playing and shrugged. "Oh yeah, she said not to tell anyone about her."

Andre looked at Shae. "You don't want us to . . . we can't tell anyone? Ryan is my boyfriend. Amy lives here." *Sort of.*

Shae stared at her. "Do not tell." Her voice was melodious yet lacked inflection. Andre couldn't tell if it was a plea or a command, but she silenced her phone. Then she texted Ryan: *"I'm lying down. Not feeling good. Left work. Gonna stay home. Will call you later."* She added a heart and hoped he wouldn't offer to come over.

Ben strummed harder, staring at Shae. "She's . . ." He shook his head. Then he stopped playing and looked at Andre. She could see mania simmering in his eyes. He wasn't okay. He was trembling, his left eyelid was twitching, and there was that pulse in his neck again. He started playing again; the sound was desperate. His guitar was a lifeline, a thumb to suck. His fingers moved rapidly over the fret-board while his other hand frantically picked. She was pretty sure if his hands weren't so busy, they would be shaking. "That—on her back . . .." He shook his head and let out a sharp-edged bark of laughter. "I have to go to *work* in a few hours."

Andre stepped towards him. "I know it's hard to take in."

The melody eased, and sorrowful notes danced around the three of them for several seconds. Then Ben stopped playing, went over to the sliding glass door, and looked out at the cluttered backyard. "I'm gonna make a run to the dumpster and buy cigarettes." He spent a few minutes loading up his car and left.

Andre watched Shae watching TV for another fifteen minutes, growing agitated, feeling like she needed to do something. The faerie seemed entranced, her head cocked, fascinated by the bats.

When Ben returned, he popped a cigarette in his mouth and snatched up his guitar and started strumming again. He shook his head back and forth as if shooing away a bug buzzing around him. "It was more like . . . she was floating than flying. Those wings couldn't lift her. It's like gravity won't affect her if she doesn't let it." He squinted. "Do you think we've just gone insane?"

"No." She put her hand over his forearm, trying to get him to cease playing even though she was weirdly moved by the sound. "But this is a lot. Just try to think about her. She's the one who must be really feeling crazy."

"Yeah, I know." His hands went still. "So . . . what are we going to do?"

"I don't know."

He pulled his phone out of his pocket. "Erik and Amy put up pictures from the Shrine . . . am I supposed to act like I'm interested?"

The world was a different place now. How were they supposed to keep this up?

He started again, playing new, light, plinking notes that drifted up around them and sailed out the window like smoke. "It's strange that she can talk," he said. "How do you think that's possible?"

Andre rubbed her forehead. There was something behind her eyes, inside of her mind now. "I don't know." She turned to their guest. "Um, Shae . . . can you please tell us what you are? We kind of need some information here."

"I am She."

"She?" Andre cocked her head.

"She. Shae," Shae said unhelpfully. Andre stared at her in the dress. She had read an old superstition once that it was improper etiquette to gift clothing to faeries and hoped Shae didn't mind.

Ben continued to play compulsively, drumming the soundboard and bobbing his head.

"I will go back to the woods now to look for the Unseel," Shae said, pulling open the sliding glass door. She was strong for her size, Andre noted.

"Oh yeah, she said there was something out there," Ben said, setting his guitar down. He turned to Andre as they followed the faerie back outside and through the gate. "A 'dangerous' one." He made quotes with his fingers. "She says it followed her here."

"What?" Andre asked sharply. "You're just now telling me this?"

"Sorry. She . . . didn't seem all that concerned. I forgot. I got distracted when she broke the law of gravity." He swallowed. "Sorry, I'm feeling a little crazy right now."

"What else did she say?"

He frowned. "That's it, I think. She went to look for it but didn't find it."

"She didn't say what it was?"

"She's not especially forthcoming if you hadn't noticed. Guess we'll find out." Ben sighed. "Maybe someone else—" He was interrupted by a call. "It's Mateo." He silenced the phone and put it back in his pocket. "Maybe someone else will find it, or maybe it will wreak havoc all over town, and we'll hear about it on the news."

"I don't know how this is going to work. We're going to have to tell Amy."

"I don't know."

She looked at him warily as they picked up their pace to keep up with Shae.

"I'm not saying we shouldn't do it. I'm just not sure we should. I mean, she did say not to tell anyone about her."

Andre followed a bird with her eyes. "Yeah." She sighed. "And when a magical creature requests that you keep their existence a secret, I feel like you should listen."

"It would blend in," Shae said over her shoulder when they caught up to her. "The woodwalker is stupid, but it knows how to hide."

"So, it's hiding from you?" Andre asked. "Is it safe to be out here?"

Shae half walked, half floated moving swiftly, the balls of her feet lightly bouncing along the ground. "I would know if it was close. It will become weaker the longer it is here. It is not supposed to be here. It cannot adapt." She slowed then and turned to face them. "I am supposed to be here." She tore off the shirt-dress, and her wings sprang out. She pumped them a few times but continued walking.

Andre pinched herself.

"This world smells awful," Shae said. "Metal stink and poison."

Andre thought this day seemed particularly clear and beautiful. Perhaps Shae just needed to get acclimated to this world and all its pollution. She studied Shae. Her wings worked to propel and steer her. When she pumped them back together with force, she shot ahead swiftly. She turned suddenly, "I'm going up to look." With that, she glided quickly away from them, rising into the trees, free, and then shooting north towards the Shellara. Ben was right; she did not seem to fly so much as to resist gravity, as if there was a switch she could turn up and down.

When Shae was out of sight, Ben turned to Andre. "Well, there isn't anything to say about that, is there?" He stuffed his hands in his pockets.

Andre laughed. "Maybe this is just the beginning. Maybe things are about to get even weirder."

"Honestly, I kind of hope that's not the case? I don't need to see anything more fucked up. I don't want to see that Unseeling or whatever the hell she's looking for."

"Unseelie," Andre said quietly. "I think she's saying 'Unseelie,' like the dark faeries."

"What are you talking about?"

"In some sources chronicling the faerie world, there are the Seelie and the Unseelie courts. I don't know how it all works, and depending on where you're getting your information from, it can be different, but generally, in British folklore, there are the good or light, faeries—the Seelie, and then there are the bad or dark ones, the Unseelie. And then some references have them sort of overlapping."

Ben didn't say anything to this, and for a few minutes, they walked in silence. He kicked at a rock. "I don't like the way she just shoots off like that. Imagine if she comes across some hikers."

"Yeah. But maybe it wouldn't be so terrible," Andre said. Ben gave her a look, and she continued, "I'm not saying we shouldn't try to prevent her from being seen, or that it couldn't be problematic, but, you know, not everyone would have a terrible reaction."

He shook his head. "I don't think people can handle this. We should try and keep her out of sight."

Andre fell a little behind and watched him. She got a text from her mother, Lydia. *"Hope you're having a good week, sweetie. Miss you. Max got first place in his swim competition!"* She sent an image of Andre's little brother smiling with damp hair.

"Neat." She texted back. *"Tell him congrats."* She caught up to Ben. "I bet there are people like us, too."

Ben shrugged.

"Okay, people like me then, since you are so anxious about this situation. I'm sure of it. So many people would be thrilled to know she exists!"

Ben slowed down, drummed his sides, his eyes searching the sky. "It could destroy religions and break the fabric of society." He pulled out a cigarette, pausing to light it.

Andre smirked. "Maybe not entirely a bad thing?" She stretched her arms up and felt her phone vibrate and knew, without having to look, that it was Ryan. She glanced at his message. He'd returned from his work trip. She texted him back quickly and pocketed her phone.

It happened when the girl came back. I'm not exactly sure *what* I did or how, but the second quarry is shot. I snagged her mind, and we are linked. And now, up in the trees, scanning and sniffing for Gray Man, I can *feel* the prettier one—the girl, talking to the serious one. They are discussing me. Concerned about whether other people should see me and what would happen if they did. I am not worried about this. The masses will never discover us. It is not part of the plan. And the plans of the court are foolproof.

I consider the serious one. He plays the music. I have to do hardly more than look at him, and he gathers up those strands of melody with ease. I do not understand how my connection to the girl is a gift. I don't like to think about it. *"You, little one, will change."* Change. Changeling? No. Never that. Neither of us is a child, and it is usually human babes or children that are given such a gift. And faerie babes that are cursed and offered as a sacrifice in reverse. I am myself . . . although, I don't have my name. There is that.

I do not see the gray woodwalker, but I catch his scent. He is already beginning to decay. I wonder how long it will take. After some time, I feel the tug to return to my little box of a building and to them: the serious one, the girl, and the furry one. I don't want to think of them by their names. I don't want to stay here long enough for it to matter. And if they are the tithe, I don't want to know them too well. It would be disagreeable to grow friendly and familiar if I am to kill them.

I look about, see a bird, and call it forth to me. Strange little being. Different from the ones I know. I do have an affinity for the winged ones, though. The birds and moths. Anything that flies like me. None of these creatures impress me much, except those bats I saw on the picture stone—remarkable beasts!

I am not truly sundered. No. I will give the serious one the music, share myself with the girl, then I will kill them and, in doing so, collect the tithe. I will do whatever else is tasked to me, and then I will find a way to get my name back. And with my name, they will give me another ball of lightning. Then I shall return to my world.

They walked without speaking for a while. Ben stubbed his cigarette out on a tree trunk and put the butt in his pocket, then he picked up a stick and slapped at branches with it while humming.

Shae appeared silently and abruptly, alighting on an oak branch not two yards away. Her greenish-white hair could have been sunlight on leaves. Her wings from this distance were the green and deep lavender of the wood.

"Oh, shit." Ben started when he saw her. "Hey."

Shae floated down to them, holding a stick in her hand like a wand.

"Did you, uh, have any luck?" Andre asked.

"It is that way." She pointed over her shoulder. "Beyond the lake."

"This might be a dumb question," Andre said, "but can it fly? Like you?"

Shae gave a slight shrug. "Everything can fly if it thinks about it hard enough. But no, it cannot fly like me." Her little feet landed lightly on the ground.

"Okay," Andre said at this unhelpful reply.

"You could fly." Shae looked at Andre boldly.

Ben laughed. "Um, no, I'm pretty sure we can't—except in airplanes. It's been proven many times."

Shae said nothing to this. Andre noticed something then; three, four, five squirrels, noses twitching, scampered over and gathered in a loose circle around them. A little finch flew in small circles a few feet over Shae's head. A large monarch butterfly suddenly landed on Shae's shoulder, its wings opening and closing lazily. Another butterfly, small and creamy white, rested in her hair like a bow. Andre almost laughed and was about to make some comment about how

Shae was like a Disney princess frolicking with the woodland critters—except there was something off-putting about seeing creatures that normally disdained humans gather around them.

"You've got . . ." Ben motioned with his hand to his shoulder, as if Shae had some piece of food on her she needed to shake off. She looked down and stroked the monarch's wings, making a little crooning sound. "Yes. I call forth the creatures."

Ben looked uneasily at the squirrels and then at Andre. "Why don't we head back?" he said.

They walked towards the house, birds, butterflies, and squirrels loosely in tow. To Andre's relief, all the critters except for the monarch butterfly stopped in the backyard, and she didn't have to explain to Shae that having wild animals in the house probably wasn't a good idea.

Shae took a honey jar and went back outside, into the shed, and shut the door. Ben turned the coffeepot back on and went up to his room to get ready for work. He appeared a few minutes later, wearing khakis and a black shirt he buttoned slowly, looking tired.

Andre sat in a chair and looked up at him with a faint smile. "I can't believe you're going to work."

He shrugged. "Yeah, well, I'm needed at the bar. It's Saturday. It's going to be slammed. If I was going to call out, I should have done it hours ago." There were faint maroon circles underneath his eyes, and his left eyelid still twitched.

He should lay off the coffee, she thought.

"Call me if anything happens, though," he said. "If I don't answer my cell for some reason, call the bar, and if whoever answers gives you a hard time, say it's a family emergency or something." He patted himself down to make sure he had the essential trifecta—keys, wallet, phone—and hesitated. He spoke, his face to the door. "I hope we're doing the right thing, keeping her here, not telling anyone."

After he left, Andre searched online for the next couple of hours, trying to find out anything else she could about Shae. Faeries were mischievous tricksters; they were tiny and helpful, or they were tall and regal, cunning and cruel. They dwelled in mystical forests or fancy subterranean courts, dancing for eternity. They existed in another dimension. Faerie was shadowy and fleeting. Elusive. Nothing fitted quite right. By the time she was done, it was getting dark, and she decided it was time to check on their guest.

She crossed the yard, shivering, thinking of those wings: grotesque and exquisite–the thin, membranous jeweled skin pulled tightly over a network of bones or cartilage or whatever made up Shae's body. Andre hesitated at the door of the shed. *If she was going to hurt you, she would have done so by now. And she's a third of your size if that.*

Andre knocked lightly. There was no response. After a few seconds, she opened the door. Shae lay curled up on the floor like a wet dragonfly at the side of a pool. Andre stood over her and stared at her for a long time. "Of course you're exhausted," she murmured. "You traveled all the way from the land of make-believe."

Andre got another text from her mother: *Hi honey, thanks for suggesting those vitamins! I already feel better. Give me a call when you get a chance. I'd love to catch up.*

Poor Lydia. She was trying so hard these days. Her mother's world was so much more stable now than it had been when Andre was growing up. Part of the twins' early childhood had been spent in a women's shelter after her parents had split, and Lydia's next boyfriend had been abusive. Then they'd all lived in her bi-polar, chain-smoking, packrat grandmother's home. They hadn't had a shower, just an old stained bathtub that she and Amy had shared.

But the twins still probably would have continued living with Lydia if she hadn't become utterly insufferable when she first accepted Christ as her savior at age thirty. A newly devout Lydia and a feral, pre-pubescent Amy were oil and water. It came to a head when Amy had first run away at age twelve. Moving to the west coast to live with their father had been the best thing for Amy and Andre, but Lydia had come a long way too in the intervening years. She had a good job, a nice home, a new family. And she'd mellowed out with religion.

Andre sighed. She texted her back. *I'll call you soon. Love you.* It would be hard to have a normal conversation right now.

She made popcorn and watched an old black-and-white *Twilight Zone* episode, feeling profoundly lonely, when there was a knock on the door. She tensed. It was not often anyone dropped by this late without calling. She pulled out her phone. The battery was dead. She muted the television and crawled out from the blanket she was snuggled beneath. It could only be Ryan. Amy had a key. Still, she went through the kitchen and peeked out the curtain next to the front door. The porch light was not on, but she saw the silhouette of a large familiar figure.

He held up a fist of fragrant purple flowers when she opened the door. "You're avoiding me, so I'm stalking you."

Andre shoved her face into the petals and inhaled. "Ooh. These smell amazing."

"What are they?" Ryan asked, following her inside. "I was over at my parents. I just stole some from Mrs. Edgelow's yard."

"Lilacs, I think," Andre stood on her tiptoes to open a cabinet and reached for a thick glass vase on the third shelf. He stretched over her easily and handed it down. "You stole flowers from an old woman?" She shook her head.

"It's a huge bush. There's plenty. Besides, she owes me. Seth and I have mowed her lawn every summer for the last I-don't-know-how-many years."

She filled the vase with water from the sink and put the lilacs in it. She plucked a flower and brought it right up to her nose, so the soft petals brushed against her face and breathed in the sweet, indigo scent.

"You mow her lawn—that's nice."

He shrugged. "So, you're sick? What's the matter with you? Are you dying? I tried to invite you to dinner tonight." Ryan was a nice guy who was always having nice dinners with his nice parents.

Andre hesitated. "I don't know. It's a stomach thing. I was throwing up yesterday. Ben had it too. I'm feeling better now, though." She went back to the living room and sat on the couch. "You probably shouldn't stay, I don't want you to get sick." She glanced at the back door. "Believe me—you don't want this."

"Yeah, actually I had food poisoning a few years ago, and it was pretty awful. But I'm willing to expose myself for my Bumblebee. I've missed you." He plopped down next to her.

She rested her head on his shoulder. "How was Arizona?"

He shrugged. "I don't know. Hot. I was working nonstop." Ryan was a chemical engineer and the hardest working person she knew. He had only been two spots away from being valedictorian at their huge high school and had graduated with honors from Stanford two years ago. He was looking into grad school at MIT. He wasn't a moody musician or flaky artist like most of their little tribe. He was a sweet, card-carrying dork built like a football player. His hobbies outside of his demanding job were playing video games and reading science fiction. In the beginning, his appearance in their circle of friends was as rare as Andre's, but there had always been a little something there. They'd both been somewhat shy back then, but two years ago, he'd asked her out for coffee, and they'd slowly started dating.

Her eyes drifted to the back door again. For a flash, Andre thought of telling him. She swallowed, felt a little shiver down her spine. She stretched her arms and feigned a yawn until it became real. "Well, I'm going to go to bed now."

"All right then." He sounded disappointed.

Andre felt a tug, looking at him. *The world is different now. I don't know how I will keep this from you.*

Ryan pulled out his phone. "Seth was going to have some people over maybe. I might head over to his place." Ryan's brother Seth was two years older and also an engineer.

Andre slept fitfully that night. She sweated and tossed and turned from vivid dreams of a night in the woods. There were bats and butterflies in the moonlight amidst the trees. They fluttered around, taunting her.

CHAPTER FIVE

The following Saturday, Ben woke to the soundtrack of a dream, the plot of which evaporated as he opened his eyes. The ballad in his head was grave and urgent. He'd been a participant in an epic saga comprising danger and sacrifice on a dazzling, cinematic scale.

He plopped into his leather swivel chair at his desk next to his bed and tuned his guitar. He knew he should call Andre and check in with her; he should take Hammer out, he should go look to see what Shae was up to. But he needed to play.

This was the third song he'd collected in the last few days. They came in his sleep or while he was doing something mindless. Lyrics were not formed, but he knew their shape and where they would fit. He sat for two hours slamming and plucking in bliss, his eyes half-closed playing the new song over and over. Eventually, he laid the guitar on his bed, went over to his keyboard, and played it there, making alternating tones and beats at different parts like dabbing colors and highlights to a painting. Then he went back to the guitar and started a different one.

When the last strum dissipated in a brassy cloud, he sank back into his chair, his mind pleasantly barren except for the vague craving of a cigarette. He picked his phone up off the dresser. Ben exchanged a few texts with Mateo and then finally made a long-overdue call to Ricardo to hear his firsthand account of the Shrine festival and how Stepfather's gig went at the Cloud Lounge.

He then went downstairs and made coffee and toast. He was vaguely aware that he hadn't been eating much. He glanced at Hammer, basking in the sun in his usual spot on the faded blue rug beneath the kitchen window.

Hammer waddled over to him and put his face in Ben's lap. "What's up, buddy?" Ben rubbed his head. "Let's go outside." He checked the shed, but Shae wasn't there. She had wandered the park alone yesterday, so he figured she was just out and about somewhere again.

It was a perfect summer day; the sky was cloudless cobalt, and the temperature was like bathwater. He grabbed a tennis ball from Hammer's ancient clapboard doghouse. Hammer didn't use it much these days, preferring his spot on the blue rug in the kitchen.

Ben held the ball aloft as he opened the gate, and they entered the park. Hammer jumped halfheartedly and barked. When they reached the bottom of the incline, Ben hurled the ball off into the trees, and Hammer bounded after it. The past few days, he usually just brought his guitar outside and played while Hammer lay in the yard.

They struck off left, going down a narrower path than the one he'd taken Shae along. It led to the same stream but took a little longer to get there and led to a broader expanse of water. As he took the damp ball from Hammer's mouth, the song rose inside him again. He'd not brought his headphones, he realized. Ben usually listened to music. He *always* listened to music, but he hadn't needed to put his headphones on since discovering Shae.

This path rose in a steep but small hill before it meandered back to the stream. He grabbed an overhanging limb to steady himself, and it snapped off.

"Here, boy, Hammer!" he called, and Hammer trotted along the top of the hill, running parallel to meet him. The path down was a little overgrown but cleared up as they got closer to the water. Ben threw the ball, and Hammer took off after it through the trees. From somewhere Ben couldn't see, Hammer began barking. Then he emitted a rare, primal growl, which Ben had only heard a handful of times in his life. The fine hairs on his neck rose. There were several more barks, followed by silence. A far-off rustling sound grew closer. Hammer bounded back, barking urgently, slamming his front legs into Ben's. "What's up? What's the matter?" Then his dog ran back up the hill with more speed than Ben knew was still possible in the old dog. When Hammer reached the top, he turned, panting, and looked back to Ben. He barked and tossed his head in the direction of home. The message was clear.

For a few seconds, intrepid curiosity rooted him to the spot, and Ben stared in the direction he'd last thrown the ball in. Nothing. Then he heard branches snapping. The sound grew louder and took on the distinctive rhythm of approaching footsteps. Breaking into a sweat—it had become rapidly hotter in the last few minutes—he scanned the wood. Then he went cold.

Some two dozen yards away was another impossible creature: a humanlike stick insect around seven feet tall. It was hideously thin with long claw-like hands, and it was heading in his direction on rickety legs.

Ben couldn't move. Useless mutterings escaped like trapped birds from his mouth—sounds which tried to be words but failed. It came closer, swinging its head from side to side like it was looking for something. The monster's mouth hung open, displaying long, pointed teeth. Its nose was two vertical slashes in its face, giving it the semblance of a burn victim. Its roving eyes were black pits; the pocked skin the gray tone of rocks or thunderclouds, more hide than flesh. It moved with alarming speed, taking huge staggering steps. There was a smell accompanying it—a sweet, rotting sulfuric odor.

Ben gaped, paralyzed until a rush of adrenaline allowed his legs to work again. He stumbled into a run back up the hill, teeth clenched. His shoulders tensed at the thought of the creature leaping onto his back. Amidst all of it was a weirdly glorious thrill. He stopped once, his hand to a tree trunk, and turned around to confirm it was still there, that it was real. And when Ben saw its repulsive, magnificent form a bit farther away, his mind sang with terrifying glee.

It tilted its head up towards him. Their eyes met. Ben's knees turned to water. He bolted away. "*Fuck, fuck, fuck!*"

Amy's long legs were draped over the arm of one side of a kitchen chair, and she rubbed a bandage on her ankle where she'd gotten more ink added. "I'm not sure how much to pack, that's the only thing."

"Do you really want to do this? I mean, it's so last minute, and you don't even know them that well." Andre stirred honey into her tea. *Don't leave, Amy. I need to tell you something. I need to show you something.*

"Oh, come on. I finally have some sort of a job, and you don't want me to go? It's going to be fun. I get to travel with the band and just work at the shows selling the T-shirts and CDs—apparently, some people still buy CDs. They're going all over. They're going up to Alaska. I've never *been* to Alaska. And don't worry. I've known Morgan for a few years. The rest of them are nice. And Margot plays bass so I won't be the only girl—"

They heard quick, pounding footsteps from the back porch, and in the next instant, the door slid open, and Hammer leaped inside, followed by Ben, who slammed it back shut so hard Andre was worried for a second that the glass would shatter. He locked it then dropped to his knees, panting. He kept his eyes clamped shut for a beat and hunched over, hugging himself. A thin streak of blood ran down the side of his face. He looked up, his eyes wild.

"Shit." Amy sat up. "Benny?"

Andre quickly poured a glass of water for Ben. It was a habit she'd obtained from her mother: a glass of water was the panacea for any crisis or distress. She handed it to him. Hammer rubbed against her legs, nasally whining. She knelt and stroked the dog's neck.

Ben opened his eyes, took a couple of quick gulps, then frowned at the water, and thrust the glass back at her as if he didn't know why she'd given it to him. "Thanks."

"Dude, what's wrong!" Amy cried. She pointed to the scrape on his face. "And what did you do to your face?"

"Huh?" He rubbed his cheek, then looked at his fingers. He shook his head. "Scraped it on a branch or something."

He stood up and staggered around the living room, looking disoriented. Amy went to the back door, unlocked it, and started to open it. "What—"

"*Don't!*" Ben shoved her out of the way and slammed it shut again, locking it once more. "Don't go outside! I saw—there's something out there. Someone."

"What? Who did you see? What's wrong?"

He shook his head rapidly back and forth, "I—I can't."

In Andre's mind, she heard a lovely voice they must obey: *"Do not tell."*

"Ben." Andre swallowed, kept her voice deceptively casual as she looked at the back door and wrung her hands. "Sit down. C'mon, it's okay. What did you see?"

He went over to the fridge, opened it, stared at the beer inside, then closed it without taking one and slumped down at the kitchen table. "I . . . saw—there was a naked guy in the woods."

Amy laughed. "A *naked* guy?"

There was a long pause. "Yeah."

Andre shuddered and looked at him, bright-eyed, urgent. He looked away.

"We-ell, did he seem like he needed help? Maybe we should go see if he needs help."

"Nope," Ben said decidedly, shaking his head. Then he muttered, "I need a cigarette."

Amy opened her mouth, looked from one of them to the other. She appeared about to protest but just looked speculatively at the back door. "I've got some in the car," she said. "Can we go out the *front* door, you think?" She grinned and shivered. "Some weirdo is wandering the park. That's creepy. I wonder if he's the one killing animals."

"Killing animals?" Andre looked up sharply.

"Yeah, there was something about it on the news we saw this morning. They've found a few deer that were like, dismembered." She frowned. "Or, oh, he's probably from the Harven! Maybe he got lost."

Fifteen miles north was the small resort and nudist colony built around the natural springs occurring a few miles north of the Shellara lake.

Amy laughed again. "*Man,* would that suck!"

The three of them went out the front door, Ben walking with Amy to her car, glancing right and left anxiously while Andre waited for them on the porch. When they got back to the porch and lit their cigarettes, Amy took a drag and ventured, "Ben?"

"Yeah?"

"Can you tell us what happened?" She giggled. "Did he try to assault you?"

He flicked his ash, his eyes scanning the yard. "You're hilarious."

"Oh, come on. It's just really weird. And I don't understand why you're scared to go out back."

Ben looked off onto the road and followed the distance with his eyes. "It was far away, but it was walking towards me."

"It?" Amy frowned.

Ben shrugged. "I couldn't see him very well, but he didn't look . . . right."

"But you're sure it was a guy, right? Did you see his cock? I mean, how old was this person?"

Ben shook his head. "Look, just forget it."

Andre gave him a meaningful look and tilted her head towards Amy, but he gave a tight shake of his head.

"This is some weird shit." Amy laughed. They smoked quietly for a minute, and then Amy stubbed out her cigarette. "Well, I've got to pack."

"What for?" Ben asked.

"She's going on tour with Morgan Cross's band," Andre told him.

"The Ransom," Amy said. "You've heard them, right?"

"What are you, a groupie now?"

"I'm going to help with selling merchandise, asshole."

"You're leaving today?" Ben glanced at Andre. "How long are you going to be gone?"

Amy shrugged. "Couple of months. I can take a Greyhound home if it gets crazy."

Half an hour later, Amy left carrying a backpack and a small suitcase. When she was gone, Ben slumped down at the table with a beer. "Well, that takes care of whether or not we tell Amy. I can't look for Shae anyway right now. I'm not going back outside today. Not even to the shed."

Andre sighed and sat across from him. "So . . . what happened?"

Ben tapped his phone a few times, frowned, then sat back, crossing his arms. He looked at her. "It wasn't a person. It was this horrible monster thing. I don't know what the hell it was."

After a moment, she asked quietly, "Was it like her?"

He shrugged. "I mean, no. It was the most horrifying thing I've ever . . . it was a fucking *monster*. I don't know what else to call it." He laughed. "Jesus, if you weren't here, and if you didn't see Shae and know about her, I would check myself into a mental hospital. I would think I was completely bat shit."

Andre chewed her lip. "What did it look like?"

"It was tall and really skinny. It moved fast and had these huge sharp teeth." He looked around anxiously. "Where's Hammer? Oh." He relaxed upon seeing his dog drowsing at the foot of the couch. He got up and pulled a yellow legal pad and a pen from the small drawer between the refrigerator and sink. "Here, I'll draw it for you."

Andre had always admired Ben's artistic skills. Amy, too, was a talented artist; she'd designed most of her own tattoos, and Ben could render images with almost photographic accuracy. It came in handy during games of Pictionary, but otherwise, he was too consumed with music to put much energy into this other gift. He slumped in the chair and leaned the legal pad against the side of the table, resting it on his stomach. He drank his beer while scribbling, his head turned to the side, frowning in focus.

"We should ask her about this," Andre said.

"Yeah, I'm pretty sure what I saw today was the 'Unseelie,'" he said drily.

"Maybe we should think about calling the police. If there is something out there that is killing animals. It could hurt people too . . ."

He furrowed his brow as his hands quickly dashed lines "The only way to get anyone to believe us would be to reveal her. I've been thinking about it."

While he scribbled, Andre flipped through an encyclopedia of magical creatures she'd checked out of the Arroyo library. She was on the letter *C*: Cerberus, Changelings, Corrigans. "I'm having the *weirdest* dreams lately," she said quietly. "They are so vivid, but when I wake up, it's almost completely gone . . ." She looked up at him, but his eyes were on the page he was working on. "I get these impressions kind of leftover in my mind, though. I think I keep seeing animals."

"Uh . . . I don't know. Yeah, it probably does mean something. I've been getting these songs in my head."

She sat up straighter. "I was going to say something about that! I've heard you playing. It's awesome, Ben."

"Yeah. It's never happened like this before. And there's this pressure. Like, I have to grab the song and play it, or I almost feel sick. It's fucking weird." He put the pencil down and stared at the image. He looked up at her and then back at the page, then back at her, hesitating.

"Are you done?" she asked. "Let me see."

He scooted the pad towards her. "It looked pretty much like this."

For a second, she just saw a gray mess on the page, but once the ragged lines materialized into a coherent image, she flinched. It looked like some monster from the imagination of Lovecraft rendered by Arthur Rackham. She imagined seeing it in the flesh alone in the woods. "Jesus," she whispered.

"Yeah," Ben muttered. "It was like . . . a corruption of nature. It wasn't right. I don't want to see anything like this ever again."

"This is *horrible*." Her voice rose a few octaves. She glanced at the back door and looked at the windows, suddenly wishing she was crouched in a closet under covers. She wished Ryan was there. "You *saw* this?"

"Yup."

Andre traced the edge of the paper with her finger.

Ben stood and gently took the pad from her. "I wasn't able to get its eyes right . . ."

They both jumped at a knock at the back door. Shae stood there, expectantly. Her wings were closed. Ben got up and opened the door for her, looking warily outside for a moment.

"It is not usually locked," Shae observed.

"Hammer and I were out in the park, and this thing was wandering around." He held up the picture. He hesitated, waiting to see her response, but her expression was as chill and detached as a cat's. "I think this may have been the thing you said followed you? The woodwalker?"

Shae studied the image. "How did it seem?"

"Uh . . . horrible? How do you mean?"

"How did it seem? Was it sick? Did it have trouble—" she made a swimming motion with her hands "—moving around?"

Ben frowned. "No, I don't think so. It seemed like it was moving fast, actually. And, there was a really bad smell."

"Yes. It is rotting. The Unseelie will grow weaker because it cannot adapt."

"Well, I guess that's good," Ben muttered.

"You said it followed you," Andre reminded her. "Why?"

"It jumped into the light with me. I do not know why. It is not nice to be here. The woodwalker is stupid."

"Well, we've got to do something about it," Andre said. "It's been killing wildlife. We can't risk it hurting anyone. What if it killed a hiker?"

Shae shrugged. "Not all animals die from violence. Some get sick. And the woodwalker doesn't collect a tithe. I will not let it do that."

"What the hell does that mean?" Ben asked.

Shae ignored him.

Andre asked the next question. She'd asked it several times now and had yet to get a satisfactory answer. It was getting frustrating, but she couldn't help but feel she must tread carefully. "Shae . . . where did you come from? How . . . *where* did you come from?" she repeated.

Shae blinked a few times rapidly and swayed from side to side. "I come from elsewhere."

"Okay." Andre leaned her elbows on the table and rubbed her temples. "So did you come from uh, outer space or underground or another dimension? And *why* are you here?"

"I come from elsewhere, and I am sundered. I am here to bestow gifts."

"What do you mean?" Andre asked, trying to ignore the distraction of her beautiful voice. "Gifts for who?"

Shae shook her head. *"No more questions."* She took the honey jar and went back outside to the shed.

Ben slept in Andre's bed that night. It was a little awkward. They kept a big space between one another. And though neither of them could fall asleep for a long time, they didn't talk much but lay like quiet sentinels side by side.

CHAPTER SIX

I sneak into the pretty one's room where they both sleep tonight because they are afraid of the woodwalker. I look at pictures of the Ryan and the Amy. Then I go to the serious one's room and smell his clothes and bed. I run my fingers against his guitar strings and plunk at his keyboard. Then, because I can't spin much glamour in the house, I go back out to my shed. I can transform that space into a glittering little jewelry box.

Serious one—my music boy, has seen the woodwalker. Smelled its rot. The creature cannot collect the tithe. It's not how things are to be done. And I feel the strain of it now: *My other task.* I must orchestrate their deaths somehow. And it doesn't make sense. What point is there to bestow these gifts upon them if I am only to snuff them out? Will I kill the serious one, or the pretty one, or both? Someone else entirely? I lay on my bedding and watch the flowers I've conjured sway in a little breeze. I close my eyes and imagine butterflies fluttering down the pleached alley. *What do I do?* I envision the sides of the alley and all the flowers there.

They don't have so many colors in this dreary world. There are butterflies here, though. And those strange, little bats. Ugly and precious.

How will I do it? I think of different ways. I saw Andre eating mushrooms once. I could take some from the wood—the ones with the poison smell . . . I could sneak them into their food and let them die this way. But they have to get their gifts first, right? My wings constrict, and I ache for my name. I wonder if I'll ever enter the lightning again. If I'll ever see my home again.

CHAPTER SEVEN

Late July

Andre squinted at the page. She hadn't been sleeping well and couldn't focus. She was attempting to read another book on the physics behind the theory of parallel dimensions. The last one had been more accessible; armchair science written for the layman. This dry tome made her eyes cross. She'd been a good student, but science was never her forte. Ryan would comprehend this sort of thing better. And he now sensed something was up. He didn't connect it to the journal Andre scribbled in constantly or the volumes on folklore and woo-woo sciences she was reading all the time.

She looked up when the back door slid open, and Shae stepped in. It was a hot morning, and Shae looked damp and dirty. An oak leaf was pasted to her chest and a small gray feather to her collarbone. The monarch, a constant presence now, was on her shoulder. Andre couldn't shake the notion it nursed from Shae's skin, the way it latched on to her, slowly flapping its wings.

"Have you been out all night?" Andre asked, closing the book. It was becoming apparent that Shae didn't follow a circadian rhythm.

"Yes." Shae closed the door behind her. She wore the little dress with the open back Andre had purchased for her a couple of weeks before. It was tattered now, and, Andre realized, too small. Shae was growing. Andre had been suspecting this for some time, but now she was certain of it. Shae was a few inches taller than she had been when she first arrived.

Andre didn't ask what Shae had been doing or if she'd seen the "Gray Man." Shae was not inclined to talk about it. Half the time, she wouldn't deign to reply to inquiries concerning her monitoring of the Unseelie. At best, Andre received one-word answers or clipped claims of ignorance before Shae would disappear into the shed.

Shae spent long stretches there when she wasn't out in the wood. Andre hadn't entered the shed in weeks. There was an unspoken rule that it was now Shae's space.

"Want some honey?"

Shae nodded, went to the cabinet, and pulled out a jar. She unscrewed the lid, dipped her finger in, and sucked on it. Shae went through a jar a day. Even with Andre's discount, it was getting expensive.

Shae gulped down a few swallows of honey, secured the lid, and put it away. She headed for the back door, and Andre was seized with a sudden and desperate desire for Shae to stay, for her to throw Andre a bone, for *something* to change. "Umm, hey, wait . . . do you want to go somewhere today?"

Shae stopped and turned around. "I have been through the river and the hills all over the park. I have been as far as where the road begins again. I always stop there." It was the most she'd spoken in days.

"I've got an idea," Andre said. She went upstairs to get Ben.

An hour later, Andre stood at the front door, waiting for Ben and Shae. She wore a tank top, sandals, and jeans, and her backpack containing a hooded sweatshirt, two thin beach towels, a paperback, her wallet, sunscreen, two pairs of sunglasses, and a small bathrobe for Shae. At her feet was a small cooler filled with water, cucumber sandwiches, and figs. She saw Ben had added a beer. She opened the front door and peered out at the empty road anxiously. Her idea seemed reckless now, but she didn't want to change her mind since Ben had actually agreed even though he had to work later that night, and he was usually super paranoid.

"I hope this isn't completely stupid of us," Ben muttered. Andre jumped. He'd come up from behind so quietly and now stood looking at the road with her. His acoustic was slung over his shoulder.

"We'll look for a secluded spot, and we can always leave if we start to feel uncomfortable, or if it's too crowded, or whatever," Andre said, fidgeting.

Shae came around the hall corner. If Andre had been feeling more lighthearted, she might have laughed. Her ears were the biggest problem after her size. A knit beanie had been fished out of Ben's sock drawer and took care of that problem. Andre had found children's sunglasses and a small green cardigan at a thrift store a few days before. She couldn't find any shoes narrow enough for Shae's feet, but

Shae went barefoot all the time anyway. "You look great." Andre grinned. From a distance, Shae could pass as an unfashionable, odd-looking child.

"I can't believe we're doing this," Ben said, shaking his head.

"We need to," Andre replied. "We're all going crazy here." She opened the door and stepped out onto the porch. "Coast is clear."

They made their way quickly down the lawn to Andre's car. She had drawn the driving straw since the trip was her idea and because she already had a full tank of gas, and Ben claimed his was empty.

Ben looked around anxiously. *This is insane*, Andre thought as she opened the back passenger door and motioned for Shae to sit down. She reached over her tiny lap to grab the seat belt and fasten her in. "She'd probably be safer with a booster seat," Andre said.

"This is likely the rarest being in the world. She should not be driven around on the freeway in a twelve-year-old Honda on the way to a public beach," Ben said.

"But maybe she's not," Andre said, settling into the driver's seat. "How many others could be hiding in people's attics or sheds right now? We have no idea." She put on her seat belt, checked her rear-view mirror, and peeled quickly out onto the road.

Shae stiffened slightly, but otherwise showed no sign of alarm at being in a moving vehicle. Ben had given her a brief explanation of what a car was and how it worked before they left.

As they got north of Arroyo, the sky darkened a little. On an exit that ended in a red light, they saw a dead deer off to the side of the road. Andre made a whimpering sound.

"Shit. That sucks," Ben said, taking off his sunglasses and sitting up.

When they crossed a bridge, Shae sat up and stared over the water. Thirty minutes later, they merged onto the stretch of road that led to a supernal landscape. Larger clumps of miniature gray mountains surrounded russet, alabaster, and green hills. The road dipped and wound, turning precariously, while little valleys and paths snaked off into gradient shades of green and gray in the distance half-covered in cottony fog. Ben rolled down his window, letting in salty, cool air. Occasionally other cars came towards them on the opposite side of the thin road. Andre rolled along at a near crawl around several looping turns. Bicyclists in tight, garishly colored bodysuits and large sunglasses whizzed by like large bugs, going faster than the cars in both directions.

They rounded a few more turns, entered a copse bordering the beach, and were suddenly engulfed by cars and people. A man in a khaki uniform waved his hand for the cars to come through. Opposite him was a small box of a building where someone sat taking money for parking.

"Fuck." Ben clenched his fists and brought both hands to his forehead. "Let's go. Let's get out of here. Andre, turn around."

"It's okay." She chewed her lips and looked around, ignoring her pounding heart. "All right, so it's more crowded than I was expecting for a Wednesday." She glanced back at Shae. The faerie had removed her sunglasses, and Andre hadn't noticed until now.

"Put your sunglasses back on," Ben hissed.

Shae obliged, slowly.

"Ben, chill out," Andre said in a light voice far calmer than she felt. "It's going to be fine." She took a deep breath and looked ahead while her hands fumbled in her purse. "We'll get right through. It's six dollars for parking. I've got exact change."

Ben's voice was soft, incredulous. "Are you seriously doing this?"

"And it's okay, if—"

"If someone *sees* her?"

Andre pulled up a little farther in the line of cars. There were four in front of them waiting to pay. "So what? What are they going to say? 'Hey, you there! Little woman! Get out of the car! You're not one of us!' This isn't the airport. They aren't going to even look in the car. Besides, she seems fine at a glance."

He groaned and ran his hands over his pockets for cigarettes that weren't there. A moment later, the ruddy-faced woman took Andre's cash and mumbled, "Have a nice day."

Ben shook his head. "Okay, sorry. I'm not used to this."

"You have to stop thinking we're doing something wrong." Andre pulled into a spot much farther down the graveled parking area than the other cars. "We have every right to be here. Shae is . . . our cousin. She has a . . . condition? She has every right to be here."

Getting out of the car wasn't a big deal either. And as soon as they stepped out, it was clear they weren't likely going to need the towels or the sunscreen; it was gray and chilly, the mercurial weather of the West Coast. Andre slung on her backpack, and Ben grabbed the cooler. They were at the edge of a wooded area that bordered part of the beach. The main path to the water was cordoned off by ropes, making a sort of guardrail along the sides of the wooden steps leading up to the top where the ocean spread out below. They took a smaller trail, amidst clusters of ferns and purple wildflowers to avoid other beachgoers. It was steeper, and at the top, they were rewarded for their trek.

Andre took a deep breath and flung out one arm in a mock-grand gesture. "The Pacific!" She was relieved to see the nearest people were still several hundred yards away. Below them was the slate gray and creamy white ocean. Waves pounded softly against the shore, soporific.

Shae took her sunglasses and hat off. Andre sucked in her breath but didn't object. Ben only frowned and looked away, coughed once, and stepped closer to Shae. In the overcast afternoon, her eyes were dark golden pools. Wind rippled her white hair out behind her. Even with her wings hidden, she looked unearthly. She looked down at her feet and wiggled her toes in the sand. Andre followed her example and removed her sandals. They wandered down, sat on a little hummock of grass, and stared out at sea. Andre rummaged in the bag and pulled out the food. Shae nibbled a fig while Ben and Andre munched on cucumber sandwiches. He opened the beer.

Shae sifted sand through her small fingers.

"So, what do you think?" Andre asked.

Shae scooped the sand in her hands and let it sprinkle down. She gazed toward the sea. "This is nice."

"Does it smell bad here, too?" Andre asked, encouraged.

Shae looked at her and then back at the water. "Yes."

Andre said, "So it didn't smell where you came from?"

Ben gave her a wary look.

"I cannot remember very well," Shae said. "Days ago, I could remember more than I do now." She looked at Andre, and although her voice never wavered, Andre thought her eyes were sad. She looked back down.

"What about the Gray Man?" Andre asked gently. "Do you remember anything about where the Unseelie came from?"

"The Unseel will die. A Woodwalker will only rot here."

"How come?"

"Because it cannot adapt."

"Is there anything we can do to help you?"

"No. I do not think so."

They snacked quietly for a few more minutes, and Ben finished the beer. Andre pulled out her phone. She took pictures of the water, of gulls, some pods of seaweed. After a rudimentary explanation of what the camera feature was and how to use it, she gave it to Shae to play with. She snapped pictures of Andre and Ben and little purple-and-yellow wildflowers amidst tufts of grass above them before the sand started. Watching her, it occurred to Andre that other beachgoers might utilize the zooming capacity on their own devices. She glanced at Ben, wondering if he was thinking the same thing, but he was just squinting at Shae with the same look of keen desperation he'd been wearing the last couple of weeks.

"Here, Shae." Andre sat up and held her hand out. "Let me take a picture of you." She snapped a few of Shae by herself, and then she motioned for Ben to stand next to her. He obliged, awkwardly placing his arm over her tiny shoulder. The monarch fluttered above his head. Andre stepped around them, taking several shots. She stopped and dropped to her knees in the sand. She scrolled through the images though it was hard to see them, backlit. "Shae, you are photogenic!" She looked up. "Uh, that means you look nice in pictures." She got a text from Ryan:

You are at the beach

I am inside an office

Bet beach is better

Shae turned and stared at the ocean. "You want to walk with me?" Ben asked. She nodded. They started toward the water. He looked back at Andre, "You coming?"

Shivering, she shook her head and sat back down on the towels they had spread out and wrapped her arms around her knees. She tried to recall if there was a time it had ever been warm enough to swim in. The ocean was nothing like the silky, comfortably cool Shellara, but Triton Beach was a majestic change of scenery.

Ben walked along slowly with Shae, who moved with almost a normal deference to gravity for once. His feet made prominent marks in the sand as it got darker and wetter. He shoved his hands in his pockets. There were people in closer proximity than he was comfortable with. They came to a large piece of driftwood, and she hopped gracefully over it. "Don't fly, okay?" he said before he could help himself.

"I won't," she said. "I know."

"Sorry." They stopped at the shore, their feet sinking into the cold sand, and waited for the next wave to run over their feet. Shae closed her eyes, swaying. Ben sucked in his breath as freezing water ran over his feet, splashing up against his hairy shins. Shae clutched the sides of her dress but gave no sign of feeling the cold even though the water came up to her thighs. A gust of wind whipped her hair up and around her face. As the tide retreated, sucking sand away from their feet, Ben felt the vertiginous thrill of moving backward he'd been so amused by as a child.

He startled when her little, almost amphibian hand grasped his arm. She looked up at him and searched his face. "I have to collect a tithe. I don't think it will be you. You will play the songs." Her voice sounded like it came from inside a shell held up to his ear.

He stepped back, trembling from something that wasn't the cold. He blinked a few times and shook his head against the feeling he'd narrowly escaped some disaster. He swallowed and looked out over the water, felt salt sting his eyes. He should ask her what she was talking about, but he found himself only nodding, and then he half walked, half staggered away from her.

When Ben reached their spot, Andre was talking quietly on her phone to Ryan, lying on her back with her knees up and her extra sweater covering her face. He sat down and stared out at the water and tiny Shae, with her white hair rippling like a peace flag. "Where the fuck did you come from?" he asked to the wind. He got a text from Mateo. *"Added some new stuff to the Dropbox. Check it out. Can't wait to visit so we can jam."* Ben suddenly craved normalcy. Of playing music, he and his best friend made together. He sensed it wouldn't be the same when they did jam together again. This new stuff possessed him now. Other music felt flat lately.

Andre lifted the sweater off her face and sat up. "Okay. Love you too. Yeah, we do need a beach day together. I'll talk to you later. Bye." She set her phone aside and lay with arms up, her elbows covering her eyes.

After a few minutes, Shae came back to them. Her dress was soaked. Andre held out a towel. "You're not cold at all?"

Shae looked down at herself as if just realizing she was wet. She shook her head, then looked up and licked her lips. "Salty," she said. Andre ushered her back over to where their things were. "Ben, here, hold up this towel." He shielded them while Andre helped Shae out of her clothes and wrapped another towel around her, quickly covering up her folded, wet wings. She rummaged in the backpack. "So glad I brought this," she muttered. "I almost didn't." She pulled out a child's blue cotton bathrobe. Shae was a little tall for it now, although she hadn't been when Andre had purchased it the previous week. The monarch fluttered around their heads; apparently, it had avoided getting wet. Andre wrung out the wet dress and laid it on the sand. "Was it freezing?" she asked Ben.

"Yeah, Hammer could probably have tolerated it, though."

"I told you he could come," Andre said.

"I know. Just didn't want to add anything extra to the day, you know?"

Andre and Shae scooped and sifted the sand and started on a little pyramid while Ben played his guitar. The monarch fluttered around him a few times before perching on Shae's shoulder.

"I wish I knew what you are, Shae." Andre was confessional, almost desperate. She made a deep trench in the sand with the side of her hand. "It doesn't make sense to us. You're like magic, you know."

She did not expect Shae to reply, but after a moment, the faerie said, "On your TV . . . I saw . . . about animals—bats? They fly at night?"

Andre nodded. "They are kind of like birds . . ." She frowned, then laughed at herself. "Except they really aren't. They are totally different from birds."

Shae waited for her to say something else, and when Andre didn't, she continued. "They have a sense that people and other animals do not have."

"Sonar." Andre nodded, frowning. "Bats have sonar."

"Yes, It's like that."

"Do you have sonar?" Andre asked.

Shae shook her head.

Andre took a deep breath, squinted at the horizon, and a slow lapping wave. She wanted to be careful, but this was the most that Shae ever talked to her. She had so many questions. She turned back to the sand and scooped some more over the mound they had formed. "What are the people—the *beings* like, where you come from?"

Shae sniffed and looked up, her eyes following the monarch fluttering around their heads. "I do not know anymore. I do not remember."

"And what about the woodwalker? Is it killing those animals in the park? If it doesn't die soon, then we can't leave it out there to hurt someone."

"They are not all dying from the woodwalker. Some of them get sick." The monarch rested in her lap, and she stroked its wings. "I have to do work here, and I have to give you gifts and collect the tithe."

"What do you mean? What is the tithe?" Andre asked.

But Shae did not reply, and Andre found she was rather afraid of the answer. She wanted to ask Shae if there were mermaids where she came from. She wanted them to be real too. They looked at one another, and Andre felt a flare on the tendril between them. It was a singular feeling, an etheric string; slight, but growing more tangible each day.

Andre shivered at the sound of Ben's playing and watched him. He'd always been talented, but his songs possessed something different now. It was like he'd entered an unexplored territory of melody. His music made her skin erupt in goosebumps, and her eyes burn with unshed tears. There was something deeply manipulative about it.

She was about to comment to him about the song when she felt the first two droplets. In seconds they were being sprinkled all over. Shae opened her robe, allowing the monarch to rest against her chest, then covered it up. Ben stood. Andre stretched and began gathering their stuff. "I don't feel like working tonight," Ben said.

Andre tilted her head back to look up at the sky and immediately felt dizzy. "Ben, do you mind driving home? I'm a little lightheaded."

They skipped the scenic route this time and took the faster way going slightly south. Andre pulled out her phone and sent Ryan a couple of pictures of the sand pyramids she and Shae had made. Merri texted her, asking if the Chestnut was out of a specific brand of Melatonin someone was looking for.

Andre felt something on her arm. An ant. She flicked it off and then found a few more on her ankles and neck. She squirmed and searched herself, hoping no more were hidden in her clothing. She pulled the Dictionary of Creatures out of her backpack. She'd set it down for a couple of weeks to read other stuff. She was on the letter G. She skimmed the pages: Genies, The Gentry, Ghouls, Goblins, Good Folk, Green Man, Gremlins. After a few minutes, she tilted her head back, closed her eyes, and napped until they got home.

She looked around sleepily when Ben parked back at the house. "Coast is clear," he said. They quickly got out, slamming the doors, and darted up to the house. Ben started up the coffee machine. Shae pulled out something from the pocket of her robe. A starfish, the circumference of a post-it note, lay in the palm of her hand. She set it on the table.

Andre frowned. "You brought that all the way home with you? How did you find it?"

"I draw the creatures to me."

"Poor thing. It's probably not going to make it. Even if I brought it to the lake . . . it needs saltwater anyway, right?"

Ben looked disturbed. "Can you just like, make that go away? I've got to get ready for work."

Andre plucked it up gingerly between her thumb and forefinger, wrinkling her nose at the salty, fishy smell. "I think it's dead now anyway." She stood up. "I'll take it outside."

There was a moment when Andre opened the back door to dispose of the starfish, as Ben was pouring his coffee when he knew something was wrong. Maybe he registered on an unconscious level that Hammer had not toddled up when they got home.

Andre came stumbling back inside. Ben had heard the description before of someone's face "draining of color," but he'd never actually seen someone go sickly white from the top of their forehead down as Andre's did just then. Her left hand was pressed against her stomach, and her right was clamped over her mouth.

"What is it?"

She shook her head back and forth and cried, *"Oh god, oh god, oh god!"*

He reached for the back door, and she grabbed his arm. "Don't! *Wait!* Don't look, please!"

It was like a different day. He hadn't noticed it as much when they'd gone up and into the house, but now the contrast from the atmosphere of Triton Beach compared to Arroyo was dramatic. It was at least ten degrees warmer, and the sun was out. It was disorienting and made the day seem sliced up and sewn awkwardly together. The afternoon was still. There was scarcely a breeze.

It was more blood than he'd ever seen; huge crimson patches everywhere as if a barrel of wine had been sloshed around, and the entire contents spilled. It was all over the doghouse and the trunks of the incense cedars. The deck had been mostly spared except for a few feet of the left corner. A patch of bloody fur sat next to one of Hammer's overturned bowls. Ben blinked. It took a moment for the shape to make sense as it wasn't large enough to be *all* of Hammer.

His pulse filled his ears like the pounding of the surf. He was vaguely aware of Andre crying behind him. He stepped down from the porch and stared at what was roughly the front half of his dog. One of Hammer's eyes was gone, and there was a gray film over the other. Later, Ben would consider that this had given him a strange little comfort. Hammer was *very* gone. There was no trace of a soul, no vestiges of suffering in that face. He stood and stumbled back onto the deck. He grabbed Andre's arm and found his voice. "Go back inside."

"You come too!" She looked around, her eyes filled with tears, strands of black hair sticking to her face. In a shaking voice, she asked, "Where is the rest?"

Instead of going back inside, they wandered the yard for a minute, stunned. They found more of Hammer behind the doghouse. Organs and entrails were flung around. Flies already swarmed over the glistening piles of gore. After a minute, Andre vomited up cucumber sandwiches into the bougainvillea.

Then Ben couldn't form sentences. He just whispered, "Jesus, fucking, fuck, the fuck . . ." He saw the Gray Man's face in his mind, the black eyes and long sharp teeth, the claw-like hands to stab and tear with. Once Hammer had gotten a piece of glass in his paw, and he'd whined terribly. The sound of his dog in pain had been awful. Ben could not let himself imagine what his companion had suffered today while he'd been admiring the ocean.

Andre straightened up and wiped her mouth with the back of her hand. Ben noticed Shae then. She'd followed them out into the yard and was crouched in front of Hammer's head. She placed her hands on either side of the dog's face, her skin becoming marked with its blood.

Ben stepped over to her. "Don't touch him," he said through clenched teeth. He didn't recognize his own voice. It sounded like someone else, someone older. He wanted to yank her away, but whether it was out of a desire to protect her from the filth, or because he blamed her in some way, he didn't know. But he forced his hands to stay at his sides.

She let go and stood and looked up at him. For once, he thought he could read something in her face, in her huge eyes: she was surprised. She'd not known anything was amiss while they'd been out. "I should not have left," she said softly.

CHAPTER EIGHT

Ben woke to the sound of Andre knocking on his door and calling his name. He pressed his face into the damp pillow. Piercing light from behind the blinds. Muscles, sore from digging. Acknowledgement of another hangover. And then he remembered. There were no songs in him just then. "Ben?" The door opened, and she poked her head in, timid. "Sorry to wake you, but I've got to go to work, and I wanted to talk to you." There was a hitch in her voice.

He sat up on his elbow and looked at her bleary-eyed. "What's up?" His voice came out phlegmy. He coughed and cleared his throat.

She stepped inside, closing the door behind her with her foot and offering him a glass of water in one hand and vitamins in the other. She had on a long, loose-fitting dress of dark material. It was not the sort of thing she usually wore. Her hair was pulled back in a low bun that rested on the nape of her neck. She sat down at the foot of his bed and stared down in her lap, looking so much like a demure girl from another century that he wanted to laugh. "It's just awful. I'm so sorry. I should never have suggested we go to the beach. If we hadn't left . . ."

He swallowed the pills, grimacing, and chugged the water. "Andre, just don't. It's not your fault. I shouldn't even have to say it."

"I can't stop thinking about it. I couldn't sleep for forever last night. And then, when I did, there were these intense dreams. I saw bats all around the yard, and they scared me, and there was this beautiful land beyond our house, but I couldn't get—"

"I was lucky," he muttered. "I passed out."

She wiped her nose, blinking rapidly. Her gray eyes were pretty when she cried; they turned a vibrant, metallic color. Her lashes were long and wet, her lips so red from her biting them. Ben flushed, mortified that his standard morning hard-on wasn't going anywhere. He shifted the sheets around, desperately wishing she would leave the room.

"It wouldn't have happened if we hadn't taken Shae away from here." She sniffled.

"We don't know what the hell would have happened," he said miserably.

Shae was the only reason they hadn't called the police. After seeing Hammer in the yard, she'd informed them that she would, "Go and kill Gray Man." Then she'd gone back inside and grabbed a big kitchen knife before bolting off into the woods.

Ben called his work, saying bluntly, "My dog died. I'm not coming in." He hung up before his boss could offer sympathy or ask questions. Then he ingested a regrettable amount of alcohol over the next several hours while they debated whether or not to involve authority figures, ultimately deciding not to since they didn't know where Shae was. They spent the rest of the night with the wretched task of disposing of Hammer and hosing down the yard.

Andre wiped her eyes. "We've got to do something. If Shae doesn't come back soon . . . if we don't know if she's taken care of it . . . we can't leave that monster out there to hurt anyone else." She pulled her phone from a pocket in her dress and quickly stood. "I've got to go. Will you try and talk to her today? I saw her last night after you passed out. She landed on the porch just for a second. I asked her if she'd found him, but she didn't answer me. She just looked around and flew off again."

"How shocking." He chugged the rest of the water. "Yeah, of course, I'll try to talk to her if I see her."

Andre turned to go, and it occurred to him that he should see her safely to her car. The Gray Man had attacked Hammer in daylight. There was no reason it couldn't snatch Andre in the front yard. "Hang on." He got up carefully, so his back was to her, and grimacing at the discomfort, he shoved himself into his jeans and followed her downstairs. "You look like you're in mourning," he said.

She opened the front door and paused. "Well, I am." She tucked a loose strand of her hair back. "I'm going to stay at Ryan's tonight."

Ben nodded, scanning the yard. "Listen . . . thank you for cleaning up with me yesterday."

She gave him a quick, tight hug. He walked her down the driveway and stood with his hands in his armpits as she got into her car and drove away.

He turned back into the house and made coffee, wishing he wasn't awake. He grabbed a baseball bat and went out to the back-yard. The view at a glance was deceptively pleasant. There were still a few dark spots on the grass where large pools of blood had been, but otherwise no signs of slaughter. When Ben's gaze fell on the doghouse and the two empty stainless-steel bowls, his first thought was that he should fill them with food and water. Then he burst into tears.

Clutching the baseball bat, he sat on the deck and sobbed as he hadn't in years. When he was spent, he pressed his palms into his eyes and stood to go back inside, and that's when he saw her— watching him. He'd not heard her land softly on the grass several feet away.

Shae was dirty. There was a little scrape on her neck. "Good morning." She stepped towards him.

His heart pounded at the sound of her beautiful voice. He wiped at his face angrily, but he ached to hear her make another noise. He wanted her to talk at length or sing. There was a tugging sensation in the muscles of his arms and chest. And then it went lower, and he felt himself flush again, stirred once more. He broke into a sweat. The female form was tormenting him this morning. Lust and sorrow made a weird, shameful pair; first, his stepsister and now someone who wasn't human. How many taboos could his desire involve to-day? She stepped closer to him and smiled. "Gray Man is dead." She dropped something from her hand then–a black, egg-shaped, slimy sphere that smelled like sulfur.

Ben stepped back from it. "What is that?"

"His eye."

Andre couldn't get the image of Hammer out of her mind: the blood, the smell, the mysterious innards strewn about—parts of the dog hidden for all the time she'd known him so gruesomely revealed. As she stocked shelves, she read the labels of products to help the organs function: liver, kidney, and colon cleansers, teas, capsules, and tinctures to assist the nervous system and rejuvenate the body. She thought of her own fragile, wet insides wrapped up in her skin and shuddered at how vulnerable mammals were, soft and breakable.

When Ben texted to inform her that Shae had come back and that she'd killed the Gray Man, she'd crouched behind the counter and cried with relief. She tried to call him a couple of times to hear what happened, but he didn't answer, and then the afternoon flow of shoppers picked up.

And when Andre was feeling like she could barely keep it together, like if things got any weirder, she was going to implode, the giantess appeared in the shop amidst a small flurry of other customers. After everyone left, Andre paced manically back and forth behind the counter with the uneasy feeling that the woman was connected to everything. And she finally admitted to herself what she'd been thinking subconsciously since she first laid eyes on her: she didn't look human. Andre wanted to kick herself for not getting her name. But what reason to ask? It might not be wise to draw any attention . . . And what if she was Unseel? Andre knew nothing about her.

She chewed at her lip and batted away a little brown moth that fluttered around her head. How bizarre that their sizes were the inversion of one another. What if Shae hadn't come from far away? Andre doubted this, though. Shae seemed very much a non-native to their world.

Toward the end of the day, light streamed through the glass front of the shop as the sun burst out from behind a cluster of clouds, and Ryan's figure appeared in the doorway, followed by the chime of the door once again. Andre darted out from behind the counter and hugged him. The night before, she'd let him know that they'd come home from the beach to find Hammer dead, but she hadn't gone into details. She'd said he hadn't been eating well the last few days and had died peacefully during an afternoon nap.

"Man, you look grim, Bumblebee. I'm so sorry about Hammer. You need some cheering up. Want to go to a movie?"

It was exactly what she needed—a nice, stupid film to distract her and dinner at a restaurant afterward. She was relieved that Ryan didn't ask about Hammer. She was able to briefly pretend that she was once again living the same pleasantly mundane life she'd had at the start of the summer. But while Ryan didn't press her, there was something between them now. She knew he was aware of the amount of time she spent with Ben. Of their clandestine texts and phone calls. When they got back to the apartment, she immediately changed out of her clothes, donned sweatpants and one of his T-shirts, and began reading once again while he picked up where he'd left off on Call of Duty.

After an hour, Ryan paused his game, stretched his arms up over his head, and turned around to look at her. He leaned over and grasped the top of the book she was reading and lowered it to look at her face. "Hey."

"Hey." She laid the book down.

He smiled. "I wish you didn't change out of that dress so soon. The Puritan look is weirdly sexy on you."

She rolled her eyes.

His expression changed. "Do you want to be here right now? You don't have to stay here if you'd rather go home . . ."

"I want to be here." She sat up straighter and kissed him, hoping it would end the conversation, but he pulled away from her.

"So, what is going on with you?"

Her eyes filled with tears.

"Oh, shit. *That's* not good. Andre, what is going on?"

"I'm—I'm just sad about Hammer." She turned to look out the window. There was a single diamond in the sky, and she absently wondered if it was a planet or the North Star. She didn't know what direction they were facing. Ryan's décor was Spartan, but there was a wind chime on the porch, and they could hear it from his room, making soft, pebbly sounds, soothing and, somehow, sad. "It's like we lost a part of childhood, you know?"

He frowned. "I am very sorry about him. But you've been acting weird since before this happened." He looked about to say something else and hesitated. "You used to talk to me about everything."

She pulled her hair out of the bun and started playing with it. "I know, I'm just . . . a little distracted."

"Andre . . ."

She kissed him and started fumbling with his shirt. *I can't tell you, my love.* "Nothing you need to worry about."

I arch my back and put my fingers to the place between my legs and gasp, thrusting my hips up and down. There is a wondrous sensation, and I shiver at a feeling like running water down my back and between my legs, charging through my veins. It *is* blood in my veins, not nectar, not ichor. It's different from theirs, not so iron-rich, but still full of minerals and velvety red.

I feel no shame. I am not inclined to such feelings. I am not invading her privacy. I am following the strand between us and having a vicarious exchange I am entitled to. And it is wonderful, and for a short time, renders my space and surroundings meaningless. And how I love him, this sweet boy.

Eventually, the fragile, slender worm of energy loses its current and goes still. I lay on the blankets in my room and stare at the monarch, slowly beating its wings on the back of my hand. The abyss threatens me. The longing for elsewhere is a heavy weight. The tendril between us is growing stronger, and the pretty one is now pining for it too, aching for it in her sleep. I can share some of the burdens with the girl now, but not too much, or she will see what is to happen.

I'd told them that the Unseel could not survive in this place, and I wonder if the same is true for me. What if I cannot adapt?

I squint, trying to fool my senses with glamour and pretend to be elsewhere. I imagine that long dome of greenery leading to the doorway to the wood and the lake. And beyond it, there are the vaguest flitting images: rich, orange sunlight through trees, regal falls. And then there were the ones like me but tiny as a fingertip, and others as tall as the trees. I can almost remember them.

The monarch flutters away from me. A veneer of enchantment lies over the room. I am like a spider, proud in my web of finely wrought silk. I've covered the walls and the ground of the shed. Grass now blankets the floor. The branches and sticks I brought inside have melded to the walls becoming three-dimensional trees. If one was to put their hand where the water seemed to be on the wall, their skin would come away wet. I have succeeded in willing the space into a lovely illusion. There is even a scent I've conjured—the echo of a flower which teases my shattered memory, buffets against it like a moth to a windowpane. Glamour sustains me. Barely.

I try not to think of my keepers and what I will do to them: Pretty one and Serious one. Andromeda and Benjamin. Andre and Ben. I can't hide from their names anymore.

My arrival is miraculous to them, and yet I am familiar. My image is in their dreams and art like the moon and the ocean. Their collective mind has already created me a thousand different ways. I shudder and grind my teeth to think I might be only an imaginary thing, somehow fertilized into reality.

I'd brought nothing—only the Unseel; a dark companion who traveled with me through lightning between adjacent worlds. And monstrous as Gray Man is, he is the *only* thing I recognize. And for this, my hand was stilled when it came time to destroy him. And so I'd gone up to him, startled that his face and carriage was now influenced by the humans. He was trying to adapt and looked something like a man now. Ugly as ever, but with a nub of a nose and rudimentary ears and gray lips. And so I hissed at him and screamed at him to leave off, and with a knife gouged out one of his eyes and hacked off one of his arms. But I left his head, and he'd howled after me.

I will collect the tithe. Not him. When the time comes, I will know what to do.

And I will kill the Unseel. It must be done, of course. Not all the animals dying near the Shellara are victims of the woodwalker. Some suffer sicknesses from this world. But the Unseel is malevolent and destructive. When the next opportunity comes, I must not hesitate, but every time I've spied him so far—pitiful and hateful and alone— wandering madly through the hills, or squatting, all long limbs and sharp angles, huddled up by a rock, I do nothing. I cannot tear my eyes away from his form or bring myself to end his life, because at least he helps me remember: I can almost see him standing on a rocky outcrop, in the setting sun of another world.

PART TWO

CHAPTER NINE

Merri hauled bottles of iced teas from their cases and loaded them into the refrigerator. She shot a glance at Andre, "Are you okay?"

Andre held up her hand, blinking, as an ant ran between the slight webbing between her fingers. She wiped it off on her pants. "I didn't sleep well."

The morning shipment had come and gone, but Vivian was in one of her conserve-and-consolidate binges and had them doing various projects. The Chestnut was empty but for the two of them. Andre went to the front of the store and started to take down the sparkle stand. Vivian was getting rid of most of the "sparkle" and replacing it with soaps and candles that sold better.

After Merri left, Andre grasped an orange crystal hanging from a thin strand. She stood by the windows and held it up against the glass as sunlight irradiated the color. She let her eyes un-focus and fought down an almost overwhelming urge to put it into her mouth. She moved to a blue crystal. She'd read somewhere that it was the most popular—most beloved color in the world. Blue was pure. She held up more crystals, and her eyes feasted on them.

Humans don't appreciate these lovely things, Andre thought. The world was saturated with visual wonders now. *Shine* had been cheapened. Once upon a time, it had taken people somewhere sublime— just looking at sparkling color under the sun . . .

Right before she was about to close the shop, as she was finishing ringing up a bottle of Fenugreek for a woman with a tiny baby in a colorful wrap, one last customer came through the door. The setting sun beamed through the glass around her. The height and bearing formed an unmistakable silhouette.

"Hi. Can I help you find anything?" Andre asked. Her heart pounded. She swallowed.

The giantess removed her sunglasses. "I'm here to see you." Andre sucked in her breath. The woman's eyes were silver and too big. Definitely too big. Andre wondered about her ears, but a scarf covered them. She cocked her head at Andre. "I was right. I can smell them on you." She removed her gloves, and Andre saw her fingers were too long. "I've been drawn here for weeks. I felt the change in electricity one night. I knew someone had arrived, but I wasn't sure where. You're keeping them?"

Andre wrung her hands. "How did . . . who—what *are* you?"

The giantess gave Andre an unsettling smile. "That *is* the question, isn't it? I would say you don't need to be afraid of us, but that's not quite true."

"Can you stay while I close up? Please? Or we can meet somewhere after? I don't even know your name." She held out her hand. "I'm Andre—Andromeda." The woman's enormous hand engulfed hers.

"I'm Grace." She shook her large purse off of her shoulder and pulled out a phone. "What is your number? I'm free tomorrow evening."

Andre gave it to her, stammering. "Will you be able to explain?" Her voice caught. She realized she was practically panting.

Grace spoke, staring into her phone. "I will try. I will try to help."

Andre nodded. "Okay. I'm really happy to meet you. You have no idea."

As she was going out to her car, Ben called. "Her room—I mean the shed—you've got to see what she's done."

"What? Just tell me."

"It's like she's been decorating. That's all I'm gonna say about it." He sounded oddly defeated.

"Okay, "I'll try and peek at it when I get a chance. I'm heading over to Ryan's. Look, I've got some news too. Shae isn't the only one. Do you remember that super giant lady I told you about before? She's some sort of faerie—or whatever the hell they are. A . . . nonperson. I'm going to meet her tomorrow night. Come with me."

Ben groaned.

"What?"

"I can't take any more."

"Relax, it could be . . . a good thing."

More of her clothes found their way into Ryan's apartment, and Andre now claimed two dresser drawers. She had deodorant, a toothbrush, and a bottle of lotion in his bathroom. He left before she did in the morning, but they got up at the same time and drank coffee or tea together while sleepily perusing the Internet on their phones or laptops.

Unless he was deep into a project, he usually got off work right before she did and would meet her at the Chestnut. Then they would go out to eat or make something at his apartment. The resolve she and Ben once had to make sure one of them was always at the house dissolved over several weeks.

But it had become a fairly common occurrence that Andre would suddenly stop whatever she was doing and announce she had to leave. That night, she was in bed reading when she knew she wouldn't be able to sleep without seeing what Shae had done to the shed. She closed the book, laid it on top of the *Dictionary of Creatures*, and lifted the covers. "I'm going home."

Ryan lay next to her, reading Old Man's War for the third time. It was the way their evenings usually ended, reading together until they got sleepy, or her reading and him playing Call of Duty or Halo until his eyes got bleary. "But you're comfortable," he said, not moving his eyes from the book.

She stood up and tugged on her T-shirt and jeans. She couldn't stop thinking about the shed. She had to see whatever Ben was talking about. "I shouldn't stay here every night. It's not my home, and I miss my room."

"It could be your home." He glanced up at her. "C'mon, don't go."

"I've got my stuff—most of my stuff, over there."

"You could move it over here." He set the book down. "Why don't you just move in already?"

It was a conversation they'd been having before the start of the summer. Before Shae had come, they were getting close to taking the next step and living together. "I've got all that storage space in the parking garage downstairs, and I don't use most of it. Plus, I could get rid of a lot of junk in the hall closet. We'd have room for all your books and magic potions from the store."

"Magic potions?" She laughed. But she was barely listening. She was already halfway home in her head. It came on her abruptly at times, like she was being pulled. He sighed and went back to his book.

"I'm sorry." She crawled back on the bed and pecked his cheek. "I'll stay over tomorrow night."

The house was chilly, but something else made her shiver when she got home. She didn't know why she had the notion that she'd tempted fate, running up to the house alone in the dark. The Gray Man was dead. Andre went through the house, slid open the backdoor, and stepped outside. As she approached the shed, she saw there were golden, horizontal cracks along the bottom and top of the door.

She opened it after knocking twice and gasped.

The initial illusion was that the room was not just bigger, but that it was no longer a room. It was almost not an *inside*. A line from a book of her childhood popped into her mind: *And his ceiling hung with vines, and the walls became the world all around.* Trees appeared—almost, but not quite, three-dimensional. Tiny birds fluttered around them. Purple flowers and toadstools sprouted along what might have been the edges of the wall. The floor was now covered in moss. A hazy, circular light was suspended in one corner, suffusing the room with a suggestion of orangey sunlight that caught little glimmerings, as if there were gemstones or shards of glass scattered randomly about, spangling the floor and walls.

Andre's eyes darted around, feasting. And then she blinked, dizzy as if she'd been spinning around in a circle with her eyes closed. "Oh my god." She could feel a dopey, helpless smile on her face. "Hi, Shae." Shae sat on the floor, braiding a wreath of white blossoms, her triple-jointed fingers moving nimbly. The monarch flitted from her, circling over Andre's head, before returning to rest on Shae's shoulder. "This is . . . amazing."

Andre sank to the floor on her knees. She ran her fingertips over the moss and gazed at the little stream running where the corners of the wall *almost* were, where they should have met. Small fish swam there. She blinked, puzzled. Was there a hidden aqueduct? "How did you do this?" she finally asked.

"It is my space. I make it look the way I want it to."

"Could you change our whole house to look like this? Or any building you are in?"

Shae frowned, shook her head. "Too much work."

A blue butterfly came up to Andre's face. She held out her hand, and it landed on the tip of her finger, going in and out of focus. Then she noticed bats in the corners and frowned. They didn't seem to fit.

"I can take it back, too," Shae said. The butterfly vanished. The lights winked out, and the room darkened and gained squared-off contours again. Andre was sitting on a hardwood floor. The heady feeling was replaced by a cold, dank wave of reality. She'd read enough about faeries to know of glamour, to know she was just in a dark, empty shed with a small, strange creature. She shuddered, sickened at the frailty of the illusion.

"Can you make ball lightning?"

Shae's face was only partly visible in the back-porch light through the open door. "No. If I could do that, then I wouldn't be here." She took on an expression of focus once more and pulled the room back into its shimmering form. Andre felt buoyed once again, but beneath it was despair. Exquisite as it was, this shed was a prison of sorts and Shae, an inmate who'd covered the walls with cutout pictures of flowers.

"What is between us, Shae?" Andre asked softly. "Why do I feel you? Why do I almost feel your thoughts?"

Shae looked away. "I do not know. It is part of your gift. I think you will have a wish come true."

"And there will be a cost to it, won't there?" Andre didn't understand how she knew this. It was a notion that came from Shae.

"Yes." Shae met her eyes again. "There is always a cost. There is always a tithe."

CHAPTER TEN

"We should get going," Ben said the next night. He was pacing back and forth in what Andre had come to recognize as his itch-to-play-the-music movement.

Andre glanced up at the clock over the stove. They were going to meet the giantess. Grace had texted Andre her home address. She lived in the Fallory Hills, which meant she was rich. Andre looked at Shae, who was absorbed in drawing some sort of elaborate structure of curlicues in her sketch pad. "Ready, Shae?" Andre asked. "You sure you want to do this?"

"Yes," Shae said without looking up. Andre couldn't shake the feeling that Shae was wary.

The Fallory Hills bordered the next town. They went up a long, winding road, past the hot springs, small farms, and wineries. The Shellara sprawled out beneath them briefly on the right before they turned up and away from the vista. The open land gave way to a hilly wood punctuated here and there by mansions. Ben drummed on the steering wheel and bobbed his head. He let out a soft whistle as they passed an ostentatious palace on the left with a huge fountain on the front lawn. Andre sat up in her seat and followed it with her eyes. "What kind of people *live* here?" she wondered.

"Uh, giant faerie people?" Ben said.

They'd occasionally made their way up the Fallory Hills for one reason or another, even if it was just to take a drive and gawk at the homes.

"Mateo's cousin Leslie has a friend who lives up here," Ben said. "Iris? I think her name is Iris. She was weird. I came with him and Leslie once, and we hung out in her Jacuzzi. A bunch of us went, actually. Andrea McCoy was there."

"Hmm." Andre murmured. Andrea McCoy—the tragic high-school celebrity; she'd hanged herself midway through their junior year.

Andre hoped Grace was not dangerous. *I would say you don't need to be afraid of us, but that's not quite true.* At least they might finally have some answers, though. They slowed and turned left onto a small gravel road and wound along it for a quarter mile through dense live oaks and eucalyptus before approaching a wrought iron gate. Beyond it was an expansive lawn leading down to an enormous house.

"Shit," Ben muttered.

"Wow," Andre whispered.

Shae unbuckled and moved to the middle of the back seat between them, her little hands on the back of their headrests. The gate theatrically opened inward, and they passed through a tall arched trellis dripping with wisteria and turned up the huge driveway towards the house. Grace had texted they could park anywhere, so Ben stopped a little more than halfway around the circular drive, and they got out of the car.

It was completely dark out now, but soft floodlights revealed lush bushes with fist-size roses. They walked under an arched stone walkway—the surface of which sparkled like glistening frost—towards the high, double doors. Grace was sitting on a bench on the porch, waiting for them.

"Oh," Ben said under his breath. "Oh, wow. Yeah . . . she's . . . uh, not normal."

Andre and Ben hung back a little as Grace stood, and Shae moved towards her. When they were only a couple of feet apart, Shae tilted her head up. Grace put out her hand, and Shae put her small palm against it. They both had the four knuckles on each finger, but Grace's was less pronounced. Shae's whole hand and outstretched fingers filled Grace's palm. The monarch circled over their heads. Andre and Ben glanced at each other uneasily.

When they dropped their hands, Grace spoke, "Does the smell bother you?"

"It was hard at first. It is not so bad now."

Grace looked at Andre and Ben. "They treat you well?"

"Yes."

Grace stepped towards Ben. "I've not met you." She put out her hand.

"Benjamin," he said quietly. "Nice to meet you."

She smiled. "Grace Foster."

"You have a beautiful home," Andre said.

Grace shrugged. "Thank you. It feels a bit much these days, but it affords freedom and privacy." She turned and opened the door. Golden light illuminated a large, spare entryway with hardwood floors partly covered by Afghan rugs. Spotless white walls with crown molding bordered the high ceilings. Cavernous, pristine rooms lay to the right and left. Slightly off to the right and in front of them was a winding staircase—the stairs wider at the bottom than at the top.

On a slim little table by the door lay a silver tray. Upon it was a decanter of wine, a jar of honey, four glasses, and little white cakes topped with pomegranate seeds. Andre's mouth watered. The giant-ess lifted the tray. "Come with me," she said. "I want to show you a part of my home most people don't get to see."

They followed the giantess down the hallway until she stopped halfway and turned to the wall. She pressed the corner of a picture frame on the wall, and a hidden door opened inward. She stepped inside, and they followed her. At first, it seemed like a closet lit by a pinkish light in the center of the ceiling. The walls were cream-colored and satiny. Grace pressed a peach-colored button on the wall, and they began to descend. An elevator. Ben glanced at Andre with a wary smile.

When the door opened, they stepped onto a cement entranceway into fuzzy yellow light, like a car garage at night. The air was cool and smelled of minerals. A few feet ahead was a green silk curtain. Grace pulled it aside. Andre gasped. Ben whispered, "Holy shit." His voice echoed throughout the space.

Before them was a cavern. Shimmering jeweled stalactites dripped down from the high ceiling like melting stone and hovered over pools. Somehow, there was greenery amidst it all. Vines wrapped their way along the floor and walls. Moss and flowers covered patches of the cavern floor, making it a subterranean garden.

Andre swallowed and squinted and shook her head a little to see if she could lose any of it and see where she really was, but the veneer of glamour was firmly in place. She breathed in the scent of stone and water. The air was cool, but there were drafts of steam that rose from some of the pools. "This is so beautiful," she whispered. *Maybe this could be enough. If I never travel to the land that inspired it, perhaps this illusion will suffice.*

Ben stepped over to a small brook where a butterfly fluttered above a huge, peach flower with crystal-studded pistils. He squatted down and put his hand over the surface of the water. "It's warm," he said.

Grace slipped off her shoe and dipped her toe in. "This is my sanctuary. As long as I've been here, and as much as I've changed, I haven't lost my ability to glamour spaces and people."

Shae had yet to comment on any of it, Andre noticed. The monarch seemed feistier than usual, frantically flapping in loose circles around her head.

"Please." Grace gestured for them to sit down on one of the two benches covered with soft moss and set the tray on the long stone coffee table in front of them. "Help yourselves." She sat down on the bench across from them.

Andre leaned forward and then hesitated. How many stories had she read warning against the partaking of faerie food? It was *never* advisable. But this wasn't faerie food. She wasn't in another world. She was just in a home in the Fallory Hills. She glanced at her friends. Shae sat unmoving with her hands in her lap. Ben grasped the decanter. He poured and handed her a full glass, poured another one for Shae, and then himself. Grace had her own full glass. She sipped and watched them. Andre reached for one of the little cakes and closed her eyes as she bit into it. A slightly spicy, irresistibly sweet flavor filled her mouth. *Am I going to shrink now?* She wondered. *Or grow so big my head hits the ceiling?* She took a drink of the wine and almost swooned.

"Wow," Ben said, smacking his lips. "That's good." He sat between Andre and Shae. Andre leaned past him trying to look at Shae, but she kept her head down. "That's the best wine I've ever tasted."

"It is," Andre agreed.

Shae took a sip, then set the glass down and reached for the honey.

"So," Grace said. "I don't have all the answers for you. But I can tell you my own story and as much as I know."

"That's good you have your memory," Andre said. "Shae seems to have amnesia."

"Well, I remember little of *elsewhere.* It has faded, but I know what I am and why I came, and I remember what happened when I got here." Grace stared at Shae. "You don't remember anything?"

Shae held the monarch in her hand and stared at it, stroking its wings. "When I saw you, I remembered your kind, for a moment," she said quietly. "And there are other moments like that. Sometimes I can see the light and the trees. Sometimes I can almost hear the songs."

Grace nodded, turning a ring on her finger. "I don't know the year I arrived, but the land was wild and untamed. It was anguish to be sundered from my world and thrust here. I slept a lot at first. I suffered from the smell, too, and this was before the pollution of today. Eventually, the sickness passed."

"How were you, sundered?" Andre asked.

"They took my name and sent me through the lightning. It was Beryl, my husband, who named me Grace—many years later."

"Shae knew her name," Ben said.

"Did she?" Grace looked at Shae. "I don't think so. Am I right?"

Shae stared into her lap.

Andre sat up straighter. "But—"

"I think she spoke one of the names for *what* she is," Grace explained. "A *Sidhe*. And perhaps it came a little bent out of her mouth. She has no name now. It was taken when she was sundered. But Shae is charming. Worth keeping, I suppose, if nothing else comes to you."

Andre squirmed, at war with herself on whether or not to ask questions. But she felt like the best thing to do was listen.

"I stayed near the lake. I spent a lot of time in the wood, but I craved stone. I craved the *below*. Caverns, caves, the smell of minerals, even sewers call to me. I couldn't find any, so I looked for shelter. There were barns and shacks, but I didn't stay in them much. I'd watched humans, and I was wary of them. There were fewer people and the ones that were here . . ." She sighed. "There was a ruthlessness back then. It was a harder life. I couldn't reveal myself. I knew this.

"I looked much different than I do now. These days I appear odd, and to the glamour-discerning eye, not human. But in the last seventy years, I've shrunk more than a foot, and that is only after I started paying attention. But my stature aside, I was different." She ran her long index finger from her jaw up to her temple. "I had . . . gems embedded into my face. They were beautiful. At some point, they fell out. It was only a little painful, perhaps like a child losing a tooth." She paused. "We are creatures of adaptation. *Most* of us can evolve enough to live here permanently. Not all of us, though. And not the unlucky few who are tasked to be changelings."

Grace addressed Shae. "We are not the same kind, obviously."

"I'm in the trees," Shae said softly.

"I think she's like, arboreal?" Andre blurted. She couldn't help herself. It was a good word. "If I had to classify her, I'd say she was a dryad?"

Grace smirked. "Oh, she's *not* a dryad." She gave Shae a curious look and didn't offer any other category.

Andre was about to suggest perhaps Shae was a sylph, but she decided to stick to her plan of staying quiet and listening.

"What about the Gray Man?" Ben asked.

"The who?"

"That monster that killed my dog. Shae said it followed her?"

"An Unseelie came with you?" Grace asked Shae.

Shae nodded. "A woodwalker—" She frowned, thinking. "Tall and ugly . . . it wanted only to kill."

"Ah. Pesky, base creatures. They don't know what fate they are poisoning themselves with. They cannot adapt either."

"It was trying to," Shae said. "It was trying to be a man."

"I presume you took care of it?"

Shae nodded.

"Not before it did some damage," Ben muttered.

"Oh, I'm sure it was eager for destruction." Grace mused. "I'm sure it was trying to help you collect the tithe."

Andre frowned. *That word again. Faerie tithes.* She was about to ask what she was talking about when Grace stood up and continued. "The barriers are thin here. Just as they are in various places all over the world." She paused a moment, stared at each of them in turn. "We come for myriad reasons and to keep the between-space from atrophying. If an adjacent world is no longer accessible, it might be the end of us all. There must be a . . . porousness, some steady flow between, and so the court plucks some unfortunate being, whenever they see fit and sends us here. Sometimes it is for reasons simple but crucial. Someone must be at the right place at the right time—one, ten, fifty years from now—and it takes a great deal of cosmic maneuvering involving *us*, outsiders, to make it happen. Our courts watch your world, and you imagine us. Gentry, Greys, Faeries, Sidhe—we wear many faces and don many sizes. We have different reasons for coming and different tasks once we arrive; mixing our blood with yours, serving as muses, making changelings, and collecting tithes . . ."

Grace clasped her hands behind her back and began pacing. "The masses don't know about us; that is the way of things, circumstances will always twist to hide us, but individual encounters can be inconvenient. I experimented with revealing myself. I was afraid to, but the tithe compelled me. I spotted a woman hanging up laundry on a clothesline one day." She sighed. "It did not go well. She ran to the house, screaming. I kept moving towards her, hoping once I got close enough, I could communicate. I should have given up, especially when a man appeared from the doorway. He had a rifle. I can still see him: sunburnt and scrawny with missing teeth—scared out of his mind . . ." Grace bent down to re-fill her glass.

"He shot at me. The sound was enough to startle me, and I finally took off. I remember the woman yelling at him to stop. He shot again, and I was hit in the shoulder—not a very serious injury, but it stung and frightened me and made me angry. I healed up quickly and did not make another attempt at contact for some time. But the tithe weighed on me more and more, so I had to seek out humans out again."

Andre admired Grace as she paced; the smooth way she walked almost as if she rode on wheels rather than stepped with her feet, the subtle motion she made with her hand when she spoke—it was like a statue startling to life with the fluid control of a dancer.

Ben finished his wine and poured himself more. He raised his eyes and held the decanter up to Andre, and she let him top off her glass.

"I made a few more attempts which accomplished nothing more than terrifying some other poor souls. But eventually, I found some people who were not afraid of me." She looked wistful. "Harold and Rosie. They were seven and five years old, and they lived in a little cabin.

"I saw them coming down to the woods to play in the creek. Rosie, the younger one, was a chatterbox with a big imagination. She always got completely dirty. Harold was a somber little boy, wiser than his age. It was the first time I was able to observe children up close. I would spend hours hiding, just watching them play. They came day after day to the same place at the creek. One day I let myself be seen."

She smiled at the memory. "Rosie marched up to me and demanded to know if I granted wishes. Poor Harold was alarmed, but at least he didn't scream or run away. After that, I saw them nearly every afternoon for months. Rosie and Harold were my first companions. They taught me a great deal. They told me of the world from their perspective, brought me books to read. I brought them shiny rocks I found and made them flower necklaces . . ."

"What happened?" Shae asked a little sharply.

"They died," Grace said, setting her glass down. "They were the tithe."

"Huh?" Ben sat up straighter. "How? When?"

"They drowned. When they were still young children, I'm afraid. I wasn't there when it happened, but I drew them further into the wood and showed them the deeper part of the lake. One day, they went by themselves. I imagine Rosie fell in, and Harold went after to try and save her. I knew they were gone because I felt a great relief from the pressure. The tithe weighs on us until it is paid. Squeezes us, holds us in thrall."

"That's . . . terrible," Andre whispered. She glanced at Ben. He was staring at Grace, his jaw clenched.

"Yes," Grace agreed.

"So, we're in danger, aren't we?" Ben asked. "Are we a tithe? Me and Andre? Or one of us?"

Grace stared at him hard before answering. "It's quite likely. But truthfully, I don't know. It depends on what Shae is tasked to do here. But it will be someone who has been in her vicinity. It could be just one soul or a few. Often it's two or three." She studied Shae. "It hasn't happened yet—I can see. You still feel the pressure of it?"

Shae gave a tight nod.

Andre looked at Shae, heart pounding. *What are you going to do to us?* She felt both alert and weirdly tapped out; maybe it was a buzz from the wine and the cloying glamour. It was all just too horrible and surreal. "So it's like the tithe to hell I've read about?" she asked. "So there's a real heaven and hell? Like actual places?"

Grace shook her head. "Oh, the folklore gets almost everything wrong. That is the church's influence trying to make it always about God. No, it's just death. No one is sent anywhere but to a grave. A tithe must be relatively young. I've never heard of anyone over the age of thirty being tithed. We don't usually kill by our own hand, but we . . . manipulate events and circumstances in order to create a tithe. It is humanity's tithe to *us* for our gifts, not something the fae gives away."

Andre could feel Ben tensing next to her. "What the hell?" He cried. "How is that right? You guys are the ones who—who I don't know . . . *trespass*. And humans have to die for it? Why?"

Andre looked at Ben and tried to agree with what he was saying. He was right, wasn't he? Why did she feel like the gifts and the tithes mattered more than their paltry lives and feelings? "Yeah. It's—it's messed up," she added weakly.

Grace shrugged. "It is the nature of our relationship. It is fair. We give gifts, and we collect a tithe for it. Humans are enamored of the notion of sacrifice: your Christ, your sacrificial virgins and lambs, your martyrdom fetish. Anyway, sometimes I fear our influence is not powerful enough any more to save this world from itself. And if it does turn to rot, it could make a ripple effect into elsewhere."

She stepped over to them, smiled tenderly, and placed her large, soft hands against the side of Andre and Ben's faces. "But, I understand this worries you." Andre's heartbeat slowed. A feeling of tranquility surged through her, and her mind and muscles slackened. Her thoughts slid away from the unpleasantness. The giantess's voice was a silky drug. "And so it's best you two don't recall too much of this conversation."

Grace stepped away from them and resumed pacing. Andre blinked and rubbed her forehead. *Something* had just happened. Even though she'd been riveted to every word Grace spoke, she had spaced out. She frowned at the drink and set it down.

"After the children were gone, I continued to reveal myself from time to time. I had a sense of who was safe and who wasn't. Usually, the very old or the very young could handle me. It was a different world then. For the most part, life is better these days. It's safer and certainly easier in a lot of ways, but there are things I miss about that time—"

As if to emphasize the obnoxiousness of modern life, Andre's phone rang. She pawed at her pocket and pulled it out, grimacing. *Amy*. Then she saw there were two texts from Ryan. One from Lydia. She didn't read them. "Sorry," she muttered.

Grace continued, "After some years passed, I came to an abandoned house. Or so I thought. No one was staying there at the time, and so I took up occupancy, although the beds were almost too small. One morning I woke up to a young man sitting on a chair against the wall, watching me. He looked nervous but also excited."

Grace paused and turned her wrist slightly to look at a watch Andre hadn't noticed until then. "I'll spare you my full autobiography. Beryl was just twenty years old, and he was completely fascinated by me. He became my guardian, my friend, eventually, my partner. He slowly introduced me to the civilized world. His father had died a few months before, and he'd inherited a bit of money and the house. I lived with him there and hid whenever people came over." She smiled. "We cared for one another. He is the one who named me." Grace sat back down, and a large white Persian suddenly appeared from behind the bench and rubbed against her legs. Andre briefly wondered if it was a real creature or part of the glamour. Grace leaned down and picked up the cat. Andre was hypnotized by her huge hands, stroking it. In Grace's lap, it could have been a kitten.

"While I was adapting and becoming more human-like, eventually we realized that I don't age, at least not at the rate as everyone else. So we lived a secret life. To the outside world, Beryl was a bachelor until he was an old man. He passed away four years ago next month. So, my keeper is gone, but this is still my home. This is where I raised my children."

Andre blinked. "You have kids?"

"I have two children."

"How did . . . ?" Ben trailed off.

"Beryl was their father."

"Are they . . . like you?" Andre asked.

Grace smirked. "They are tall, and they have a unique look, but they are 'normal' to the rest of the world."

"Where are they?" Ben asked.

"Aurora is in Europe till the end of the month, and Alexander, my youngest, just moved back from college on the east coast. He's staying in the city with friends right now."

Andre rubbed her face. "This is . . . amazing."

The cat jumped off of Grace's lap. "Our children didn't come until late into Beryl's life. He was surprised by my first pregnancy. I was not. That was my task, along with the tithe. It was the reason I was sent here. We put our blood together from time to time. Link our worlds through flesh."

They were quiet for a moment, and then Ben asked, "Are we the first people to see this place?"

"My children have, obviously, and a few friends. I made this years ago. Back then, things were different. In the sixties and seventies, we hosted parties down here. There was a lot of . . . spirituality. Psyche-delics were rampant; a lot of people were open-minded, and"—she added drily—"none of them had cell phones. Quite a few of them knew me for, if not what I am, at least what I'm not. It was our little golden age, I suppose. Most of those people have since passed away or are infirm at this point."

Andre looked up at her. "How do you know who to tell? Shae said not to tell anyone, and we've been so afraid to expose her, but it's gotten hard. I want to tell—I *need* to tell my boyfriend and my sister."

"Shae is right to be cautious," Grace said, sparing the smaller fa-erie a glance. "That's our instinct, but if you trust them, tell them and only them. I would not reveal Shae to anyone else for now. If too many people know it can get . . . messy. And I would ask that you do not tell them about me—not just yet."

Andre nodded. "My god, my sister, would love it here."

"We should probably get going." Andre was relieved to hear Ben say it. They needed to get back home. She looked up at him. In the strange light, their eyes met. She couldn't tell if it was just the shad-ows, or if his eyes were dilated. She wondered if hers were too.

The three of them were silent for the first few minutes of the drive home. Andre tried to rally her excitement over this new develop-ment, but there was a pall of worry about the evening. She knew there had been things Grace said that had unnerved her. There was something about a tithe, about a sacrifice. It was as if the answer was perched on a little hill in her mind, and she couldn't climb it because it was too slippery.

And Grace herself made Andre sad somehow. She'd molded her nature to live in their world. Her underground sanctuary was a rep-lica, a deception, a place to play pretend. Grace wasn't fooled by what she'd created. She had done as best she could out of necessity, but she would always be an outsider.

CHAPTER ELEVEN

"It's hot. You want to go swimming?" Ben sat on the back deck. The pages of the music magazine he'd been trying to read were too glossy under the sun. His guitar was upstairs beckoning him, along with his keyboard, with siren songs that his fingers itched to play. He was testing himself, disturbed by the pull on his will. He looked up at Shae, shading his eyes. It was sweltering, and he didn't want her to leave, and he didn't want to be outside unless he could be in the water. It was the first week of September. The last of the dog days.

Grasping the top of the back gate, Shae turned, hovering a few feet off the ground. She'd been about to catapult over the fence and into the woods, where she would spend the next who knew how many hours or days. It occurred to him that she might have already been to the lake on her excursions. She dropped lightly down. "Where?"

"The Shellara. It's just a short drive. We can swim, and there are some secluded spots."

Shae wore a sundress, a large brim hat, and sunglasses. Ben filled a backpack with towels, sunscreen, a few snacks, and a water bottle. In the car, they passed vineyards then went up a winding terrain of golden hills spotted with clumps of oak trees. They passed farms with lethargic cows and tranquil-looking llamas. Ben had taken Hammer on this ride many times over the years. His dog had lived a good life, Ben told himself. He tried not to think about how it had ended.

They parked at an overlook with a view of hills undulating off into the distance, covered here and there with patches of wood. Beneath them, the wide lake wound through the trees, and several larger patches of blue lay scattered in the distance like giant puddles. The only other vehicle was a battered pickup truck several spaces away. Ben was glad it was a weekday. Weekends were crowded with swimmers, hikers, and families come to camp and barbeque. Two trails lay before them heading down towards the water. They started down the dusty, steeper one.

They walked for a quarter of a mile, avoiding the first few places to swim in favor of somewhere more private. He'd learned over several high school summers where the best spots to skinny-dip or smoke pot were. Shae followed behind him, and he glanced back from time to time to see her effortlessly skipping upon rocks as if they were springboards.

When they got to the bank, Shae undressed and entered the water, wings closed, and slipped beneath the surface. Ben set the backpack on a rock, kicked off his shoes, yanked his shirt off over his head, and plunged in. He swam out in the butterfly stroke he'd learned so many years ago, exercising latent power in his shoulder muscles.

Ben did a backflip, accidentally swallowed some of the loamy lake, and coughed. He treaded water and looked around. He couldn't see her. The minutes passed, and he started to wonder if they had ever spoken with her about water. She'd been okay when they went to the beach, but she hadn't slipped under the waves. He was turning back to head for the shore when he heard that singular voice call his name, softly, from just a few feet behind him.

Her opalescent hair was plastered against her head and shoulders. Her huge eyes glimmered green and gold. And then she did something he'd never seen her do before. She smiled. Not the little smirk that appeared on occasion, but a huge grin that was jarring on someone usually so expressionless.

"Hey," he said. She bobbed up and down a little and moved towards him treading water; her limbs seemed gracefully separate from her, like some bit of plant life beneath the surface. He backed away, acutely aware of her nipples, now only a couple of feet away from him. "How long can you stay underwater like that for?"

"A long time. I am strong. I am stronger than you." She laughed, and it made a little explosion in his brain, a disorienting burst of cymbals and flutes and wings flapping about, trying to escape.

He shook his head, dazed. "Not surprising," he muttered after a moment. "Can you do me a favor? Can you let me know if you're going to be down there for a while? I'm a mere mortal, and I can't stay under for more than a minute or so. I also can't see very well."

"Alright." Her face was once more unreadable, and Ben wondered what right he had to keep her on a tether because of his limitations?

"I mean, just be careful, okay? You can swim all you want, but we can't stay more than a couple of hours. I've got to work tonight." The notion was ridiculous. How on earth could he leave a beautiful lake where he swam with a real live nymph to serve the local plebeians food and beer? It was torturous, unthinkable.

Shae sank beneath the surface again. He swam alone for a little while before it occurred to him that he'd forgotten to apply any sunscreen. Andre was usually good for those kinds of reminders. He made his way back to the rocky little shore, sat down, and stared out over the water for a beat before digging around in the backpack for the sunscreen.

He looked up, and she materialized, walking toward him, dripping naked. She'd grown so much, more than half a foot since they'd first discovered her. She turned back to look at the water. Her wings were carefully folded into her back. She picked up little rocks and skipped them expertly into the water, each one bouncing off the surface at least three times. Then she went over to him and sat a few feet away, crouching down with her hands wrapped around her knees. The monarch fluttered from a tree to a rock a few feet away from her.

"Maybe you should wear some of this?" They hadn't put any on the day they went to the beach, but it had been chilly and overcast then. He stepped over to her, took her hand, and turned and opened it, so her palm was facing up.

"What is it?"

"Sunscreen. It protects you from the sun."

"It's dangerous?"

"Well, yeah, it can burn you." He squirted a fragrant white blob into her hand, hoping she didn't have any allergies to the chemicals. "At least it can burn *us*. Here, rub it on your shoulders and face and stuff." She daintily dabbed some on her face. He swallowed. "Do you want me to help you put some on your back?" They sat down, and she scooted close and turned her back towards him.

He'd never touched her before. Her skin was soft and cool. There was no tremulous, hummingbird-like whirring beneath the surface of her flesh as he'd been half-expecting. If he was not looking at the ridge of her wings tucked into her back, he wouldn't know it wasn't just a small human he laid his hands on. He gently spread the lotion all over her back and neck, feeling the slight indention of her ribs. He avoided her wings and did not let his fingers linger anywhere, but discreetly coated her as best he could. She didn't move until he was done, and then she ran her hands over her arms. "Is this why people do not go outside very much because they will be burned by the sun?"

Ben leaned back on his elbows and looked out over the water, "Not really. People go outside. It's just, we live indoors and work inside for the most part. At least in this country. People do go camping and hiking and stuff. And there's . . . you see, there's this ozone layer?" He sighed. How to explain the complexities of their problematic planet to Shae? "And so, if you're going to be in direct sunlight during the day, it's a good idea to wear sunscreen." He finished lamely.

He felt sorry for her. Was this place a wasteland where the inhabitants lived stifled lives in bunkers, and everything was processed and polluted? He didn't think of the world that way. "I could show you the really big trees," he said. "There are some close to us, but for the biggest ones, we have to drive north."

She turned to him. "You and I will go to those trees in winter." And when she spoke, her voice put that glaze over him so that he couldn't form a reply or ask what she was talking about.

His phone rang from his backpack. He dug it out. Andre. "Hey, what's up?"

"Where are you?"

"At the lake." He hesitated, and after a beat, added, "With Shae."

"Can you come home? We need to talk. We've got a problem."

CHAPTER TWELVE

Back at the house, Andre felt Shae's desire through the string and pulled out a jar of honey from the cabinet and handed it to her. "Here, you haven't tried this kind yet. It's raw orange blossom."

"I thought they still had to go through Washington," Ben said, leaning against the kitchen counter.

"She's taking a train back. I guess she's tired of sleeping in a van. But that's not all of it. Mateo is coming too. He's stopping by on his way down the state. He's only in town for the weekend, so you'll need to try and hang out. *And* he's staying here, *and* we're all going camping tomorrow. I'm supposed to tell you to get your shifts covered."

"He hasn't texted me"—Ben started to say when, right on cue, Creedence rang from his phone. Ben turned the ringer off on his best friend. "That was him. He's going to want to crash here."

"I know. That's what I said." Andre sighed.

"What are we going to do? He can't stay here. What should I tell him?"

She bit her lip, "I think it will be fine. We just have to make sure Shae stays out of sight." She glanced at Shae. "She's quite good at that."

Ben turned to their guest. "You can't stay in the shed. I mean, you can, but don't keep it, uh . . . activated or whatever. We can't chance Mateo or Amy opening the door to Narnia."

She didn't say anything but looked at each of them in turn, sipping the orange blossom honey, inscrutable. The monarch was perched on her shoulder. Ben's phone rang once more. Mateo again.

"Answer it," Andre directed him with a note of authority. "Tell him it's okay to stay here."

Ben slept ten minutes through the alarm though it had pricked him in his sleep, irritating his dreams without actually waking him. He quickly showered and dressed, strummed his guitar once, and went downstairs to make coffee, fighting the urge to play. He checked his phone. He should have been excited to see Mateo. He should have been looking forward to a weekend camping and hanging out with friends, but all he wanted to do was follow Shae around and play music. He'd even managed to get his shifts covered easily. There was a crop of new employees hard up for cash with the way they grabbed any available hours. The lack of money was going to sting, though. He'd bought a bunch of new music online that he had yet to listen to, new effects pedals, and he'd been late on his car payment last month.

The back door opened, and she appeared, lovely and absurd. Andre had acquired a few new pieces of clothing for her— a green halter top that didn't constrict her wings, and ugly polka-dotted skorts found in the clearance section of a children's department somewhere. The monarch slowly flapped its wings like a mechanical corsage on her chest. "Your friend is coming."

He wasn't sure if she was making a statement or asking a question. "Yeah. I'm sorry. You don't have to go. I can still tell him it's not a good idea. It's not too late. He can find somewhere else to stay." The words were out of his mouth before he could stop himself.

"I will be fine," she said. She floated over to the kitchen cabinet and pulled out a honey jar. "Andromeda says you are going to the lake."

"Yeah. I don't know whose idea it was, probably Amy's. We used to go there all the time. Like since we were kids. Where will you . . . what will you do while we're gone?"

Cocking her head, she sucked honey off her finger. "I will be around. They will not see me." She went out the back door, taking the jar with her.

That afternoon Ben was pulled away from the song he was entrenched in by a brisk, familiar knock. His best friend broke into a grin when he opened the door. Mateo was tanned, bald, and had gained some weight. "Hey, man!" They high-fived and did the quick, lean-in-smack-on-the-back hug.

"When did you do that?" Ben pointed to Mateo's head as he stepped inside.

"Last week." Mateo set down his guitar case and backpack in the living room and rubbed his scalp. "It's been so hot. It feels good; just wish I didn't have such a lumpy head." Ben went to the fridge, pulled out a beer, and handed one to him. "Thanks. So, we're doing the Shellara tomorrow?"

"That's the plan, I guess." Ben hesitated. "Maybe we should go somewhere else, look for a new spot."

Mateo frowned. "Why? It's so close. I was looking forward to not spending so many hours in a car for a couple of days."

There was no place that was just as nice and wasn't inconveniently far away for them all to camp. The weather was perfect, and it would be the same group of old friends together for who knew how long till the next time. They were all slowly drifting away into adulthood. Hanging out didn't come as naturally as it used to. There was more planning involved. And Mateo lived in another state now. *And* the lake was a place where they could engage in illicit behavior without the fear of being happened upon by park rangers or families. He couldn't think of a remotely good reason for discouraging the camping trip.

Ben suddenly imagined telling Mateo everything. He could go find the picture he'd drawn of the Gray Man and say that he'd seen this monster in the flesh. He could tell his friend that the world was different than everyone thought it was, that monsters and faeries were real; he could try and find Shae . . . The thought was exhilarating, and part of him felt sick to think of what Mateo would say. He had no idea. Then he considered that they'd told Shae to stay away, and without her around as evidence, he and Andre were basically crazy people. Although . . . perhaps both of them telling the same story would make it sound less crazy.

"Everything okay?"

Ben was staring at the back door and nodding to himself. "Huh? Yeah, fine. I was just thinking . . ."

"That's not like you." Mateo looked around. "Hey, where's Hammer?"

Ben turned away and shook his head. There was a long pause. "I had a lot going on. I don't know how I didn't call you."

"Oh, no."

"Yeah. I lost him a month ago."

"Oh *shit*, Ben." Mateo rubbed his head. "Seriously? Dude, I'm so sorry, really. I—I can't believe I didn't hear about this. That's terrible. How are you holding up?"

Ben cleared his throat. "Uh, it sucks. I miss him, but he was getting old. He had a good life. Anyway—kinda don't want to talk about it."

Mateo waited for a beat, then said, "Sure. I understand. Just—I'm so sorry. I know how you loved that dog. *I* loved Hammer, and I'm not a dog person. I know it's hard to lose an animal. Remember, my mom had to put her cat down right after my grandma died? She was a basket case." After an awkward pause, while they stared at their feet, Mateo nodded at his guitar. "You wanna jam?"

He'd missed Mateo. They turned on their amps and returned for a couple of hours to the power-chord-heavy, adrenaline-and angst-fueled ballads from high school. When Mateo made a dopey, open-mouthed face—the perfect impression of how their old friend Jessie-the-mouth-breather had looked when he'd played bass—Ben laughed so hard he fell onto the couch, his guitar digging into his ribs.

After they were tired of the old stuff, Ben listened to some of Mateo's new material. It was good, he thought. Mateo's strengths had always been his technical skill and stage presence. When he asked Ben if he'd been working on anything new, Ben nodded but quickly changed the subject, reluctant to share it.

They went out, and while they drank cheap beer and ate fish tacos, Mateo talked about school and his life in Oregon, and a girl named Cecily he'd been dating for a few months. Ben had seen pictures of them together online. She was cute, with shoulder-length hair and a heart-shaped face. "I wish she'd been able to come, but she had to visit family in Vancouver." Over the next twenty minutes, Ben learned more about her than he cared to. She worked in a little boutique and lived in a house she rented with two other girls. She was starting her second year of grad school in the fall. Her dad was Canadian. Her mother was Japanese. She loved music, hockey, YA novels, and sushi. She wanted to be a special-ed teacher. Ben realized, without his friend saying it, that Mateo was smitten. "She's making me think about my major, you know. I mean, I plan to be a music teacher, but it would be something else to teach kids with special needs. I think that could be awesome—like fulfilling, you know?"

Ben thought it sounded horrifying, but what the hell was he doing with his life? He was a server and sometimes bartender at Cedric's Bar and Grille with no other prospects or ambitions beyond playing music in his bedroom with the vague hope of starting up a band again. "You seeing anyone?" he asked Ben eventually when Ben only nodded in reply.

"No, I've just been making music and working a lot."

"Well, sweet, I hope I get to hear this music at some point before I go. There isn't anyone at Cedric's?" Mateo sounded disappointed.

Ben shrugged. He thought of the leggy new hire he'd seen in the last week. He couldn't remember her name.

Mateo raised his eyebrows. "I talked to Amy for a while the other day. She said Merri's got a thing for you."

"Really?" He wondered if it was true. "Merri's . . . nice."

"And speaking of Amy . . . so she's finished with that Veronica chick, and it's Ricardo now?" Mateo looked skeptical.

Ben rolled his eyes. "I have no idea. You know how that goes."

Mateo snorted. "Nothing against your sister, man, you know I love Amy, but I hope he just soaks it up and enjoys the ride while it lasts."

Fickle and innately polyamorous, Amy wasn't made for long-term relationships. Ben was aware Mateo had slept with her at some point. He was not as close to her as he was to Andre, but it wasn't something he particularly cared to hear about.

They drank more beer and ate more tacos—although Ben didn't have much of an appetite—and during this time, he felt it wasn't possible that Shae, Grace, or the Gray Man existed. It was as if the real world was contingent on who he was surrounded by. And for a little while, he felt tremendous relief, and the depressing ennui, of his old life.

It must happen soon. I will put the tithe into motion this night. Gray-Man must stay out of my way. He has grown sicker, but he's not decaying fast enough. I finish the jar of honey and take the crackers from my pocket and nibble on them. I want more than honey right now. I want salt.

"Yup, good, fine, whatever," Andre spoke into the phone wedged between her cheek and shoulder while she handed a barrel-chested man with a white beard and ponytail a slip to sign. She gave him a plaintive look, motioned to the phone, and mouthed, "Sorry."

"Cause it's going to be tight since Erik is coming after all," Amy said. She'd gotten back the night before and was calling to inform Andre that they were short a tent since Ricardo had pulled his out of storage that morning to discover a huge hole in the bottom of it. At this point, there was going to be nine people sharing two tents. It was going to be a tight fit. Andre, however, was not concerned with everyone's comfort.

"All right, I'll see you in a couple of hours." She heard Amy start to say something else but hung up. "Sorry," she said again to the man as she handed him a brown paper bag containing a bottle of aloe and Dr. Bronner's soap.

He smiled. He was like a summer Santa Claus, wearing a Grateful Dead shirt and flip-flops. It occurred to Andre that this was what some of her friends might look like in thirty years.

"That was my sister. We're going camping after I get off work." Andre had no idea what compelled her to tell him that except she sometimes yapped when she was anxious or distracted, and for some reason, she was feeling anxious about their camping trip.

"Well, have fun. It's a beautiful weekend for it."

"It is. Thanks. Have a nice day."

A few more customers came and went, and when the store was finally quiet, Andre hunched over on the stool, sapped by the steady flow of banal pleasantries. She pulled her phone out again and called Ben.

"Hey." Then there was laughter and Amy saying something in the background. "Hold on a second—" Several seconds passed. "What's up?"

"We shouldn't do this," she said. "I don't know why, but it feels dangerous."

"What do we do?"

She tugged at a chapped part of her lip. "I don't know. Maybe . . . oh, I'm sure it's fine. Right? I don't know why. I'm—I'm just worried."

"Nothing has happened since—" He lowered his voice even more "—since she killed that Unseel thing, right? I don't know how to get out of this."

"Yeah." A gray moth fluttered around her, and she flicked her hand at it, frowning. She heard the chiming of the door opening again, looked up to see Merri, and gave her a quick little wave. "Merri's here. Is everyone else at the house now?" She hated the thought of it. What if someone went into her room and saw her stack of books and the notes in them? What if someone peeked inside the shed when it was actively enchanted? She didn't know why she was paranoid. That was Ben's job.

"Yeah, she's riding here with you, and then she's probably going to ride to the Shellara with you and Ryan, or Raf says he'll drive too. We're still figuring out the car situation."

Andre sighed. "Alright, I'll see you soon." She hung up.

Merri slung off her backpack and plopped it on the counter. For the next half hour, they hung around the store, waiting for six o clock to approach so they could leave. Despite being worried, Andre kept glancing at the cloudless sky and finally started to feel a little eager for their adventure. She hadn't hung out with anyone but Ben, Ryan, and Shae in a long time.

Merri sat on an extra stool behind the counter and played a game on her phone as Andre walked down an aisle to the row that had arnica and aloe at the bottom, and expensive bottles of all-natural insect repellent. She frowned at the price. Even with her discount, it was expensive, but she brought one to the counter, wondering how many flashlights they would have and if there would be enough firewood.

The bell chimed once more, and she turned to see Ryan walk in. "You're on the wrong side of the counter," he observed.

She held up the insect repellent. "For tonight."

He laughed. "That's an overdue purchase." Lying in bed the night before, he'd found a ladybug marching down her spine.

"Yeah, the critters love me lately for some reason. I'm kind of over it."

"We just have fifteen minutes!" Merri cried. "This is going to be fun!"

Andre made a weak noise of agreement, trying to ignore a nebulous voice in her mind that said something was wrong.

Back at the house, she quailed to see Ricardo, Erik, and Amy, where Shae so often hung out these days. They walked out onto the back porch where Ben and Mateo sat cross-legged with guitars in their laps, sharing a joint. It was hot and bright and felt more like early afternoon than early evening. If they left right away, they would still have a couple of hours of daylight once they set up camp.

"Relax." Amy gathered a bunch of Andre's hair at the nape of her neck and tugged lightly. She could always tell when Andre was ill at ease.

"I was just thinking about Hammer," Andre said.

"Oh, I know, right? I keep expecting him to come out of that damn doghouse. It's tripping me up. Speaking of that, shouldn't we get rid of it? It's kind of depressing just sitting there."

"Not getting rid of it," Ben said in a flat voice that broached no argument.

Amy rolled her eyes and shrugged. "Okay, so we're all here, why don't we get going?"

In the car, Andre rolled down the window as her eyes flickered over the swiftly passing trees. She imagined Shae, perched somewhere, golden eyes seeking them out.

They made camp a quarter-mile from the cars in an area a little ways back from the water—a good distance from the regular campgrounds and facilities. Ben and Ryan each took one cooler; Mateo and Rafael hauled the firewood. Other victuals and snacks were carried in various backpacks and tote bags. Erik, Ricardo, and Amy immediately started with the tents.

Genevieve leaned against an oak tree. Her eyes were closed, her head tilted back under the sun. Raf came up to her, put his hand on her shoulder, and spoke quietly.

Andre wandered away, taking a little trail that forked off the main one leading down to the water. She saw several squirrels and a lizard. An unsettling number of finches stayed within mere feet of her. Ben came up behind her. "Hey."

"Look." She pointed to a small turtle making its steady way towards them.

A funny look passed over his face. "Lots of animals around."

Andre bit her lip and looked over Ben's shoulder back towards their friends, setting up the tents. The skunky scent of marijuana floated towards them. "That's nice, Mateo is here. It's been a while."

"Yeah, we had a good time jamming yesterday." Ben looked around distractedly.

Andre watched Mateo talking to Genevieve and Raf. He nodded, crossing his arms, listening to something they were saying. "He looks different," she said. "He's acting different too—a little less cocky or something." The realization was oddly poignant as Andre realized how much her friends were changing in general.

"I'll be glad when he leaves, though," Ben said. "Not that. I mean when this is over—when we don't have to hide her anymore." He tilted his head back to peer at a hawk sailing overhead, and she saw dark shadows beneath his eyes. "I wonder where she is right now."

Andre suspected Shae was somewhere nearby. She closed her eyes and tried to feel Shae, but it was one of the times she was cut off. There was no indication as to her proximity or whereabouts. Ricardo bellowed something in a low voice, and there was laughter from the direction of the tents. Ben kicked at the dirt. Andre saw Ryan then, his hand shielding his eyes from the sun, looking around. When he saw her, he raised his hand tentatively. She waved back and started towards him. "You should go talk to Merri," Andre called to Ben over her shoulder.

"Uh, Mateo said something about her too. I haven't really seen her in a while, you know."

Andre smiled. "Well, you should go talk to her," she repeated.

"Oh." He was about to say something else when they heard footsteps behind them.

"Wassup?" Amy appeared, coming up from the part of the trail that led to the water, followed by Merri. "We're going in for a dip. Get ready." They walked back to the erected tents, where the rest of the group was gathering towels and stripping down. "So, I was just

telling Merri about that naked man Ben saw a while ago." At everyone's incredulous faces, Amy repeated the story once more while
Ben kept a tight smile on his face.

Mateo shook his head. "Dude, that's some weird shit."

Andre went inside one of the tents and undressed quickly, piling
her clothes neatly in the far corner. She still had the yellow-and-black
two-piece she'd gotten in high school. She slipped it on, running her
hands over her pale stomach, self-conscious. She slipped shorts over
the suit and brushed out her hair and tied it back.

They'd brought the smaller cooler down to the little pebbled shore
where they gathered to swim. Andre smiled to Ben waist-deep in the
lake with a bikini-clad Merri on his shoulders. Amy was on Mateo's,
and they were trying to knock each other down while Ricardo and
Erik watched them. Ricardo grinned at the sight before him. "This
is awesome. I feel like I'm in a beer commercial."

Andre caught Ryan's gaze and backed away, giggling. She fumbled
to get her shorts off before they got wet, and tossed them on the
ground by a rock just as he grabbed her by the arms and hauled her,
laughing, into the lake. The water was wonderful. She swam beneath
the surface, stretching her limbs. When she bobbed up, Ryan disappeared below, and a couple of seconds later, she was being lifted up,
his head between her legs; the unshaven skin on the sides of his face
against her inner thighs tickled. He stood, and for a second, she
grasped his hands for balance. And then she was wrestling in the air
with Merri, who'd just knocked her sister and Mateo over in a big
splash that sent water spraying into Ryan's face. She squealed and
bucked as Merri grappled with her while Ben hollered out encouragement. "Get her, Merri! It's just Andre! She's a weakling!"

Andre held steady and then shoved Merri hard, knocking her
backward off of Ben's shoulders. "And daaaamn!" hollered Ricardo.
"Is this a dark horse in the running? The winner appears to be
Miiiizzz Andromeda Waters!" He set his beer down and complained,
"Man, why don't I have anyone to play with?"

Erik smirked. "I'm not too heavy."

Suddenly Amy was back up on Mateo's shoulders. After several
seconds of grunting, giggling, and feints, she and Andre knocked

each other down in a tie, after which point the game devolved into splashing. Then they all came dripping out to raid the cooler. Andre poured white wine into a plastic cup and then sat on a rock and stared at the glow of the setting sun gilding the surface into rippling metal around her friend's silhouettes. Ricardo and Ryan threw a Frisbee. Someone turned on a portable speaker, and Naked Snakes blasted into the atmosphere. She sipped her Chardonnay. It was yummy, like oak and pears, or maybe she was suggestible to the description she'd read on the label. Amy sat down and rested her head on Andre's shoulder. "Good times, huh?"

Andre nodded. "Yeah, this is so nice." And it was true. She wasn't worried anymore. And she realized how isolated she and Ben had been the last couple of months.

Then impulsively, she said, "I need to talk to you about something. But maybe not right now because I need to show it to you."

Amy raised an eyebrow. "Oh yeah?" Then she laughed. "Don't look so worried. You know you can't shock me, right?" After a moment, she said, "So . . . uh, do you want to take some ecstasy?"

Andre blinked slowly, turning to her. "You have some?"

Amy leaned back on her elbows. "Yeah, we got some from Ricardo's cousin, Charles. Do you remember him? You met him once, I think. Kinda tall dude, widow's peak?"

Andre shook her head. Amy knew more people than Andre could ever keep track of.

"I've still got some." She grinned. "I just took one a little while ago."

Andre looked at her cup of wine. "I've been drinking . . ." Andre felt loose. She wanted more of that feeling. She wanted euphoria. "I haven't had it since the summer after graduation. It made me throw up, remember?"

"This is quality stuff. You'll be fine. If you take it now, you'll be back to normal before the night's completely over. You'll be able to sleep."

Andre chewed her lip and stared out over the water. Then she gave Amy a long, conspiratorial look. "Alright."

"Ha! Yes!" Amy went over to her tote bag and pulled out a tin from a side pocket. She came back over and dropped a little pill into Andre's hand. Andre quickly swallowed it down with her wine.

"I hope I don't throw up, I've done enough vomiting this year." Ryan walked over to them. Andre squinted up at him, shielding her eyes from the setting sun. "I just took some ecstasy."

He looked from her to Amy, startled. "You think that's a good idea?"

Andre threw up her hands and laughed. "Too late now."

Amy smiled up at him. "I've got more. You want one?"

He rolled his eyes and looked out over the water. Then he grinned. "Sure," he said. "Why not?"

CHAPTER THIRTEEN

Andre stared up at the stars and the full moon. Floating on her back, she languidly kicked her legs in the water. Every few seconds, another jolt of manic joy pulsed through her synapses. Some part of her knew it had gotten too cold, but cold water was liquid crystal, wrapping her in shivers. It felt good. Everything felt *good*. She sucked in her lips and swished her head back and forth and went upright once more. Treading water, she looked about with exquisitely amped up glee. All sorts of bulbs had flipped on in her brain.

The music playing from the speakers by the shore was poignant, a familiar soundtrack to that moment. Andre didn't want to leave the water. *Why would anyone leave the water?* Instead of working, instead of having jobs and governments and running water and dental appointments, why didn't everyone just take baths all the time and spend their hours in amniotic bliss? This was the best time ever. She would never be able to thank Amy enough!

Ryan's arms came around her waist, and he slowly appeared in front of her. How long had he been away? *A minute? An hour?* She laughed. His eyes reflected what she felt. "Hey, be careful out here." The sound of his voice was magical.

She ran her hands over his face and pulled him toward her. "I am careful." Her voice sounded like her ears were plugged. "You're *mmmmm*." She bit his shoulder.

He laughed. "You are peaking, Bumblebee." They kissed. "So, you feeling good?" he asked when they pulled apart after several minutes.

She nodded and kept her head moving up and down. It felt wonderful to nod.

They dipped under the water. It grew completely dark and colder, and Ryan coaxed her from the lake. They split another pill. Amy's disembodied voice came from somewhere, and laughing said, "Keep an eye on her, she's not used to this. Looks like it hit her pretty hard."

At some point, Genevieve and Raf appeared and stood at the edge of the water, watching everyone. Andre sensed that they were sober and in a very different mood. They were from another planet.

Joints. More wine. Perhaps it was because they had not all been together in so long, or it could have been the nature, the atmosphere of a summer night, but something flicked on a hedonistic switch. Layers of inhibition and habitual proprieties peeled away with clothes and bathing suits. She kissed Merri and Erik, and Ryan didn't mind because they spent most of their time making out and murmuring things so brazenly sentimental they would never be repeated.

They were a long time in the dark down by the water. Flashlights roved around, and the orange tips of cigarettes and joints. In the distance, a little fire flickered near the tents. It beckoned with the slowly dawning suggestion of warmth. Ryan leaned towards her, and when she made out his face, she was flooded with affection for his familiar features. And then she felt a wave of tenderness towards everyone. Ryan said, "Let's go to the tent."

A revelation! What a brilliant idea to be in a new setting! She squeezed his hand and leaned against him as they walked uphill. "I want you to meet someone."

"Hmm? I want me to meet them too."

"I want to show you. You've got to meet her," Andre said again. Then she tripped, hard, her knees smacking onto the cold, hard surface of rock beneath her. "Oh," she said. "Ow." She laughed.

Ryan helped her up and turned her by the shoulders to look at him. "Are you okay?"

"Yeah, I'm fine. What? Hey, c'mon. I'm fine." A bit of the sparkly fog faded, and she pushed away the dull pain in her knees that would probably turn into bruises tomorrow. When they got to the bonfire, Mateo was playing guitar, and Amy was dancing in nothing but her bikini bottom and a robe that was loosely tied at the waist and hanging off of one shoulder. She swayed, a hypnotic Salome, twisting her hips and coiling her arms. Andre suddenly wanted to hear Ben's music. Her eyes wandered around, looking for him. He wasn't there, and neither was Merri.

Ryan watched Amy but turned and smiled down at Andre when she looked up at him. She felt herself easing down from the pinnacle, and part of her was relieved. She grinned back at him and lightly bit his arm. "We should take some B vitamins tomorrow."

Amy stopped her sexy belly dance and started doing deep plies and rising onto the balls of her feet. She laughed. "I am *really* in love with my legs right now." Beaming, she ran her hands over her thighs and knees. "They just work so well, you know? You all should try this."

Ryan procured a bottle of water from one of the smaller coolers, and they turned toward the tent. Inside, they sat cross-legged in front of each other, sipping the water under the gleam of a weak flashlight. Andre sucked the tip of the bottle and ground her teeth. He took a ribbon of her damp hair and studied it under the flashlight. "Weird. It almost looks blue in this light." He dropped it and stared at her. He ran his fingers along her shoulders. She closed her eyes and felt something tickle her face. Without looking, she knew it was a moth.

Outside the tent, a guitar began strumming steadily, and Mateo began to sing. There was shuffling and talking too, but she could not attribute the voices to anyone in particular. They were like birds or crickets, although Amy's laugh pierced through it all here and there.

Then they lay naked and tangled together. For a long time, her mind was away, her thoughts moved in loops, and she hitched on and rode them like a merry-go-round. She didn't know how long they stayed there, but after what seemed like forever, Andre felt herself surface. She sat up and felt around for the water bottle. "I'm so thirsty," she murmured. Ryan turned on the flashlight and squinted at her. "What?" she asked.

"Nothing, just looking at you."

She swallowed and licked her lips. "I feel weird. My head . . ."

"Mine too."

Andre nodded. "But it was nice. It was awesome, actually." She stared at him, at the dramatic shadows the flashlight made on his face; he looked like a different version of himself. "Probably something we shouldn't make a habit of."

"Yeah, that's for the best. So . . . who is this person you want me to meet?"

Andre closed her eyes. *Shit.* "I don't know. I got really out there. I was talking nonsense." She didn't look at him but stretched her arms, straightened her legs, and leaned forward in a pike position to grab her toes. "I should put some clothes on." Her voice still sounded strange in her ears. She fumbled around for her underwear and shorts, then straightened out the blanket and lay down, yawning. "I'm just going to close my eyes for a few minutes."

Ryan laughed. "You mean you're going to bed?"

"No, I'm just going to lay here for a bit."

"Mind if I leave? I'm starving. I'm going to see if there are any snacks or anything. Ricardo had some jerky."

"Ew," Andre said, her face pressed against the pillow.

He kissed her temple. "Love you, Bumblebee."

She napped without dreaming, slipping out of the blankets and rolling into a corner of the tent, so only the thin vinyl was between her and the cold ground, and her face was pressed into the wall. She stirred at the sound of the zipper. Ricardo spoke, "I missed you so much, Amy, you're so—"

"I'm awake!" Andre sat up quickly, rubbing her eyes. "Please, you guys, don't have sex next to me." She groped around for the water bottle but realized it was empty when she put it to her lips. She tossed it aside.

"Huh," Amy said. "You're not one to be telling anyone not to screw around in a tent."

"We didn't," Andre said. She blinked at the flashlight Amy turned on. She was suddenly completely awake, on the upswing to sober.

"Right," Amy smirked.

"What's everybody doing? What time is it?" Andre asked.

Amy sighed as if it was information Andre should already have. "Merri, Ben, and Ryan are down by the water, I think. Genni and Raf are in the other tent. They're trying to sleep." She added under her breath, "They've been total downers all night. I don't know why they even came. Mateo and Erik are by the fire."

Fire. That sounded appealing. Shivering, Andre slipped out of the tent and went over to the cooler to grab a bottle of water covering her hands with the sleeves of her sweater and holding the bottle between the fabric. She wondered how long she'd stayed in the water after the temperature had dropped earlier, and if she was going to get a cold. "We need to make sure we collect all our beer and water bottles to recycle," she said softly, mostly to herself.

"Oh, hey. I thought you were asleep," Mateo said when she sat down in one of the flimsy lawn chairs circling the small fire.

Andre wrapped her sweater around herself and smiled tightly, hunching forward. She put the bottle between her knees, stretching her hands out to be warmed. "Yeah, I took a little nap."

Erik started laughing and shaking his head. "Oh, man, I smoked too much. I forgot you were even here, Andre. I was like, who the hell is this girl?"

She laughed.

Mateo plucked the guitar, and gradually a familiar tune emerged. It was one of his and Ben's first songs. He was playing it slowly, interspersing it with a couple of beats between notes by thumping his leg and lightly slapping the soundboard. Andre sat back in the chair and grew nostalgic. She glanced up and saw Mateo was looking at her. He smiled, genuine and disarming, and she'd not realized until then that she'd missed him. "Brings back memories, huh?" he said.

She nodded, and her eyes wandered to the flames. "The good old days," she said quietly.

"Yeah." He plucked a series of high notes. "I miss it here more than I thought I would."

Erik snorted. "I need to get away so I can say the same thing."

"I think we're really lucky to live here," Andre said.

"Yeah, you're right, but—" Mateo leaped out of his chair and yelled, "Jesus! Ah! What the fuck!" a small black shape swooped in front of him in a flurry of flapping wings. He stumbled forward, and his foot brushed the fire, sending a spray of smoke and cinders into the air.

"Shit!" Erik yelled, ducking his head as the winged creature darted towards him.

Mateo swung his guitar through the air, trying to smack it away.

Andre curled into herself, squeezing her eyes shut and putting her hands up in front of her face. She opened her eyes just in time to see it come towards her. Shrieking, she felt a wing brush her cheek—a primal, too-close-to-nature sensation.

The tent unzipped, and Amy shouted, "What the hell is going on?" A flashlight roved over them. They stood gasping, looking around.

"I think it's gone," Mateo said after a few seconds.

"Dude! What the hell?" Ricardo appeared next to Amy. "You guys scared the shit out of me." He laughed nervously.

Andre tried to force her hands to stop trembling. "It was a bat. I'm pretty sure it was a bat."

"Geesh." Amy huffed. "You guys are so dramatic. I thought it was a mountain lion or something."

"Yeah," Ricardo said. "I thought I was about to hear someone getting eaten."

Andre shivered. "Why would there be bats? I've never seen bats out here before." Far away, she smelled a hint of sulfur.

"They're pretty common, right?" Mateo said. "My grandma had some roosting in her attic a few years ago."

The other tent opened, and Genevieve and Raf appeared over the glow of another flashlight. "You sure it was a bat, not a bird?" Raf asked.

"What are you guys talking about?" Ryan said, walking up the path towards them with Merri and Ben. Staggering drunk, Ben collapsed into one of the chairs.

Mateo proceeded to tell them about the "attack."

"I think I did see some earlier," Genevieve said suddenly. She looked at Raf. "Remember? When we were down by the water?"

"Yeah." he nodded. "I thought they were birds, though."

"Well, one of them tried to steal my joint," Erik said, flicking the end of it and blowing on the tip to keep it alive.

"Maybe it liked my song," Mateo said, his voice just a tad high. "That was pretty fucking creepy." Then he broke into a loud, familiar strumming and belted out, "I see—a bad moon rising!"

Amy laughed and started dancing out of the tent, and Ricardo reached for her.

A few feet from the tent, Andre thought she saw a snake slithering away into some bushes. She squinted, unable to trust her eyes in the dark. *She calls forth the creatures* . . . She looked at Ben. His eyes were half-open. He was wasted. She kept her hammering heart to herself and leaned against Ryan.

"Well." Genevieve coughed and quietly said, "I'm going back to bed, you guys. Maybe try to keep it down?"

Next to her, Raf raised his eyebrows and gave a little wave, and then they returned to the tent.

Merri stood shivering still in just her bathing suit top and shorts. "Aren't you cold?" Andre asked.

She blinked and looked down at herself. "Yes. I'm freezing," she said through chattering teeth. Andre went back into the tent to find something for her. She pulled out a hooded sweatshirt of Amy's and handed it to Merri. "Oh, thanks!" She pulled it on over her head, ran her hands through her hair, and looked at them in the firelight. "Oh, no!" she cried. "Oh shit! No, no-no." She put her hands on top of her head and groaned.

"What's wrong?" Amy asked.

"My ring!"

Merri wore it all the time. It was a large, antique sapphire in an ornate silver setting, a family heirloom. Vivian had given it to her two years before on her twenty-first birthday.

"It's all right," Ryan said. "We'll find it tomorrow."

"No." Merri shook her head. "I can't leave it."

"You lost it?" Andre asked.

"No. I know right where it is. I took it off to go in the water. It's a little loose, so I didn't want to swim with it. I put it on a rock."

"Why don't you wait until morning?" Andre suggested, not liking the thought of anyone walking back to the lakeshore in the dark.

"Except a bat might steal it," said Ricardo.

Ben roused himself and said, a bit reluctantly, "I'll go . . . come help you look if you want." He stood up slowly and then stumbled.

"I'll take her," Ryan offered. He turned to Merri. "I saw where your stuff was. Right beneath that big tree, right? Behind the cooler?"

Merri nodded. "Ugh. What if it's lost now? What if a bird grabbed it or someone knocked it into the water by accident? Ugh. I'm such an idiot."

Amy lit a cigarette and took a deep drag and said, "Don't take too long, you two. If you can't find it quickly, just come back, and we'll look for it in the morning. You've got ten minutes." Andre studied her sister in the firelight and had the impression of Amy as the leader of a bohemian tribe. The night was doing funny things, amplifying everyone, turning them all into caricatures.

Ryan put on a sweatshirt and grabbed an extra flashlight. "We'll be back in a few."

Ben sat down again, looking relieved. Mateo shrugged and continued playing. Erik yawned and disappeared into the tent that Genevieve and Raf were in. Amy sipped from a flask and resumed dancing. Ricardo, apparently having lost his chance to get laid, started rolling another joint. Ben bobbed his head along to the music, holding a cigarette he forgot to smoke. A few minutes passed, and he looked up blearily and said, "You guys saw a bat?"

"Yeah, it was wild," Mateo said. "Fucker was crawling on me for a second, I think."

Ben dropped his head and let out a snuffling noise. It took Andre a few seconds to realize he was laughing.

"What?" Mateo asked.

Ben shook his head and wiped the outer corners of his eyes. Andre stared at him. *Don't.*

"There's a lot *wilder* stuff out there, believe me."

"Oooh!" Amy cried. "He's being all mysterious now." She tapped her cigarette, tossed her head back, and blew out smoke. "What are you babbling about? Your naked fellow?"

He pointed at Andre. "She! *She* knows what I'm talking about!"

Andre let out a calculatedly bored sigh. *Please not here. Not right now.* She forced her voice to sound light, almost distracted. "I don't think I do know, Ben. Please enlighten me."

"You—"

He was cut off by a throat-flaying scream.

CHAPTER FOURTEEN

For a beat, they were all deer in headlights. Amy was frozen, the end of the cigarette she'd just lit between two fingers by her mouth, her other hand was clenched in a fist–a creature poised for fight or flight. Genevieve and Raf appeared once again from the tent, arms wrapped around each other, their faces accusing. Then everyone began shouting and talking at once.

"What the *fuck* was that?" Ricardo cried, his voice going up several octaves. "Was that Merri? What the hell?" They scrambled for flashlights and phones, trying in vain to get signals. Mateo, Ben, and Erik, muttering expletives, summoned courage long dormant in their safe lives and staggered onto the path that led to the lakeshore. Their walk was both urgent and halting, like reluctant but motivated Frankensteins. "You guys stay here," Ben said to the rest of them.

Andre grabbed a flashlight and darted after them. Mateo turned around. "Go back, Andre. We don't know what's going on."

"I appreciate the chivalry, but I'm coming with you."

A few minutes later, they heard Merri sobbing as they neared the water. Andre let out a breath she hadn't realized she'd been holding. She skidded down the little path faster now, passing all the guys. One of them tugged on her sweatshirt, and she batted him away. A branch poked her painfully in the chest, and she gasped.

And then Mateo's flashlight illuminated Ryan carrying Merri and running towards them. "Good, you have light," he said. "It knocked our flashlights in the water."

As they got closer, Andre saw that they were both splattered with blood. The smell of sulfur was strong now. Something went still inside of her as she looked up at the moon sailing above them, a perfect silver coin mirrored in the wavering surface of the lake. The water wasn't still, and she imagined creatures beneath the surface swimming around. *I call forth the creatures.* She shook her head and came back to the present.

"What the hell happened?" Mateo cried.

"Are you guys, okay?" Ben asked.

"We'll be fine. Let's just go! Go! Go!" Ryan cried, moving past them. "We need to get the fuck out of here." Andre had never heard him panic like that before.

Her voice thick with hysterical sobs, Merri said something Andre didn't catch. Ryan answered her, "No, it wasn't. Shhh, it was just a homeless person or something."

"No! It had claws!" she shrieked. "It had fucking claws! Did you see? Did you see its *face*?"

Merri sat trembling violently in a chair, clutching the bottle of water Andre had shoved in her face. Genevieve kneeled on the ground next to her, murmuring and pressing a cloth against her left cheek to stamp the flow of blood from the large gash. Genevieve turned back to the rest of them. "We need to get her to a hospital. She's going to need stitches."

"We should call the police, too," Raf added.

"And get the hell out of here," Ricardo said.

"—the next thing I know, she's screaming, and being like, dragged off into the trees." Ryan was telling them the story while they frantically packed up the tents. Raf stood frowning by the fire, trying to get a signal on his phone.

"I don't get it," Ryan continued, shaking his head. "It was like, a man, but—" He swallowed a long drink of water before continuing, his face shined with sweat. "—He wasn't right. He was super skinny and *crazy* tall. I only got a glimpse of his face. I think he was missing an eye, and I don't know if he was deformed or had some—"

"No, no, no!" Mateo cried. "Are you serious? Let's get the *fuck* out of here. This is a horror movie! We are *in* a horror movie!"

"Shit!" Ricardo yelled. "Mateo is right. It's the Slender Man!" He yanked a pole from the ground and grappled with the tent, looking around for someone to agree with him. "Right? Doesn't that sound like the Slender Man?"

"Pipe down, guys," hollered Amy, tossing her head in Merri's direction. "Let's just get the hell out of here."

Merri started wailing again.

"Look, I don't know what I saw. There was a fucking bat attacking us, too, all this flapping. It was chaos. I think there was something else in that pill too, Amy, because it doesn't make any sense. I saw this . . . I thought it was a little kid at first. I don't know. Some small person that moved so fast and jumped on him like a monkey and pulled him off Merri—like dragged him away, I guess." He shook his head. "Shit. This sounds insane. I must have been half hallucinating. It was dark. I don't know what the hell happened."

"It's got to be the same guy you saw that time, right?" Mateo asked Ben, who was staring at Ryan in horror.

"That doesn't make any sense," Genevieve said, standing up. "Who would be out here without any campsite nearby? This isn't a place homeless people squat. They go to cities. How could someone survive out here without any clothes or food?"

"That's why he was trying to eat campers!" Ricardo cried.

"We've got to get out of here!" Merri sobbed.

"She's right," Ryan said. "We need to go, *now*." They all moved quickly to gather up what supplies they could find and tear down the tents.

Ben went up to Andre and grasped her elbow. "Let's go," he whispered. "Let's just leave right now. "She would go back to the shed. I'm sure of it. We've got to check on her."

Andre looked around. Ryan was hoisting a backpack and a cooler, Mateo had his hands full of stuff too. Everyone was preoccupied. "They're going to want us all to leave together," she said quietly. "We can't just ditch them."

"Screw it," Ben said. "Stay if you want. I'm leaving."

He grabbed a flashlight and bolted off down the path that led to the cars. He might have been hopped up on adrenalin, but he was still drunk. She bit her lip and looked around. Once they saw his car was gone, they'd know they left. She grabbed her backpack and went after him without a word to anyone.

"Shit, Ben. How long has the light been on? Why didn't you get gas on the way?"

"We were in a hurry. Amy wanted to get there asap. I figured I'd fill up on the way home tomorrow."

She clenched her fists on the wheel. He *always* put off getting gas. They filled up at a station, and Ben grabbed an energy drink. When she got back in the car, she could hear her phone buzzing and ignored it. They came home and went to the shed, but it was empty. Andre closed her eyes and felt on the string. "She's coming." She nodded at him. "I don't know how I know. She's on her way. She's . . . something's happened."

They went back into the house and stood in the living room. Ben swallowed. He'd been afraid at the campground, but the fear in his eyes now was something more primal. "Is she okay? Is she going to be okay?"

"I don't—" And then suddenly there was pounding up the porch steps. A knock, and Mateo opened the door. "Hey, guys." He looked back and forth between them, obviously confused. "Genevieve took Merri to the hospital, and Ryan went with them to make a statement to the police. Why the hell did you guys just jet like that? Andre, Ryan, was worried. He wasn't going to leave until we came back and told him Ben's car was gone."

Ben looked at Andre. "I needed to come home right away. I felt sick. She drove my car."

Mateo raised an eyebrow. *What the hell kind of answer is that?*

"Where's Amy?" Andre asked.

"They went back to Raf's. Genevieve and Ryan, I guess are gonna be at the hospital until Vivian gets there."

"Well, I'm going to bed," Andre announced. "I'm wiped out."

"Yeah, me too," Ben said, nodding.

"Dude, I don't feel like I can sleep after that shit. I mean, what the hell, right? What *happened* tonight? Merri says a monster attacked her. Ryan says he doesn't know what he saw, but he thinks he hallucinated. What a weird, fucked up weekend."

Neither of them responded to this for several seconds. "Yeah, it'll probably make more sense tomorrow," Andre said finally. "Here, Mateo." She moved to the hall closet and grabbed a couple of blankets. "Let me find you a pillow."

Leaving Mateo downstairs wired and baffled, Andre and Ben went upstairs where he chain-smoked out the window, and Andre sat crouched on the floor, her back against the wall, trying to call to Shae. The string between them was clamped down tight. *What happened tonight, Shae? What did you do?*

An hour later, they slipped downstairs to find Mateo snoring on the couch. "If she's not in her room, we're not going to panic,"

Andre whispered as they cut across the yard. Several birds shot up and away from the ground in front of the shed, and she shivered.

"I knew tonight was a bad idea." Ben hesitated when they reached the door.

"It could have been worse," Andre said. "Nobody's dead. And she's tough, remember?" And even though she spoke the words, Andre felt that something worse than Merri being maimed and traumatized had occurred that evening. It was becoming a familiar feeling, this numinous dread.

"If she's not in here . . ." Ben opened the door.

The shed was dark and cold; the old stale scent had returned. The glamour was gone. They turned on their flashlights, shivering. Andre sucked in her breath when the flashlight landed on Shae. She lay in a corner of the room and was covered in a dark substance like mud. Nearby lay a large kitchen knife. Her clothing was in scraps, almost entirely gone, as if in one night they'd withered to rags. The room reeked of something rotten and sour. Shae turned her head toward them and opened her eyes.

Andre went over to her and dropped to her knees, raised her hand over Shae, and then lowered it, unsure if she should touch her. "Are you all right?" And then Andre flashed the light over her and saw she was definitely *not* all right.

"Oh shit. Oh, no, no." Ben had come up behind Andre. "Oh, fuck. Oh god, what do we do?"

Shae held her arm out and away as if to distance herself from the unsightliness. Her joints were normally slightly hyperextended, but now her right arm was bent at a perfect right angle in the wrong direction. The skin was torn open, and violet and blue veins appeared glistening around jagged, startlingly white, exposed bone.

Andre took a deep breath and met Shae's eyes. They were distant. "Okay, okay, okay," Andre whispered. "You're okay. We're going to take care of this." She put her hand to Shae's face. Her skin was cold.

Ben groaned. "What the fuck happened tonight?"

"Shh. Calm down," Andre said. "We've got to figure out what to do. "Okay." She bit her lip and nodded to herself. Shae's eyes were half-open. Her breathing was shallow, but considering one of her arms was barely attached by a flap of skin, she seemed to be doing okay.

Shae spoke, "Gray Man is dead now."

"What are you talking about?" Ben asked. "I thought you killed him weeks ago."

"I did not. He was not dead before. He is dead now. I took off his head." She made a hissing sound.

Andre looked around, shivering. "Ben, can you find me some scissors?"

"Huh?" He was still staring at Shae.

"Scissors, there should be a pair in the drawer by the kitchen sink."

"Oh, yeah, sure."

He left and returned quickly with a pair of orange-handled shears. Then he stood up and faced away from them as Andre cut away the unrecognizable remains of Shae's clothes. She was splattered with smelly black slime that Andre was realizing was not mud or blood. "What is this?" Andre wrinkled her nose.

"The Unseelie," Shae said.

Andre went still for a second, closed her eyes, and swallowed. The smell was unbearable, like sulfur and rotten meat. They would have to clean her before they did anything else. Shae lay with her eyes averted to the ceiling while Andre looked over her to make sure there weren't any other serious injuries. "Ben, can you do me another favor? Go upstairs and draw a bath."

He said nothing and disappeared once more. Andre pressed Shae's left hand between both of hers. They looked into each other's eyes and the connection pulsed. Andre felt pain in a sharp reflection in her arm and winced. Shae slipped her hand away, and the connection broke. Andre noticed a dark bruise on Shae's chest that had been hidden in shadow, roughly the size of a plum.

Ben opened the door. Andre grabbed an ancient green throw blanket from the corner of the room and tried to ignore the gore as she tucked it around Shae's chest.

"Okay." She looked at Ben. "We're going to have to be careful of her arm. I'm going to take a closer look before we bring her upstairs." She focused the flashlight and steeled herself. She studied the exposed bone, broken in thin slivers like sharp teeth surrounded by green veins with pink tissue puffing out of her skin like foam. And it was dirty. The filth that covered Shae had gotten in her exposed flesh.

Andre could recommend all sorts of herbal and dietary remedies for common ailments, but she'd never cleaned anything beyond a surface wound. She'd never made a poultice or set a bone. "We're in over our heads, Ben," she said quietly.

Shae kept her face turned away. Andre wondered if she was in shock. Could this kill her? One small comfort was there didn't appear to be much of Shae's blood. There was a good amount of crimson staining her arm, but it seemed to be under control despite the lack of a tourniquet. Maybe Shae had a different system of coagulation, or maybe her body contained less blood.

"The tub is going to be full soon," Ben said.

"Okay, let's get her into the water."

"I've got her." Ben nudged Andre out of the way and gingerly gathered Shae up, so her broken arm was facing out. They went inside the house quietly and up the stairs, grimacing as they passed Mateo asleep on the couch. The bathroom was bright and warm with steam. Ben knelt and eased Shae out of the blanket and into the water. Then he stood up, went over to the toilet, and puked. Andre grabbed the glass sitting on the bathroom sink, filled it with water, and handed it to him. "Sorry," he muttered. His hand trembled as he took the glass from her.

The water enveloped Shae's broken arm. Andre had no idea if it was wise for it to be submerged, but she didn't know how else they could clean it. Shae's face slipped under. Ben made a noise and pointed.

"It's okay; she's okay," Andre said as she knelt and lifted Shae by the shoulders. She looked at the sticky splotches in Shae's hair and made a decision. "Okay, we can't get her clean like this. I'm going to get in there with her."

Ben nodded. His eyes were bloodshot, but he was alert. He held Shae's head above water while Andre peeled down to her underwear. She grabbed a bar of soap, stepped into the warm bath, and sank down, opposite Shae. She let out a shuddery breath realizing that the water acted as a sort of conductor to their connection. She felt a dull throb in her arm, and she felt . . . *Shae*. She felt her strength, her loss—that agony of her sundering, the mysteries buried. She felt the pull of winged ones in her mind and the call to pay the tithe. And she felt Shae's mind shying away from her own, felt her resisting the connection. The water was hot, and her scalp started to sweat. She leaned forward. "Shae?" Shae's eyes opened and closed sleepily. "I'm going to wash you, okay?"

Shae nodded, then hunched forward almost languidly while Andre soaped her up. The room was balmy. Ben sat on the toilet seat and stared at the tiles. For several minutes no one spoke while Andre carefully ran a shower puff over Shae. She scooted Shae around so she could wash her back and neck. The wings were another matter. The delicate appendages were tucked tightly into her back. Andre wasn't sure if she should attempt to clean them. Were they sensitive? Was it a breach of privacy? There was no part of her anatomy she could use as a comparison, but Andre could see, in the tight accordion fold, that they were dirty. She clicked her tongue, and before she could ask Shae about it, the faerie's ribcage expanded in a deep breath, and she tilted forward more so her wings would have room to slowly spread.

Andre sucked in her breath. She'd never seen them so close. It was against Andre's instinct to touch them. They looked fragile, like rice paper over a network of spider-web bones, with tiny veins pulsing slightly beneath shimmering colors: green, pink, gold, indigo—like oil on asphalt.

Andre dipped the washcloth into the soapy water and very gently dabbed it over Shae's wings. At first, she wiped so gently that none of the dirt came off, but as Shae sat there, quiet and stoic, Andre gained more confidence and realized that although the wings looked delicate, like the rest of Shae, they were built of something tough.

Ben now watched them unabashedly, a little smile on his face. Andre continued cleaning until the wings were spotless. "Okay," she said, sighing, sitting back in the water. "That looks much better."

Shae's wings stretched out just a little farther then, going taut and trembling slightly before retracting neatly back between her shoulder blades.

They now sat in a pool of cooling, dirty, gray water with dark oily spots, a soup of monster gore. Andre shuddered. She still needed to wash Shae's hair. She pulled the plug. Shae leaned back against her, her broken arm resting on the side of the tub. Andre glanced at Ben. "You should check on Mateo." When the water drained, Andre refilled it and soaped and shampooed both herself and Shae once more. "Shae? Let's do a final rinse in the shower. Can you stand up for that?"

Shae rose easily as if some invisible force plucked her up by the nape of her neck. When Andre finally turned the water off, some of the adrenaline she'd been running on for the last few hours sifted down the drain along with the water. For a moment, Andre wilted against the shower door, utterly spent and unsure of what to do next.

Ben was waiting with towels for each of them when she opened the door. She led Shae out of the bathroom and into her room. Shae sat on the bed while Andre fetched sweatpants and a tank top for herself. Back upstairs, she gingerly dried Shae off. She felt she should dress her in something, but she was scared to slip anything over her head. Blankets would have to do. Shae looked up at her, her eyes becoming more alert. "Water—I need water."

Andre nodded. "Yes. Hold on a second." She padded down the stairs, running lightly on the balls of her feet, past Mateo, to the kitchen. Early morning light gave the kitchen the air of a cloudy fish tank.

"Andre?" She went still. Mateo grunted. "Is that you?"

She took a deep breath. She didn't trust her voice. She strained to sound sleepy, bored. "Yeah, it's me."

"Oh, okay." Then to her dismay, he sat up. "You're not asleep? What time is it?"

"I'm going back to bed now." She hoped she only imagined the crazed, singsong note in her voice. "I'm just getting some water." She waited several seconds while he drifted back to a reassuringly horizontal position, then grabbed the glass of water and darted back upstairs.

Andre gently held up the cup for her to drink while Shae's wrecked arm was flung out and away from her like a broken kite she wanted to let go of. Ben sat on the floor with his head in his hands. She glanced at him. "It's ridiculously irresponsible for us to have Mateo here."

"Your idea to let him stay," he said, yawning. "Want me to wake him up and kick him out?"

Andre ignored him, sat back, and met Shae's detached, injured-reptile gaze. The light was growing brighter through the blinds. A mourning dove began its melancholy coo. Andre didn't like the way the sunlight was juxtaposed with the lamp. It was distracting some-how, as if the world could not decide if it was night or day. She got up and switched off the light, and turned the blinds slightly.

The sight of Shae's arm against the morning light repelled her eyes. "We need to set it," Andre said grimly.

"Uh . . ." Ben rubbed his face. "How . . . who . . . do you know how to do that?"

"Nope." She looked at him. "Do you?"

"What do you think?" he muttered.

She shrugged. "You were in Boy Scouts, right?"

"Ah, that was a million years ago, and wilderness first aid doesn't exactly cover this."

"Too bad," she said, gazing out the window. Daytime was approaching in a bright, overwhelming avalanche of the *real* world, and Andre knew they had to act fast because she wouldn't be able to keep it together for much longer.

"The hospital?" he asked miserably.

She shook her head. "C'mon, Ben." She took a deep breath. "Let's get my laptop. We'll look up how to set a bone."

"Jesus Christ."

She sighed. "Got any other suggestions?"

CHAPTER FIFTEEN

It could be worse. My keepers have cleaned me and wrapped up my arm. It will heal quickly. People have seen me and the woodwalker, but the masses will still not know of us.

I would not have been compelled to save the girl, but *just* as I'd called forth the creatures to set the tithe into motion, Gray Man came along to make mischief. And that wasn't right. It would have been messy—complicated everything. And there should be no more bloodshed than is necessary. I cannot regret the monster's death. He killed the furry one and still didn't heed my warning, even after I took his eye and his arm. He'd been rotting and was only days away from his demise, but he was strong enough to snatch the girl and then to snap *my* arm. I'd not expected that. But after I'd torn him off her, his head had sloughed off with ease, and he melted into a sticky sludge. What a mess. And how my arm stings!

I strain for glamour, but I am weakened. I do not feel good about the tithe. Why isn't the pressure letting up? Yes, the forces of the court are approving, but I am wary. I am not supposed to have any regard for my quarry. Would I feel this bad if I still had my name? Likely not. I am doing as I was tasked to do, but it does not feel good. Nothing feels good anymore.

Andre walked down a corridor of greenery—a pleached alley. She was trying to get there. Elsewhere. That wild and shining place. But she struggled to get farther as if she walked on a conveyor belt. She started to run. The pumpkin-colored light and the trees in the distance beckoned her. On the ground on either side of her were flower beds. The flowers burst from their stems and rose into the air to take the form of butterflies. She reached out. No, please, no! *The butterflies grew larger, darker. They were birds. No, they were bats. They traveled farther than she could—faster and farther down the pleached alley. The winged ones would help her get there. Once the tithe was paid. They were the key; she just had to follow . . .*

Then she was nowhere, in black space. The darkness was punctured by fireworks that became radiant stained glass mandalas, twirling in perfect symmetry. Something was thrumming in her chest, running through her blood; her body was vibrating, changing—

Andre felt a hand on her shoulder. She sat up with a jerk. No one had touched her. She was alone in her room. There was a knock— another knock, she realized. "Hold on just a second." A circus in stained glass evaporated from her mind. She was sticky from sweating in her sleep.

"It's all right," Mateo said through the door. "You don't have to get up. I'm just saying goodbye. Ben wanted me to wake you up before I left."

Andre opened the door. "Hey, what time is it?" She brought her hand to her mouth. Her jaw was tender. She'd been grinding her teeth something fierce.

"Almost two." Mateo was dressed, wearing his backpack.

"Where's Ben?"

"He's passed out. He went to bed a few hours ago. He kind of insisted I wake you up before I headed out. I don't know why."

She pulled her hair back in a ponytail, as the pieces of the last twenty-four hours fell back into place in her mind. "Have you been up long?"

"A couple of hours. I've been watching TV. I ate some of your Chia cereal." He smiled. "It was pretty disgusting."

"It's an acquired taste." She yawned, covering her mouth. "Have you talked to anyone else? Any news about Merri?"

He shrugged. "I talked to Amy, and she said Vivian took her home from the hospital." He looked uncomfortable. "I heard your phone going off like crazy this morning. Ryan called me, asking for you earlier. I told him you were okay. That you just went to bed. You might, uh, you might want to check in with him." Then he sighed and looked at the floor. "Poor Merri. I think she's kinda traumatized. Sucks."

"Yeah." Andre rubbed her face.

"You know, since I've been here, I've had this feeling that something is different. I don't know. You and Ben . . . you guys *look* different."

Every time Mateo spoke, it took her a beat longer than it should have to comprehend what he was saying. There was a fog in her mind. When had Mateo become so astute? If he sensed something, what must Ryan think after all this time? She stretched her arms over her head and yawned again. "I don't know, Mateo. Nothing has changed much around here. Ben is pretty absorbed in his music these days. Have you heard any of it? It's really good."

He brightened. "Oh my god, yeah, this morning. Well, just part of one song for a minute, and it was freaking amazing. I wish—I wish he'd let me hear more." He looked like he was about to say something else, but stopped. He smiled. "Well, I've got to go. I'm meeting my friend in SoCal. It was great to see you. I've missed you guys."

She hugged him.

He laughed. "You know, last night was pretty anticlimactic. A bunch of people camping and getting debaucherous in the woods with a deformed attacker lurking around? It should have ended in a proper bloodbath."

"Yeah," she agreed with a weary smile. "We make a pretty dull horror film."

"I hope Merri's okay."

"I know. Me too."

She followed him down the hall towards the front door and realized that the Shellara would never be the same to her. *It is where a monster roamed sick and lonely until his blood was spilled as bats converged. The lake is where it starts.* She shook her head. *Where did that notion come from?* Last night was already taking on mythic dimensions.

She followed Mateo up to the front door and hugged him again, then stood in the doorway and watched as he walked, fast and effortless, though his backpack was enormous, and he carried his guitar. He dropped his burdens in his car, waved once more, and drove away.

She closed the door and found her phone in her backpack, which was hanging off a hook next to the doorway. There were seven texts, all from Ryan except one from Amy an hour ago. She read them.

Where are you?

Why did you leave without saying anything?

Is everything OK?

I'm feeling really weird right now. I wish you were here.

Please call.

Whatever. I'm over it. Have fun with Ben.

Her face burned, and a knot twisted in her stomach. She called and got his voicemail and left a desperate, choked message to please call her back and that she was sorry. Then she hung up, wiping away the tears now running steadily down her face, and looked at the message from Amy: *Why did you and Ben leave Mateo? Did you forget about him? Kinda rude! Anyway, hope you're feeling okay. Call me when you get a chance. (Wasn't last night totally fucked up?)*

Andre drank a glass of water and brushed her teeth. Her knees were bruised and aching from where she'd tripped on the path the night before.

She stood at the back door for a long time before she crossed the yard and opened the door to the shed. Hugging herself, she stepped inside. Patches of moss gleamed here and there, verdant once more. In her peripheral vision, a bird fluttered around the ceiling, dissolving when she looked directly at it.

Shae lay on her back, limbs splayed. Her face was peaceful. The monarch sat on the center of her chest, right over the bruise, which had faded to a yellow-green color. Andre couldn't recall seeing the butterfly the night before and wondered where it had been while they'd taken the bath. She sat down and watched Shae's chest rise and fall. The scrapes on her skin had faded. Andre wondered if she was dreaming. What did she dream about? What memories were buried inside of her?

A breeze wafted in from somewhere in the room. Carefully, without touching it, Andre leaned over and studied the splint she'd fashioned out of a ruler, cotton, and electrical tape. The skin was not red or swollen.

She went back to the house and made a cup of black tea. She texted Ryan to please call her, then pulled out some of her books and perused them through watering eyes. Her mother texted her. *Hi, sweetie! Hope you're having a good week. Max started eighth grade. I can't believe it! Would you please tell Amy to call me sometime? I miss you girls.* Poor Lydia.

Andre cut an avocado in half and ate it with a spoon in her room while scribbling notes in a trembling hand. Part of her knew it was busywork, pointless research. And yet . . . little snippets here and there, from different sources, seemed to paint a picture she could almost grasp the delineation of.

She turned up the same stories over and over: the disappearance of Robert Kirk, Brigit Cleary—an Irishwoman who was immolated by her husband, who believed she was a changeling, Rip Van Winkle. There were plenty of eye-roll-worthy anecdotes from the New Age community and tales of faerie and angel "guides" coming from middle-aged women who owned an unlawful number of cats. Hogwash. *Shae* was real. She was tangible, not some diaphanous spirit to be glimpsed only between sleeping and waking on a full moon in Libra after the proper incantations are chanted.

And there were plenty of unsettling stories of human suffering at their hands. Tales of death by grief and pining away, people cursed with being blinded, hunchbacked, drowned, rapidly falling into old age. There were faerie "tithes"—human lives stolen to be sent to hell. There were the changelings and hypnotized wanderers who were never seen again . . .

Andre tried calling Ryan again. When he didn't answer, she grabbed her keys and headed over to his place. His car wasn't there. She texted him: *I'm at your apartment. Where are you? Please let me explain. We need to talk.* Nothing. Twenty minutes later, she left.

Amy called after she got back home. "I tried to call Merri, but Vivian said she was still asleep. Vivian sounded . . . kinda pissed."

"That sucks."

"It's been a weird weekend," Amy pronounced brightly.

"Weird, yes," Andre agreed.

"Did Mateo leave?"

"Yeah."

"Aww. I wanted to see him before he left again. Did you talk to Ryan? He called me this morning to see if I'd talked to you. I told him you were probably sleeping." There was a multitude of unspoken questions in the pause after her words. Andre suddenly wanted to get off the phone. "So apparently the police did go to the lake to check things out, but they didn't find anything. They think we were just fucked up. It didn't help that Merri never stopped insisting the guy wasn't human." She sighed. "She's gonna have a scar, poor thing."

As evening approached, Ben finally emerged from his room, looking strung out, clutching his guitar. "You check on her?" he asked Andre as she was attacking the upstairs bathroom with bleach instead of the plant-based spray she usually cleaned with.

"She's sleeping." Ben played guitar, watching her warily. She wiped out the tub, making frantic circles with the sponge. Her bun came loose, and her hair fell in sweaty streaks against her neck. She sneezed.

"Are you okay?" Ben asked. It was only when he stopped playing that she realized she'd been in a trance. The new song was stark and *so* beautiful. He had no words, but he hummed and sang vowel sounds.

"I'm fine. I just want everything to be clean." It was an understatement. She wanted every particle of the Gray Man gone. She could not shake the feeling he was still there—that one little drop of him would be toxic to them. "Can you please play some more?" Her voice caught. Her hair refused to stay up and kept slipping down into her face, black vines strangling her. She fantasized about chopping it off and whimpered. Her hair was a nuisance and a security blanket.

She tried to call Ryan again once Ben left the room, but it went to voicemail. She took another shower.

Shae turned to them as they opened the door. Andre hung back in the doorway, swaying, light-headed, clutching a jar of honey. Her hair was still damp. She smelled like jasmine lotion, but beneath it all, she could swear there was a hint of rot and sulfur on her.

"Shae," Andre said softly, and then she felt a weird shiver of pleasure as the chord between them sang.

Shae sat up smoothly, without using her arms, like a robot waking. The monarch fluttered from her chest to her shoulder. "I'm better."

Ben looked from one of them to the other. He stepped towards Shae. "Well, that's good—that's awesome, I mean."

"Why don't we take a look at it?" Andre asked.

Ben scratched his head. "That's probably not a good idea? Shouldn't we give it a few days?"

But Andre stepped into the room, knelt, and set down the jar of honey. She spoke without taking her eyes off Shae's arm. "I just want to see it. Shae, do you mind if I unwrap it for a second?" Shae held her arm out, obliging. Andre would not have been surprised if she'd found it perfectly healed, the bones melted back together, and the skin stitched neatly with no sign it had ever been broken. It was better—remarkably better—but still unsightly. The bones fitted together like teeth, but the skin had not fused. "How do you feel?"

Shae looked down impassively while Andre wrapped it back up. "There is pain, but it is not bad."

"Here," Andre said, opening the honey jar.

Shae took it with her left hand and drank some. Then she lay back down in the same position and turned her face to the wall. The monarch fluttered around her for a few seconds before settling back onto her chest. Shae closed her eyes.

"C'mon." Ben nudged Andre. "Let's let her be."

"Well, good thing we didn't take her to the hospital," Ben said. They sat at the kitchen table, drinking tea. Andre was starting to sense exhaustion, like a huge wave in the distance coming to pull her under.

He flipped through one of her books, frowning. "Do you think she's immortal?" he asked abruptly.

Andre chewed her sore lips. "No. But she's vastly physically superior." She looked down at her notes. What a case Shae was, a lone traveler from another world with no way of returning. She tried Ryan's cell once more. Her eyes stung when she heard his voicemail come on. She hung up and texted him. "*I'm so sorry, Ryan. Please give me a chance to explain. Please answer the phone.*"

"God, I feel awful," she said. She pressed her hands to her face. She had forgotten to take her vitamins. She went over to the cabinet, pulled out a bottle, and popped a B12 under her tongue, followed by a spoonful of honey.

"You know, maybe she's better off here." Ben stood and leaned against the counter, and Andre noticed that his face had changed. He was gaunt now.

She looked down at the open book in front of her. Her eyes unfocused, and the words blurred as the vitamin tingled and dissolved under her tongue. She tugged a ribbon out of her hair and began braiding it. "Have you talked to Merri?"

He shook his head.

"You should call. Just ask her how she is. Tell her we're here for her if she needs anything. You know." She sighed heavily. "Be a friend."

He put his head between his hands and stared at the table. "I don't want her to get the wrong idea about us. Could you do it? I'm not a good friend right now. To anyone."

"Me neither," Andre said softly. "I don't want to call her either. But god, Ben, calling her to see how she's holding up isn't giving her the 'wrong idea' whatever happened last night."

He groaned and put his hands over his face.

"Did you sleep with her?" Normally she wouldn't have put him on the spot like that.

"It got close, but no."

"I can't get on your case," she said, blowing her nose in a napkin. "I'm a shitty girlfriend."

"No, you're not. You just can't lead a double life, Andre. It's not working. You've got to tell him about Shae. I mean, he's already seen her—kind of."

"It would help if he'd answer his phone. I keep telling myself that it could have been much worse." She stood shakily and turned on the hallway and living room lights. "I feel like I'm losing my mind." She rinsed out her teacup and started gathering up her books. A silverfish fell out of the middle of the spine of one of them. She yelped and jerked away and then felt a tickling in the crook of her elbow. An ant. She clawed at her arm, and then she snatched up the book and threw it against the wall. Ben stared at her, eyes wide. She clasped her head in her hands and started crying.

He moved towards her. "It's—it's going to be okay, Andre."

Several seconds passed before she could speak. "I think something awful is going to happen. She hiccuped. "I don't know. Ben, what did the giantess tell us? Do you remember? I feel like she said something upsetting, but then she . . . distracted us or something. I know something isn't right. I *know* it, but I can't tell what it is."

He hesitated, seeming to decide whether or not to hug her, and settled on patting her on the back, awkwardly. "I don't know. I think Grace said something about these little kids drowning, and it was sad. I think . . ." He frowned. "I think she could have helped them, but she didn't or something? That's the only bad thing I remember. She said it happened a long time ago, right? Maybe it's just the shit we dealt with last night and the ecstasy and the drinking. It can mess with your head."

She nodded, wiping her face with her sleeve. She wondered about Amy.

As if reading her mind, Ben said, "Amy's like an elephant. Nothing affects her. She's got neurons of steel or something, extra dopamine; I don't know." Amy was just Amy. Amy never got heartbroken or hungover.

Andre wiped her eyes. This wasn't going to end well. She knew the stories of the selkies and mermaids and fair folk of the wood—beguiling creatures mortal men pined for. The older stories, before they were steeped in honey and hacked up with happy endings tacked on. And there was *something owed*. Andre could feel it. She went into her room. She texted Ryan that she loved him, that she was sorry again, and good night. Then she lay listening through the open door to the beautiful music coming from Ben's room.

CHAPTER SIXTEEN

Vivian called Monday morning saying Merri wouldn't make it in to give Andre her lunch break. She offered to come herself, but Andre told her boss not to bother. It was overcast. Years of daily weather-influenced rhythms told her she'd have no problem finding a few minutes to eat the sandwich she'd packed at the counter. "Thank you, honey. I've got another favor to ask. Will you come by this evening after you get off? I'd like to speak with you in person."

Andre peeled the corner edge of the catalog in front of her. She'd wanted to go home right after work to check on Shae because Ben was closing at Cedric's Bar & Grille. "I—okay, sure. I just can't stay too long." After she hung up with Vivian, she tried Ryan's cell and got his voicemail again. She was slipping from contrition into anger and finally did something she'd only done once or twice before; called him at work. She rubbed her temples, feeling idiotic and desperate as she waited for the receptionist to put her through.

There was a long pause, and she was about to hang up and call back when he answered, "Yeah?"

"Don't hang up!" She waited for a beat.

"Andre, I'm *really* busy right now."

"Can't we please talk? I'm sorry about Saturday night. I'm sorry about how I've been in the last few months. I need to tell you something I should've told you a long time ago. It has to do with what happened the other night—with what you and Merri saw."

There was a sound like a door closing. "I can't deal with that right now. We can talk in a few days, but I'm consumed with a project that just came in. Everyone is sick or on vacation or having a baby. It's crazy here. Haskins asked me to take the spot for New York this week. I'm leaving in a few hours. I'll be back on Friday."

She sighed. "Okay, we can talk then—you promise?" In a less anxious, selfish part of her mind, she was aware that this was an opportunity for him. He was an entry-level engineer at the firm.

"Yes. We can talk then. But look—I'm angry with you, and I just want you to leave me alone right now."

"I can't stand this. Answer the next time I call, please?" Her voice cracked. "You need to let me—I can explain."

There was a pause. When he spoke again, his voice was warmer. "All right, but I need to focus over the next few days. We'll talk when I get back, okay?"

"I love you."

"I've got to go." He sighed. "I love you too, Andre. But you can't do this to me anymore."

It was still light out but unseasonably chill and overcast when she left the store. Summer had ended abruptly. She wondered if it was going to rain. Even though she'd known them for years, Andre had only been to Vivian and Merri's home a handful of times. She'd always felt a little strange there, seeing Vivian and Merri in the context of their small, slightly run-down apartment off Foothill Road, between Andre's house and the Chestnut. Vivian opened the door, clutching knitting needles engaged in garish orange yarn. "Come on in, honey." Andre followed her down a hall plastered with photos of her and Merri.

In the living room, Vivian announced, "Andre's here," and tossed the yarn and needles onto the sofa. Knitting did not seem like the right pastime for Vivian. She was a restless woman who didn't like to sit still—a quality Merri had inherited. *Merri.* She sat very still now, in a recliner covered in a quilt. She was staring at the TV screen and slowly pulled her glazed eyes away from it to look at Andre. A bandage covered one side of her face.

"Hey, Merri!" Andre forced a smile. "How are you feeling?"

Her friend shrugged one shoulder and turned back to the television.

"She hasn't been much for conversation today." Vivian put her hand on Andre's shoulder. "Come into the kitchen with me." Andre followed her, warily. The kitchen window was open, and cool air swept in. She shivered. "You want anything to drink?" Vivian asked, pouring herself a glass of iced tea.

"I'm okay, thanks." Andre stuffed her hands into her pockets. "I can't stay too long."

"Well, I need to talk to you," Vivian said tartly, and indicated Andre sit down at their little table.

"Merri's not well. I'm very worried about her."

"I'm sorry."

"They gave her Xanax and suggested she get psychiatric counseling. The doctor was more concerned with her mental state than the injury on her face." She held Andre's gaze for an uncomfortably long time before turning to look over her shoulder out into the other room. She lowered her voice. "She wet her bed last night."

Andre glanced at the window, longing to escape into the night and leave what was undoubtedly going to turn into an interrogation. "Well, Merri did say someone attacked her. Ryan thinks he saw something, too. A—a sick-looking homeless guy, maybe? He's not really sure."

"And you didn't see anything? The rest of you didn't see anything?"

"No. We just heard them yelling and went down to meet them at the water. We saw a bunch of bats, though, and I thought I saw a snake near the tent. It seems like there's been more animals around than usual." Something tickled her inside her shirt. "It was a weird night." She discreetly tugged at her collar and lifted her bra strap. A small white moth fluttered off. "Huh," she said softly. "I'm harboring winged ones, apparently."

Vivian waved at it distractedly. "That's strange. I wonder if it's an environmental thing. This damn planet . . . Look, I don't know what happened. I doubt I will ever get the full story, but it sounds suspicious." She looked hard at Andre. "Honey, you're like a daughter to me, and I don't want to put you in a difficult position, but I'm worried about Merri."

Andre held her hands beneath the table and cracked her knuckles, waiting.

"I realize that when you kids have your concerts or campouts or whatever, there are probably things going on that I wouldn't approve of. But you are all adults."

Andre smiled weakly. "I don't go with them to concerts or big parties. I don't like crowds, and I'm usually work—"

"I was young. I know how it is. I just want to know if *you* think Merri has a problem. What happened on Saturday . . . should I take it as a sign? You don't have to go into details, but I respect your opinion."

Andre waited a few seconds, and then slowly said, "I don't think so, Vivian. I think she's going to be okay."

Vivian sat back, frowning. "Then *what* happened? She got that awful cut on her face somehow. Either she got out of her head on god knows what drug and injured herself, or there really was some psycho in the woods who attacked her, in which case I want to find the son of a bitch."

"I—I don't know what else to tell you. That group—our group can get a little wild, but I don't think there is anything you need to be worried about with Merri."

Vivian frowned. "And she lost the damn ring. My *grandmother's* ring."

"Maybe we'll find it?" Andre looked through the doorway. All she could see were Merri's feet in pink fuzzy socks propped up in a recliner in front of the TV. The rest of her legs were under a blanket.

"She insists it was a monster, not a person. And she said there was an *elf* too. What am I supposed to do with that?"

Andre squirmed. "If she believes what she saw, maybe making her think she's wrong or crazy could make things worse." She stood up to leave. "I gotta go home. I need to check on something. Don't worry, Vivian. She'll be okay."

When Andre got home and went out to the shed, Shae was still sleeping, the splint was gone, and there was only a trace of lilac-and-green bruising along her skin. She got a text from Amy: *Hey, it's been a crazy week. You needed to tell me something last weekend before all hell broke loose? When did you want to talk?*

On Tuesday, Ben closed at Cedric's again, and the house was quiet once more when Andre got home after work. Inside the shed, Shae was up and able to move her arm with ease. "I'm going out." She tossed down the flower chain she'd been making, and it turned to gossamer dust on the floor.

"Can I come?" Andre asked impulsively.

Shae gave her a long, thoughtful look and nodded. When Shae reached the end of the yard, she stopped, rolled her shoulders, reached back with one hand, and tugged the zipper down her dress. Her wings spread out and beat, languidly, as if the muscles were relieved to be used.

Shae rose a few inches off the ground, glanced over her shoulder at Andre, and sank down again. She took a few steps and opened the gate. *Polite, Shae.* Andre followed her. A breeze picked up and rustled the branches. It was not dark yet, but the night seemed to seep out from the trees.

They started on the trail; Shae's step was light, her wings bouncing and swaying behind her like part of an elaborate costume. Andre's heart squeezed a little at the gloaming; a twinge of morosity at the death of another day. She plodded along, feeling clumsy and lacking. Andre expected Shae to take off, but after a few minutes, she stopped walking and turned around. The monarch fluttered from her right wrist to her left. "Do you want to try?"

Andre looked around. "Try what?"

Shae stretched her wings out and pumped them. "This."

"I can't." She laughed. "Unless you've got some pixie dust or a magic feather or something."

"I can hold you up."

Andre swallowed. A bell began to ring softly inside of her. You weren't supposed to fly unless you were dreaming or dead—an ethereal creature skimming along the night sky, sailing above the trees. Was there a greater wish of the earthbound human? "How could you? I don't even know how those wings hold you up." If Shae had been like a bird, more feathers than meat, it could work, or if her wings moved rapidly as a hummingbird's . . . but Shae just sort of floated. She was dainty, but not enough to be borne aloft.

The wind rustled up a little tornado of oak leaves. Shae reached a hand over her shoulder and stroked the tip of her wing. "They allow me to move around, but I can get up without them."

Andre chewed her lip. "How do you do it then?"

Shae went up to her with a raised index finger. Andre winced as Shae poked her between the eyes.

She stepped back. "Okay, so it's a mind thing? A third eye thing? I still can't."

"*You* can."

Andre smiled and shook her head. *Of course. I'm the special one! That's me. Go on.* "I wish."

"You don't have to do anything. Close your eyes and I will come and hold you." Shae looked more eager than Andre had ever seen her. Her uncharacteristic enthusiasm made Andre hesitate.

"Okay, so . . . should I just close my eyes and try to space out?"

"Yes. Let me come to you."

Andre closed her eyes, aware of the cold earth under her feet, of its solidity—filled with the bones of animals and ancestors. The wind rinsed out her senses. She was pricked by the thought that her cell phone going off would seriously break the spell and was glad she'd left it inside. Minutes passed. Her mind wandered. She itched here and there and tried not to think about itching, which made her itch more.

Then Shae grabbed her hand, and Andre was falling. She opened eyes and gasped as terror and elation warred within her. The wind washed over her as they sped up, and she was aware of a huge, mad grin on her face. She clutched Shae's hand so hard, despite the clear new feeling she had: *Gravity can't hurt you.* She was a creature of the skies who had a right to be there.

They went up to the treetops and slowed, and bobbed, and Andre felt the leaves sighing around her. For an instant, she felt a surge of sickness and said to Shae, "You know, my life is in your hands, literally." She looked at her feet and kicked them lightly.

They moved forward again, staying above the trees, with a silky blanket of air over them. She looked up for stars, but as usual, only a sprinkling could be seen, though it was dark now.

It was easy—a simple trick, Andre realized. Not an ability to be mastered, but a switch simply not yet flipped on in people. She looked below. It grew colder under the eye of the waning moon.

And after just a short time, there was a tug, and they began to sink back down through a break in the trees. She didn't want to. She kicked her legs, resisting—a swimmer trying to reach the surface. They turned, so they were going down at an angle, in the direction of the house.

Andre's feet touched the ground, lightly at first, and then her hand parted with Shae's. After a couple of staggering steps, she fell hard on her knees, once more shackled by gravity. The link was not entirely gone, the thread remained, but it was weak once more. She looked up and saw Shae was on her knees too, wings sagging on the ground, her forehead against a tree. She was panting.

Andre stood shakily, limbs heavy. "Are you all right?" she asked Shae.

Shae nodded and stood slowly, her wings retracting.

Then Andre turned and bolted for the house, turned on the lights, and sank onto the couch, hugging a pillow and rocking back and forth. She wanted human voices and electric light; she wanted to smell greasy food and hear familiar music. She wanted to rub her face against the mundane. And the next moment, Andre ached to disappear into the dark, into the trees, into the lake. She rubbed the spot between her eyes.

When she looked up, Shae was stepping inside, watching her. "Why do you shut me out sometimes?" Andre whispered.

"What do you mean?"

"You know what I mean. I feel you. I feel your thoughts. I see what you see, and you see what I see, but you've got control. You can shut me out. I know you shut me out when you're giving Ben the music, but it's not just that. You are hiding something. What are you hiding?"

Shae only stared at her. "None of us can change our fate."

"What the hell does that mean? What are you doing to us? What is going to happen?" Andre whispered.

Andre wasn't sure if she imagined fear in those golden eyes. Shae looked down. "I am doing whatever I am supposed to be doing. I am giving you a gift."

"I'm not sure I want your gift," Andre whispered. She stood up, went into her room, and slammed the door.

In my box, I dim the lights, and the flowers and butterflies dissolve. I am a glowing spotlight in a dark room. It is becoming a strain to hold glamour. It tires me. Just as flying with the girl has tired me.

And where does that whim come from? Why do I feel the increasing urge to usher the likes of some human into my arts?

I bring the monarch to my lips and kiss its fluttering wings. I kiss the back of my hand. I rub the spot between my eyes and try to comfort myself. The tithe has started, and that is something, but it moves slower than I expected, biding time in the bloodstream. I fear for them. And I fear their knowing of my betrayal. Will they remember the giantess's words and know I am the cause? Yes, they will. There will be no hiding from it. I must accept that I will know what to do when the time comes. Grace made it through her tribulations. I am an agent of the court, and whatever I am tasked to do will happen smoothly. It will work out in the end.

Ben opened the door to a dark and quiet house. He took a beer from the fridge. It had been a rough night at the restaurant. He was finding it hard to deal with people. Coworkers and patrons were testy with him for being flaky and aloof, but he couldn't help it. The songs were distracting him. There was little room in him for extra sides of ketchup and refills on water, for banter.

He went out the back and stood in front of Shae's shed. He wanted to open it, but didn't. He pressed his forehead to the door, wishing he could catch a hint of her scent. After a few minutes, he went back inside and upstairs to his room.

He played on his keyboards, but it was one of those awful times when he couldn't get the song right. He struggled for an hour before finally giving up. He lay awake for a long time with a cramp in his gut and tenderness in his jaw.

When he finally did fall asleep, he had nightmares. He woke in the morning, covered in sweat. Someone was calling. He grabbed his phone to see who it was. He answered, frowning. "Hey, Merri?" How's it going? Everything okay?"

"Hi, Ben." She sounded hesitant, sad. "Are you doing anything right now?"

"No. I just woke up."

"Do you think you . . . would you want to come over?"

CHAPTER SEVENTEEN

Andre was in the kitchen, adding a huge dollop of honey to a cup of tea as Ben walked in late from work on Thursday night. She wore a ratty bathrobe. An open book of fantastical art sat on the table. He wasn't sure what was going on with her research project—or whatever the hell it was, anymore. She was constantly reading and scribbling in her notebook and perusing dubious material online. She smiled at him. Her lips were discolored and chapped. Her eyes were bloodshot. She looked withered. He noticed two silver hairs in the loose black bun that perched atop her crown like a second head.

"Shut the door. It's freezing. It's like fall came out of nowhere." She shivered. "Are you okay? You look spooked."

Ben forced himself to smile, and it turned into a dark laugh. "I'm just great. You know I wrote a new song?"

"I can't wait to hear it. How did it go visiting Merri yesterday?"

He hung up his keys and unbuttoned the top two buttons on his collared shirt. "She was pretty quiet. She asked me if I remembered anything. I think she would have talked more, but Vivian was hovering, so we mostly just watched TV." He sat down at the table. "I had a shitty night at work. There were so many assholes . . ." He probed a tooth with his tongue and pointed to his jaw. "Toof ache." After a moment, he asked, "Do you ever think we've handled everything wrong?"

Andre blew over her drink and took a tremulous sip. "Maybe, but then again, who knows? Why do you think I'm trying to figure it out all the time?"

"I think you're trying to figure it out all the time because you're trying to find a way into fairyland."

Andre winced and then went perfectly still. Ben regretted the words right away, as though they were obscene and cruel, but he would have been hard-pressed to explain how. After a few seconds, she took a deep breath and shrugged it off.

"And where do they come from? She had to come from *somewhere*." Andre looked up at the ceiling as if she was trying to determine something. Then she stood up, closing the book. "I've got to go to bed. I've got to try to sleep. Look, I'm going to have Ryan meet her when he gets back on Friday. Amy too. I don't care what Shae says. We can't keep this up, and it's time."

CHAPTER EIGHTEEN

Early Friday evening, they arrived at the giantess's gate and found it barred. The lights were out. Of course. They got out of the car and stared at the place for a few minutes. It had the air of an abandoned gothic fortress. Andre shivered. It was getting cold. She was the one who insisted they should come—that they make an impromptu visit after Grace hadn't replied to any of Andre's texts. Amy and Ryan were supposed to meet Shae, and both Andre and Ben were apprehensive for reasons they couldn't name. They were feeling something slipping. A bit of knowledge they still needed to get from her. Some clarification on things she'd said before.

As they walked up the driveway back at their house, Andre wished she could glean what Shae's feelings were about the impending encounter, but when she felt along the string between them, she got nothing. Shae was closing her off. *And I'll be leaving her in a few months. How will that feel?* She and Amy traveled to the east coast every December for the holidays to be with Lydia, their stepdad Preston, and half-brother Max. What would it be like to be so far away from her? How could she leave Shae and Ben alone for a week and be across the country?

Ben groaned as they approached the door. "Andre . . . I've—I've got to go upstairs and play before I do anything else. Just for a few minutes, okay?"

The porch light was off, but she could still make out his face in the dark. He was grimacing. She nodded. "Sure."

Amy sat on the kitchen table with her feet on a chair. "Well, speak of the devils!" she cried. "We've been waiting for you guys for like an hour. You said you need to talk to us, remember? Tonight's the big reveal or something?"

Ryan was leaning against the counter, arms folded. He looked tired. Andre immediately went up and hugged him tightly. He responded hesitantly, stiff at first, then draping his arms loosely around her. He put his face into her hair. "Bumblebee," he murmured. When they pulled apart, his eyes wandered over her, frowning.

"Hey, man." Ben bobbed his head. "How was New York?"

"Awesome. How you been?" Ryan moved towards him, and they performed a painfully awkward and stiff half-hug.

"So, what the hell is going on, you guys?" Amy looked from one of them to the other, and then her eyes went wide. "Whoa. *What's* wrong?" She pressed her fingertips together and laughed. "Did something happen? Did you guys have to hide a body somewhere?"

Ben looked at Andre. "It's not . . . it might not be all bad. We just need to show you something." Neither of them spoke or moved for several seconds. Then he said, "Uh, so, I—uh, I gotta go upstairs for a little while. I'll be back down in a few." He nodded at Andre. "She can fill you in till I get back. Then we'll go outside?" He disappeared, and a moment later, they heard his feet pound up the stairs, and his door slam.

A pink sphere of bubble gum bloomed out of Amy's rosebud lips. "So, the suspense is killing me," she said dryly, raising an eyebrow. Amaryllis Waters did not beg for information. She sucked the bubble back into her mouth, popping it softly and turned her hand over to inspect her nails then looked up at Andre, cocking her head. Her eyes were glassy. "Oh, I've got some news too. Did you hear? Genevieve is pregnant."

"Really?" Andre frowned. "Since when?"

"Since like, almost three months ago or something. They've been keeping it to themselves."

"Oh, wow. That's—that's crazy. I guess that's why they were all low key the other night. Are they happy about it?"

"I think so. I talked to her yesterday. She said it was a surprise, but she's excited. They're going to get married too—something small in a few months. I mean, it makes sense, I guess. They've been going strong for like four years." Amy shrugged. "Still don't see why any-one would want to lock themselves into an outdated union."

Andre looked at Ryan. "Did you know about this too?"

"Yeah." He smiled. "And you would have known if you ever went on social media. The news was opened to the public yesterday."

"Huh," she said softly.

Amy squinted at her and cocked her head. "You look different, sister."

Andre ignored this. "Are you high right now?"

Amy blew another bubble, shook her head. "Well, Erik and I smoked a bowl a few hours ago, and then his brother came by and gave me half an Adderall. We went over to Carlos's, and I whooped his *ass* at table tennis." She grinned, chewing. "Why? Am I going to freak out or something?"

Andre took a deep breath. "Maybe. Um, okay, so we've been trying to have it so that one of us is always here at home. That hasn't been happening lately, though, as you know . . ." She paused, then opened her mouth to continue but closed it once more and shook her head. "Let me start over. It's about the other night when we were camping . . ." She started trembling and suddenly wondered if she could physically do it; or if Shae had done something to prevent the words from coming out of her mouth. "I'm sorry—I, I can't."

She walked over towards the stairs saying over her shoulder, "Let's just wait here and listen to the music for a minute, okay?" Frowning, Amy and Ryan followed her, going halfway up the stairs and then sitting down, Amy two steps above Andre and Ryan. They waited in silence, coiled like a spring for a couple of seconds before the sound of the keyboard overlaying a thrumming acoustic drifted out of Ben's room. Andre got chills.

"We need to wait for him to finish? What the hell?" Amy shook her head. But then a thoughtful look came over her face, and for the next few minutes, they all waited, spellbound by the melody. When the song drew to a close, Amy said, "Oh god, that's so good. *Damn.* He's always been talented, but when did he become a fucking Mozart? This is the new stuff Benny's been writing? He was saying something about it the other night." She looked meaningfully at Andre, raising her eyebrows. "And *speaking* of the other night . . ."

Andre's throat got tight, and she was seized by the notion that she was making a terrible mistake. She rubbed her forehead. "Ryan . . . do you remember what you saw with Merri, that creature, that weird tall guy?"

He looked at her with an expression she couldn't quite interpret; he seemed almost afraid. "I don't know what I saw. It was dark, and we were messed up. I thought he looked deformed or something, but I can't trust my senses from then. I do remember . . . there were a couple of bats around. They were kind of attacking us. And there was this horrible smell. I thought I saw a . . . I don't know." He shook his head and added quietly. "I've pushed it out of my head to deal with work this week."

She took a deep breath. "Do you guys remember like maybe four months ago, or I guess at the beginning of summer—" She frowned. "Oh yeah, it was the night of the Shrine show—"

"Yes," Amy said, inspecting her nails before bringing them to her lips to chew. She spoke in a flat voice. "You got sick or something. Ben was going to come with us, but we couldn't find him." She frowned. "Was that the same night you saw the UFO or lightning ball or whatever? I remember you kept going on about it."

"Yeah, that's right," Andre said, impressed. She turned to Ryan. "Remember, when I saw that weird light? I told you about it."

"I think so, yeah. I remember you were sick when I got back from Arizona."

"Ben was sick, too," Amy added. "You both were." Ben opened the door to his room suddenly, startled to see them all so close. He gave Andre a questioning look, but she just shrugged. Amy rolled her eyes. "Okay, Andre, let's not lose momentum here. You saw a light outside, several months ago, and now . . . what? You both gained X-Men powers or something?" When they didn't reply, she leaned in towards Ryan and muttered, "If they didn't look so miserable, I'd say they were enjoying this."

"You're not that far off, Amy," Ben plunged ahead. "We found something supernatural the next day. Well, more like someone. We found a . . . sort of a girl. She's been staying in the shed in the back-yard ever since. And she has affected us. She's not a regular person."

There was a beat of silence. Amy's face contorted in disbelief as she looked from one of them to the other. Ryan looked wary. "Ugh!" Amy finally cried. "Do you have *any* idea how crazy that sounds? Is she . . . what? Is she homeless or something?"

Ben looked at Andre with bloodshot eyes and shook his head. "There is no adequate preparation for something like this. We just do it." Heading down the stairs, he said, "Why don't you guys just come meet her?" He went into the kitchen to the fridge to grab a beer first.

Andre realized that along with or despite her great trepidation, she was feeling something else. She was feeling relief; they were finally doing this. As Ben opened the back door and led them outside, she said, "Listen, if you had any other plans for tonight, you both need to ditch them."

"Why's she's staying in the *shed*?" Amy asked, incredulous. "That's messed up."

Andre followed her out, and in the porch light, she saw a tattoo of a swan at the base of Amy's hairline. Fine blond hairs grew over it. Andre wondered if it was new or if she'd seen it before and had forgotten. *Not on your neck, Amy. Mom is going to flip when she sees that.* She stumbled over a small familiar hillock in the yard and glanced back at Ryan. He put a hand to her shoulder. "Clumsy Bee."

They reached the shed, and Ben hesitated. He appeared about to say something but changed his mind. He turned and knocked on the door. "They're here, Shae. We're coming in now, okay?"

He opened the door.

The room was in full, sparkling form: birds singing, butterflies flitting about, the little stream against the wall, chuckling. Shae stood in the middle of the room. She'd taken off her clothes, and her face was partly covered by her opalescent hair. She lifted her chin at them and spread her wings—something Andre had never seen her do inside the shed before. She rose a couple of feet into the air and pirouetted. Ben cleared his throat. "Amy, Ryan, meet Shae."

Amy made a startled noise, something between a gasp and a squeak. Her hands shot to her mouth. Ryan stood utterly still, expressionless. Andre took his limp hand. Amy took a step towards Shae.

And then, for too long, nothing happened. The silence following the introduction went from uncomfortable to unbearable in seconds, before it was finally pierced by the shrill note of Amy's hysterical laughter. Andre glanced plaintively at Ben. He shrugged. Ryan stepped backward, unable to look away from Shae. He bore the pained expression of a child watching a scary movie they don't really want to see. Andre tightened her grip on his hand, trying to keep him in the room and put her other hand on her sister's shoulder. "Amy, please."

Amy's laughter subsided, and she dropped to her knees and started to hyperventilate. Ben kneeled next to her. "What. The. *Fuck*!" She pointed up at Shae. "What the fuck!" She pressed her hands to the side of her head and shook it back and forth and started laughing again. "Oh, my god. What the fuck!"

"You're doing fine," Ben said, patting her on the back. "I couldn't believe it either when I first saw her."

Shae dropped to the ground, the balls of her feet touching the floor before her heels. The monarch sat on her shoulder, wings beating lazily. "Hello," she said in her musical voice, reaching a finger up to stroke the oversized insect.

Andre turned to Ryan and tugged his arm gently, trying to get him to look at her. His eyes slowly drifted from Shae and met her concerned gaze. "This is who you saw last weekend? The other one?" she asked. He didn't answer. Looking into his shell-shocked eyes, she whispered, "Are you okay?"

He swallowed. His hand trembled as he pointed at Shae. "This is real?"

She wasn't sure if he was asking her or making an observation. She nodded and squeezed his hand. "Yes, Ryan, this is real."

"Well, now you guys know," Ben said, throwing his hands up.

Ryan pulled away from Andre and put his hand over his abdomen. "Sorry. I'm going to be sick." He turned and stumbled out into the yard.

Behind him, Amy said, "Oh shit, me too. I'm going to throw up."

Andre looked up at Shae, "Thanks. You did good. Sorry, we'll come back when they feel better." She and Ben followed them back into the house. She looked sideways at him and smiled. "We did it," she said softly, and then she went into the kitchen to pour glasses of water for Amy and Ryan.

"Sorry," Ryan muttered a little while later, wiping his face with a damp washcloth held in shaky hands. "This is gross."

She hugged him from behind and said against his back, "Why don't you go lie down?"

He didn't reply but let her lead him by the hand back to her room. "This happened before you know," he said. "Right after that night camping. I threw up when we were all in the hospital, but I thought it was just from all the partying. This is worse, though. It's brutal, like food poisoning."

"Oh, I know. It happened to me at the beginning of summer. You wanted to stay over and take care of me after you got back from Arizona, remember?"

"You should have let me."

"Maybe you're right."

He sat down on the bed but then stood back up. "Mind if I take a shower? I sweated through everything."

"Sure."

Amy appeared in the doorway, swaying. She was pale, but Andre thought both she and Ryan were rallying fairly well—mentally and physically. She pinched the bridge of her nose. "You know, you could have given us a warning. I had spicy Thai for lunch. That shit burns coming back up."

Andre grimaced. "Is it still bad? Here, let me go get you guys more water."

Amy sniffed. "I think the worst is over." Andre followed her out of the room to the kitchen. Amy walked a little unsteadily. "I feel hella rude, you know, becoming violently ill right when you meet someone."

Andre refilled their glasses directly from the sink. She handed one to Amy who took an epic drink, gulping loudly, keeping her eyes on Andre over the rim of the glass. When it was drained, she slammed it on the kitchen counter and belched. They stared at one another. Amy was trying to play it cool, but Andre saw her eye was twitching, and her hands were trembling just a little. "Some things make sense now." Amy smiled tightly. Then she reached over and tugged Andre's hair at the nape of her neck. "This all seems about right, yes? Haven't you always been waiting for something like this to happen? You've always believed in magic. You should have told me sooner, sis." Her eyes were shining.

"I wanted to. We were scared. We didn't know how to handle it. It seemed safest not to tell anyone. And then you went on the tour . . ." She laughed. "You should have seen Ben. He was so freaked out."

"He's still scared of her," Amy observed. "Maybe not quite that, but something."

"Yes." Andre agreed, not bothering to ask how Amy knew this after having barely observed Ben and Shae together. "Or something."

"Aww. I kind of want to go back out there. I barely got to look at her before I got sick. She's so beautiful." she sighed, then abruptly pulled Andre into a tight embrace. Amy never said a heartfelt word to her twin or anyone for that matter, but this was something she did instead–these aggressive, spontaneous hugs.

"Hey." Ryan looked pale and feverish when he came back to the room after rinsing off. But he smiled at her. Something tugged at Andre, a hint of anxiety she couldn't place the source of.

She lifted the sheets. "C'mon and lie down."

He took the towel off from his waist and put his boxers back on. "You should have told me to bring a change of clothes."

"You dropped your stuff off at your place? I thought you came straight here from the airport."

"I did. But my bag's still in the car, and everything's dirty." He lay down on the bed and closed his eyes. "I know I should be asking a ton of questions, but I'm jet-lagged, and I'm also pretty convinced I've lost my mind, and we aren't even having this conversation."

"I know," Andre said quietly. "It's really weird. It changes everything. It changes reality."

He opened his eyes and reached up to stroke her hair down from the top of her head to her waist. "I guess I'm not scared if you're not." He frowned. "Why do you have all these suddenly?" He pulled her hair out for her to see the several grays she'd noticed but had given little thought to.

"I don't know." She grinned. "Maybe the stress of my jerk boyfriend giving me the silent treatment."

"You should have told me sooner." He pulled her towards him and onto the bed, so they lay spooned on their sides. "But, I'm sorry. And I kind of like the gray."

"Thanks. I think being around Shae is doing things to us."

"Yeah, like this?" He flicked an ant off of her arm. "And . . . Ben's gotten skinny. I noticed it a little last week, but more tonight." He sighed. "We have no idea, Andre. This could be the first human encounter ever with an alien species. She could be dangerous."

"You think she's an alien?" Andre laughed. "Ben thought the same thing. She's not. She's a faerie. She's a Sidhe."

"She's a she?"

"A Sidhe—it's pronounced, 'shee.'"

"Oh. How do you know that?"

"I just do. Listen, you have to promise me you won't tell anyone about her."

He was quiet for a moment. "People should know about this, don't you think?"

"No!" She sat up and loomed over him. "*No*, Ryan. Promise me. Do you trust the government or the FBI or whatever, to be cool about this? They might erase our memories. They might do experiments on her; anything could happen! We're not taking any chances."

"Okay, okay." He held his hands up. "I think you've seen too many movies, but you have a point. I won't tell anyone. I promise."

Relaxing a bit, she nestled against him again. "Thank you. You can start staying over here now. In fact, instead of me moving in with you, why don't you bring your stuff here? We've got more room."

I lay panting in the dark. I had a small glow a moment ago. But I can't hold anymore. I went all out, and now I am fatigued. I wanted to give them something. To show off as Grace did in her cave for Andre and Ben. They should witness all my power and my beauty. It was fun. They were so stunned!

The tall girl is bolder and more lovely than Andre but not as permeable at all. And the other boy . . . a sweet one there. I tug on the string and close my eyes and lean into the feeling of him. I love him even though he fears me. I can almost taste him.

That night Andre dreamed of a cavern deep underground. A place with gemstone walls and sparkling pools. It grew dark. As the lights dimmed, she looked up and saw the stiff bodies of bats hanging upside down, shrouded in their wings between the stalactites. She shivered at the familiar sensation of a bug crawling on her arm. She smacked at it, and when she squinted closer, she saw with horror that it wasn't a bug, but a very tiny faerie. She'd killed it; smearing its delicate, infinitesimal body onto her skin.

PART THREE

CHAPTER NINETEEN

November

"I'm telling you, they don't mind." Ryan stood up and brought his plate to Andre, who was starting to wash the dishes.

"You should come," Amy said to him with her mouth full. She licked her fingers. "Andre, what is your problem?"

She fiddled with the faucet until the water ran steamy. The heat felt good on her hands and face. "His mom will miss him. I don't want them to resent me."

"I have spent every single holiday with my parents," Ryan reminded her. "Twenty-seven years I've spent Christmas with them. I can miss one. We're doing a dinner and gift thing the Friday before anyway because Seth's birthday is on the twentieth—poor guy always gets shafted that way—and I told you, I'll get the tickets."

"You don't have to do that." Andre's eyes followed a soap bubble gone adrift that was heading up the window. "My mom and Preston might have already bought them. That reminds me, I need to call her. And you know if you do come, we'll probably have to keep separate rooms, right? My mom's super Christian."

Amy snorted. "She's probably still afraid of Andre losing her maidenhead." Amy and Ryan collected the rest of the bowls on the table and brought them over to the sink. "I hope you can come, Ryan," Amy said, sighing. "You can take some of her attention off of me. I can't wait for the inevitable, 'what is Amy doing with her life?' conversation."

"I really want you to come, but—" Andre looked at Ryan skeptically "—you say they don't mind, but I got a different impression the other night."

"You're imagining things." He shook his head.

The night before, they had eaten a nice dinner over at his parent's house, and afterward, they sat in the Carpenters' cozy living room by the fireplace sipping port while his mother, Candace, showed Andre old photo albums. They reminisced and told her old family stories. It was a good night.

But right before they left, Ryan had mentioned his plan to accompany Andre to Virginia for Christmas, and Andre was sure she hadn't imagined Candace looking hurt at the suggestion. Andre had no idea what it was like to have such a relationship with one's parents. They saw Lydia once a year for about ten days, and that usually felt sufficient to her. Being around the Carpenters gave her the uncomfortable notion that perhaps she was missing something essential.

"We've got another month to decide," Andre said as the back door slid open and Shae appeared from the darkness outside barefoot, wearing a pink cotton shirt and skirt with a gaudy butterfly on the front—cheap children's garments Andre had purchased for her at a thrift store. It was cold out, but Shae never seemed to suffer from temperatures. She clutched a poppy and twirled it between her fingers. The monarch was perched on her wrist. A finch had followed her into the house, and she tossed her arm out and made a little trilling sound to compel it to go back outside. Andre watched her. *She calls forth the creatures.*

"Not really," Ryan pointed out. "If I want to get a good deal, I need to book tickets now."

"What happens in a month?" Shae asked.

"We travel to the east." Amy sighed.

Shae stepped lightly over to the table. She levitated in the house less often. "Is there snow there?"

"Sometimes," Andre said, setting another plate in the drying rack. "A few years ago, there was a huge blizzard." She tried to be nonchalant about Shae talking so much and asking questions.

"I'd like to see snow," Shae said. She went up to the cabinet and pulled out a jar of honey.

"We could take a road trip somewhere," Andre suggested.

"Yeah!" Amy hitched herself up on the counter. "I love road trips. Did it snow where you came from, Shae?"

Andre tensed. It didn't matter how many times she'd told her sister that Shae didn't remember her world; questions came flying out of Amy's mouth whenever she got curious. Shae didn't appear to be bothered by it, but she didn't answer with more than a shrug and a frown. She opened the honey, sipped it, wandered into the living room, and picked up the remote.

Andre gazed out of the window over the sink. In her mind's eye, she was walking down a path of snow-covered trees with glittering icicles dripping down under the moonlight. The trees grew close overhead, forming a dome that became the same pleached alley of her dreams—except this time, the greenery all glistened with frost. The air smelled of snow. She could hear bells chiming in the distance.

"Bumblebee?" She jumped at his hands on her shoulders. She'd been standing with her hands in scalding water and washing the same plate over and over. The icy images in her mind had countered the heat. She pulled her hands out and wiped them on a dry washcloth. The sting of the burn evaporated, and her lobster hands faded back to pale almost instantly. "I've got to remember to request time off work," she said, adding cold water to the hot and quickly resuming her cleaning.

Amy frowned. "You need to stop being such a slave to that place. You've made this trip every year since the dawn of time. They should expect it by now."

"They do. But it's not always the same number of days or at the same time every year. This time I want to make our trip shorter because I want to go to some other places next year."

The last few nights, she and Ryan had laid in bed, contemplating vacation spots that might help her research. Andre wanted to go to Europe. She knew it was probably pointless; Shae claimed not to feel any affinity towards Ireland and Scotland when Andre showed her images of the landscape, but it couldn't hurt. And she'd never traveled overseas.

It was something she planned on bringing up to the giantess the next time she saw her. Grace had not mentioned any experience visiting ancient, supposedly faerie haunted places and spiritual landmarks, but from everything Andre had read, the British Isles were where the Sidhe originated from. Andre wondered what her opinion was. She imagined Grace was well-traveled.

The house was more crowded these days; Ryan had brought his essentials over, and Amy too had resumed residence in her old bedroom. Overall, the two of them had handled things well—better than Andre had expected. Amy was endlessly amused and delighted by Shae. Ryan was wary but fascinated. He was still not convinced Shae wasn't an alien, or at least that being a Sidhe and an alien weren't different names for the same thing. And though he was too busy with work to do much of anything, he understood and was appreciative of Andre's research. He now spent his own free time looking for legit reportage on alien encounters, though, like Andre, he was discouraged by how scant anything helpful was.

There hadn't been an increase in the havoc Shae's presence seemed to wreak. Andre—and especially Ben, had both grown thinner, but the presence of the insects had tapered off slightly with the onset of the cooler season. Ryan and Amy weren't showing any changes or signs of exposure to being around Shae since that first night when they got sick.

But Andre's connection with Shae was growing stronger. There was nothing she could compare it to. Ryan was her partner, Amy had shared a womb and a childhood with her. Ben was her closest friend and had grown into a sibling in the last fourteen years. But an aetheric, live wire was burrowed inside of her, connecting her to Shae. When Andre was at work, she would sometimes feel the wind on her face, and her steps became lighter, and she knew Shae was flying. When she stopped eating halfway through her lunch, it was because Shae wasn't hungry anymore.

And then there were times the bond was thin. Sometimes hours went by without any feeling. She wondered about the trip and what the change in their physical proximity would mean.

The front door opened, and Ben walked in, hunched over, his phone to his ear. He nodded at them and held his hand over the mouthpiece. "The bar was dead. They cut me early." He went quickly past them, up the stairs to his room.

"Do you still think it's a bad idea to tell Merri?" Amy asked, cocking her head and staring at Shae. "I saw her the other day, and she was asking me about what I remember. She said she doesn't understand how Ryan could not have seen what she saw. I didn't know what to say. I mean *I* didn't see the monster, and I didn't see Shae *then*, so telling her I didn't see anything that night isn't exactly a lie, but it's kind of messed up."

Ryan said, "It's probably true that the fewer people who know, the better, but like I've said, she knows. She's already seen her. She just doesn't know what she saw. I think we should tell her. It's kinda cruel not to."

"She hasn't mentioned it to me." Andre set the last plate in the rack and wiped her hands on a towel. "At least not recently. Not since the first couple of days since she came back to work."

"Yeah," Amy said. "But that's because everyone convinced her she was wacko."

Shae didn't appear to be paying attention to the conversation. She had turned on the television and was watching a home improvement show while plucking the petals off a poppy. The monarch abandoned her wrist and flew to Andre's shoulder. She shied away from it.

"I still feel like it's safer to not tell anyone else," Andre said.

"Ricardo thinks there's something up," Amy said.

Andre groaned. "No. We are *not* telling Ricardo. You haven't said anything, have you?"

"Of course not. But he wants to come over to play with Ben now. I let him hear that song we recorded, and he practically jizzed his pants." She rolled her eyes. "He thinks it's groundbreaking or something, and he wants them to play together again."

"He's right," Ryan said. "It is *really* good. Ben needs to get it out there."

Andre was about to say something else, when, on cue, music poured down from up the stairs like a golden trail. Ben had recorded keyboard and drumbeats along with his guitar. They all stopped talking and sat still, held in thrall by the sound.

When he finished the song, Ben lay on his back on his bed next to his guitar. He felt his phone vibrate and saw Mateo had sent another text: *Hey, I'm in town again next weekend. Let's hang out.* Ricardo had sent Mateo that recording, and now he wouldn't stop talking about it. They'd also had a few long conversations via text about Mateo's plan to propose to Cecily over the holidays. Ben thought it was too soon, but he didn't say anything to discourage Mateo. What the hell did he know?

Right on the heels of this text, Merri sent one saying: *goodnight.* They'd only gotten off the phone a few minutes ago. She wanted to be invited over. He could sense it from talking to her, but it was out of the question while Shae was around. Ben berated himself. He'd never intended for anything to start up between them, but in the last several weeks, their visits and texts had evolved into more. His feelings for her weren't strong, but he'd grown fond of her. And they'd started sleeping together.

She was sweet and eager, and though Ben was becoming self-conscious about his scrawny chest and bony shoulders, being with Merri took his mind off the pain of the music—just a bit. It went a small way to quell the desire that set him to aching and shaking if he couldn't get the tune out right. He knew he shouldn't let it turn into anything. They'd agreed they were just friends, and the sex was casual.

On some level, he knew she adored him, but he wasn't in a position to be someone's partner. He wouldn't want to do that to her. Because when they were moving against one another, he was picturing Shae's golden eyes and hearing music. And he felt his body wasting from whatever it was Shae was doing to him.

CHAPTER TWENTY

Afternoon at the Chestnut popped with a wave of customers. Regulars came in for their usual supplements, along with many first-timers sniffling with requests for non-pharmaceutical relief. Temperatures veered from warm to spiky cold, and the shifts wreaked havoc on immune systems. Andre had just finished helping a customer when the door chimed, and Merri walked in. She wore a black scarf, gray sweater, and black gloves. Her hair was scooped over her right shoulder, not quite covering the shimmering pink scar running down her face.

As Andre ate her lunch in the back office and sipped a bottle of coconut water—mermaid piss as Ben called it—she saw her mother had sent a text when the store had been busy: *"Yes, that's fine if Ryan comes. We'd love to finally meet him! You won't believe it when you see Max. He's gotten so tall!"* Then she got a group-text from Genevieve inviting everyone over for dinner that weekend.

Andre sent Ryan a thumbs up, an airplane, and a heart emoji, then replied yes to Genevieve's invite. She walked to the front of the store just as a customer was leaving. Merri stood at the window, following the person with her eyes. Andre looked down at the honey gleaming like amber under the sun. "Do you know why this is moved up front and marked down?" She pointed.

"Huh? Oh . . . we're not going to carry it anymore."

"What? Why?" Andre huffed.

Merri shrugged. "I don't know. People buy honey at drugstores at a fraction of the cost with a squeezable lid."

"But this is a health food store. We're supposed to sell local honey. And raw honey. Drugstores don't have that. And people do buy it. *I* buy it all the time."

"Talk to my mom if you feel so strongly about it."

"People need it for their allergies. You know Carla? She uses it all the time."

"It's at the Farmers' Market too," Merri added. "A lot of people get it there now since they opened that one up in Darryville. And you can buy it online." Merri turned back to the window. "It's not allergy season anyway," she added under her breath. "Call her if you want. Maybe you can change her mind." She sounded doubtful.

"No." Andre caressed a jar. "It's her store. She knows what she's doing."

Merri pulled her phone out of her pocket and glanced at it.

"Are you all good? Can I go?"

Andre nodded. Merri got her bag from behind the counter, wrapped her scarf around her neck, and walked towards the door.

Andre asked, "Oh, you're good to cover me for a week next month? Our trip to the east coast is coming up."

"Sure."

"Great, thanks. Oh, did you see the invite from Genevieve? You should come. I don't know if Ben has to work, but if he does, you can ride with me and Ryan and Amy."

Merri's expression softened. "Sure. I haven't hung out much since . . ." She looked down and pointed up to her face. "That would be nice." She sighed heavily and rubbed her index finger along her scar. "So, Ryan thinks what we saw was a man?"

Andre squirmed. "He hasn't talked about it much."

"And the rest of you didn't see anything?" There was a desperate note in her voice. "You didn't *smell* anything?"

"I did smell something strange, Merri." Andre heard that melodious voice in her head. *"Do not tell."* But she opened her mouth, about to. It wasn't fair to Merri.

"I smelled something *awful.*" Merri shook her head. "I've gotta go." Andre watched her walk away, her head bent down into the cold.

"That hurt?" Ben asked.

Amy was lounging on a beanbag chair in the living room, massaging Aquafor into the new ink on her right arm. The vibrant peacock blooming across her skin glistened.

She frowned. "Not really."

He strummed, twisted the pegs, strummed again. He was agitated. He kept getting teased with a song that wouldn't quite land in his mind. Andre was sitting in the recliner reading. Shae was crouched over a map of the world spread out on the floor. The monarch was asleep on her shoulder. She sat up on her knees suddenly and leaned over, inspecting Amy's arm. "I like it." They all looked up.

Amy beamed. "Thanks!"

Andre gazed at her own pale arms. She vaguely desired a tattoo, but she struggled to commit to any particular image being permanently sewn into her skin. "How much was that?" she asked.

"Oh, Zach's my friend. He hooked me up," Amy said lightly. Amy got a lot of things for free for being Amy. She got out of traffic tickets and never paid for drinks. She set strangers to bumbling nervously.

Ben suddenly quit tinkering and struck up a song. The melody crawled under Andre's skin and into her brain. She closed her eyes and saw mountains, an orange and lavender sunset, and the shadows of tall, tall trees.

When the song ended, Amy cried, "That's *so* good, Ben. I love it!"

"Thanks." He smiled shyly. His hand drummed the soundboard.

They all turned at Ryan opening the front door. "Sorry, I'm late." He nodded at Ben, "Cool, you're coming then?"

"Yeah, I switched shifts. I'm working the floor tomorrow afternoon. Gonna lose some money, but—" He shrugged, picked up his guitar again, strummed it once more, and set it back down. "We should get going. I told Merri we'd pick her up 20 minutes ago."

Andre realized too late that she didn't feel like socializing. She stared out the car window wishing she was somewhere else.

"What is Ricardo going to do when they get married?" Merri wondered as they pulled up to the apartment.

"You mean, what will he do when they have that baby." Amy laughed. "Poor fellow's going to get smoked out of there. Oh well, he'll probably move in with Erik and Spencer. He's *not* moving in with us."

Pippin set to barking as they came up the steps. "Ugh. That little fucker," Ben muttered to squeals of objection from Merri and Amy.

"How would you like it if someone called Hammer that?" Merri asked, making Andre wince slightly.

Ben raised his chin and said, "No one would talk about him that way. He was a real dog."

Following shouts at Pippin, the door opened, and Genevieve appeared wearing an emerald toga dress and holding a goblet of something crimson. With her big belly, she looked like a pretty, green egg. "Hello, everyone! Come in! Come in!" she exclaimed and hugged Amy with one arm. In answer to something, Amy asked, she laughed. "Cranberry juice with a squirt of tonic water. I'm obsessed with cranberries these days. I made cranberry bread yesterday. There's a bunch of leftovers. You should take some back home with you when you leave."

Ricardo, Raf, and Mateo were already there. Mateo jumped up at the sight of Ben and started talking excitedly to him about the music.

On the coffee table was a spread of food and drinks: hummus, pita bread, wedges of melon and cheese, bottles of red wine, sangria, and one of something golden colored. "Ooh, what's that?" asked Amy, pointing.

"Mead," Genevieve said. "Ricardo got it at the Garlic Festival last summer."

"It's made from honey, right?" She nudged Andre. "We should get some for Shae. I wonder what she's like after a few drinks."

Andre gave her a smoldering look, but no one was paying attention. Everyone was talking at once.

Andre watched Genevieve go up to Merri and gently move Merri's hair back so she could inspect the scar on her face. She murmured something Andre didn't catch. Merri nodded and tapped at her temple. Genevieve said something else, petted her hair, and then Merri laughed and hugged her.

When the car pulls up, I turn off the TV. I don't understand the show, but it is weirdly compelling: silly humans running around talking urgently into their cell phones, arguing passionately, creeping around corners, clutching weapons between their hands with their backs pressed up to walls. I hear Andre, Ben, and Ryan walk up to the house. Amy is not with them. I know this because Amy is the loudest.

I deliberate a moment and then slip outside. Tonight I want to be alone, though often lately I find I prefer to be near them. And when Ben plays his music, I listen, my eyes half-closed in contentment. And I sense I am doing my job. I feel the caress of unseen forces, approving. I hold my mind against the pain I am causing him. And against the hurting to come.

I might be an agent to harm, but I do good, too. I know their air, know their land, better than they do. I know the creatures—I know their joys and sicknesses. I know where the squirrels hide their treasures and what the breeze intends when it comes from different directions. I immerse myself for hours in the lake, until I feel my body will dissolve, giving nourishment with my decomposition. I am a bee pollinating, a worm burrowing in the soil. My presence and my work will enrich this world.

On Monday, I sit at the kitchen table, nibbling cranberry bread. Lately, I am hungry for more than honey. Andre and Ryan have gone to work, and Ben has departed on some errand or other or to see his girl. Amy comes downstairs, yawning. Smiling, she wraps her arms around me. She is the only one who does this. Sometimes she even lifts me like a child and carries me around. Andre and Ben admonish her for this, but I do not know why. It is rather nice, being treated like a cherished doll.

"Wish I could hang out. I've got to get groceries. I promised Andre I would." She checks the cabinet. "You all set with honey? Need a different kind or anything?"

I shake my head.

After Amy leaves, I go outside, slipping a sweater on over my small dress. Not because I require the protection, I tell myself, but because it feels soft on my skin. I walk a long way before taking it off and hanging it from the branches of a tree. I stretch my arms, savoring the sensation of my wings unfurling.

It is something I can never explain to them, the pleasure of these appendages. I told Andre wings were not needed for levitating, and this is true. But they are necessary for propulsion and all movement other than floating. I could never describe the wonderful utility of them; the delicious spray of nerves throughout the webbing and bones, sensitive as the whiskers on a cat.

I fly, I swim—though the water is beginning to sting me with its chill. I collect stones and inordinately perfect leaves. I drape myself on the arm of an oak tree and stare up at the topaz sky through the boughs. My eyes follow a Stellar's jay that bursts from a hidden perch and darts after something. A month ago, I would not have wondered if I'd be able to catch it. I am slower now. And I am bigger. And I don't want to think about what this means. Humming one of Ben's songs, I grow drowsy and close my eyes.

It is nighttime in a teeming place in the middle of the wood. Colored lights are strung along the stalls and among the trees. There are bonfires and the smell of spices, meat, and mischief. The sound of laughter in different tones and tongues. Light from the fires catches the surfaces of trinkets and gem-studded goblets. Music blooms like bubbles from flutes and cricket-drums.

Beneath a spangled night sky, I am surrounded by beings of myriad sizes. There are snouts and warts, wings, and glowing eyes, feathered faces. The grotesque and the beautiful sting my eyes.

This place is familiar. I walk along, speaking to a friend with red eyes and gleaming yellow skin. "How am I here if I was sundered?"

"You are in a dream, and you won't remember upon waking." If she were human, she might have looked apologetic at this, but this faerie seems only to find the conversation distasteful.

"What is my name? Oh, please tell me," I ask before I can stop myself.

The yellow girl looks surprised by the question. Delicate antennae are sprouted on her brow and move with her face and eyes, adding depth and nuance to her expression. "I can't tell you. Why fret on it? There is a friend for you in her fine home. And you are doing well with your quarry, and the tithe will soon be paid."

I see something else in her eyes. Something she is hiding from me—my own place in this story. The yellow faerie starts to turn away. I catch her arm. "When?" And then I realize I don't know her name. I scarcely know what we are speaking about.

Her garnet eyes are opaque in the light. She laughs as if it is an absurd question. She hesitates and lowers her beautiful voice—it is lovelier than mine now. "What is it like to change? We all wonder."

The air in front of me shimmers, and all is dark. I am falling. I land on all fours, though the pain is sharp when my knees smack the ground. I gasp, my wings half open and drooping over my shoulders. I stand quickly, glancing about. I could have been seen. I looked up.

Trembling, I brush dirt and leaves from my knees as the dream drifts from my mind like rings of smoke. I have never fallen out of a tree before.

"You must accept whatever happens. None of us can change our fate." Grace kicks her long legs in the water. We sit in one of her pools, drinking mead again. This is not the first time I have come to see the giantess alone. I gaze around the cavern and watch my monarch hovering over one of the flowers. "I spoke of you to my children."

I draw my gaze away from the butterfly and look up at Grace. "Will I make them sick?"

"I don't think so. It's in their blood."

I nod. "My keepers are fragile."

"Yes," Grace agrees. "All of them are. Their lives are gone in a nap or two." She tilts her head to the side and wrings out her wet hair. "Time is so fast here. They are such a feeble variation of us."

"You've known a lot of them to die?" I ask.

"Yes. And I can see my own end up ahead—not for some time probably, but it's there. My pulse may go for another century or two, but I feel my mortality now."

I cup water in my hands and let it fall to the surface in a little splash. I feel almost as low as I did after the sundering. "We live almost forever—but not forever, and some are killed from the violence, I remember that at least."

"Yes," Grace says. "At times, it was vicious." She sighs. "But . . . the *music*. And those great parties." We look at one another, both holding fragile, gossamer threads of memory.

"I'm thinking of leaving them," I tell her. "I could find another shed somewhere. I could make my own treehouse . . ."

Grace fixes me with a sad smile. "There is nothing to be done. To use a phrase you are likely not familiar with: the die is cast, my child. Has been since you killed the woodwalker, am I right? You started the tithe that same night. It is on its way. I have scried it in this water. Although, I do not know how. I can't make it out." She leans forward. "Tell me how you did it."

The monarch flaps in front of my face, and I grasp it, too roughly, and toss it out into the air a few feet away. Some swear word burst out of me, from muscle memory, in a forgotten language. It twists my tongue to make the sound, and I cover my mouth with my hands. I whisper, "The creatures, the winged ones, they—" But I stop. "No. I won't speak of it. I dread it so."

Her eyes widen as suspicion grows. "They will know you compelled it to happen. They know you call forth the creatures. They will blame you." She takes a sip and cocks her head. "You can stay with me when the time comes."

Ben lay on the sunflower bedspread, squinting at his phone. He was trying to read a review of a new album and trying not to forget that he needed to reply to Mateo's texts. His best friend had been asking for more music. Mateo was excited and was sharing it with some musician friends up in Portland, who were enthusiastic about what they'd heard. But he couldn't concentrate on anything. His right lower jaw was killing him.

He glanced over at Merri, absorbed in her phone, frowning. She set it down and sat up, so the window was behind her. She played with the zipper on her sweater. "Is your tooth still hurting?" she asked tentatively.

"Yeah." Ben looked back down at his phone. No matter how he did it, it was going to be unpleasant. He'd been intending to since the night of the dinner party but hadn't mustered the nerve. It didn't help that he wanted her just then. Despite his physical discomforts, his libido wouldn't let up. But he had to do it—he had to break it off.

He was going to miss being with Merri in her bedroom with the sunflower bedspread and curtains, above the circular, sunflower rug covering the hardwood floor. In the last couple of months, he'd spent many hours in this room. They had sex and watched movies, and she'd listen to him play music for hours. Ben didn't know if sunflowers had a scent, but to him, they smelled like her. She dropped back down on the bed, curling up next to him. "That sucks. You should go to the dentist."

He ran his fingers along her forearms for a few seconds, then stopped himself. *A dentist can't help me, Merri. No one can help me.*

After he'd gotten home from the dinner party—a week ago now, he'd smoked a joint that went swiftly to his head. Alone in his room, about to play the music he *had* to play, he suddenly thought again of Genevieve's round belly, and he had the jarring realization that the same thing could happen to Merri. They hadn't been using condoms. He didn't even know if she was on birth control. It was the sort of hyper-paranoid reality check he was grateful to the herb for. He'd put his guitar down and lay on his bed in the dark, heart-pounding, and vowed to himself that he would not take another chance. How could they be so irresponsible? What was he doing with the poor girl? And why did Merri even want to be with him? He wasn't great company. He was brooding and sickly, and the last thing he could handle was some terrible accident no matter what she would have decided to do.

"What's wrong?" She propped her head up into her hand and leaned on her elbow. She looked at him, subconsciously drawing her hair over her scarred cheek.

He sighed. "I—I don't think we should do this anymore."

Ben was distracted by the throbbing tooth, and it must have shown because he got poor tips. Servers at the Cedric's Bar and Grille were not required to do any side work besides giving the mahogany tables a last wipe down with hand towels. He worked slowly, lingering over the wooden surfaces. Another server, Maya, who was either terrible at reading social cues, or else feigning her obliviousness because she wanted to run her mouth at anyone's expense, drifted over to him. "Last week, I got stiffed by those assholes. Did I tell you about it?"

"More than once."

"What is it about the lunch hour? I swear it makes people bigger jerks. Both times I've been stiffed, it's been during a day shift."

"Uh-huh." *Go away. I don't care about your muggle problems.*

"They shouldn't go out to eat if they aren't going to tip!" She huffed and wandered over to the bar to find someone more sympathetic. He moved to the next table and made slow, methodic rings with the rag, watching the way the light of the dining room lamps made the moisture on the surface of the table into thousands of tiny golden beads.

A song that had been sprouting in snippets over the evening now poured into his mind in powerful, clear waves. It was a balm over the pain in his jaw and the unpleasantness of the day. Notes surged forward, then marched, mincing, backward; they rose and fell, and made a declaration. He heard where the synthesizer would stipple along the sides of the refrain just so. His eyes glazed over as he swirled the rag over the table in sync to the music. The song reached a crescendo where the table met the wall. He sighed heavily and realized he was hunched in the booth, panting. He looked around self-consciously as a new thorn of pain bloomed in his jaw.

On the drive home, he told himself that it was good he'd cut things off with Merri. He'd hated it—was trying desperately not to think about it.

She'd tried to be stoic. She'd flinched, but then nodded and blinked rapidly and said only, "Okay, okay." She had not asked questions, only stifled her tears. It was a shame, but he could live more honestly now.

All that mattered was for him to be near Shae. She had brought the surge of music. He'd always known this. He'd just never allowed himself to think about it. The songs thrummed in his brain, in his gut—a wonderful and terrible virus that he was the host of—and that he *craved* being the host of. He couldn't do anything until they ran their course and infected others with the sound. Ben had not given much credence to the notion of a muse before, but now he knew he was cursed with one. He was a slave, and it was getting worse.

At home, he walked down the hall, passing by Andre's room, faintly aware of her and Ryan's quiet presence. He wondered, too, what was happening to his stepsister. Was he imagining that strange, nimble quality in the way she moved? An odd counter to how she was growing increasingly daft and dreamy?

He undressed, took a quick shower, and then sat down at his keyboard, and with painful relief, he played. He dug around in his hands and his mind for the right notes to match what was in his head. He knew where the vocals would go and what they would do, and the sound of them, but he didn't know the words yet. After a minute, the song appeared in full, and he closed his eyes and rode the waves.

An hour later, he stopped and went outside to smoke a cigarette. Shae emerged from the shed and stood for a long time, watching him. She stepped closer, spread her wings, and hovered above him, wearing an expression he'd never seen, something like tenderness. His mouth watered. She smelled like rain on stone and freshly turned earth, and something else—something sweet like a flower from another world. Ben reached out and put a hand to the side of her face. "Come upstairs with me, please," he pleaded.

It did not surprise him that she was gone when he awoke the next day. Ben sat up, lifted the bedclothes, and inhaled the sheets, pressing his hand against his screaming jaw. They had gone up to his room and coiled together—but it was a fuzzy enchantment he only half believed in. He couldn't remember clearly. His body felt bruised, his skin weak and fragile as if it could be easily torn. The song wasn't there, and he felt a moment of panic, until he found it again, faint now, but steady.

How typical that she was gone. This was what they did, wasn't it, creatures like her? He winced again, and tears sprang to his eyes at the pain of his tooth. He thought of the toll then, the sacrifice that had been alluded to here and there. It had remained on the edge of his mind like a bad dream he couldn't quite remember. *It's me*, he thought. *I'm fucked. She's going to kill me.*

He dressed, his teeth chattered and aggravated the toothache, but it wasn't just him, he realized. It was winter, and the heat wasn't on. Someone, likely Amy, was in the shower. He left quickly so he wouldn't have to see her, and wondered vaguely when the last time he ate was.

It was gray out, and a fog laid above the trees in the distance. Ben missed Hammer as he walked down the path. He started whistling, then stopped. Began again, stomping his feet along in an unconscious beat. Slowly, without him quite noticing, the song began to grow again. A little hop came into his step. The soreness in his muscles eased up. He moved faster and stopped when he reached the clearing. He was sweating, and his heart pounded. He looked around, drank from his water bottle, and shivered.

Of course, he wouldn't find her. She would appear again when it suited her, and there was nothing he could do. Ben slugged water, grimly contemplating a future of crippling longing that he would never get relief from. He started whistling again to purge the music that ran through him. He had to whistle or beat his hands against his sides. If he stifled the music, there was an icy flare of pain in his tooth. Snippets from the night before came back like the way her skin had felt when she'd moved against him like a fragile, teasing breeze.

He stumbled and groaned, grasping his jaw and probing his tooth with his tongue. There was an awful pop followed by a rush of warm, salty blood. He spat his tooth out and whimpered, staring at the little white square among the crimson speckled leaves.

CHAPTER TWENTY-ONE

December crept up insidiously, and then possessed a punishing chill, rare to their region of the west coast. Andre, usually organized, didn't remember to switch her calendar until halfway through the month when Ryan reminded her they had a holiday dinner at his parents' house the next day. This time there would be aunts, uncles, cousins, and a matriarch in her nineties. It was to be a sort of semi-formal, extended-family affair, the likes of which she'd never experienced with her own relatives. She imagined dining on china by candlelight and people primly patting their mouths with unabsorbent cloth napkins.

Andre was wary for the gathering; she didn't trust herself these days. She got honked at when she stayed put at stop signs, waiting for them to turn green. She got lost, staring at the way the light hit her fork or the nubs on a pinecone. She was hypnotized by shiny surfaces and busy textures. One morning she was late for work because she got stuck peering inside the sparkly alcove of a geode that had been on her windowsill for years. And the rest of the time, she was underlining scraps of theory in the dubious volumes she'd procured off the internet. She took meandering walks in the woods and very long baths.

One night she had taken a bath and fell asleep in the tub, although she never *felt* like she'd fallen asleep. But she must have because she woke up to Ryan pounding on the door. Dripping, she'd hopped out to unlock it, and he'd cried, "I was about to break the door down! I've been knocking and calling you." He'd pulled her towards him, holding her face against his chest, and she realized, with embarrassed dismay, that he had been seriously panicked. She apologized, wondering why she hadn't heard him. And why had she locked the door? She never locked the door. None of them did.

On a whim, she'd bought a dress for the dinner. It was made of a velvety white material with a scooped neck and back—the upper half-formed to her like a leotard. Andre could not stop staring at herself in the mirror. Amy twisted her hair up into two ebony buns and dabbed her face with vibrant gold eye shadow and dark liquid liner, and put on two coats of mascara. The makeup was dramatic, but she couldn't shake the notion that something else had changed about her face. She leaned forward to frown at the white streaks in her smooth, pinned up hair.

When Ryan got home from work, he gaped for a few seconds.

"She cleans up nice, doesn't she?" Amy observed, folding her arms and leaning in the doorway.

He smiled, but there was wariness in his gaze. "You look . . . amazing. I've never seen you wear makeup like that."

Andre pointed at Amy. "She did it."

"Well, she's good for something then."

"Thanks, Ryan," Amy smirked.

"No, really, you did a great job. Did you do her hair too? It looks awesome." He put his hand on Andre's back and gently turned her so he could see the back of her head.

"Yeah." Amy looked admiringly at her work. "I keep telling her if she's not going to cut it, she needs to do something with it once in a while."

Dinner was served forty minutes after they arrived. The food was delicious. Conversation was engaging. Andre was not ignored or overly focused upon. She relaxed and enjoyed herself more than she'd expected to. When they were readying to leave, she was pleasantly buzzed, and everyone hugged her.

"Well, that wasn't so bad," Ryan said when they reached the car.

She stood on her tiptoes and kissed him. "They're great. That was nice." But she felt daunted on the drive home, thinking of how she would spend the rest of her life engaging with people who didn't know the truth about the world. *I've flown. How will I ever feel normal again?*

When she pulled up to the house after work the next day, Ben was on his way out. Head down, jittery, hurrying to his car; he muttered,

"Be home by ten. Got the early shift so I can take you all to the airport in the morning."

"Thanks." She watched him drive away.

Inside, Ryan was on his laptop, and Amy was making a playlist on her phone. Ryan's vacation had officially started that day, so he hadn't gone to work. Three suitcases rested, pyramided in the living room. Andre was impressed. Usually, Amy was scrambling to get packed right up until they were about to leave, and Andre would have to help her. "I ordered pizza," Amy told her. "It should be here soon. I did laundry, too."

"Okay, thanks." Andre trudged up the stairs to finish packing, nursing the anxiety she always felt before flying, and all the hassles entailed in traveling.

As she sifted through her drawer, pulling out the essentials: socks, underwear, favorite jeans, blouses, and sweaters, Andre realized something else was gnawing at her; she was afraid to leave Shae alone with Ben. She scratched at her arm, and her fingernail hit something hard. She'd snapped the casing of a ladybug. She flicked it to the floor, went to the bathroom, and washed her hands.

In the dark hours of the morning, Andre lurched up in bed from a nightmare of the airplane plummeting to the ground. Heart hammering, she looked at the clock. It was 2:00. Ryan lay on his side. Her heart slowed as she looked at him. He was sweet when he was asleep, like a giant child. She lay back down and tossed and turned for an hour before sleep claimed her again.

She had been walking down a pleached alley, following the bats and butterflies, but she couldn't get any farther. Not until the tithe is paid. And then she was disembodied, and there was only beautiful music. She gathered it up like spools of shimmering thread churning inside of her. Silky to the touch, silky to the mind. She sent it into him. Into his mind. He drank in the song, and then he looked at her, and he was sickly and beautiful, and he grasped her by the arms and pulled her towards him.

Andre arched her back and woke herself with a little moan. She gasped and shuddered, and then her face burned. *Oh god.* She grimaced. She wanted to take a shower and wash the dream away. *Keep that out of my head, Shae.*

She looked at the time. It was 5:59–two hours before the alarm was set to go off. Their flight wasn't until noon. She kissed Ryan's temple and got up, feeling a tremble of anticipation. Shivering, she quickly stuffed her legs into sweatpants and threw on a T-shirt that was draped over the desk chair, and went downstairs.

Ben was just coming in the back door as she walked into the kitchen. It was still dark out, and the only light was the dim orangey glow from above the stove. His eyes gleamed, cagey. They stared at one another. *Not just a dream then.*

"Shut the door, it's freezing," she said finally.

He closed it behind him. "You're up early."

"So are you." The words hung between them. Finally, she turned away to the cabinet and pulled out two mugs. "I dreamed that the plane crashed."

"That won't happen," he said quickly.

She turned her back toward him, measuring out the coffee with a teaspoon. "Probably not, but something bad will happen soon, right?"

"Yup. Pretty much got that feeling too." He slumped down into a chair at the kitchen table and put his head in his hands.

She pressed the button to start the coffee machine and waited for the comforting gurgling sound of it percolating. She leaned against the counter and crossed her arms. "So, when did it start?" She nodded towards the back door he'd come through.

His eyes narrowed. "Did you really have a bad dream, Andre? Why are you up this early?"

"I had a *nightmare.* I have weird dreams all the time. Usually, they are about animals. Anyway, what the hell, you're . . . *with* her now?"

He scratched his face. "It's because of the music."

What the hell would happen to him now? Poor Benny. "She's dangerous . . . whatever she's doing to you . . ."

"I know," he said quietly. "I don't know what to do. Andre, I can't explain it. It hurts." He clenched his fists, and she noticed how prominent the veins in his hands and forearms were. He'd lost a scary amount of weight.

She poured them both coffee. When she sat back down, she asked softly, "What about Merri?"

He looked confused. "I ended it a couple of weeks ago. She didn't say anything?"

Andre shook her head. "She's been very quiet at work."

"This only just started. It might have been building up for a while, but I'm not a total asshole."

"We should tell her about Shae," Andre said quietly. "It's not fair not to, Amy's right. I think it's messed her up, thinking she's crazy."

He sighed. "I know, it's just . . . awkward for me, with those two."

They sat quietly for a minute. "Are you going to Mateo's for Christmas?" Andre usually felt a little bad leaving him alone for the holidays, but over the last several years, he'd developed the tradition of spending Christmas with Mateo and his mom Sandy.

He shrugged. "I don't know. I don't think so this year." Both Mateo and his mother had already extended the invitation for Ben to come over, but he hadn't replied to them.

"I don't want to go," Andre whispered.

"It'll be fine. It'll be good for your mom to meet Ryan," Ben said. He felt for her, though. He was glad he didn't have to travel.

CHAPTER TWENTY-TWO

"Stupid, awful news." Amy glared at her phone. "Okay, time for some cute sloth videos." She was slumped in the pleather seat to Andre's right. They were camped at the gate, waiting to board. Ryan was on her left with his laptop open. Andre turned back to her paperback, but she couldn't concentrate. After reading the same paragraph three times, she laid the book down on her lap and looked around. Except for herself, a young guy reading a magazine, a baby and an old man who were both napping, and two middle-aged women reading the same hard copy of the current bestseller, every single person she saw at the packed gate had their face in a screen. Ryan put in his earplugs, and she could faintly hear the recording of Ben's music.

She looked down at the faded cover of her little book—a yard sale purchase from early in the summer. She loved the dated artwork, the coffee-colored pages, and the sweet, musty smell. When a voice announced it would be time to board soon, she dug in her satchel and pulled out the tiny vial of flower essence she'd somehow been allowed to keep through security. She opened it and tapped a few drops beneath her tongue.

"Gimme." Amy held out her hand, not looking up from her phone.

Andre handed it to her. "It only works if you believe in it."

"Yeah, yeah, I believe in everything."

Ryan glanced up and pulled out one of his ear-buds. "What's that?"

Amy held it up for him to look at while Andre answered, "It's flower essence. We sell it at the store. It makes me feel better. I get flying nerves. It's homeopathic."

He frowned. "Does it work?"

Andre shrugged. "It does for me. It does *some*thing."

Despite her anxiety, shortly after they surged into the air, Andre grew drowsy. She declined the coffee and peanuts that Amy and Ryan accepted and nodded off.

There were creatures on her, mosquitos drinking her blood. She looked down at her chest and saw a huge butterfly. Its wings thickened and grew sinewy and black. It was not a butterfly after all, but a bat . . .

She jerked awake, rocking slightly back and forth from the turbulence. She blinked and rubbed her eyes. Ryan was reading a space opera, his headphones still on. Seeing she was awake, he smiled. "Good nap?"

"I guess . . . another bad dream, though. Nasty little winged ones." *They've got a madness inside them.* She yawned.

"What's that?" He took out one of his earbuds.

"I don't know, never mind. What time is it?" she asked, pulling her phone from her purse to answer the question herself.

"Almost three. You've been out for the last couple of hours."

"Yeah," Amy piped up. "You were snoring. I've been jealous."

During the two hour layover in Atlanta, they used the bathroom, got food from vending machines, and drank beers at a pricey airport restaurant. They didn't have a big meal because Lydia had texted Amy and suggested they would all go out to dinner. The next flight was just over an hour, and before she knew it, Andre was experiencing the familiar ache of complex emotions that always accompanied the sight of her mother.

Lydia wore a salmon-colored blouse with a silk scarf, nice slacks, and flat slippers. A black coat was slung over her arm. She was only forty-four. For the first time, Andre thought she looked kind of close to her age. The network of fine lines around her eyes now deepened as she broke into a tearful smile at the sight of her daughters. A blend of the two of them, she was the same height as Amy and wore Andre's raven hair in a new bob cut. She hugged her daughters, gathering them both in her arms, making a little moan before pulling back to smooth their hair down and look at their faces. "My girls!" Her eyes flicked back and forth between them. Then she looked over Andre's head and said, "And this is the Ryan I've been hearing so much about for the last few years?"

"It's so nice to meet you," he said, smiling down at Andre while she hugged him.

"Where's Preston and Max?" Amy asked as a tall young man—almost unrecognizable from the one she'd seen a year ago—came through the sliding glass door that led out onto the dark, cold night beyond the dropoff and pickup area.

Andre gaped. He easily towered over her now. Lydia had mentioned several times that Max had had a growth spurt, but Andre hadn't been paying attention. He was not permitted much of an online presence, so she hadn't seen any recent pictures of him. It was hard to reconcile the lanky thirteen-year-old walking up now in trendy clothes, and shaggy hair with the cherubic little boy she and Amy had played with back when they used to return to the east coast for whole summers at a time.

"Holy shit!" Amy nudged her laughing then went up to embrace her little brother and ruffle his hair. Andre glanced at Lydia, who was beaming at the reunion of her children and dabbing the corners of her eyes. "Oh my god," Amy said, "How did this happen? Look at him, Andre!" Max smiled awkwardly, trying to keep his lips over the metal in his mouth.

Andre gave him a quick, tight hug. "You've gotten so tall," she said.

"Yeah, that's what everyone says," he replied in a squeaky, tortured-violin voice.

There was a sprinkling of pimples on his forehead, but that, along with his braces, didn't take away from the fact that he was going to be a heartbreaker. She stepped back. "This is my boyfriend, Ryan. Ryan, meet my little brother, Max."

"Good to meet you, man." They shook hands.

"Well, C'mon," Lydia said. "Let's get your bags. You must be tired and hungry. Preston is waiting in the car."

"So, Andre tells me you're an engineer," Lydia addressed Ryan after they ordered drinks and appetizers in the dimly lit Mediterranean restaurant. "That's a great career, quite demanding, I'd imagine. How do you like it?"

Ryan swallowed a sip of coke with some difficulty, coughed, and removed his arm from around Andre's shoulder. "I love it. The hours are long, but that isn't a problem if you're engrossed in what you're doing—which I am." He explained what his company did, which was to develop software for medical technology. Preston asked him a few questions about the project he was currently working on, grunting, seeming in his subtle way impressed.

Lydia turned to Andre. "How is the health food store?"

Andre shrugged. "Okay, I guess. Honestly, sometimes I feel like Vivian isn't so into it anymore."

"Hmm." Lydia nodded. "I imagine running your own business in this economy is difficult—long hours, lots of taking your work home with you."

Andre nodded, taking a bite of bread. But really, she was doubtful. Vivian was at the store less than ever these days, and while she did have work related to the business to do at home, it wasn't like she didn't have a life. Andre had been some months away from social media, but from the impression she used to get, her boss appeared to be living it up, always talking about the latest movie, hiking every week with her friends, plenty of time for political debates. She seemed to be enjoying her middle age now that her daughter was older, and she had Andre pretty well in place to run the store.

"What about you, Amy?" Lydia asked as she buttered a piece of bread. "Have you figured out what you want to do yet?"

Amy took a sip of wine and set it down, twirling the stem. When she looked up, her eyes were half-lidded, and she gave Lydia a strange look. Andre wondered with a sinking feeling if she'd taken something stronger than flower essence. "I'm thinking of getting into adult film."

Andre snorted. "Here we go." She addressed her mom, "Actually, Amy's been at Cedric's, you know, the restaurant where Ben works? She's been waitressing a few nights a week." She gave Amy a piercing look.

"I was a groupie for a couple of months this summer." Amy grinned, straightening up. "I was the merchandise girl."

Lydia sighed. "I'm not trying to give you a hard time, sweetheart. I'm just concerned about your future. At least Andre has a degree."

Andre winced; she could feel Amy's hackles rising. It was like an allergic reaction. Why they couldn't both learn how to shut up and speak in platitudes, like she did, Andre would never understand.

"Ah, yes," Amy said. "And that Bachelor's in English is doing her so much good. Maybe someday, if I work hard, I too could aspire to a job behind a counter, working for minimum wage, selling quinoa and colon cleansers." She looked at Andre and said, pointedly, "Sorry. No offense."

Groaning, Andre leaned against Ryan's shoulder and said to him, "see what you've gotten yourself into? Aren't you so glad you came? This is what you're stuck with for Christmas."

"You're young and extraordinarily beautiful, Amy." Lydia sighed. "I'm sure you'll get along fine for a while longer."

"Wow, thanks, Mom."

Andre cleared her throat and addressed her little brother. "How's school going?"

He shrugged. "Pretty good."

"What is your favorite subject?" asked Ryan.

Max drummed his fingers against the table, and the motion reminded Andre of Ben. She wondered how he was doing just then and if he was okay. Max frowned, thinking. "Probably algebra."

"Good for you," said Amy. "I hated algebra. I used to copy Andre's work all the time."

"As I recall, you hated all your subjects," Lydia said.

"How would you know? We'd left you by the time we were his age."

Andre rolled her eyes, feeling a surge of annoyance at both of them. "Amy, we've been here like twenty minutes. This is already starting?" She glanced at Lydia but looked quickly away at the stricken expression on her mother's face.

The drive back to the house from the restaurant only took a few minutes, and fortunately, Max and Ryan's discussion of a video game they both played broke up some of the tension. It was frosty and dark out as they pulled up to the trim brick townhouse nestled in a maze of cookie-cutter homes. A garland of white Christmas lights lined the roof and door. The single dogwood tree in the yard was strung with colored lights. Her family had lived here for the past five years, but the development still seemed new to Andre.

The house was spotless and smelled sweet from something that had been baked earlier in the day. Andre, Ryan, and Amy trudged up the clean, white, carpeted stairs and set down their suitcases. Andre looked at Ryan and confirmed something she thought she'd noticed before—that he'd lost a little weight. He hadn't eaten much at dinner. She put her arm on his shoulder and stood on her tiptoes to kiss him. "Are you okay? You look exhausted."

He shrugged away from her, annoyance flickering over his features. "Yeah, Andre, stop it. I'm fine."

"Ryan?" Lydia appeared in the doorway. "I think Andre told you; you're welcome to sleep in the spare bedroom in the basement."

Andre rolled her eyes. "*Mom*. He was helping to bring our stuff up. We're just talking. Don't worry; he'll sleep far, far away from me."

"Er, Andre—it's okay," Ryan said.

Lydia grimaced. "I have no problem with him being alone with you here. I just thought he might want to get his stuff put away and see where he's going to sleep. I'm only trying to make him comfortable. I do ask that while you are here, you sleep in separate beds, but I wouldn't dream of chaperoning you two every second. I'm sorry if I was interrupting something."

Andre looked down at her feet. "Sorry."

Lydia addressed Ryan. "If you two are talking, Andre can just show you down later."

"No, it's okay," Ryan said, giving Andre a look she didn't care for. "I'd like to get settled; I appreciate you having me here."

Andre closed the door after they left the room, kicked her shoes off, and plopped down onto the bed. The shower in the hallway turned on. Amy always managed to snag the bathroom first. Andre gazed up at the ceiling fan, her eyes following one panel in a lazy, steady circle for a few seconds.

She tentatively tapped on the string to check in with Shae. It was muted somewhat, but Shae was awake and active. Andre sensed that much. It was a relief to know thousands of miles apart couldn't cut them off entirely.

Then she remembered she hadn't let Ben know they'd arrived safely. She dug her phone out of her purse and sent him a quick text. A few seconds later, he sent her back a thumbs-up emoji.

Amy appeared in the doorway, wrapped in a towel, her hair darkened with water. "Mmm. I forgot how much better the water pressure is here than at home." She stepped into the room and squatted down to rummage through her suitcase. "It makes me feel cleaner." She rubbed Andre's vanilla-scented lotion into her long legs, and Andre wondered why everything was better on Amy than on her. She could swear Amy smelled better using the same products.

After her shower, Andre dressed in comfy sweatpants and a tank top and went downstairs, dragging a comb through her hair.

Lydia and Amy were in the family room, watching Max and Ryan play a video game. Seeing her brother and her boyfriend together was sweet and weirdly unmooring.

"Wow, Andre," Lydia said. "I hadn't realized how long your hair has gotten." She frowned, "Is it a lot of work to take care of it?" Andre could feel her noting the gray.

She sat down cross-legged on the floor and tilted her head down, running the comb through the black waterfall of hair. "I don't mind it," she said.

"You think maybe it's time to cut it?" Amy asked. "I mean, it's pretty, but I can't decide if you look like a Disney princess or a sister-wife."

"Where's Preston?" Andre changed the subject.

"He went to bed," her mother replied. "He has to be at work at five-thirty."

Andre nodded. Preston always dwelled in the background when they came to visit. Andre liked him alright, but she didn't ever feel like she knew him very well. He'd always—probably wisely—stayed out of the way of Lydia's complicated relationship with her older children.

"Max, you should think about getting to bed soon too."

He didn't appear to hear her but gritted his teeth and cried at the screen, "Oh, man, oh, man! C'*mon*!"

"That's a good idea," Amy said, standing up and stretching. Andre saw her mother frowning at all the new tattoos, but to Andre's relief, she didn't comment on them.

"Are you sure, honey?" Lydia asked. "I thought with the time difference, you would all be up late."

"It's probably just the wine and the long flight. Night, Mom." She pecked Lydia on the cheek and patted Andre and Max on the head.

Andre sat for a while watching Ryan and Max's muscled avatars slaughter beasts and wander through a primeval landscape while she combed out her hair. Lydia kept glancing at her, a sort of eager look on her face as if she was trying to figure out the right thing to say, or was thinking of a question she could ask Andre to spark conversation. After a little while, Andre stood up. "I'm going to bed too."

"Okay, then." Lydia sighed. "I'll see you in the morning. I thought we could all go shopping in the town center or maybe do a matinee?"

Andre shrugged. "Sure, a movie might be nice."

Amy was lying on the bed with her head propped up on the pillows. Andre could just make out her eyes open and glittering in the dark. Andre lifted the covers and climbed in next to her. They always engaged in uncharacteristically twin-ish behavior when they made this trip. They cloistered themselves away in the room and conversed more, whereas at home, they generally just coexisted. This trip always fused them together, temporarily.

"I don't like being away from her," Andre said. "It makes me scared that she doesn't exist. Like, we'll go home, and the last six months will have been a dream."

Amy sat up on her elbow and fixed her with a strange look. "What are you talking about? Like who doesn't exist?"

"You're hilarious." She sectioned out a ribbon of her hair and began braiding it.

"Oh, don't worry. You'll get to see Tinkerbell again in a week. At least you have Ryan here."

Andre laughed. "Yeah, but I can't sleep with him." She frowned then, genuinely resentful. She could go a week without sex, but his physical presence was almost essential to her sleeping at all these days. There was something solid and comforting in Ryan. Something about being next to him that made her feel safe despite all the weirdness surrounding them. He didn't stop the dreams, but when she woke up from them, he was a warm, life-raft of normalcy.

"You think there are more?" Amy asked suddenly. "You think faeries or Sidhe, or whatever she is, have come before?"

Andre thought about Grace and bit her lip. She needed to be careful. Amy was good at sniffing information out of her. "I think it's possible."

And still, the tithe isn't paid! She felt her muscles squeeze painfully, and then her mind skirted away from the thought, and it evaporated, leaving her with a nameless ache and wariness. Her thoughts drifted to Grace again. It would only be a matter of time before Amy found out about her.

They were quiet for a few minutes. "Can you believe Max?" Amy said. "Isn't he so adorable?"

"I know." Andre sighed. "He's sweet. I just love him. I wish I knew him better."

"I know what you mean. Looks like Mom's doing a better job this go around."

"Preston has been a good thing for her too."

"True," Amy said, yawning.

"What about you?" Andre asked. "What about Amy's love life? I haven't noticed you hanging out with Ricardo as much . . ."

"I don't know. I need freedom. I need someone who isn't freaked out by what I look like." Amy handled attention well, quite enjoyed it overall, but she'd had a couple of boyfriends and one girlfriend who grew obsessed and possessive.

Long after Amy fell asleep, Andre, having tossed and turned to madness, finally got up. The door to her mom's room was shut now, and soft Christian rock music drifted from Max's. Shivering, she crept downstairs. White Christmas lights ran along the empty fireplace setting a soft glow beneath the family photographs on the mantle.

She opened the door to the basement and went down, holding the banister, not turning on the light–she didn't need to; her eyes were remarkably sharp in the dark. The guestroom was open. She went in and looked at Ryan. She thought he was sound asleep, but when she sat down on the bed, he jerked awake. "Shh. I didn't mean to wake you."

"What's up, Bumblebee? Animal dream?"

"Nothing. I just wanted—" She straddled him suddenly. "C'mon," she whispered.

"No." He was fully awake now, leaning on his elbows. She leaned down and let her hair run along his bare chest. He shivered. "Go back, Andre. Stop it. We're not teenagers. I don't want to disrespect your mom." He sighed, kissed her back. "Why are you doing this? It's not like you."

She pulled away and then lay beside him, suddenly overwhelmed with sorrow. "I just wanted to be near you right now, that's all." They lay, chastely spooned while he drifted back to sleep, and she cried silent tears she didn't know the source of. There was pressure inside of her—a worrying throb in her mind. After an hour, she slipped back upstairs to sleep next to Amy.

Early in the morning, as the sun rose, Andre went into the bathroom to pee. After flushing the toilet, she caught her reflection in the mirror and frowned. She leaned closer, studying how the silver was advancing over her crown at an alarming rate. *But that isn't right.* She squinted at her scalp, then her heart started to pound. The hairs weren't silver; they were *white.* Her hair wasn't thick enough for her to have noticed at first. She turned toward the bathroom window. Clutching a few strands together, under the winter sunlight, she saw sparkling amidst the white, all the colors of the rainbow.

CHAPTER TWENTY-THREE

"Hello." *Finally, an answer.* But the voice on the other end surprised Andre. She sat up. "Shae?" She'd never talked to her on the phone before. "Hey, I've been trying to call all day. Is everything okay? Is Ben there?"

"Ben is driving." There was a muffled sound, and Andre could just make out his voice in the background. "He asks how your trip is going."

"It's fine." *How is he, Shae?* She waited for a beat and then asked— as Shae was unlikely to offer up any information unprompted, "So . . . what are you doing?"

"We are going north. To the bigger trees. We will see the stars better."

Andre closed her eyes. She wanted a night sky without light pollution. She wanted the cold wind on her face and branches above her, but she was thousands of miles away, stuck in the suburbs. "It will be freezing," she said. "What park?"

There was another muffled sound. "What did you say, Andre?" Shae asked.

Andre winced. Shae's voice was strange and echoed. "Which park?" she repeated. But there was a muffled sound like Shae was saying something to Ben, and the line hung up.

Ben sat on the back-yard porch, smoking. He looked up at her, hungry as always, then closed his eyes, his head bobbing to the music she brought him. He'd been stuck in the same song for three days, but he felt another coming nearby, coming soon.

"I want to go away."

"Don't." His voice was pitiful, and he hated himself for it. "Don't go, please." He licked his lips, and he knew she could smell panic coming off of him, like rotting citrus fruit and anxious, jumbled musical notes. He stood up and came towards her, limping. "I will do anything. Tell me what to do."

She lifted off the ground then and went into his arms, resting her head on his shoulder. The monarch abandoned her wrist and fluttered around her head, stirring up a little breeze in her hair. "Come with me," she said finally. "Take me. Not for long. A day, or two, or three. I want to see the bigger trees—the redwoods."

"Yes, okay." He nodded, stroking her hair with wiry hands. "I will take you there." *I will take you wherever you want to go.*

Ben packed water, candy bars, trail mix, two jars of honey, and an apple. He regretfully decided against the extra weight of any beer. He gathered a blanket and a sleeping bag, but no tent. He had the tentative notion of a park a couple of hours north. Their chances of privacy would be good since it was going to be frigid, and he doubted many people would be there the day before Christmas Eve. He was vaguely worried about freezing his ass off, but he was more afraid of not being with Shae.

Shae sat on the kitchen table while he got everything together, staring pensively out the window at the pale light, her arms wrapped around her knees. The butterfly rested at her feet. Her hair was like snow. Ben caught himself staring and wondered if he would ever get over the sight of her. She was so much bigger now, but she was still impossible. Shae turned to him and said, "You will be cold."

"I've got extra clothes packed." He wore his backpack and carried the tote with the food. The sleeping bag was slung over one shoulder. He strummed his guitar once then put it in the case. It was the last thing to go with them. "You ready to go?"

She blinked and got down from the table. She wore a sundress and children's tennis shoes. She donned a soft white button-down sweater that was draped on the chair behind her and plopped the large blue hat on her head. "Yes."

She was silent during the car ride, sitting in the backseat even though Ben had told her it was fine this time to sit up front with him. He stole glances at her in the rearview mirror and tried to ignore the encroaching headache. He watched her eyes carried along by a passing tree or telephone pole and sliding back horizontally to another object. It was a hypnotic thing to watch—those shifting orbs reluctant to abandon whatever it was they were latched onto. *What is happening, Shae?*

"Andre is doing the same thing right now," she said.

"What's that?"

"Her eyes, but in a circle, above her. The wheel spinning in the ceiling. Right now." She blinked slowly, then looked away from the window and met his gaze in the mirror. "I like riding in a car." She gave him a small smile. Ben doubted there were cars where she came from. He imagined her traveling in some palanquin of sticks and moss if she didn't just fly wherever she wanted to go.

She leaned forward, and he felt her little hand—neither warm nor cold—touch his neck. He turned his face towards her, and then she moved her fingers to touch his ear, then his chin. He was unsure of whether the touch was inspection or affection, but he didn't care. He would have it, whatever it was.

After Shae's brief talk with Andre, Ben silenced his phone and shoved it down into his bag, only then recalling he was supposed to work that night. He considered pulling it out again to call in sick but decided he just didn't care. He suspected it didn't matter anymore. It was a wonder he hadn't already lost his job. He wasn't a popular figure at the restaurant these days: constantly seeking to get his shifts covered, a moody, taciturn waiter who clearly never wanted to be there.

He sensed they would be gone for at least one night, and he thought of his Christmas a year ago, spending the day at Mateo's drinking Bailey's and eggnog, jamming out "12 Days of Christmas" on their acoustics while Mateo's mother Sandy made them a feast.

Mateo had called a few times over the last week. He'd left Ben a message and then texted a few times, asking if he was coming for Christmas. Ben had gotten distracted with a song and forgot to reply. There was a concert they could go to, Mateo had mentioned. And Ben was supposed to meet Cecily. And he wanted them to jam together as they had since they were twelve years old and first started playing music. His last text had been, *"You even there? Everything okay? You got a new number?"* Ben hadn't gotten any more texts from him in the last few days.

I am being the shittiest friend. I'm sorry, Mateo. Ben knew he would have to explain himself soon, but he was with Shae, and there was nothing more important than being with Shae. And there was more music for him up ahead. *Maybe I'll be dead before I have to explain myself*, he thought. *Maybe Mateo will never know what happened, but he'll know something happened. He'll forgive me.* And then Ben thought of Merri. He hoped she didn't think poorly of him. Despite everything, despite the music and Shae, he realized he had missed her in these last few weeks. He imagined her in her sunflower bedroom, and he hoped she was okay. *I'm sorry I wasn't better to you, Merri. I'm sorry, I couldn't be more for you.*

Two hours later, he turned on the GPS as they entered the winding roads where mountains of redwoods gradually encompassed them, the claret-colored pillars rising majestically, scraping the sky. He felt the songs he was so desperate for right ahead of him, and he almost salivated. Just a few more—they dangled, teasing at the edges of his mind like goblets of water sparkling under the sun in front of someone parched in a desert. And at the center of these feelings was the fear and the terrible weight of the *cost* of them, the cost of having Shae come. The cost of this gift she was giving him. What had Grace said that he'd forgotten? There was a dark word floating somewhere in his consciousness that he couldn't remember.

It would be growing dark soon, and he would lose the signal on his phone. He gasped as a pain lanced through his jaw. A headache threatened on the front outer ridge of his skull.

They reached a parking entrance with no one in attendance and a gate barring them. Ben got out of the car, hopped over the gate, unlatched it from the other side, and pulled it back. He got back into the driver's seat and pulled the car through, then got out again and closed the gate. *No one knows where I am. No one will find us.* Shae had told Andre they were going to the redwoods, but that could mean a lot of different forests. They parked at the end of the lot. *How long till the car is found?* He got out the backpack and sleeping bag roll. *How long till my body is found?*

Shae stepped out of the car, her face tilting up at the trees. Then she began walking lightly and swiftly into the forest. Ben followed her. He didn't bring a map. He drummed at his sides, breathing in the cold air, and felt the music coming.

CHAPTER TWENTY-FOUR

"You do realize this is literally the *worst* possible day to go shopping, right?" Amy sniffled and put her feet up onto the coffee table. She was buried in a hooded sweatshirt and blankets. "A misanthropic wacko with an assault rifle might show up and shoot everybody. In fact, I'm surprised it hasn't happened yet."

"There's been shootings at malls before," Andre said.

"Not on Christmas Eve," Amy muttered. "Yet."

Andre rubbed her forehead, feeling claustrophobic, just imagining a crowded mall. Her stomach ached, and her ears, nose, and throat were turning on her fast. And she was trying not to think about the strange phone call with Shae. She kept texting Ben, but he wasn't replying. Cell phone service was scant in a lot of the state parks, but she was still worried.

"Are you sure you don't want to come?" Lydia looked plaintively at them.

"Are you kidding?" Amy asked. "Have you forgotten how Andre gets in a big crowd? You'll need to bring a paper bag for her to breathe into. It's why she doesn't ever go to concerts with me. She can't bear all the energy of the public—affects her constitution—a delicate flower, this one." Amy sneezed again. "Ugh. How is this happening? I never get sick."

Preston spoke without looking up from his business magazine. "Medicine cabinet is in your bathroom. Has all kinds of stuff."

"I don't think you should participate in the consumerism madness," Andre mumbled. "It's not fair to the people who work there."

"Oh, it's not like it's Christmas day, and I'm sure they get time-and-a-half or something," Lydia said. Not for the first time, Andre caught her mother's eyes roving over her with a frown. "Andre, you look very peaked and thin. Are you eating enough these days? You look . . . you almost look like you've *shrunk*."

"I'm fine, Mom. I just have a cold."

Frowning, Lydia moved to the foot of the stairs and hollered up them. "C'mon, Max! It's just us, then. Your sisters aren't coming."

It had been a good visit, overall. They had gone ice-skating, attended a local ballet production of The Nutcracker, had a popcorn movie marathon . . . but now Andre and Amy were getting colds, and Ryan had developed a bad headache the night before. A few minutes after Lydia and Max left, he came upstairs from his guest room in the basement, grimacing. Andre leaped off the couch and hugged him tightly.

"Good to see you too, Bumblebee. It's been like, what, an hour?" He frowned. "Are you okay?"

But she wanted to ask him the same thing. His eyes were bloodshot, and she could tell without asking that the headache had worsened.

Late that afternoon, after Lydia and Max returned, it started raining hard. "If there has to be shit falling from the sky on Christmas Eve," complained Amy, "it would be nice if it was snow. Can someone put on the heat, please?" She sneezed.

"I'm going to take a nap," Andre mumbled.

"Me too," Amy said.

"Are you all still not feeling well?" Lydia asked.

Andre nodded, shivering. She found Zinc and Vitamin C that morning in one of the kitchen cabinets and taken some along with the cold medicine, but she was feverish. The tenderness in her throat and pressure in her ears was getting worse. She trudged upstairs, following Amy, who immediately sprawled out Vitruvian-Man-style on the bed. Andre curled up on the side. "I'm sick." She sniffled.

"Get away from me then."

Andre shoved her lightly. "You're sick too. Move over."

Amy acquiesced, to her relief. "Is that why you're so bummed out?"

Andre was quiet for a moment. When she spoke, she could feel a hysterical edge creeping into her voice. "I think something bad is happening. I feel this . . . strain in my mind and my body. I'm so worried about Ben. We shouldn't have left him. He was looking really sick. I've texted him so many times since yesterday. I don't even know which park they were going to."

Amy sighed. "Try to stay calm, Andre, you're getting yourself worked up. I'm sure everything is okay."

Andre nodded miserably. She closed her eyes and felt for the string. It was delicate as a spider web, so insubstantial she couldn't tell if she was imagining it being there at all. *Where are you, Shae?* And then she sensed her, deep in the forest. Ben was there. *Music.* She couldn't get anything else.

Amy's phone buzzed in her pocket. She pulled it out. "Ricardo again? I already talked to you, buddy." She turned the ringer off and put it back in her pocket. After a few minutes, Amy sat up. "Okay, I can't sleep, I'm going to see what they're doing downstairs."

Andre slept for an hour, then got up, went to the bathroom, and took a Benadryl from the medicine cabinet. She changed into thermal underwear and looked over the gifts she was going to give her family while she ran a comb through her hair. Every box was neatly wrapped in blue and silver paper and shiny ribbons.

She moved to the window. It was still raining. In the dark, Andre could make out the dreary backyard getting drenched in water and moonlight. A couple of lean shrubs were tucked into the corners of the fence. The yard was tidy, but Preston and Lydia didn't do much with it besides keeping it mowed. Andre wondered why they had never gotten a dog for Max. It seemed a little unfair. He was pretty much an only child.

"Andre?" She hadn't heard Ryan coming up the stairs, and his voice made her jump. "You should come down. We're watching 'It's a Wonderful Life.'"

"I—I'm good. I think I just want to be alone."

He hesitated. "It's Christmas Eve, and you don't see them very often."

She was about to snap at him for trying to make her feel guilty when he stepped farther into the room, and she got a look at his face. His eyes were shifty and red. He looked pained, and he'd dropped a few more pounds in the last week. "God, you look awful! Do you have a fever?" She reached towards him, but he jerked away with a vehemence that startled her.

"I feel shitty, yeah. Headache is killing me, but I think we should be down there with your family."

The weight bore down, and the pressure gripped her in a spasm. Andre sucked in her breath. "I know. I'm sorry. Tell them I'm sorry. Tell them I went to bed because I don't feel well."

He looked like he was going to argue, but after a moment, he shrugged and left the room.

CHAPTER TWENTY-FIVE

"Merry Christmas! C'mon, get up!" Max cried.

Andre burrowed her face into the pillow and moaned. She pried open her sticky eyes, and when she croaked out, "Hey," it hurt just having a noise come out of her face. Her sinuses were tender, mucus-filled cavities.

"Merry Christmas! C'mon get up, you guys!"

Andre peered balefully at her brother. Apparently, regressed in age, he wore a Super Mario T-shirt and was, jumping up and down. She half expected him to announce that Santa had paid a visit during the night.

"We're coming down in a minute. Now shut the door!" Amy yelled right by her ear.

"Hurry! Mom made breakfast."

"Merry Christmas, Max," Andre said. Her throat felt like it had been rubbed with a cheese grater. "God, I'm so sick."

"I feel like shiiiiiit," Amy groaned.

Max huffed. "What is wrong with everyone? Ryan is sick too."

Amy leaned up on her elbow. "Is everybody up?" Her hair tickled the back of Andre's neck, which for some reason, compelled her to sneeze.

"Yes. Mom says, we can't start opening presents until you guys come down, so hurry up!" He turned and bounced down the stairs. "You snooze, you lose!" He called over his shoulder.

Amy's head dropped back down on the pillow. "Did he actually just say that? What a dork." She yawned. "He wasn't this annoying before. Christmas brings out the worst in people." She turned to Andre and patted her on the head. "Speaking of which, Merry Christmas, Andromeda."

Away in a Manger on violin drifted from Bluetooth speakers by the television. The weak filter of Andre's clogged sinuses caught an imagined hint of holiday spice from the candles by the window. The dining room table was neatly set with china and a poinsettia in the center. The living room was sparkling with the same decorations she'd seen all week, somehow made shinier by the significance of the day. Beneath the tree was a modest assortment of gifts, prompting her to remember the presents she'd forgotten to bring down from her room. Andre turned around to go back upstairs and bumped into Ryan. She gave him a quick peck. "Hey, Merry Christmas."

He looked feverish and hyper-alert. "Merry Christmas." He jerked slightly forward as if an invisible rope tugged him.

"I left my gifts upstairs. Be right back." She hurriedly gathered her presents from the room and returned swiftly to place them under the tree.

"Alright!" cried Max. "Why don't I go first?"

"Not so fast." Lydia walked out from the kitchen bearing a circular tray with a mandala of sliced fruit. "Why doesn't everyone grab something to eat first?" She set the plate down on the dining room table and lifted the silver lid of another platter, revealing fluffy scrambled eggs. She smiled at Andre. "These are fresh from my friend's farm, so I can personally attest to the comfortable quality of life of the hens." There were English muffins, sausages, bacon. The only thing that appealed to Andre was a crystal decanter full of orange juice.

"This is so nice, Mom. Thanks. But I'm not hungry."

"Yeah, too bad, we've got the plague," Amy said, swiping a napkin off the table and wedging it into a leaky nostril.

Lydia looked from one of them to the other. "Still? All three of you?" She rolled her eyes, her gaze landing on Ryan, and she frowned in concern. He sat on the floor against the wall next to a chair. His knees were drawn up to his chest. She stepped closer to Andre and lowered her voice. "I'm a little worried about him. He looks awful."

"Hey, Mom, this has my name on it, can I open it?" Max held up a fist-sized box wrapped in shiny red paper.

"Whoever is hungry, get a plate." Lydia sighed. "I guess it's just the three of us."

"I already had some sausage," Max said without looking up. "Alright, I'm just gonna open this."

"Max, knock it off," growled Preston. He set his magazine down and got up to get a plate of food. He looked at Ryan and said, "Hey, why don't you have a seat?"

Ryan tossed out his hand as if to block the offer. He shook his head and opened and closed his mouth before speaking. "No. That's alright. Thank you."

Preston hesitated, then went over to the table and began piling food onto his plate.

Amy poured herself orange juice. "I wish this was a mimosa," she said longingly.

"You want a mimosa?" Lydia asked. "I have some champagne." She went over to the fridge.

Amy and Andre looked at one another. Their mother did not drink and never kept alcohol in the house to their knowledge. "You have champagne?" Amy's voice practically cracked with hope.

Lydia pulled the bottle from the fridge. "Yes. I almost forgot. I bought this a couple of weeks ago."

After watching her struggle for half a minute, Preston took the bottle from her. "Here, let me get that. Merry Christmas!" The pop made Ryan jerk. Andre grimaced. The sound bothered her, too, more than it should have—like a bursting balloon startling a toddler. She shivered.

"This is awesome, thanks, Mom." Amy held up her glass, and Preston poured the smoking champagne in.

He held it out to Andre with a question on his face, but she shook her head. "Maybe later." She already felt doped up with mucus and medicine. She went over to Ryan. "You call your family yet?" she asked him quietly.

He kept his gaze to the floor as he answered her. "It's early on the west coast."

When they had all moved back to the living room, Lydia said, "Alright, fine, Max, why don't you be Santa Claus?"

"Yeah, go ahead, squirt." Amy blew her nose. "Why don't you open a few? Most of them are for you, anyway."

The next half hour was spent opening gifts, the majority of them for Max. He got video games, clothes, an advanced Lego set, and art supplies. He seemed genuinely excited by the books Andre got him. Interspersed between his gifts were various things for Andre and Amy: candles, handcrafted soap, gourmet chocolates, scarves, a silky green blouse for Amy, and a black one for Andre. Lydia gave them a large picture frame containing several photos of them as children that Andre had never seen before. "I found them in a box in the garage," Lydia said, looking like she was about to cry. "I'd thought they were lost."

Amy and Lydia crooned over the jewelry Andre had bought for them at a gem faire early that spring. Andre gave Preston an award-winning book on the Civil War, which he grunted at in apparent interest. She was pleased to see him become utterly absorbed over the next hour, ignoring everyone as he pored over it, sipping his coffee. Amy gave Andre a poison holder ring and Max a box-set of anime films.

Ryan was doing a laudable job of appearing interested in watching her family open their presents. "Andre." He said her name a couple of times. "Andre, I've got something for you."

She bit her lip and pointed to a couple of unopened packages beneath the tree. "You can go ahead and open yours."

He scooted over. "You want me to go first?"

She looked around—Max had gone to get some more breakfast, Amy and Lydia were talking to each other, and Preston still had his nose buried in his book. She nodded.

He carefully unwrapped each gift, sci-fi books, and a nice sweater. His movements were economical and painstaking. He responded with a satisfying degree of enthusiasm, but he seemed preoccupied. "Thank you so much, Bumblebee."

She said softly, "What's wrong? You really don't feel well, do you?"

"Headache . . . I feel pretty bad. I threw up this morning." He shook his head as if to rid himself of something, and when he looked up, his eyes were clear again. It was like the sun coming out from behind clouds. "Now open yours." He held out a small square gift.

She carefully tore off the ruby red paper to find a small, velvet jewelry box. For a split second, she panicked that it was an engagement ring, but then she realized that if Ryan was going to propose, he wouldn't do it in front of her family on Christmas morning. She opened it and saw a large, tear-drop emerald in a silver clasp.

"Lemme see! I helped pick it out!" Amy appeared beside her. She stroked the chain with her finger. "Nice. Very nice."

Lydia came over to look as well. "That's a beautiful stone."

Andre removed the necklace from its velvet bed and held it up to the light. The green gleamed like seaweed. It almost made her thirsty. "Here." Ryan scooped her hair over her shoulder and tried to fasten it around her neck. "Damn." He grunted after several seconds, struggling.

"Here, let me do it," Amy said. "There." She pulled Andre's hair back.

"Okay, next one." Ryan hesitated, and for a moment, he looked shy. He reached beneath the tree and handed her an envelope.

Andre opened it, and it took her a moment to understand what she was looking at. "Tickets?" She studied them again. They were plane tickets to London. "What?" She looked up at him, aware there was a stupid grin on her face.

"We're going in February." He smiled, waiting for her to say something. "Glastonbury, Cornwall, then onto Scotland and Ireland. It's eleven days. We've got a lot to cover."

She clasped her hands over her mouth and said muffled beneath them, "Oh my god! Thank you so much!" She hugged him.

Amy stood up. "Lucky devils." She went over to the table and made another mimosa. "But how are you going to bring Shae?"

"Who's Shae?" Lydia asked.

"No one." Andre glared at her twin.

"Just a friend of ours who needs to trace her ancestry." Amy winked.

"Don't worry about the store," Ryan said. "I talked to Merri, and she checked with Vivian. You've got the time off."

Andre shook her head. "I can't believe this." She hugged him again, but this time he stiffened up at her touch.

"We won't be able to see everything on your lists, but it's a start."

"I'm so excited." She bit her lip, grinning. "I've never been out of the country. I'll need to get a passport."

"Wish I could go." Amy sighed. And truthfully, so did Andre. Amy would be fun to go romping around Europe with.

❦

After they had cleared away the dishes and debris of Christmas gifts, Ryan went to lie down. Preston lounged on the couch with his book, and Lydia continued tidying up while Max played one of his new video games. Amy watched a movie on her tablet. Andre looked up the places she was going to visit, then tried texting Ben once more. She took a bunch of Vitamin C and drank some water. Then she went downstairs to check on Ryan, found the door closed and decided to let him rest.

She went up to her room and fell into a deep, sweetly dream-free sleep, preceded by thoughts of travel. When Andre woke up hours later, she took a long, hot shower. Feeling markedly better, she wandered downstairs to find Max still at the same video game and Lydia setting the table for an early dinner.

"Perfect timing. I was hoping you'd be up soon. Dinner is almost ready. Maybe you'll eat something this time? I made a turkey."

"Thanks, Mom." She hugged Lydia. "You didn't have to go through all this trouble."

Lydia straightened a plate. "I checked on Ryan while you were in the shower. I'm tempted to take him to urgent care. He wouldn't let me take his temperature, but I'm sure he's got a fever. I sent him up to your room because I thought he might be more comfortable with the fan and being right next to the bathroom." She looked like she was about to say something else, but didn't.

Andre poured a glass of water for him and went upstairs. The heat was blasting, and that, combined with the oven on for so long, made the house almost too warm. The fan was turned off. She flicked it on, thinking the breeze would be welcome. Ryan lay on his side, his underarm holding his stomach, and his other arm was across his chest, his hand in a fist. His eyes were open. His breathing was visibly fast and shallow. She put a hand to his head. He was running a fever. "Hey," she said softly.

He looked up and glared at the ceiling. He batted his arm at the fan. "Turn it off. God, turn off the fan, please!" He grimaced. "How's it going, Bumblebee?"

"Fine. Jesus, what's wrong with you?" She touched his head again, but he winced and leaned back from her. "You're not going to be able to fly tomorrow if you get any worse. I think we should take you to the hospital."

He sat up. "I'll be. Fine. I just . . . I want to get home." His head twitched, and then he looked around as if he heard someone else in the room say something.

"Why are you moving like that?"

He rubbed his forehead. "I feel so strange. My head, ugh. I feel really weird for some reason. Kind of—kind of nervous."

"Here." She nudged him with the glass of water. He took a shuddering breath, his hand trembling as he grasped it. He swirled the water around a bit and handed it back to her. "I can't."

"C'mon, you're going to get dehydrated."

"What time is the flight tomorrow?" He tugged around the collar of his T-shirt. "I can't remember."

"We should be ready to go by six-thirty. Our flight is at eight thirty-five. I'll pack your stuff up. Have you taken anything? Here." She handed him the glass again.

"Not since last night." As Ryan brought the glass up to his face, his hand started shaking, spilling water on the comforter. He gagged. "Fuck! Just please—get it away!"

Andre took the glass from him before he dropped it and stepped away, her heart pounding. He wiped his mouth with the back of his hand and stared ahead at the doorway, hyper-alert.

She flicked on the light. "I'm worried about you. We are taking you to the hospital first thing when we get back if you're not better— right when we get off the plane."

"Please don't turn on the fan again." He looked up at her and then quickly down. She turned it off again. The hall and bathroom light illuminated them well enough to see each other.

"You should take something to bring the fever down. At least Tylenol?" She prodded him to move to the other side of the bed and sat down next to him.

He attempted to laugh and grimaced. "Don't you have any eye of newt or herbal shit to give me?"

"I couldn't smuggle much onto the plane—just my flower essences. You want some of that?"

He laid back down and looked up at the ceiling, blinking. "Nah." He spoke with an effort. "I tried to take Tylenol an hour ago. I just can't take anything right now." Andre petted his shoulder, and he tensed beneath her touch. "It could be a virus," he said. "Maybe you shouldn't get so close."

Andre was about to remind him that she was sick too, but she realized that wasn't quite true anymore. She was feeling a little better, and he'd developed a fever. Ryan had something different.

Amy appeared in the doorway. "How's it going, kids? So, home tomorrow. Can't wait." She said to Andre, "Mom is asking if we should just have that picture frame mailed. Otherwise, we have to pack it up now and check it before the flight. I say we mail it."

"Sure," Andre agreed.

"Is this from the faerie?" he asked them suddenly. "Is this from Shae?"

Amy smiled tentatively. "What are you talking about, Ryan?"

Andre bit her lip. "He's sick."

When he jerked again, Andre's pulse quickened, and she experienced the flash of a notion that she was the butt of some terrible prank.

A little while later, Ryan lay on the bed between Andre and Amy. Amy patted his leg. "You look like utter shit. I'm with Andre. I think we should take you to the hospital."

"No. I'm getting on the plane. I'll go to St. Luke's when we get home if I'm still bad tomorrow." He closed his eyes. "I'm just going to try to go to bed. Wake me up tomorrow if I don't die in my sleep."

"Oh, *please* do not ruin everybody's holiday," Amy said, lightly shoving him.

A few minutes later, Amy and Andre moved to the room he'd been occupying in the basement, squeezing together in the twin bed. "This isn't comfortable." Amy sighed. Then she said, "I'm kinda worried about him. He was all . . ." she didn't finish the thought but plucked up a tissue and blew her nose. "I'm feeling a little better. I think the worst is over."

"Me too. I hope the flight isn't a nightmare for him."

"And just another couple months, and you'll be on a plane again."

Andre looked at her. "You should try to come with us. I could use your help. It's going to be as much a research trip as a vacation. If I find someone I trust, I'll show them a picture of Shae."

"And you really think you're going to find someone who can help? What, like some old storyteller in a pub? Like some ancient

Celtic hedge-witch who can tell you how to find the portal? You know it's not people from the 17th century who live there, right?" She laughed. "And she came here. I mean—to California. So it seems the 'border'—she made quotes with her fingers—"would be there."

Andre sighed. *Yeah, yeah, Grace said as much.* "I know. But the history and legends of the Sidhe originate in the British Isles. And it can't hurt. I hope we find something." *And Grace didn't tell us enough and hasn't talked to us since* . . . "Shae has forgotten almost everything. It's tragic."

"For you or for her?" Amy asked.

Andre rolled over to look at her sister. With the moonlight through the window, she could just make out Amy's profile, the elegant, sloping contours of her perfect face, her cheekbones. "It makes me crazy to think there is an entrance to another world somewhere if I just knew where to look. How can you not feel that way? Don't you want there to be more than this?" She waved her arm around pointlessly in the dark.

"Yes." Amy sighed. "I think it's all beautiful and dangerous and sparkly. I can almost see it."

"Are you making fun of me?" Andre turned her head towards the ceiling and yawned. "I can't tell."

"I'm not sure," Amy replied sleepily.

Andre suppressed the urge to blurt about Grace. "I'm so worried about Ben."

Amy was quiet for a long moment. "Me too. It's like a fairy tale, huh? Ben and Shae. She's the nymph, and he's a lowly human bard."

Andre laughed. "Aww. He's not a lowly bard."

"Yeah, but he didn't start making musical heroin until she arrived."

The pressure and the sorrow squeezed Andre, and she fought back tears. "Yeah, well, he's got a muse now."

CHAPTER TWENTY-SIX

The court shimmered and melted away, the figures, losing edges and resolution. They had been moving and speaking a moment ago. And she could see, in the background, they were crafting another ball of lightning! But now they were dream-stuff, dissolving with her waking, except the most pertinent message. You will return to us!

Shae opened her eyes. She was *not* sundered . . . and they were pleased the tithe was coming. *The die is cast, my child–has been since the night you killed the woodwalker.*

Burrowed in the sleeping bag, Ben breathed into the music and held her close. *You didn't let me die—not yet.* She wrapped her arms around him. She was the only thing that kept him warm. She felt more substantial now—like a real girl, not some pretty little goblin. Her hair was soft against his face. "It's Christmas," he said. A wispy, ancient memory of his mother's voice floated through his mind—an auditory ghost. *"Feliz Navidad, mi muchacho."* But that wasn't right. It was the day *after* Christmas. He'd been in a trance of songs. He could scarcely count the days.

Shae tugged on the zipper, slicing open their cocoon of a sleeping bag, and sat up. The monarch fluttered from their little nest to the low hanging thatch of nearby fern. Ben watched it. There was no way it should have still been alive. And how it survived the cold, he couldn't begin to imagine. Then he realized how cold *he* was, and started shivering violently.

Shae shivered too. Sitting up, she pulled her shoulders back and raised her chin. Ben stood up and stumbled away from her. Backing up against a redwood, he breathed on his clenched fists through chattering teeth.

"I can return to my world. They will let me back in."

He stared at her. "I thought you were—s-sundered. I th-thought Grace said—"

"She doesn't know everything. Let's go home."

Ben was entering a darker phase of starvation. He'd eaten only a few handfuls of trail mix in the past few days. He was freezing. His toes had lost feeling, and his fingers were too numb to play his guitar. He was close to the point of frostbite. But the headache and the pain in his jaw were gone—the absence of which almost made him euphoric. He was better. Shae had done what she was going to do with him, and he wasn't going to perish out here in the wilderness. After all, he had to share his songs, didn't he? And he felt them all inside of him now. All the songs he'd written since she came. They were jewels he could hold in his pocket—a priceless treasure that would transform his life. Albums that would change the world somehow.

And if Shae spoke true, part of him wanted to tear at his clothes and howl like an animal at the thought of her departure. But when he started weeping, it was with relief. The *weight* was lifting, even as the music still poured through him. They packed up and started walking. For the first time in a long time, he thought maybe things were going to be okay.

Once his blood was flowing, he rummaged through the backpack and tore into a candy bar. It was rock solid and hurt his teeth, but it tasted wonderful. He washed it down with the last of their water after offering some to her. "I don't know what it means for me." He managed finally. "You leaving."

She held her hand out in front of her face and turned it back and forth. "It is strange. Now that I have become so good at adaptation." Then Shae did something shocking: she tripped over a rock in her path. It was cringe-worthy, like seeing a ballerina stumble. She went still, looked up at him, and then quickly away, hugging herself.

Less than an hour later, they reached the frost-covered car. Ben had no idea they were so close. Some of their wanderings must have been in circles after all.

When pools of moisture began to clear up the windshield as the heat blasted, he thawed with shuddering, teeth-chattering, violent relief. He was sore with spent muscles, his feet were killing him, and he was dizzy with hunger, but a sweet, existential joy swept through him. Ben hadn't expected to drive again. He hadn't expected to make it back. He found himself grinning through tears at a beautiful December morning. *I'm going to live. The world is mine again, and I've got these songs to share!*

Twenty minutes into making their way down the winding roads back to civilization, his phone started buzzing in his backpack, loud and accusatory with all the missed calls and texts—a neglected mob of pent up correspondence. He ignored it. He'd call everyone back when he got home. He glanced at Shae here and there, but something had changed between them. The power had shifted, and she wasn't quite the addiction she had been.

His songs were tucked neatly in his mind. Accessible to him if he wanted to pull them out and let them play. And he couldn't wait to play them for real—to play them with different instruments backing him up. After he got home and had a hot shower and ate a real meal, he would attack his keyboards for a bit. Then he'd call his friends. He would start up a band again with Mateo and recruit Ricardo too—Stepfather was disbanding anyway he'd seen on social media since the lead singer was moving to Boston.

During the ride home, Ben was consumed with thoughts of his future. He'd been given a sublime gift, and he would share it with everyone now. He was deep into a fantasy of playing in a huge stadium in front of a roaring, adoring crowd of thousands and didn't notice the maroon Subaru parked in front of his house when he pulled up. In his consuming fog, it lacked meaning. He parked behind it, and just as it registered as odd, Shae spoke, "Ben, someone is here."

He turned his head. "Oh shit." Walking swiftly down from his front porch and toward them, was Merri.

Amaryllis Waters was not used to feeling vulnerable or distressed. Even as a child, she was never scared of being alone in the dark. She never cried. Before these last couple of days, it had been years since she had gotten sick. Amy was cushioned with extra layers of pluck and luck, but the flight back to the west coast was the worst experience of her life.

They'd woken late. She'd slept through her alarm, and Andre, who used to be the responsible one, had been useless and flaky and fretting over Ryan. Amy heard them in the upstairs bathroom when she went to fetch her phone charger. "If you're seeing double, we need to go to the hospital."

"No. It's stopped. Please, Andre. I can do it. It's just a day of travel. I want to go home. *Please, I just need to get home.*"

Amy had spared only a moment to see that Genevieve and Merri had both called late the night before—after she had gone to bed. She saw there was a voicemail but didn't check it as she was scrambling to get them all out the door. There was a text from Ricardo, too: *Call me as soon as you get home. It's important.*

They had rushed, getting themselves ready and trying to help Ryan, who summoned some inner strength to thank Lydia and Preston, give a fist-bump to Max, and say goodbye to them. They'd made it to the gate just under the wire.

There was a quick bounce of a layover, and they bolted again to make the next flight, all the while, Ryan kept periodically gasping and making jerky movements. Amy finally called Genevieve back while they sat on the runway. Her friend had answered, sounding distracted and upset, insisting for Amy to just call her back right away when they landed. First thing. She had said something odd then, something that didn't quite make sense, and then, "Don't go anywhere. Don't even go home. Go right to the hospital and call me."

"Hold up, Genevieve, slow down, *what* did you say?"

But the pert flight attendant asked her to get off her phone and please fasten her seat belt. They surged up into the clouds while she ran over Genevieve's frantic words. Then, at one point, it crystalized, and several strange and awful fragments fell into place. And now she was trapped, thousands of feet in the air, in a torturous tunnel of time. There was nothing she could do.

I am okay. I am better. Andre is okay. Andre is better. We just had a bug, and it has passed. It happens in the winter when people travel. It's a coincidence that we got colds. She kept telling herself this over and over. Amy was pretty sure she was going to be okay because as stressful as the morning had been, she'd woken up feeling better—feeling like the cold had lifted and run its course. She'd drunk a big glass of orange juice—no mimosa this time—and took a very hot, albeit short, shower. She felt pretty much right as rain—physically, at least. And Andre was okay too. She had even stopped sniffling.

But sitting between them, Ryan was deteriorating, and she didn't want any part of him to touch her. It took all of her willpower not to recoil from him. And as she watched him cover his face and shake his head in panic when the flight attendants offered refreshments, *she knew*. As he clenched his fists and tried to contain his suffering, *she knew*. Amy was always quicker on the uptake than most people.

She couldn't look directly at either of them. She could not let herself relay the message, for what point would there be? It would only terrorize them. Only once did she meet Andre's gaze, and when she did this, she saw that her sister's eyes, which were fighting back tears, were also changing color.

Ben's first craven instinct was to turn the ignition again and peel away, but Merri walked in front of the car, and though he could have thrown it into reverse, the damage was done. She could see Shae in the passenger seat. Merri muttered something, a dark, disconcerting smile on her face. "Ugh." Ben put his face in his hands and groaned. "Not like this."

"It's okay." Shae sounded resigned. "Open the door."

He turned the car off and got out, raising his hands above his head as if a gun was pointed at him. "Hey, Merri." He closed the door with his knee. "I—I didn't know you were here. Did you call?" Arms crossed, she ignored him and went over to the passenger's side window. "Don't." But he knew it was too late.

Merri said something too soft for him to hear.

"What?"

"You were gone all night," she repeated.

"You were here *all* night?"

"No. I stopped by late last night, and then I came again this morning. From this, I deduced you were out all night." She was looking at Shae through the glass, and her voice was eerily calm, but he could tell that she'd been crying. Ben tried to get between her and the window, but she leaned past him as he tried to block her. "I thought I was crazy. Did you know that? I thought I was *completely* fucking crazy. I've been seeing a shrink. They've been trying to get me to take anti-psychotics!"

"Look, I'm sorry. But let's go inside, please."

She tore her eyes away from the car door window and searched his face. "You don't know, do you? You don't know what's going on." She shoved him to the side and, leaning down, shouted through the glass, "Get out of the car!" She kicked the door and hollered at Shae through the window. "Let me see you! Get out! Get out of the car!"

Ben grasped her arm. "Merri, take it easy, c'mon."

She shoved him again as the door opened, and Shae emerged quickly, unceremoniously. For a few seconds, Merri and Shae just stared at one another. Merri blinked away her tears, nodding. "It *is* you."

Shae gave a tiny nod.

Ben sighed. "Merri, this is Shae. She's a . . . friend."

"Shut the fuck up, Ben. Don't say a word. Don't say *anything*. You're good at that." She took a step closer to Shae. "You've changed." Merri reached a hand up slowly as if she was going to touch her, and then she lowered it. "You've grown so much. Where are your wings?"

Shae removed her hat and tossed it up onto the roof of the car. She pulled off her shirt and rolled her shoulders. Her wings opened. She rose a few inches and moved away from the car so she could beat them slowly. Merri trembled, then she swayed. Ben put a hand on her shoulder. "Don't touch me," she snapped. Then she sighed. "Sorry, I'm not going to faint, though." She closed her eyes. "Shit. She's *real*." Then she opened her eyes and addressed Shae angrily, "Is this happening because of you?"

Shae looked away down the street and then up at the sky. "Yes," she said almost in a whisper. "In a way."

"No, but you *saved* me; it's that monster, isn't it? It's from that monster?" Merri's voice cracked.

"What are you talking about?" Ben asked.

She finally turned to him, tears swimming in her eyes. "Where have you been? Where have you been for the last couple of days? We've been trying to get in touch with you." She shuddered. "Oh god, it's so awful. It's just so, so awful." She put a hand to her mouth. "I knew that camping trip was fucked up."

Shae said two words.

"What?" Ben looked at her.

"The bats," she repeated. "I draw forth the creatures." The monarch fluttered from her wrist to her shoulder. "I have to collect the tithe—you knew this. And I felt a sickness in the bats."

Merri nodded, wiping her eyes. "Yeah—a bat. That's what they're saying—the doctors, the people from the CDC. They're the most common carriers in North America, and the bites are so small people don't even realize it's happened." She was speaking quickly. "We were all so fucking wasted, too. And it can take months to show up . . ."

"What are you talking about?" Ben asked again, uneasily.

Merri looked him up and down. "You look like hell, Ben. But please tell me you're not sick. Once symptoms appear, there isn't much they can do. You have to come with me *right* now. We need to go to the hospital. You need to start the PEP shot." She ran her trembling hands through her hair. "Oh, God, the twins, and Ryan . . . they should be getting back any minute. We're trying to get in touch with them."

"I'm not sick. Please, Merri, what the hell is going on?" A hot panic was starting to roil his empty guts.

Merri wiped her eyes with her sleeve and then looked at him with pity. She took his cold, veiny hand in her warm ones. "Ben, I am so sorry. Mateo was put into a medically induced coma a little while ago, and he probably won't come out of it."

The alarm at seeing Merri, the tiring obsession of Shae, the hunger, the fear over his fate, the music—everything that had been churning inside of Ben, stilled. "What?" he whispered.

"He was admitted to the hospital a couple of days ago. They weren't sure at first . . . He had . . . strange symptoms." She let go of his hands and started wringing hers. "His girlfriend said he'd been acting weird for a few days. He was paranoid, and he had a fever and muscle spasms . . . they were doing tests. And then yesterday they realized he couldn't drink anything. He got upset when they tried to give him a cup of water." She met his eyes, then looked away.

A memory floated through Ben's mind: Shae, so tiny and beautiful standing in front of the ocean. He heard the pounding of the surf in his ears. *"I don't think it will be you. You will play the songs."* His throat got tight. "What—" But understanding was unfurling in his mind.

"It's called hydrophobia. It means fear of water."

Ben started shaking his head and became dizzy. Little metallic maggots swirled in his peripheral vision. *Sick bats, people from the CDC, he couldn't drink anything . . . No.* It was a dated fear in this part of the world—as absurd and unlikely a threat as falling into quicksand or getting razors in Halloween candy.

"They did a test, and it came back positive for rabies."

He looked at Shae, and she returned his gaze, stroking the monarch on her shoulder, her golden eyes, unreadable. "What have you done?" he whispered. "No." He started shaking his head again and staggered back away from both of them. "No, not like this."

Merri moved towards him and grasped his hand. A fat, shining tear rolled down along the line of her scar. "Come on, please, Ben. We need to go."

CHAPTER TWENTY-SEVEN

Pumpkin colored sunlight sparkles through the arch of the pleached alley. The doorway is burgeoning—a pinpoint in the distance. Beyond the door is a wood and water. "It is alright, little one. You have almost reached the end. And you have almost reached the entrance. Your friends are playing and napping on the boughs, on the banks of the silver stream, amidst the grasses and flowers. You will soon feed on the sweetest nectar. When the suns set, they will play sorrowful and wondrous music under the moonlight. Your heart will beat in rhythm to the cricket drums. The ball lightning comes, and you will soon be given back your name!"

Andre's hands flexed, then grasped the blanket. She moaned. These were almost worse than the nightmares had been—these mystical snatches of wonder and relief followed by waking up sundered all over again. And then consciousness socked her like a punch to the gut. She gasped and sat up.

"Everything is okay," Merri said quickly. "Well, I mean nothing has changed," she amended. "Amy and Ben left a little while ago. Here." She held up a plate with a sandwich on it. "You should eat something."

Andre took the plate and stared at it. She wanted to go into the kitchen and drink a jar of honey, but she didn't want Merri to see her do it. What else could she eat? Perhaps a little salt? She licked her lips. Her stomach was perpetually clenched in the forty-eight hours they'd been back. She took one bite then set it down.

Merri watched her warily, and after a moment, tentatively reached up to touch Andre between the shoulder blades. "How is it feeling?"

"No different." Andre had developed a pain there, and it was worrying everyone. Unidentified pain at various points in the body was another one of the many early symptoms. She had started the PEP shot, but she'd started it late, considering all the time and depth of her exposure to Ryan. Andre was worried about a lot of things, but coming down with the virus wasn't one of them. She stood. "I'm going back to the hospital. Your mom is at the store?"

"Yeah."

When they'd gotten off the plane and rushed to the hospital and learned what was happening, Andre had been a mess. And now everyone looked at her as if she were a broken-winged bird dying on the sidewalk. And there was something else in their gaze too—wariness at her appearance.

By the time the plane landed, Ryan was hunched over, gasping from muscle spasms, and spitting the saliva he couldn't swallow into a cup. The flight attendants notified the airline and had an ambulance waiting when they deplaned. He'd been disoriented but lucid on the gurney at the hospital. He'd tried to answer questions, but when they asked him if there was any way he could have been bitten by a bat, he understood and started crying and asked for his parents. Then he started struggling to breathe, and the white coats herded Andre away and sedated him. He didn't get to see his parents. It had all happened quickly.

Andre had a panic attack, and they'd given her sedatives. Since then, a protective web of numbness surrounded her. Her eyes leaked randomly, but she was calm. Of all the unbelievable things that had happened that year, this was the most unbelievable.

It was the oldest and most lethal virus in the world—and their friends were undergoing the current protocol to treat rabies, which involved putting them into medically induced comas in an attempt to give their brains a small chance to survive the symptoms that ravaged them.

But they *were* going to survive this. She was certain. All the worry and foreboding, all the pressure and anxiety over the last couple of months had been about something ridiculous. Who succumbed to such a thing this day and age? A quick search had told her tens of thousands of people annually, actually, just very few in first world countries. She'd stared at her laptop, and something crumbled inside of her. *How soft we are. How oblivious we are to the poverty the world is still mired in.* She skimmed over abysmal statistics for survival and the subsequent failures of the Milwaukee Protocol after it was first introduced. In response to the cold hard facts, a protective bubble of disbelief formed around her, and then the information slid off this veneer. Everything was going to be okay. There was no way a stupid, archaic illness was going to kill her boyfriend and Ben's best friend. It just couldn't happen. She took the worst possibility and wrapped it up, put it up on a high shelf in her mind, and refused to think about it. *They were not a tithe.*

But the prognosis was bleak. The doctors looked grave. The parents were heartbroken and horrified. No matter that no one blamed her, Andre could scarcely look at Candace and Barry. She had not protected their son from Shae. She had taken him away for the holidays and brought him back rabid. And Mateo's mother—poor inconsolable Sandy—a single parent and Mateo her only child.

There had been questions. Lots of questions. There were needles, gloves, and masks, and swarms of somber-eyed, dead serious white-coats. The events of the night were relentlessly rehashed in an attempt to mark the location and timeline of exposure. Merri, Erik, Ricardo, Ben, Amy, Raf, and Genevieve all took turns making statements of what they could recall. They left out the ecstasy but not the pot and alcohol. And they left Shae out of it. The airline was alerted, and an investigation was put forth to determine if anyone had been at risk on the flight. Lydia, Preston, and Max were all advised to get vaccinated just in case, and so were seventy other people—coworkers, family, and friends—who were considered remotely at risk. They didn't take chances with rabies. Genevieve had initially balked at taking the vaccine while pregnant, and she was sure no bat had touched her. But she didn't refuse it.

Notices were put up at the Shellara lake to report any sightings of bats. The public was alerted to the threat. Two reports of rabid raccoons had been reported the previous month, but no animals since. An abandoned barn, some miles away from their camping spot, was found to be the host of the culprits. It was fumigated by a pest-control management company. There were no more human victims. It was a freak occurrence—a grisly spot of fucking bad luck.

Andre remained standing, not making any further movement. She just stared. Her phone buzzed on her dresser. There were a bunch of messages that she had ignored or skimmed through. She supposed she ought to make some calls, but the thought was daunting. She would let people connect with her through the filter of Amy.

Merri picked up the plate with the sandwich in one hand, grasped Andre's hand with her other, and led her out of the room. "Look, I've got to head out, but if you need anything, we're here for you. Me and Mom. She's running the store. You can call us; you know that, right? Even if you just need someone to . . . bring you takeout or something."

Andre stopped walking and turned toward her. "I'm sorry, Merri. I'm sorry we didn't tell you before. And I'm sorry you got hurt, too."

Her friend tensed and blinked rapidly for a few seconds. "Don't worry about it." They kept walking down the hall. "But . . . thank you."

"Whoa." Amy moved her knees down from the dashboard and pulled her sunglasses on top of her head. "You know, I *felt* like this was here. Something about this place is . . . not *familiar,* that's not the right word, but like, appropriate?" She shook her head. "I can't explain it."

Neither of them spoke as they got out of the car and walked up the drive. Ben banged on the door. They waited a moment; then he sneezed violently before pounding on the door again. Amy watched him, frowning. "Jesus, Ben, eat a fucking hamburger, please. You look like you were just liberated from Auschwitz." As if they didn't have enough to worry about, it was his turn to have a cold. He shot her a dark look and was about to try the door handle when it opened. A young man and woman, both statuesque and striking, appeared.

"Yes? Can I help you?" the young woman looked mildly annoyed, and the young man stared at Amy, a curious smile on his face.

"We're here to see Shae," Ben said. "And Grace." He looked them up and down. "I'm thinking, that's your mother?"

The girl raised an eyebrow.

"Yes, come in," said the guy. "I'm Alex. This is Aurora." He turned to his sister. "It's okay."

"Of course it is," Amy snapped and pushed past them into the house. She looked around with a calculatedly unimpressed expression, hating that these beautiful, half-ling giants made her knees weak. Screw these creatures, they probably thought of themselves as alphas.

"Mom is indisposed," Aurora said.

Her voice, Ben thought. Yes, it carried that strange note in it although less so than Grace and Shae's. If one didn't know the giantess's blood ran through her, she would have just been an unusually alluring person.

But Ben was less affected than he would have been a few months ago. "Indisposed? What does that mean? Is she here or not? We need to see her. We need to see Shae. If they are down in the cavern, take us there. We've been here before." He glanced at Amy. "Well, her sister and I have, and she knows about it."

Aurora crossed her arms. Alex turned to her and said, "She told us she showed them. What harm could it do?"

"You should listen to your brother." Amy glared up at her and marched past them down the hall. "I'll find the secret passage or whatever. We've got time." She took a few more steps and then whirled around to face them. "Actually, that's bullshit. We have no time. It's running out while you dick around."

Ben went past her. "I know where it is. It's the panel right there by that picture."

"Here." Alex went ahead of him and led them inside the little elevator. Aurora followed, frowning. Amy stared straight ahead as they descended. She did not flush or stammer, although she was acutely aware that these two were probably weren't used to people *not* doing those things. But she could feel their eyes on her, and despite everything, she liked the feeling.

Once the doors opened and the curtains parted, she was unable to stifle a gasp. It was like stepping into a dream. The glamour was thick and heady, and the glowing cavern was breathtaking.

After a moment, they spied Grace sitting against a rock with two raised ridges on the sides like armrests. There was an open book in her lap. She wore a robe, loosely tied. She looked up, seeming unsurprised. "Ben." She nodded at him and appraised Amy with interest.

"Hey, Grace. This is Amy. Andre's sister. I told her about you." He stated the obvious in a slightly challenging tone.

"Hello. I see you've met my children."

"Yeah." Ben spared them a glance then turned back to her, suddenly unsure of how to begin. "Look, you've got to help us. There must be something we can do. That thing you told us about—the tithe? It's happened. It's happening." He swallowed, sneezed, looked around. *What am I doing? Do I actually expect to get help here?* "Our friends are sick."

"I know. It is unfortunate."

Ben ground his teeth, a sinking feeling in his gut. "Where is Shae?"

Grace slowly leaned to the side and looked down into the pool to the right of her. She glanced back up at them and then turned her gaze down at the water. Ben and Amy stepped over and stared into the pool. Shae was some fifteen feet down at the bottom, curled up in the fetal position. Her hair floated around her face. Her wings were half open and relaxed. "What the hell is she doing?" Amy asked. "Taking a nap at the bottom of the pool?" She toed off one shoe and dipped her toes in. "Mm. Warm."

"I don't know precisely, to be honest," Grace said. "She is going through some physical changes, as I am sure you are aware. The water eases her tissue, and this kind of growth is . . . painful. I suspect she won't be able to do this much longer, though."

"Well, let's get her out." Ben squatted down. "Maybe she can figure out how to fix things."

"Fix things?" Grace set her book aside. "Fix what, exactly? And how?"

"Look, we have no idea what to do," Amy admitted. "But we're not going to let them die without making an effort to help them. I don't know. Maybe we can like, sneak Shae into the hospital and . . . she can . . . do some powerful reiki?" She made a face. "That sounded better in my head."

"She caused this," Ben said, staring down into the pool with a detachment that, despite everything, was a source of great relief for him. He was no longer beholden to Shae for music. "She doesn't get to hide from it."

Grace stood, and coming to her full height, she was threatening. Ben had forgotten just how big she truly was. She took a step towards them. "Would you tear a caterpillar from a chrysalis?" Her voice filled the whole cavern. "*Leave her be,*" she snapped. It was a command. Ben and Amy shrank back as Grace continued. "Her transformation is painful enough, and still, the poor child is unaware of what is truly happening. There is nothing to be done. If your friends are somehow able to rally through the efforts of modern medicine, then another one of you will inadvertently ingest a poison or stumble into oncoming traffic."

Ben thought of Mateo's mom in the hospital, hysterical with fear. And Mateo's girlfriend—no, his fiancé now—that sweet-looking

Cecily, eyes swollen from relentless crying staring into space with the same bereft expression Andre wore. *Do it, Ben.* He'd hoped he wouldn't have to. "Then let it be me instead."

"Ben!" Amy snapped. "Cut it out."

He swallowed, his heart pounding. "No, I mean it. You guys must be able to make some sort of bargain. If you or Shae have powers to heal . . ." His voice shook. "Her arm healed so fast when she broke it. Help them, and then take me."

Grace looked at him almost sadly and shook her head. "I'm so sorry. It is very noble of you. But there is nothing we could do for them. We can't transfer our healing attributes onto another."

"But I thought . . . I thought it was going to be me."

"Oh, well, yes, the muse effect is quite taxing on the subject. It has no doubt strained your body and mind a great deal, but that is over now. No, child, you have another purpose, as I'm sure you're realizing. Your music must spread." She cocked her head and squinted at him thoughtfully. "I suspect you will have an extraordinary life, Ben. You've been given a rare gift—the kind only bestowed once or twice a century."

"If this is the cost, then I don't want it." But it hurt so much to think of surrendering it—like lowering the golden treasure of his soul down a bottomless well. Offering his life had been easier. But he plunged ahead. "Take the music back and let them live. Use it for the tithe."

The giantess sighed. "You are under the impression I possess some influence in this situation. I don't, and even if I did, I'd not interfere." She paused. "Grieve. It's part of being a human. Grieve as you must and then move on. Be grateful it will be no worse than this. People die all the time. Even young people. Your music will do great good in the world, or if not that, then it will at least prevent some catastrophe."

The route to the hospital was becoming familiar after going back and forth so many times over that couple of days. Andre knew the best lot to park in. At first, it had seemed like some awful labyrinth with the walls closing in on her the further she walked down any hallway.

But now she understood the layout of the building, where the cafeteria was, and the closest restrooms were.

Andre stepped through the sliding glass doors and realized she'd left her water bottle and the bag of snacks Merri had insisted she take in the car. She had the vague idea her body was begging her for some sustenance, and she'd been neglecting it like a forgotten pet. She found a vending machine and put in some change to get a bag of potato chips and absently shoved the greasy chips into her face as she walked the long corridor. The floor was flecked with gray, white, and salmon-colored slashes. The walls were a soft grayish-white. It smelled like mothballs and disinfectant. It made her think of sharp needles and rigid protocols.

She tilted her head up and looked at the ceiling. This place was so calm and efficient as wars were being waged in so many rooms. Cells were mutating, bones were struggling to mend, immune systems were being ravaged while medicine was administered to alleviate the suffering of the afflicted. It should seem more dramatic. Violins should be playing.

To her right, a wall of glass revealed a courtyard and part of an adjoining building. A walkway down one side led off to another parking lot. She knew it was cold outside, but the sun had come out, and the space looked inviting. The grass was a deep green flanked by bunches of boxwood. Potted plants were interspersed between pillars and benches. Some people in scrubs sat laughing and eating lunch out of Styrofoam containers. Andre wondered when the form-fitting uniforms and prim little white caps from the first half of the century had been replaced with these pajamas. A dour-looking man appeared in the courtyard, rolling an old woman in a wheelchair with a pink knitted blanket on her lap.

Andre stood rooted to the spot. The sunlight warmed her, and she did not want to move. She wanted to freeze time and not go any farther into the future. Better to stay static in this moment forever.

I spring up, spitting out a stream of water. Then I gasp for air I've never needed so badly. I hunch over the ledge and rub my eyes. When I pull my fingers back from my face, I stare at them.

"It happens when your skin is in the water for a long time." An echo trails behind Grace's voice. "Don't worry. It looks like wilted fruit now, but it will go back to normal." She is several feet away at the edge of one of the fish pools. She lays on her side with her head propped up on her elbow, reading a book. Her body goes on forever like a mermaid's.

"Does it happen to you?"

"Only if I'm immersed for a whole day. *You* were only down there for an hour." Grace turns another page of her book.

I stretch my arms and wings, making droplets on the surface of the pool. Then I hug myself, soggy to my core. I panic, my eyes dart around before I even know what I'm looking for. I leap out of the pool.

The monarch appears from the back of a stalactite. There is an eagerness in the way it flutters to me, alighting first on my forehead then moving to each shoulder before settling on my wrist.

"Have they come?"

"Yes. You just missed them. They will come again, likely soon. They are upset, as is to be expected. And we must tell them again what they already know—that there is nothing we can do."

After I'm dried off, Grace points to a plate with a sandwich and a bottle of juice. I eat and drink greedily, wiping my mouth with the back of my hand. "Do you know . . . when?"

Grace stands, removes her robe, and steps into one of the pools. "No, but soon."

My eyes sting. "Ryan feared me, I think. I saw him looking at me, sometimes. He was afraid I would hurt her." The words come fast and wobble in my mouth. "But he was kind. Once, when they weren't home, he set out honey for me." *And I recall his touch, his smell, his love for me—no, not for me. For her. For Andre.* "I do not know the other one. He was at the house when my arm was hurt . . . Ben loves him, though." I finished eating and look up in desperation. "I need more food."

She shrugs. "Help yourself to anything in the kitchen." She looks at me, and I wonder if I'm seeing mockery in her eyes. There is something. Scorn? Pity? I feel like the walls of this cave are shrinking and going to close in on me. I see that I am adapting, but something feels wrong. My wings hurt where they meet on my back. My skin hurts. My mind is confused and filled with sorrow.

After I eat, I am restless. I'm tired of being at Grace's. I want my shed. I want my own glamour and my own space for this uneasy time I'm having.

I breathe heavily, the way *they* do when they are winded. Resisting gravity is harder now. It takes me longer to reach the house than it should. I hesitate when I approach the fence and peer through the cracks. Ben and Amy sit on the back deck, their feet resting on the grass below. They look sad and tired. Ben opens a pack of cigarettes, puts one in his mouth, and offers one to Amy. They sit smoking together in silence.

Finally, Ben speaks. "Maybe we should have demanded to talk to her." He is grinding his teeth.

Amy blows out a long, gray cloud of smoke. "I hate it, but I think Grace was telling the truth." She flicks ash. "It's so fucked up. This? This as the tithe?" She shakes her head. "What a vile way to go about it. You know what? *Fuck* them. Fuck them, sending Shae to our world. And fuck Shae."

Ben squints and smokes. He might have grunted something in response, but I can't hear it. Amy, however, has one of those naturally loud voices. She takes a deep drag of the cigarette.

After a moment, he says, "She's leaving."

I press the side of my face harder against the fence, my ear to the crack. I am having a hard time hearing him. I wonder if all the time underwater has done something to my ears.

"What? No. What do you mean?" Amy asks.

"Something happened the night of Christmas Eve when she slept." He points to his temple. "She thinks she is going to be allowed to go back to where she came from. I guess they're going to send another lightning ball for her."

"You're just now telling me this?"

He sneezed twice. "Since you guys got home, we've been mostly at the hospital. Sorry." He makes a sound in his throat, sucks in air, and spits across the yard. "Don't give me any crap, please. The past six months have been a total mind fuck."

Amy stubs out her cigarette and pulls him into a hug. She says something else, but it is lost in a sudden breeze. She gets up and goes into the house. After several minutes of him staring at his feet, Ben gets up and goes inside too.

I am not welcome anymore.

I don't want to risk them seeing me go in. I resolve to wait until dark. I slump down on the cold, damp grass and lean my back against the fence. I gaze up at the sky until the gloaming coats the world, and I shiver from the cold. Finally, I rise and creep clumsily over the fence and slip into my shed. I try to spin glamour to give the little box light and charm, comfort, and depth. Nothing happens. I squeeze my mind, grunting with the effort. At one point, I feel a faint hum that normally preceded my pulling the glamour into place, but it dissipates before I can gain any traction. I try again to no avail and cry out as a sharp pain blooms between my eyes. I gasp and look around. It is dark, dank, and cold. And I can't change any of it.

I don't want to go back to Grace's. I don't want to go inside and risk seeing Ben and Amy. They hate what I have done. *I* hate what I have done. The stinging in my eyes becomes worse, and my face starts shuddering and becomes wet. Huddled in one of the corners of the shed, I hum one of his songs and stroke the monarch's wings in the darkness.

CHAPTER TWENTY-EIGHT

Andre was not at the hospital when the tithe was finally paid. She was home in bed, sleeping well for the first time in days. There were no dreams, just hours of lovely, dark oblivion.

"Andromeda."

She opened her eyes. Sunlight leaked through the vertical crack at the bottom of the window where the edge of the curtain didn't quite cover it. She felt weightless and warm as if she was floating in a bath. Her mind buzzed with an effervescent, buoyant relief. And she knew, right away, because Amy had said her full name and there had been a hitch in her voice.

Andre sat up, rubbed her eyes, and looked at her sister. Amy moved to hug her, but Andre shrugged her off. Then Andre took a deep breath and sighed the longest sigh of her life. "When?" she asked softly.

"A few minutes ago. Seth just called. And—and Mateo too, about an hour ago. I was going to wake you then, but . . ."

Andre threw off the blankets and stretched her arms over her head. She had slept *so* well. She felt like a seedling who'd been in the moist, dark earth and was now germinating, disoriented and shocked by sunlight.

When she tried to stand, her legs were wavering stems, which she wasn't steady on for a moment. She dropped to her knees. Despite being weak, she was hyper-alert—felt like she could crawl on the ceiling. She grasped ahold of the dresser and stood shakily, blinking at her reflection in the mirror above it: black and white hair spilling around sharp features and gold-flecked eyes. She'd grown gaunt, but not in the sickly way that Ben had.

She gasped. A massive weight had been lifted, and beneath it was a fourth-degree burn—a molten anguish she could not yet feel. She turned to Amy. "What am I supposed to do now?"

Amy draped her arm over Andre's shoulders and steered her out to the hallway and into the bathroom. "Take a shower and get dressed."

After a shower that she did not feel or recall taking, Andre went downstairs and found Ben with his head down on the kitchen table. She spoke his name. His face was beet-red and slimy when he looked up at her. He started to say something, but shook his head and put it back down. Andre wondered at his raw emotion. Her own feelings were far away and shrink-wrapped.

Amy led her to the car. Ben drove, and Amy sat in front. "We're meeting Seth at his parents' house," Amy told her when Andre asked where they were going. There had been no inquiry as to Andre's comfort. Amy hadn't asked her if she wanted to sit shotgun.

Ben's shirt was on inside out, Andre saw. His eyelids were swollen from crying. Amy snapped at him when he almost pulled into on-coming traffic, and once again, when he broke hard for no apparent reason. His hands were shaking.

"I should have driven," Amy muttered. "My bad."

The house was quiet when they arrived. It was a bright, crisp day in January—the first week of a new year. Everything looked normal. There was no pall of dreariness, nothing to indicate the massive sorrow that should have been emanating from the front door. It might've been some time in the morning, or perhaps it was afternoon. Andre didn't know. She didn't want to know very much, just then. She took a deep breath and stumbled a little. A ginger cat was on the porch, and it scampered away as they walked up the driveway.

A very pale Seth opened the door. "Andre." He said her name tenderly as if he hadn't remembered her until that moment but was pleased to see her. He reached a hand up to the side of her face. "Thank you. He . . ." But he didn't say anything else. Instead, he hugged her. For a dangerous second, she felt her bubble dissolving, but when she pulled away from him, she secured it back in place. They followed him into the house, which was clean, if not as fresh and well-aired as it had been the times she'd visited these people (who would never be her in-laws) before. It had barely been occupied the last week and a half, but the living room window was open now, allowing in cool air and sunlight. The four of them looked at one another, unsure whether they should sit or stand. "My aunt and cousins are on their way." He nodded down the hall. "Mom's asleep. She was . . . there." He ran a hand through his dirty hair. "Dad's at the morgue."

Andre flinched.

"I was going to go with him," he continued in a quiet voice. "But he wants me to stay with her." He shrugged. "It's pointless, though. She was up all night, and I'm pretty sure they gave her something strong. She's going to be out for hours."

Amy made a reply to this, but Andre didn't catch it as she wandered into the kitchen and looked out the window. She could see the side of the neighbor's house and through their window into their living room. A woman in a blue workout suit was pacing back and forth, talking on her cell phone. Something the person on the other end of the phone said made her laugh. It was strange how these big houses were so close together. It would have been difficult having Shae if they'd lived in one of these neighborhoods.

Shae. She had to find her. Andre couldn't feel her at all right now. She was completely sealed off. It was making her angry. They needed to connect. They needed to address this situation and fix it. Something could be worked out. Andre was certain of it, and just about now, she was ready for the twist in the story. There had to be one. She hugged herself and stepped away from the window as a cold voice in her mind began to whisper otherwise. She started to hyperventilate.

"I need to talk to her. Where is she?"

Amy, Ben, and Seth turned towards Andre as she came back to the living room. She saw their grim faces; she saw the dark green couch, a newspaper in a thin blue plastic bag unopened on the coffee table, the remote control, the lamp sitting on the end table—these things grounded her, threatened her. They were like frigid water leaking through cracks in her mind, attempting to pull her into the present and engulf her in icy pain.

"Mom's deep asleep," Seth said, frowning. "I don't want to wake her."

"I'm not talking about Candace!" Andre cried, grasping her head in her hands. "I need to find Shae!"

"Who?" His brow crinkled.

Amy stalked over and grabbed Andre by the shoulders and led her back towards the kitchen. Andre tried to slip out from beneath, but Amy towered over her and dug her fingers in. Andre looked up at that beautiful, infinitely familiar face and felt a flicker of terror. Amy was going to drag Andre over to the freezing water and throw her in. "She can't do anything, Andre. She couldn't help them. He's gone." And then the worst thing happened: Amy started to cry.

A moth appeared between them. It tickled Andre's face, and she whipped her head back and forth. "No, no, no. I know she can do something. This isn't it. They aren't —he can't be . . . no." She was vaguely aware of Ben and Seth speaking in the living room.

"Andre." Amy's voice was thick. She kept her grip on one of Andre's shoulders with one hand and wiped her eyes with her other. "We've spoken to Grace about it. This is the tithe. You know this."

She shuddered at the word 'tithe' but then looked up with a crazed smile. "Grace? You know about Grace? You've met her? Don't you love her house! The downstairs . . . the pools and the cavern. Did you see the cavern?"

"Yes, Andre. I saw the cavern."

"I haven't met her family. I think Shae has. That's probably where's she's been all this time." Andre was speaking quickly. She had to keep talking. Her words were her feet running over hot coals. "Isn't it neat? There are more of them! It changes things. It means there are more living in other places we don't know about." She dipped out of Amy's grasp. "I wanted to tell you about her so badly when we were in Virginia . . ." She was running out of words. "But Grace didn't want us to. She explained some things. She . . ." Andre slipped back into the living room, sat on the couch, and started rocking back and forth. Amy stood above her, arms crossed. She looked about to say something when Andre snapped, "Don't! Please, just— *don't.*"

Amy studied her and then glanced toward the kitchen where Ben and Seth had switched places with them and were now drinking beers. She dropped to her knees, so she was eye level with Andre. "You need to be careful," she whispered. "Seth's going through enough. You've always been cautious. I know it's hard, but don't mention Shae or Grace again, okay? Not right now." Amy wiped her eyes, stood back up, and went into the kitchen.

Andre brought her fist to her mouth and bit the dry skin on her knuckles until she felt it tear and heard it sing with a sting. The pain was a flimsy anchor, but it kept her from being swept away. Amy returned with a glass of water and a pill.

Andre drank, not realizing she was thirsty until that moment. And then she thought about how easy it was to drink, how the water just slid down her throat as she effortlessly gulped. *They'd had to give them fluids through an IV. Mateo—brain swollen and terrified—had gotten violent, almost hit a doctor when they'd attempted to give him a cup of water. He'd suffered from the more lurid symptoms: violent hallucinations, hours of an unceasing erection, and relentless ejaculations. They'd put him in restraints.* She closed her eyes and forced herself to breathe. "Why are we here?"

"You know why. This is what people do. They stay with the family."

Andre leaned over and pressed her nose into the silky and surprisingly aromatic fabric, wanting to burrow into the sofa.

Ben and Seth came back into the room with their beers. "What should I do, you guys?" Amy asked. "Want me to turn on the television? Just for some background noise?"

Seth shook his head, tiredly. "I don't care. Sure."

Amy grabbed the remote, turned it on, and something freakishly ill-timed and surreal happened; a reporter appeared on the screen standing in front of the hospital that had become familiar to them all over the last week. "—hour apart just this morning." The coiffed, dark-haired woman in a pantsuit said, "Sources say these are the first deaths from rabies in Arroyo and in all of Alcosta County in over fifty-three years and the first deaths reported in the entire U.S. in almost two years. Officials say the two young men, whose names have not been released, were allegedly bitten by a bat approximately four months ago during a camping trip at—"

"Fuck!" Amy turned off the television and put her hand over her mouth. "Sorry, you guys."

Seth went completely still. His face was white. "It's on the *news*?" His voice cracked. "Oh, god. My parents don't need this shit yet." He slammed his beer down on the coffee table so hard it spilled on its side. He didn't right it. He grasped his head between his hands and started weeping.

"I need to find Shae," Andre whispered. She strained her mind along that string, connecting her with the faerie. She followed it for a bit, and then it snipped off on her. Trembling, she reached for the glass of water and knocked it onto the floor. Hypnotized, she watched the liquid soak into the carpet. *I need to find her. I need to find her. I need to find her. This can't be it. This can't be the tithe. She will make it right.*

CHAPTER TWENTY-NINE

The pills softened the edges of it all. They made her foggy and detached, but a film reel of certain images played over and over in Andre's mind: The expression on his dad's face as they lowered the casket, the light breeze ruffling the clothes of dark-clad mourners on a green field of the local cemetery. At one point, Andre had looked around and felt so much like a character in a movie that she had the burning, obscene urge to giggle. She stifled it by biting the insides of her cheeks.

Back at the Carpenter house, crowds of people milled about the living room, dining room, and kitchen. They ate finger foods and sipped tea or beer. They spoke in murmurs, dabbed their eyes, and shook their heads. His mother clutched the ginger cat and stroked it aggressively with her thin, old-looking fingers. Andre envisioned her snapping its neck. The family she'd met at Thanksgiving hugged her and said nice, sad things that she'd managed to nod at and mumble responses to. Ryan's co-workers introduced themselves and murmured kind words. Andre mostly clung to her group: Amy, Ben, Erik, Merri, Ricardo, Genevieve, and Raf, but even with them, she was adrift at sea. Small things drew her attention away: the filigree on the edge of a lacy table cloth, the way light through the kitchen window hit a crystal magnet on the refrigerator, and spilled fractal rainbows over a section of tiles. She worried at the emerald pendant and rubbed it against her lips.

Mateo's funeral, the next day, was a slightly louder, more maudlin affair. His fiancé wept noisily. Ben played a favorite song they'd written together in junior high. There was a drunken gathering at the Waters' afterward. Hordes of people came over; some Andre hadn't seen since high school. She hid in her room with a jar of honey, covering her ears as a loud bass pulsed through the house.

Days blended into one another. Andre slept a great deal. When she was awake, the whole world smelled bad. She sensed, rather than experienced, the pop of media sensation that the story caused, but it still leaked into her like poison. Amy had to shoo journalists away from the house once or twice. Andre ignored the unfamiliar numbers that called her phone. It was an exciting piece of news and was contorted into a deliciously macabre object lesson. There were several articles about it online, and she made the mistake of skimming one and then drifting down to the comment section. It was flooded with savage jokes and clever observations from strangers who had the advantage of hindsight but lacked the full context of the story. They spouted their wisdom and wit:

Dumb millennials probably deserved it!

What kind of idiot doesn't know a bite from a wild animal should be followed by a rabies vaccine?

Darwinism in action!

Andre imagined them sitting smug and virus-free behind their screens. Squat and wart-covered trolls. She wished the worst upon them. It was then that Andre stopped feeling any tenderness towards her species.

Sometimes she couldn't feel anything but sensual pleasures—silky fabrics, the taste of honey on her tongue, the shiny glitter on an old poster in her room. Her mind split and ran in two veins. In one of them, she only had room for a drowsy appreciation of aesthetic beauty and a deep longing for *elsewhere*. And then other times she was old Andre again. And that was when she suffered most. The bubble trembled and threatened to pop as that tenacious hope for a twist (that even burials weren't entirely able to squash) began to dissolve.

And then it was February. Andre looked at the calendar and remembered that they were supposed to have gone to Europe. And the numbness dissolved. Ryan was never going to hold her again; he was never going to whistle while he got ready for work, never going to complain about his boss or frown in that certain way while he worked on a problem. Mateo was never going to be a music teacher, marry that girl, or goof off with Ben and tease her like a brother. Andre screamed and sobbed and twisted in her bedclothes in a belated frenzy of grief and rage. There was nothing to project her anger towards except an elusive court of beings in another dimension, and Shae, who was still hiding. Amy said Grace was protecting her from them.

She developed hives and clawed at her skin. She took long baths to ease the pain in her back. She sat in the hallway and listened to the music Ben played in his room. By silent mutual agreement, they'd barely spoken since the tithe had made itself known and scarcely at all since it had been paid. They were home together often now since he'd been fired from Cedric's Bar and Grille. The Chestnut was waiting patiently for when and if she wanted to return. Her pristine room went to hell. Piles of paper and books she no longer read, dirty clothes, used glasses, and half-empty, sticky bottles of honey were everywhere. Fruit flies—lazy but relentless—buzzed around her nightstand and dresser. She didn't care. She wasn't staying here. She was like a thoughtless guest trashing a hotel room.

One day it spun out of control.

She lay in bed, drunk on the nice wine Amy had started keeping in the house. Her phone rang. *Seth.* She didn't answer but listened to the voicemail a couple of minutes later. "Hey, Andre. Just calling to see how you're doing." *He sounded so much like him.* "You know you can call if you need anything. I hope you're hanging in there. Mom and Dad started grief counseling. I don't know what your insurance is like, but they wanted me to let you know they'll pay for you to see someone too if you think it would help."

Such nice people. And I killed their son.

She sat up, suddenly thinking of the little pills. She'd stopped taking them a few days after the funerals. There must still be some around. She searched the medicine cabinets in the bathroom, the pantry in the kitchen, and finally located the little bottle on top of Amy's dresser. Small wonder it was still pretty full. She popped a few of them and then poured herself another glass of wine.

Her phone buzzed again—her mother. Lydia didn't leave a message this time, but she'd already left several fretful pleas for Andre to call her, and emphatic reassurances that she was being prayed for. Amy was launching a desperate campaign to stop her from flying out to be with them.

Andre put the phone down, sighing. She turned on loud music and paced around her room. She finished her wine. She looked at the phone again and saw the battery was low. She went to grab one of the chargers they kept in a basket in the kitchen but forgot why she'd come downstairs when she arrived. Instead, she grabbed another jar of honey and opened another bottle of wine, carrying both jar and wine bottle back upstairs.

She looked in the mirror and tore a piece of her chapped lip and watched a small pearl of blood form. She licked it off and stared into her golden eyes. She paced more. The lines in her back wracked her with a strange pleasure-pain. She went into the bathroom to get the medicine the doctors had prescribed for it. Nice warm opiates. She took four.

When she went back into her room, her eyes landed on the objects on her nightstand: the picture of her and Ryan in the redwoods next to the one of her and Amy when they were little. Beside that was a mug holding pens and pencils. It read, "Darryville Aquarium" in a watery font bordered by silhouettes of dolphins, starfish, and seahorses. Andre picked it up and dumped the pens onto the floor. The mug made a satisfying sound—dramatic and glittery—when she hurled it through the window. The indulgence made her shiver. She stepped over to the window, her heart pounding. Cool night wind blew into her room through the shattered glass. When had it become nighttime? Shards gleamed on the floor by her feet. She bent down and picked one up, wondering if she would be able to find her jugular vein and how much it would hurt if she were to open it with the shard. She sat down on the bed, squeezing her fist so the glass bit into her palm. She squeezed tighter and tighter until it made a counter-balance to the pain in her back. Gritting her teeth, Andre dragged the shard down her hand feeling hot, sticky blood coat her skin.

Out of somewhere, Andre got a different idea and tossed the shard down. She went to the bathroom and washed and dried her hands, bloodying the towels. She opened the cabinet above the sink and closed it, frustrated. She didn't find what she was looking for, but she took a couple more pills. She was dimly aware that she should probably wrap up her hand, but she was busy looking for something. She moved to the hall closet, rummaging carelessly, streaking the clean linens with her blood. She ransacked the kitchen, searching, she took a couple more Xanax. She drank another half a jar of honey. She drank more wine. The sharp red and the sweet gold swirled in her mouth and down her throat. She clutched the bottle to her as she wandered around and finally found what she was looking for in Ben's room: scissors.

Why was it windy? Her head was being compressed. It was about to pop like a squished grape. It hurt to breathe. She tried to sit up. Daytime? Andre hadn't wanted to see daytime again. The room didn't so much spin as cause her to feel completely disembodied. Andre dropped her head and crawled to the edge of the bed to release bloody-looking vomit. She'd swallowed a poisonous sea monster. There was acid in her nostrils, and she felt like she'd been hit by a truck. She had no thoughts except the brain-stem demand for unconsciousness. Sleep called to her like a siren song, but some deep flicker of self-preservation was keeping her from passing out again. She tried to open her eyes, and daylight sent spikes into her skull. And then there were noises, voices, footsteps. The sound of her door handle opening plucked at her eardrums.

"Andre? Oh god, what the—"

She heaved over the side of her bed as more wine and honey erupted from her. She sagged, half off the bed, becoming aware of a pain in her right hand. It was too cold. She opened one eye and saw the curtains waving. It all went dark again.

"Do you think we should take her to the hospital?"

Andre groaned. *No more hospitals.*

"Nah." Amy sounded entirely too upbeat. She shook her roughly by the shoulders. "How many pills did you take? Any idea? C'mon, sit up." Andre opened her eyes and grasped the glass of water held before her with a shaking hand. She tried to mumble words but could only make a choked whimper. The water was pure and cool. She felt like she was defiling it with her noxious mouth.

Amy wrinkled her nose. "Did you break that window?"

Andre closed her eyes, lay back down, and groaned.

"Who else would have?" asked Ben.

"I know, I know. Just felt like I needed to ask. It's not exactly typical behavior for her." There was a pause. They murmured something she didn't catch. "She does look cool this way, though, doesn't she? But she's changing, you know? I mean, I know I'm not the only one who sees a freaking resemblance, right? And that's not *gray* hair. So weird. Not sure how I feel about it, you know? She's supposed to be *my* twin."

Andre wasn't sure she wanted to know what they were talking about, and asking was too much work. Being alive was too much work. She just wanted to be a little piece of light or color. Something small and lovely that had no feelings. She drifted away again, just hearing snatches.

"—Didn't recognize her." Ben sounded upset.

"—Probably took some of those Xanax too. I found the bottle on the counter."

"—Might need stitches."

The ache in her hand was becoming something bright and throbbing.

"—I don't know what time."

"—Left in the bathroom."

"—I shouldn't have stayed out last night. Went over to Merri's because—."

"—Must say, it doesn't look bad."

Andre forced her eyes open. "What are you talking about?" She moved her head. There was air on her face and neck.

Amy and Ben exchanged uneasy looks, but Amy seemed almost amused. "Do you remember what you did last night?" she asked.

Andre shook her head. The movement made her dizzy. She whimpered and touched the side of her face. She vaguely recalled throwing the mug through the window, but beyond that was a blur. "I don't . . ." She rubbed her eyes.

"Alright then, let's show you." Amy stood up. "I'll be right back." She slipped out of the room.

Ben leaned against the wall, avoiding her eyes. "Ben?" She said his name softly, hesitantly. He wouldn't look at her. "Ben?" She reached for him. She needed him just then. They'd been moving around one another with the familiar but distant ease of planets. She needed him to look at her. No one understood, but he did more than anyone else.

His voice was even and cold. "Did you try to kill yourself? Are you going to? Can you give me a heads up so at least this time it won't be a shock?"

Had she tried to kill herself? She waited a moment to reply. She wanted to be sure she told him the truth. She looked at the ceiling, and her eyes filled with tears. Finally, she whispered, "No, Ben. I wouldn't do that. I'm just . . . *very* sad."

Amy came back into the room, clutching a handled mirror. She was smiling, which slightly reassured Andre that she hadn't mutilated herself. "Check it out!"

Andre was starkly relieved to see her miserable self with pixie short, almost entirely white, hair. "I remember now," she lied.

"I love it!" Amy cried. "You did a pretty decent job considering you were three sheets to the wind."

Ben looked at her with vague disgust, then pushed off the wall and left the room. She didn't want him to go, but she hoped if he was going to his room that at least he'd play his music. Amy sat down on the bed, crossed her arms, and looked at Andre with an odd little smirk. Her sister was just too healthy and pretty. She clashed with the room. Andre preferred sickly, tortured Ben. She cleared her throat. "Leave me alone."

"Oh no, actually I can't do that," Amy said, growing serious. "Let's see." She held up her hand and ticked the reasons off her fingers. "You broke a window, sliced your hand open, almost overdosed, you've probably got alcohol poisoning, and you chopped all your hair off. You're not allowed to be alone anymore." She drew closer to Andre and squinted. "Also, I'm *pretty* sure you're turning into a faerie. And they're not the most trustworthy of creatures." She shook her head and sighed. "What am I going to do with you and Ben?"

When she woke again, it was dark once more, and she was alone, but she could hear Amy and Ben murmuring in the hallway. They were sitting just outside her room. He strummed depressing, lovely snatches of songs, and Amy sang along. She laughed and said, "You should read what they're saying about it too. This is so exciting, Ben!"

Andre sat up and turned on the lamp on her nightstand. Someone had cleaned the floor next to her and put towels down. The shattered glass was gone, and a thin towel was taped over the opening of the window, blocking out the worst of the wind. Cold air was still leaking in, but for some reason, she wasn't shivering. Hopefully, it wouldn't rain. She shuffled the pillows around, relieved she hadn't thrown up on his, and crawled out of bed.

Her head felt like a balloon, her mouth tasted horrible, her hand ached, a block of fermenting honey sat like a chunk of amber in her gut, and there were two fiery, sore lines in the middle of her back. They had taken on a rhythmic pulsing of pain. Still, Andre felt worlds better than she had when she'd woken up violently ill some hours before. She walked, wobbly, towards the door and opened it. Amy turned to her and smiled. "Look, it's alive!"

Andre stepped over them and went into the bathroom. She peed forever, then brushed her teeth, rinsed her mouth out, and washed her face. The water stung her hand, but she was surprised to see the wound had mostly closed. She looked over and saw a huge swath of black and white hair lying in the waste-basket like a dead skunk. When she opened the door to the hallway, Amy was squealing and looking at her phone. "Oh my god! Guess how many views now?" she said to Ben. "Just guess!"

"Please stop," he said miserably.

"Hey, Andre. Someone made a video to one of his songs. It's going viral; you gotta see this!"

Ignoring her, Andre stepped back over them and into her room and slammed the door closed. She lay in bed, nestled with two extra blankets and four pillows. No matter how she placed them, no matter how she twisted and turned, she could not replicate a warm body. She hugged Ryan's pillow and breathed in deeply. His scent was already fading. Old Andre's mind took the reins, and she soaked the pillow, sobbing herself back to sleep.

Deep in the night, there was a tapping on her door. She sat up. It wouldn't be Amy. Amy wouldn't knock. "Yeah?" she called. "Come in."

The door opened. There was a silhouette—familiar—but *so* much bigger. The huge butterfly sat on her shoulder.

"*There* you are," Andre whispered with venom.

Shae hesitated in the doorway, then finally stepped inside and closed it behind her. A long, dark minute passed. "I couldn't help him."

Andre put her hand against her suddenly hammering heart. "Okay." She nodded. "Okay, okay . . . There isn't any way to find him? To send a message or something?" Her voice cracked, and her eyes brimmed again, instantly.

"No."

Andre let out a small gasp as a last tiny thread of hope; she hadn't known was still there, snapped like a slender nerve being severed. She couldn't speak again for a minute. "It hurts," she said finally, her throat tight.

"I did not know who. I did not decide . . ." There was something new in Shae's voice now: a dense, prosaic tenor. It had lost the shimmery notes of *elsewhere*.

Andre squinted up at her. "I hate your fucking guts, and I wish you had never come."

Shae took a step closer to her. "Then, my changeling, turn on the light and look at this. Perhaps my pain will please you."

Andre turned on the lamp and blinked, waiting for her eyes to adjust. The monarch fluttered off Shae's shoulder and landed on the cluttered dresser. *Was it moving sluggishly?* Shae pulled her dress off over her head. She wore no underclothes. She was just a naked young woman now. And when she turned around, there were no wings— just two weeping red wounds between her shoulder blades.

CHAPTER THIRTY

Ben stepped out onto the deck, shut the door behind him, and lit a cigarette. Andre glanced at him over her shoulder. "Do you want me to go somewhere else? Or put this out?"

How much of her is even in there, right now? It fluctuated, but less and less. They no longer knew what went on in her head. She was so quiet, but her grief seemed to have been eclipsed by something else. And she had changed irrevocably. Her eyes were enormous and gold. Her short hair was opalescent and growing much faster than it should have been. She was impossibly tiny. She looked like Shae. Or, like Shae used to look. Shae no longer looked like herself. The last time Ben had seen her, the night before last, Shae had looked like a very sick human.

She shrugged. "The world smells bad, no matter what." She sounded more like herself, though, when she said it—a good sign. A few tense minutes passed, and then tired ease. "You want to do something?" she asked, finally turning around to look up at him again.

He smiled sadly, seeing it was old Andre just then. "Sure. Maybe. What did you have in mind?"

"I've been thinking about . . . I think I need to go to the Shellara . . . to where we were. I have a pull to go there."

He went still. They hadn't been there since the camping night, but the weather was getting warmer, slowly. It was the first week of March. The rain had eased up, and the days were lengthening.

"Or—you don't have to do that. I could just go by myself—"

"No. It's fine." He took a drag and rubbed his forehead with the back of his hand. "What about your back? Do you think you're up for a hike?"

She shrugged. "I go to the woods all the time lately. And the pain comes and goes no matter what I do."

He looked out over the yard, his eyes lingering on the place Hammer was buried. "Okay, sure."

Ben drove while Andre sat quietly looking out the window. Her legs were drawn up, and her arms laced around them. They turned onto Foothill and went up the windy road toward the camping area. His song reached a final climax of three striking chords. When it ended, she said, "It's a whole album, huh? More than an album. Like two?" Another song started—melancholy and silvery.

"Yeah, well, the one I'm working on now is kind of a remake of an old Shepherd's Wake tune, but it fits in somehow. There's an order. It's kind of a narrative."

He parked, grabbed the water bottle, and locked the car. They set off down the trail to the right. Andre's movements were supple, her feet almost bouncing off the ground with just the smallest beat of too much time between her steps. It was hard to look at her. And hard not to.

They didn't have much to say to each other. They were each getting their fondest wish—bitter-tasting gifts served alongside the tithe. Ben felt himself hurtling toward a horizon with blinding lights and noise and crowds. The thought of the future was more daunting than thrilling. He'd spent his teenage years fantasizing about being a rock star, but he would rather be able to walk his dog and hang out with Mateo and have Andre stay Andre and for her to have Ryan back.

He could play the music he'd been gifted anywhere. So long as there was someone to hear it. It would have been satisfying playing on a street corner surrounded by pigeons where appreciative listeners tossed change at him. Or even better, to be in a band and have friends, and be able to make ends meet from touring, it would have been enough—would have been a great life. He didn't need any more than that. It was already getting out of his hands. He was credited, but people were spinning their own covers. New videos were sprouting up every day. It sickened him to think his songs would end up as muzak playing in grocery stores. The initial reviews were embarrassingly effusive, and a phone interview terribly awkward and invasive. He felt a need to quash the part of him that savored the idolatry. The guilt festered.

The night of his twenty-fifth birthday had been spent in a quiet bar with Amy and Merri. They tried to play poker, but he couldn't focus as he quickly became too drunk to see straight. Amy got annoyed with him. "Ben, you're an alcoholic rock musician. Don't be an idiotic cliché and die in two years." He glared at her. "And don't take yourself so seriously either, geesh."

"Are you a household name yet?" Andre asked softly.

"I don't think so. Not quite. I imagine I will be soon." He did not say it happily. "You do know it's more like I found the songs, or, like they entered me, right? I don't feel like I wrote them."

Andre smiled. "Yeah, so you were enchanted. Doesn't mean you can't take some credit for being a worthy conduit."

He looked at her sidelong. "*Enchanted.* Nice way to put it."

Andre made a little trilling sound, and a finch landed on her arm. He stared at her. At whatever she was now. Less and less a person every day. Not quite Andre. Not quite Shae, though. A small being with little interest in anyone. And then sometimes, like this lucky afternoon, he could see her there, hiding in her own eyes. He could hear her in her voice. His throat got tight, and he swallowed painfully. He missed her. And *Mateo.* It was an open wound that he tried not to touch any more than he had to. He tried to tell himself that wherever his friend was, he wasn't hurting, but that was so little solace. He'd rather him alive and enjoying life, or just enduring it as Ben was.

He wanted to believe Merri and Amy when they told him there was nothing he could have done, but he couldn't shake the feeling that there had been a way to thwart the tithe, and he'd missed it. He had gone over to see Mateo's mom only once. She was sick with grief, and it was too excruciating to be around. He told himself that whatever wealth he obtained from his gift, he would make sure she was taken care of. And what else could he do but keep breathing and loathe his good fortune?

The path was still moist from the rain, and the sides of his shoes got muddy. They hiked until they reached the pebbly shore near the water. A small lizard skittered up as Andre sat down. They finished the water in a few minutes, and he felt thirsty. He wished they'd brought another bottle. That was the sort of thing old Andre would have thought of.

He looked out and thought of the day he'd come with Shae. He could almost see her in the water—a pointy-eared nymph dipping in and out of the sun-spangled lake. She came to his room sometimes at night and knocked on his door and cried silently when he wouldn't let her in. He knew this because when he'd opened the door to use the bathroom, on two occasions, she'd been sitting outside his door weeping. He gave her a pillow and a blanket, but he wouldn't let her in. She had developed a fetid odor only Andre seemed to be able to tolerate, which was odd to him as she complained lately that the world smelled bad.

After a few quiet minutes, they stood once more and walked a little further along the trail till they reached the little sandy half C of shore that hugged the edge of the lake—the place where they'd had such a great time before Merri had been attacked. Andre looked out, shielding her eyes with her hand, and then she stood up suddenly.

"Ha!" she cried, and darted over to a tree and plucked something from among the grass and leaves next to a rock.

Ben stared. Then he laughed. "Is that Merri's ring? No way! That's unbelievable. It was just right there? How did you see it?"

"Here." She held the ring out to him, ignoring the question. "You give it to her. It should be you."

He put it in his pocket, thinking of how surprised Merri would be. "Thanks." He smiled. He was going to see her that evening after she got off work. Things had changed. The week before, he'd been at a particularly low point and found himself sobbing once again in her sunflower bedroom. She'd rubbed his spiny back, murmuring for an hour—over and over—that it wasn't his fault until he fell back to sleep like a child. When he woke up again, he was alone for a few seconds before she opened the door carrying a tray with a plate of pancakes and bacon that smelled wonderful and gleamed under the afternoon sunlight. Her scar tilted vertically when she smiled at him, and two things happened at once: his appetite—although it would never be a big or healthy one—returned, and he started to fall in love with her. She had been in the background of the last several months, but he finally saw her for what she was—someone he wanted to be around. She was a comfortable and kind girl who understood what had happened to him and who was sweet and familiar in his increasingly lonely world.

"We could go by the Chestnut," Andre said. "She's probably working right now. And—and maybe I should talk to them about starting to pick up hours again?" She looked at him, questioning.

"Uh . . . about that."

She threw a rock, and it skipped three times over the water. She smiled. "I can't. I look too weird now, don't I?"

"No. Well, yes, you do—but it's not just that. The uh, the store's going out of business next month. They didn't want to lay that on you with everything else that's happened."

"What?" She whirled around to look at him, her smile fading.

"Yeah. I guess there's like another Whole Foods opening up down the road? It could be a problem, but Merri says it's really that Vivian just wants to get into something else. I think she's renewing her real estate license."

"So . . . I don't even have a job anymore?" Andre shook her head.

On the way home, Andre thought about the Chestnut. *All those remedies.* All those capsules, vitamins, and tinctures. Nothing in nature's cabinet or modern western medicine had been able to save them. Science and medicine had a ways to go when the faeries coaxed Mother Nature to let her fangs out. Then she spared a thought for the customers she'd come to know over the years. She hadn't seen any of them in months. Where would the ancient ladies get their Calcium and Magnesium? What about all those folks looking for guidance on changing their lifestyles, living with allergies, or new medical conditions? Outside of her cluster of friends, the people who came into the store were her connection to the community.

Such weak and short-lived creatures.

At the funeral, Vivian had given her a card signed by dozens of customers. Several had sent cards of their own, and a few had sent flowers. Andre had barely glanced at any of it, but she decided she would look for the card when she got home.

But she didn't.

By the time they turned back onto Foothill, she'd forgotten all about it. She gazed out the window and was consumed by the way the sun-dappled sycamore trees swished in the wind on the drive home, and her mind wandered. She thought back to her earliest memories and recalled how big the world had seemed when she was little more than a baby, how vivid and entrancing it all was just watching ants crawl on the ground and clouds drift across the sky. She remembered how she would imagine herself shrinking down, down, down, so she could swim around in a single raindrop collected in the gutters of the house in Virginia.

Then she licked her lips, thinking about the jar of honey waiting for her on the counter. *I'm like a butterfly seeking nectar. A bee. A honeybee. A Bumblebee. Bumblebee!* She gasped. Ben glanced at her warily but said nothing. She shivered and blinked and called to Shae through her mind. She wanted to sleep next to her again that night. They spoke little, but they were spending many hours together.

Andre's wrath had dissipated here and there, and she stopped hating Shae as they lay side by side underwater for twenty or thirty minutes at a time or ventured together into the woods. Shae, head tilted back, shielding her weak and watery eyes from the sun, would watch as Andre deftly climbed the trees. Shae shivered and sweated, and Andre didn't suffer from temperatures at all anymore unless her back was throbbing. Andre had spent most of the last couple of weeks either in the pools at Grace's or out in the woods with Shae. The baths made her back feel better while also aiding her shrinking, and the woods called to her. They slept next to one another every few nights.

Andre felt pity for Shae, although she was starting to lose those kinds of feelings in general. But she never would lose them entirely, and that would make her nearly-infinite life a bit more painful. It was not lost on her that she was getting the better deal. There were irritations, though. Her clothes weren't comfortable these days, and they were all too big for her anyway. Her shimmery, white hair was growing out fast. It was funny looking—dandelion puffy. Sometimes at night, she would go to the woods alone and naked. She looked for bats to kill, but she never saw any.

When they got back to the house, and Andre stepped out of the car, the pain came back—an instantaneous fire pulsing under her skin. She gritted her teeth and made a hissing sound. Her eyes filled with tears, and the corners of them went black. "Is it bad?" Ben asked quickly. She nodded and stumbled into the house, dropping to the floor on her hands and knees. She began to cry in earnest. It was the worst it had ever felt. Ben carried her up to her room. And then, that night, she got sick.

Ben didn't leave for Merri's until Amy arrived home. "I'm sorry. I've got to go. I'm not staying for this. You—you understand, right?"

Andre nodded at him.

Amy opened the bathroom door just as Andre had flushed the toilet and was sitting on it, holding her stomach. "I think . . . I have a fever."

Amy put a hand to her forehead. "Shit. You're burning up. Do you want me to get you anything?"

"No. I'm fine. Go away. You don't have to hover."

But Amy stood there looking at her, distrustful. "Andre, I know you're too weird for the hospital, but I don't care if it saves your life. Can you tell me? Would it help if you went? Could they do anything for you?" She bit her lip. "I know we're supposed to be in the clear, but it still scares me."

Between gasps, Andre said, "I don't have rabies." But she did feel like she couldn't breathe—or at least like she couldn't get enough air into her lungs.

Amy rubbed her forehead. "I'm going to be scarred for the rest of my life," she muttered. "I'm never going to be able to pet a stray cat again."

Andre made a weird sound in her throat.

"So, what's happening? Jesus, you look so weird. You're like, turning into Gollum."

"Thanks."

Amy opened and closed the cabinets. "Damn it. Where did all the medicine go? Okay, I'm going to get you some Tylenol at least to get the fever down. I think there's some downstairs. I'll be right back. Don't die, okay?" At Andre's glare, she said, "What? It would be gross. There would be a bunch of paperwork. I'd have to talk to the police and stuff, and then your room would be forever creepy."

After Andre took the pointless Tylenol, she went into her room to lie down. She tossed and turned, sleeping in fits. She called to

Shae, but there was no response. Andre woke from sparkling fever dreams, drenched. The sheets were cold with moonlight and sweat. "Okay, okay," she whispered. She looked at the time on her phone. It was four. She'd been asleep for several hours, but it didn't feel like it.

She felt bruised all over. She wished she was at Grace's. The heated pool would have helped. She could have gotten into her own bathtub, but it felt like too much work. She couldn't shake the unpleasant notion that her bone marrow was leaking into her skin and muscles. It was the contractive pain of shrinking—Grace said, having experienced a degree of it herself—the body withering, gripping inwards, and dissolving. Andre wanted nothing more than to sink back into unconsciousness.

There was a draft where the wind seeped through the fabric curtain covering the window. It was fixed, but she'd gone to bed with it open. She hugged his pillow and suddenly wished he was there to help her; to at least hold her. *I loved him once—the one I killed. No, not me. Shae.* But she couldn't always tell the difference anymore. Her loneliness was smothering until she forced herself to look out the window at the stars and think about how tiny they were. And how huge. She murmured words that were not words.

She ached for the ball lightning to come, and she craved her name.

When the pain slammed again, Andre hissed through her teeth, clamping her eyes shut. She twisted her torso so far from side to side, and her eyebrows sweated. Two sheets of fire ran in lines halfway down her upper back. She got up off the bed and began to growl in an effort not to scream. The pain that had been coming in spells for so many weeks turned into agony. It heightened and tightened and reached a crescendo.

Her knees buckled, and she cried out as her ribs stretched as far apart as they could. The skin on either side of her spine tore open, and the growths biding their time burst forth in unison. The pain was shrieking violins of unfurling tendons growing taut. Her vision blurred with tears, and her nose ran.

And then she gasped in the sweetest relief. They were like another set of lungs outside of her body, and she could finally breathe. And she thought this must be the pinnacle of all sensations in the vast spectrum of them. The air hit her new appendages, and the last discomfort evaporated and became ecstasy. They almost moved of their own accord. Her wings shivered and flapped, and she sobbed in terror and joy as flecks of blood speckled the floor around her. Her twin burst into her room and turned on the light.

And for once in her life, Amy was speechless.

CHAPTER THIRTY-ONE

A breast pump, mechanical baby swing, stroller, and an old-fashioned bassinet cluttered the tiny apartment. Towels, stuffed animals, and baby blankets coated the chairs and floor where they sat. With all of them, and with Genevieve and Raf's moms, the small apartment was thick with people. It was uncomfortably warm. A yeasty, milky scent permeated the air, and Ben felt a twinge of claustrophobia as Raf related the graphic story of the birth. After a restless night, Genevieve had gone into labor early Monday morning. She birthed her daughter at two-thirty that afternoon. The pool where Lily Esperanza had arrived had already been drained and taken away. She weighed eight pounds and 6 ounces.

"It was so hard but worth it," Raf said, cupping his hand around the tiny pink head sprouted with downy black hair.

"I think she's the one who has a right to say that," Amy said, stepping towards Genevieve, who lay on the sofa-bed, exhausted and radiant. Her curly hair was pulled back in a bun. She wore an orange and red shawl draped over one shoulder and stared at her daughter, who was avidly sucking her nipple. Amy leaned down to stroke a tiny starfish hand that gripped her mother's pinky.

"She's so cute."

"Thank you." Genevieve laughed. "Her head is still so pointy." She shifted her shoulders and kissed the little brow. "I'm so high right now. I'm so in love with her." She sighed. "Thanks for everything." She nodded towards the bag of supplies and cute little onesies they had brought as a gift. "So . . . how is Andre? I'm sorry she didn't come."

Amy kept the smile fixed on her face, but it drifted away from her eyes. *About thirty pounds and bat-shit crazy. But . . . she has some impressive party tricks up her sleeve! Quite the little acrobat.* She could feel Ben looking at her. "She's . . . you know, she's not really herself these days." The night before, Amy had gone into Andre's room and found her in the upper corner by the ceiling bobbing like a helium balloon. She was naked, save for the emerald pendant, which swung from her tiny neck like a pendulum. She'd conjured some hazy birds and butterflies that made Amy's eyes almost cross. It was weak glamour.

"She was right!" Andre cried in her lovely, weird new voice. She was beaming. "It's from right here!" She tapped the little spot between her eyes. "All I have to do is *think* it!" She pumped her wings and moved around the perimeter of the room, giggling. Amy stared at her, wanting to cry. She wanted her boring Andre back.

Genevieve made sympathetic noises and then turned back to her daughter, a smile slowly spreading over her face. Lily was like a magical creature, appearing after so much anticipation, fragile and soft.

Drunk on the overwhelming vibes, there was a collective sigh from everyone. Raf pulled out his phone and took some more pictures of Genevieve nursing. Lily sucked greedily till she fell back—milk drunk—her tiny mouth making a sucking motion and fell asleep.

Kneeling together, Shae and Andre scooped away the dirt in Grace's flower bed. The earth was moist and messy on their long fingers. Andre had the urge to bring it to her lips as if it was salted chocolate or coffee. Her ears perked up to some flux in the wind. It was like her hearing had been plied with a tuning fork. And now the sharp chirruping of birds made a weird sort of sense.

After they made a small neat hole, Shae picked up a smooth, oval-shaped stone and laid it to the side. Then, with trembling hands, she removed the monarch from the paper towel it was wrapped in and lay it in the shallow grave. Their heads tilted together, they studied it for a moment, its unfamiliar stillness, before filling the hole in with dirt. Shae laid the stone on top of it as a marker. They stood and wiped their hands on their pants, their movements synchronized, then went to a nearby stone bench, white as bone, and sat. After a few minutes, they got up and went back into Grace's house and went down the elevator to the cavern. Amy's voice carried:

"She's getting to the point . . ." Amy kicked her legs out, sending droplets flying. "I don't know what to do." She was sitting on the side of one of the pools, swishing her legs back and forth in the warm water. Alex was submerged up to his shoulders. He kept trying to tickle her feet. When Andre appeared, Amy pointed. "See? What am I supposed to do with this?"

"Changelings," said Grace, "don't stay overlapped in the same place for very long together. You know what I'm saying, right?"

"Yeah, I get it. I don't have to like it." Amy's throat got tight, and she wiped her eyes angrily. Alex tried to pull her into the water, and she tugged away from him, glaring. "I didn't know you guys were going to do this. What if it's dangerous there? And what the hell am I supposed to tell people? 'Oh, Andre just went on vacation for like, seventy years.'" She looked sharply at her twin. "What if the police think you've been murdered?"

"You won't need to worry about that," Grace said. "It should all stitch up neatly. We can glamour anyone who asks too many questions. It wouldn't take too much work for Shae to take her identity."

Amy groaned. "No. That—" she pointed at Shae, "—is not my sister. It's not going to work. And what is going to happen, exactly? A magic portal appears? A rabbit she chases down a hole? You got a special wardrobe in this big house?"

Grace shrugged. "I presume the ball lightning will come to take her."

"Whatever that means," Amy muttered. "And Shae, you don't have any advice for her when she gets there? Seriously? No berries to avoid, no hand gestures that could be interpreted as hostile?"

Shae stared blankly at her.

"It's my greatest wish," Andre said lightly.

Amy looked up angrily, but she was so glad to see in that moment that it was old Andre who had spoken. Amy hadn't seen her in days. She wanted to grab her and keep her.

Andre met her eyes, and as if understanding, she looked away sadly and sighed. "Be nice to Lydia. She's going to be . . . sad." Then she made a face. "And she's going to hate your hair." In a fit of restlessness and solidarity, Amy had shaved her head and dyed it purple. When that didn't satisfy her, she got another tattoo covering her left calf. Then she'd started sleeping with Aurora in addition to Alex. She knew she wouldn't be able to stay mad at Grace and her children. It wasn't their fault, anyway. If anything, they were trying to help. And the exorbitantly expensive, crowd-funded hospital and funeral bills had been paid for by a mysterious wealthy benefactor. Still, it seemed to Amy that by their nature, they were complicit in it all.

"I still don't understand why this is happening," Amy muttered.

"As best I understand it, Shae's task was to serve as a muse, make a changeling, and to collect the tithe. She has collected the tithe and been a muse. And for some time now she's been making a changeling. Shae came here for different reasons than I did. Shae is not like me. I was sent here to breed with a human and build enough wealth to affect this world. I still have glamour. I adapted to be a human, and I'm mortal now, but I'm still me. Shae does not have her glamour anymore. Shae is not still Shae. She was tasked to be a changeling, and she cannot adapt."

Shae looked stricken and went over to a pool to stare down at her reflection. The exchange from faerie to human was not a blessing to the faerie. Her human form was frail and feebleminded. Shae suffered in her new body. Her nose ran, and her eyes leaked. She was knock-kneed and clumsy and bruised easily. There were varicose veins all over her arms and legs and a rattling in her lungs. Her hair and teeth were falling out, and she was starting to smell like an infection. She had a vague compulsion to be near Ben if she wasn't with Andre. He tried not to be cruel, but he wanted nothing to do with her.

"For whatever reason, the court decided they wanted a changeling, and this time, they wanted Andre."

"Yeah, yeah." Amy hopped up and went over to a little table to pour herself wine. "She's a special fucking snowflake." She glared at her twin. "I don't care if she's got wings. Andre is still used to running water and central heating." She sipped her drink, looked at Andre, and shook her head. "You're fucked, you know that? You're not going to last five minutes before a woodwalker eats you or something."

Andre held up her hand, which was perfectly healed. "This should have needed stitches, Amy."

"And don't talk about some higher plan the court has. They don't give a shit about humans." She looked at Shae. "Or their own kind, apparently."

"*I'm* not human anymore." And Andre's beautiful voice sent a chill down her spine. She wasn't Andre anymore when she said it.

Amy didn't have to wait long to find out what would happen. A week later, she and Ben were up late one night watching television when Ben suddenly sat up. "Oh shit, look." Something appeared outside through the sliding glass door—a sphere of light drifting around.

When they first saw it, she laughed nervously. There was something comically strange about the little ball of electricity bobbing about. "It's ball lightning," Ben whispered. They got up from the couch, and he opened the door, and they stepped out onto the porch. It was just a few yards away. He pointed. "That's it. That's the same thing we saw the night before we found Shae."

The atmosphere outside was strange. It was warm for an evening. The air felt soupy, thick with electricity. A few eerie seconds passed in slow motion, and they saw the sphere jerk around like a fishing rod, then a beat later, it drifted up the side of the house and headed for Andre's window. It hovered in front of it, and then the window was snatched open, and the ball of light disappeared inside. Amy put her hand to her mouth and turned to Ben and read in his eyes what she'd known was going to happen. She stumbled back into the house. "No, no, no, no!"

They bolted up the stairs and burst into her room. A wall-eyed Shae sat on the bed, rocking back and forth. Amy went to the window and stared out into the night. She swallowed and wiped her eyes. "Well, then. I hope she has a nice time there. I hope it's as wild and shiny as it was in her dreams." Amy turned and slumped down next to the smelly, sickly changeling on her sister's dirty bed. "I'm sorry, Shae," she said quietly.

Shae whispered something.

"What's that?" Amy asked.

"My name. The light came for her. She took my name," Shae repeated. "My name. I am nothing without my name."

I wake after another torturous night. I am rotting, and I know what I must do. I feel the sweet pull of the lake, tugging me towards it. I ache to surrender, and I will surrender to the water. Everything hurts. Grace gave me a robe with big pockets. I stumble outside on atrophied muscles that won't take me far if I let it go much longer. I make my way along the path, and saltwater streams down my face as I recall my strength, my wings, my monarch. I think of Ben. My instrument turned against me. I love him now, and I hope his gift makes some kind of difference.

I try not to think of the tithe. I try not to picture his face or recall his voice. But I am haunted by the sweet memories I've absorbed into this decaying vessel. I remember the way he'd study something so intently, working out the kinks of a motor or a map. Thoughts of him and the other boy corrode my mind. My glamour is gone and replaced with horror and remorse. And all that is left is a flickering lucidity forcing me to acknowledge all that I have done. And all that I have lost.

I wince, wandering over the wood floor, my cracked feet, bleeding. I make my slow, plodding way to the Shellara. I pick up rocks and stuff them into the pockets of my robe. When I reach the lake, I look around this world one last time. I smell only life on the wind, and I see now how this complex foreign place has its own kind of beauty.

Clouds have filled the sky, and rain bears down. Beautiful droplets that nudge me in. I feel no fear when the water closes over me, only a hope that the end will come quickly and not be too painful.

The giantess called Amy the morning after the storm, suggesting it was time for her to report her sister missing. It would be ten more days before hikers found the body—bloated and dissolving. Scarcely recognizable as something that had once been human.

That year, a musical phenomenon crossed cultural chasms and was universally seductive—influencing the soul and articulating the angst of a new generation. The musician was worshiped and devoured, a young man with dark, haunted eyes. Amy stayed with him. *"You're not going on this ride without me!"* She quickly learned to play bass and sang backup vocals while Ricardo played drums. Ben tried to hide amongst them, but he couldn't. He tried to cling to them, and he tried to cling to Merri. But it was *his* voice they wanted to hear. It was him the world wanted to see. It was him they would consume.

Elsewhere, a delicate being—always a bit different from the rest—pumps her wings and drifts among the boughs under pumpkin-colored sunlight. At night she dances under moons and glowing torches to music that is more beautiful than what the most gifted human could create. An emerald pendant from a baser world hangs from her neck. One night she looks at the moonlight shining through the green stone, and it makes her a bit sad even though she has forgotten where it came from. She takes it off and leaves it on a tree branch. A breeze flings it off, onto the forest floor, where it becomes buried in leaves and lost to time.

In adjacent realms, Shae's quarry follows their trajectories, planned long before, by an unseen court that decides such things. The *faeries* come and go, dipping in and out of places where the barriers are thin. They harm. Help. Manipulate. They are known to a few but never seen by the masses. They bestow gifts and collect tithes. And sometimes, they make changelings.

Our sickening earth turns on its axis. And the world is none the wiser.

The End

ACKNOWLEDGEMENTS

This book wouldn't have been possible without the help of writing pals and early readers. Thank you to those who encouraged me, those who gave it to me straight, and those who did both: My first readers and indispensable writing pals, the talented O'Dell sisters, Amanda and Robin. Thank you for your wise advice, enthusiasm, and encouragement.

Christina Funkhouser, thank you for an incisive and helpful critique at a crucial point. Blythe Donham, thank you for reading at a time when I was hanging by a thread and really needed the encouragement.

I'm grateful to Jessica Klahr and Lauren Counsel for your thoughtful perspective and copy edits on earlier drafts. (And to Joanie for printing out a monster copy.)

Thanks to my pal Ryan Morris for assisting with formatting emergencies when I was in the submission process, and to helping me nail down the darn synopsis.

I'm indebted to the beta readers and the many friends and family (Uncle Russ!) who I pestered to read and give me feedback. I'm lucky to have so many talented and patient people in my life.

Huge thanks to Lawrence Knorr and Chris Fenwick for publishing my book. This was fun and I hope to do well by you.

And lastly, thanks to my wonderful husband and son for making life sweet and putting up with my occasional shrieking. I love you.

ABOUT THE AUTHOR

Natalie Pinter has been an accomplished daydreamer for most of her waking life. After working for many years as a bookseller, she started sharing her own stories. When she's not reading or writing, she enjoys taking pictures of nature and hanging out with her family. She currently resides in a swampy part of Florida surrounded by large and scary looking bugs.

https://www.nataliepinter.com/